DEATH NOTE

Also by Caroline Mitchell

DEATH NOTE

CAROLINE MITCHELL

Bookouture

Published by Bookouture

An imprint of StoryFire Ltd.
23 Sussex Road, Ickenham, UB10 8PN
United Kingdom

www.bookouture.com

ISBN: 978-1-78681-085-4
eBook ISBN: 978-1-78681-084-7
ISBN: 978-1-78681-999-4

This book is a work of fiction. Names, characters, businesses,
organizations, places and events other than those clearly in the public
domain, are either the product of the author's imagination or are
used fictitiously. Any resemblance to actual persons, living or dead,
events or locales is entirely coincidental.

This book is dedicated to the real heroes; the members of the emergency services who risk their lives to protect ours.

PROLOGUE

The lights of the Christmas tree twinkled in the dark space. On. Off. On. Off. Then the second set kicked in, sending an array of colours dancing on the walls of the dank grey basement. Despite the absence of windows, Emily Edmonds knew it was sunny outside. The weather forecast had warned it would be the hottest September in five years. She shifted in the cold metal chair. The puddle of urine had soaked into her skirt, casting up the stench of ammonia with every movement. Her wrists sent a sharp slice of pain through her nerve endings as the bindings cut further into her flesh. Something clicked into place and a low whirr ensued. On. Off. On. Off… the light sequence began again. Emily closed her eyes, the flashes still found their way into her vision. Her throat tightened as she sobbed, but no tears came. She was dry. Wept out, pissed out, sweated out. Dry as a bone with nothing left to give.

Drip… drip… drip… the noise of a leaky tap teased her. Apart from the flashing lights of the artificial tree, she had been left in darkness. But over the course of the day she worked out her surroundings. She was in a basement of some kind, a windowless cave underneath the ground. Her captor seemed at ease when she entered, not looking over her shoulder for fear of being caught. The room housed a sink. Overhead, she could hear the sounds of a functioning home: footsteps, and sometimes a muffled television. Furniture screeching, taps running, toilets flushing. Life went on as normal above her head. Even if she wasn't gagged, it was doubtful anyone would hear her screams. Her jaw still hurt from the punch she had received last time she tried it. The blood from her loose tooth had been warm, wet and left a bitter aftertaste. It was a relief to have some liquid flow down her throat. Tears finally found their way to her eyes, blurring the gaudy baubles into a kaleidoscope of colours.

Her eyes flicked up to the ceiling, squinting at the single light bulb hanging from a cobwebbed wire cable. The switch was powered at the top of narrow wooden stairs which creaked when weight was applied. It was a small comfort to know that the noise was enough to wake her when her body fell into slumber. Struggling against her bindings only made the ropes ride higher up her ankles and wrists, and her circulation was almost cut off as it was.

She stiffened as a door opened, flooding light down the stairs and into her field of vision. Emily blinked away the tears as the woman slowly took each step. *Keep calm. Whatever she wants, please God, help me get it right.* Visions of Harry, her husband, swam in her memory. How was he coping without her? He would be going out of his mind. *Don't cry. Everything will be alright, just focus...*

'It's almost Christmas,' the woman said, the childish words curling on her tongue. She looked as if she'd stepped from another era. The Victorian-style outfit consisted of a dark knee-length dress, covered by a lace-trimmed white cotton apron. Lace-up boots tapped on each step as she giggled with delight.

The woman seemed not to notice the smell, the overwhelming stench of decay. But Emily could not think about the source. It emanated from the dirt-stained floorboards which were rotting and splintered underfoot. The makeshift flooring revealed slices of blackened soil beneath, and Emily shuddered as she inhaled the offensive smell.

'I've got a surprise for you,' the woman said in a sing-song voice, jumping down the last step, both feet together.

Emily murmured a whine, her eyes wide and pleading.

'Remember our little chat when you talked about Harry?'

Emily remembered, and regretted every word. Why had she confided in this stranger? Thinking she could trust her with the secrets she held most dear? Yes, Harry could be controlling, but it was only because he loved her and wanted to keep her safe. And now look at her. This is what happened when she tried to leave him. A prickle of fear rose up from within. She would never have said those things if she had known. Lucy was deranged. And she had been wrong. Whoever this person was, she was not her daughter.

Emily's heart accelerated with each step Lucy took, until she was behind her, ripping off her gag.

'Tomorrow is Christmas Day, Mummy. And it's going to be just you and me. No nasty Harry anymore. We're going to have the perfect day.'

Emily spat out the bile in her mouth, coughing, until something resembling air entered her lungs. 'Harry… ' she gasped, the words scratching against her throat. 'What have you done with my Harry?'

Lucy's voice thinned. 'I killed him, of course, so we can be together. Tomorrow…'

But her words were cut short as Emily produced a woeful, garbled scream. 'No… not my Harry! Get me out of here! Do you hear me? Untie me right now – get me out.' She rocked in her chair, throwing her head from side to side.

'But Mummy… ' Lucy said, her face turning dark.

'I'm not your mother,' Emily screamed. 'You're a monster. I don't want you! I want my Harry.'

Lucy turned to the tree, her words cold. 'After everything I've done. You're not my mother. You're just a selfish cow.'

Emily's chest heaved as she drew in lungfuls of air. She had vowed to stay calm. What had she done? 'I'm sorry,' she said, 'I didn't mean to… Lucy? Please, don't be cross.'

But Lucy was ripping the baubles from the branches of the tree, too consumed by anger to hear Emily's pleas for forgiveness.

'I'm sorry, Lucy, please,' Emily said, her words laced with panic.

Her heart beat wildly as fear wrapped itself around her, and she strained against her bindings, desperate to escape. And then she saw it. The flash of anger in Lucy's eyes. Spittle had formed in the corner of her mouth, white and frothy. She was beyond reasoning. The urine Emily was holding trickled once more down her thigh.

Darkness enveloped them as Lucy ripped the lights from their socket, her tortured wail filling the lightless room. Emily finally deciphered the source of the smell. Inhaling one last shuddering breath, she closed her eyes and prayed.

CHAPTER ONE

With one swig Ruby knocked back the fizzy concoction that promised to ease your pounding head and provide a burst of energy. Her team were still jubilant from yesterday's result and the post-celebratory drinking session that had followed. They had taken some major players off the streets, but, just like always, there would be more lining up to take their place. She pulled up a chair, preparing to pick over the bones of the case with the familiar faces gathered around her.

'Morning all.' DI Jack Downes's voice boomed a greeting in his Northern Irish accent, his broad, lumbering frame making itself known. Coffee in one hand and croissant in the other, he spoke mid-bite, sending flecks of pastry flying onto the foot-worn carpet. Shoreditch Serious Crime Unit took up residence in the third floor of the drab grey concrete building. A man with a big voice, DI Downes had no problem being heard. His eyes lit on Ruby, and he shoved down the last of his pastry before marching over and giving her shoulder a little shake. 'Alright mucker? How are yous this fine morning?'

Ruby winced, feeling every bone in her body rattle. 'Tender, so handle with care.'

Downes sucked in air between his teeth as she turned to greet him face on. 'Ouch. That's come up in the night.'

Ruby winced as she touched the pad of swollen flesh. High cheekbones may have been a blessing in her teenage years, but not so when she found herself on the receiving end of a left hook. 'It's only a couple of stitches,' she said, the side of her mouth jerking up in an involuntary smile. 'He came off a lot worse.'

'Well, don't let me interrupt you,' he said, taking a seat. The faint smell of mint and whiskey vented from her DI's breath. Since his wife's death, his fondness for 'a wee dram' had become more frequent, and Ruby had warned him more than once that he was putting too much at risk so near retirement.

Yesterday's post-incident briefing had been a time for back-slapping. But today they would discuss 'learning points' in more detail, or what she preferred to call the 'fuck-up round-up' of the day before.

Luddy, also known as DC Owen Ludgrove, handed her a mug of sweet tea to wash down the bitter taste of Alka-Seltzer on her tongue. A likeable guy with tousled black hair, Luddy had the character of a young man who would go places one day. 'Keen but green,' Downes called him, but Ruby could not fault Luddy's enthusiasm for the job.

Ruby slid the intelligence pack from the desk she was leaning on and thumbed through the pages. 'Great job last night, guys, but there's a couple of things we need to cover before we can move on.' Her dark eyes roamed over the group of satisfied faces. All except one.

DC Eve Tanner was shrinking into her chair, her head bowed.

'This isn't a matter of naming and shaming,' Ruby added. 'It's learning how we can do it better next time. So who'd like to get started? Silence fell, and for a few seconds all she could hear was the sound of the traffic outside. A siren blared in the distance, reminding Ruby that their time was limited. Crime didn't stop just because they had a good result. 'OK, I'll make a start. What we *expected* was a group of young dealers believed to have been involved in a kidnapping. What we *got* was a small army, including five out of ten of our most wanted. You'll have seen their faces on our wall. Violent bastards with a string of offences to their names. It was a great collar, but the fact there were firearms in the flat makes us lucky we came away with just cuts and bruises.' Ruby glanced around the room, grateful her team were all present to recount the event. Battle-scarred and still wearing yesterday's crumpled shirts, they were a scruffy band of officers. All except Eve, who was immaculately dressed in her black trouser suit; her blonde hair pinned neatly in a bun.

'I'm sorry,' Eve said, her voice low. 'I should have delved deeper into the source of the intelligence.'

'And had better eyeballs on the premises,' Ruby added.

Eve would have worked closely with the intelligence support unit, but the covert human intelligence sources had been hers. However, CHIS weren't always wholly reliable, and Ruby wasn't about to publicly flog her only female DC. The fact Eve stood and watched her colleagues getting pummeled worried Ruby more than her lack of preparation for the raid. Why hadn't she supported them by getting stuck in? All the same, it had been good to blow the cobwebs off. She hadn't been in a hands-on brawl for months and had come away feeling exhilarated, barely conscious of the blood running down her cheek. But there was no point in going over old ground when they had so much to do. 'Besides not taking intel at face value, what else can we take from this?'

'To have each other's backs, and the ability to use a pair of handcuffs,' DC Ash Baker said, linking his bruised knuckles and resting them on his rotund stomach.

Ruby had a vague recollection of seeing him holding a thick-necked skinhead in a headlock, swearing at Luddy to cuff him from behind.

'Did you see the width of his wrists?' Luddy protested. 'Besides, modern handcuffs aren't as flexible as the ones back in *your* day.'

Ash took a breath to retort, and Ruby raised her hand to cut him off.

'Excuse me,' DI Downes said, skirting past her to answer his phone.

'Who was it that moaned about having TSU along?' The presence of a team from the tactical support unit, equipped with shields and Tasers, had undoubtedly saved the day.

'I was going by the intel provided,' Ash said, glaring at Eve.

'Well, it's a good thing I erred on the side of caution. If the suspects had made use of their firearms, some of us might not be here today.'

Ruby could see her words were having an effect on Eve, whose neck seemed to have disappeared completely as she shrank like a tortoise in its shell. Ruby had a couple more points to go over, but decided to leave it for another time.

'This morning we're homicide-free, so we can get on with our backlog of work. We've got a suspect in the bin for armed robbery; Ash I'd like you to deal with that. You can pair up with Luddy in interview.'

'Why can't Eve?' Ash said, making no effort to hide his reluctance to work with the newest member of the team.

'Because I asked you.'

Ash mumbled some retort about babysitting, while Ruby delegated the workload to the rest of the group. It consisted of drug-related violent crimes and a gang-related grievous bodily harm. Being based in central East London, it was nothing out of the ordinary for the team.

Heads swivelled as Downes strode from his office holding a scrap of paper with illegible writing. His eyes were bright, as if he had just picked the winning lottery numbers. Ruby recognised the look, which could only mean one thing.

So much for being homicide-free.

CHAPTER TWO

Ruby took the wheel of the grey Ford Focus to enable Downes to speak to officers over his police radio. She had left her team setting the wheels of investigation turning.

'What have we got?' Ruby said as she negotiated a shortcut to the scene of the crime.

'It's a domestic murder by the sound of it. Neighbours called it in, saying they heard a couple arguing. Uniform have just got there and confirmed a body at the scene.'

'Husband and wife?' Ruby said.

'Seems that way, although there's no sign of the missus now.'

'She's probably panicked and ran off. Sounds pretty straight-forward. Why are we dealing with it?'

'The other teams are up to their necks in it. We haven't had any homicides on our patch in a couple of days so… '

'Any intelligence on the couple?'

'Her name is Emily Edmonds, married to Harry Edmonds. His identity has been confirmed, and neither is known to us. He owns a café on Well Street.'

'That must be Harry's Café, the one across from Lidl. There's a few of them dotted about the place.'

Downes tapped his palms against his lap in a restless drumbeat. 'This is all I fecking need,' he muttered. 'If this involves a local businessman, Worrow will be crawling over it like a fly on shite.'

Ruby nodded emphatically. She used to get on with the Chief, but lately she had borne the brunt of her temper on more than one occasion. Sloppy workforce, disgusting conditions, and what was the last one? Oh yes, insubordination. There had been times when she wondered if her superior was in possession of a pair of balls. You had to be to reach promotion at Worrow's tender age. Ruby's knuckles whitened over the steering wheel. Their office might not smell of pot-pourri, but they were real coppers and they got things done. She took a deep calming breath through her nostrils and exhaled slowly as she parked up behind a police car.

The red-brick townhouse on Tresham Walk looked nothing out of the ordinary, but given its location in London, the three-bedroom abode on the quiet residential street could fetch three quarters of a million pounds on the property market. Her own recent property search had proved fruitless, and the thought of spending another year in her hovel of a flat was too depressing to face. She noticed the blinds twitch next door and smiled. Nosey neighbours were welcome, particularly in domestic murders. She listened as DI Downes received updates via his police radio. Intelligence stated there had been previous calls by concerned neighbours. Mr Edmonds had told attending officers that he was a member of the local dramatics group and had been practising his lines. Ruby rolled her eyes. Amateur dramatics indeed.

The scene guard officer dished out white oversuits and gloves at the gate, quickly jotting down their names before allowing them inside. Ruby slid a hairband from her wrist and scooped up her long dark tresses into a ponytail. Crime scene investigators were en route, and she zipped up the front of her bunny suit, keeping her eyes sharply tuned for evidence.

Slowly, she walked through the front door, admiring the small crystal chandelier as it reflected spots of light on the magnolia walls. Apart from the recent threads of police boots on the thick oatmeal carpet, the hall was spotlessly clean. The scent of lilies intermingled with a blast of warm air wafting in from outside, and she brushed past the table in the hall, avoiding the pollen-ripe stamens. The body was fresh, which was just as well given the recent spate of hot weather. At least she was spared the acrid, cheesy smell of decay. She had visited many murder scenes where the victims had been in various stages of decomposition. The dead did not bother her. It was the living that played on her mind. Ruby pushed down on the bronze door handle with the tips of her gloved fingers as she entered the living room. The crime scene investigators would not be best pleased she had beaten them to it, but the 'golden hour' was so called for a reason. Downes strode purposefully past her to the body, his tweed jacket swishing inside the paper-thin suit. He surveyed the blood splatters on the wall, while Ruby held her ground, taking in the scene. She briefly closed her eyes, allowing her senses to do the work. She could smell antiseptic, hear more than one ticking clock. A trickle of sweat ran down the curve of her back. She glanced around the room, storing the images to her memory bank. An upturned coffee table, a broken ornament; the disturbance was small but spoke volumes.

Lastly, she turned her attention to the body. The stocky man was face down on the floor, producing enough blood to soak through the surrounding carpet and dribble onto the linoleum through the open kitchen door. His short auburn hair was combed back at the sides, and a wedding ring graced the finger of his left hand. A splatter of crimson laced a copper bracelet, and his once blue shirt was now drenched in blood. Ruby cast her eyes over the puncture wound between his shoulder blades.

'See his hands?' DI Downes said as he stepped over the blood that was now congealing into jellied bubbles.

Ruby nodded. She had already noticed his clenched right fist. His left hand was gripped tightly around a black cordless phone.

'He didn't put his hands out in front of him as he fell. It's an automatic reaction. The fact his fists are clenched and by his sides suggest he could have had some seizure or heart attack on the way down. That's why his face took the brunt of the fall.'

Ruby frowned. 'Why would she stab him if he was going to cop it anyway? Surely it would have been better to leave him to die?'

DI Downes snorted. 'Ach, you know what domestic murders are like; they're rarely from a logical standpoint.'

Ruby felt a sneeze coming on and turned away as she pinched the bridge of her nose. It reminded her of the crime scene she'd brought Luddy to, the year before, when he forgot to wear a mask, and he had sneezed all over the body. His desk was covered in Kleenex for weeks afterwards by his colleagues. She held in the expulsion, sniffling, as she regained her composure.

She took in the inoffensive room. It was spotlessly clean; no alcohol that she could see; nothing to relay drugs were a factor either. Ruby surveyed the photos hanging on the wall. A much younger Harry Edmonds smiled for the camera with a small mousey woman on his arm. She looked more like his daughter than his wife, but the wedding photos erased any doubt from Ruby's mind. There were no recent pictures to speak of, and no evidence of children or pets. She tiptoed past the body to the kitchen. It could have passed for a show home. The knife block resting on the counter was full. She opened the cupboards to see every tin was facing the same way, perfectly tidy and not a crumb out of place. A slight hint of lemon cleaner lingered in the air. It made a change from the usual crime scene, where you wiped your feet on the way out.

'I'm not happy about this scene,' Ruby said, crossing her ankles as she leaned against the doorframe, 'it's all too perfect.' She caught a glimpse of silver as DI Downes slid his hip flask back into his suit pocket. She waved away his offer of a mint before he sheepishly popped one into his mouth.

'Only you could complain about being given a suspect on a plate,' he said, with a twinkle in his eye.

Outside, a chorus of voices followed by the sound of van doors slamming indicated that CSI were here.

'I should have known you'd be trampling all over my scene,' the husky voice of Bones greeted DI Downes. The stocky dreadlocked black man was nicknamed such because of the model of a human skeleton taking up residence in his office. Ruby had once overheard him talking to it and had never allowed him to live it down.

'And your partner in crime here as well! Ruby, made a start in the kitchen too?'

Ruby had the decency to look embarrassed. She knew how territorial Bones could get about his precious crime scenes. 'Sorry. We haven't been upstairs.'

Bones shrugged, watching, as his colleagues lay down the stepping plates. 'No matter. One of the neighbours saw his missus get a taxi last night, and she was carrying an overnight bag. Prima facie by the sounds of it.'

Prima facie. Open and shut case. The concept held no weight with Ruby. She narrowed her eyes in defiance. 'Don't use those swear words with me, Bones.'

Bones grinned, making a fishing rod gesture with his hands. He had reeled her in once again. Ruby snorted before leaving the building, glad to step out of the paper suit that was making her sweat. A crowd was gathering behind the police tape, and she pushed through them to the car. It was time to get back to the nick. She had that uneasy feeling in her gut. Her innate voice that whispered whenever all was not as it seemed.

Just where was the murder weapon that killed Harry Edmonds?

And more to the point: where was his wife?

CHAPTER THREE

The stairs creaked as Lucy took each step upwards, her shoulders slumped, the tips of her gloves wet with blood. Tears ran unbidden down her face: not for Emily Edmonds, but for the dream of a mother she had left behind. Emily wasn't her mother. She was just like all the others. Nothing but a huge disappointment. She would have to clean up the mess before she could even think about starting again.

Steam rose in puffs of clouds as the bath filled, and she wiped the sides of the old music box clean. Despite the mouldy tiles and the paint chipping on the bathroom ceiling, she couldn't bring herself to activate the extractor fan. She liked the steam, and the condensation dripping lazily down the walls. She could pretend she was in a different place rather than here, at home, abandoned and alone. The music box gave an involuntary tinkle as she gently placed it on the tiled window ledge.

She tutted at the splatters of blood as she slipped off her lace-up boots. She had cleaned them up before; she could do it again. 'Hush little baby, don't say a word… ' she sang. Pulling off the bloodstained apron and then her dress, she rolled down her black tights and removed her underwear. 'Mama's gonna buy you a mocking bird.' She wasn't wearing a bra. Little girls didn't need things like that. The wig was the last thing to come off, and she walked across the landing and placed it lovingly on the styrofoam head in her bedroom. The blonde ringlets bounced as it settled, and she hummed the rest of the tune, fixing the dummy's head until it was in line with all the others. Satisfied, she returned to the bathroom.

Steaming hot water sloshed over the sides of the roll-top bath as she eased herself in. She would need to wash again after she disposed of the body, but she didn't want to think about that. She needed to go to a happy place now that the rage had subsided. She wound her music box, allowing the tinkling tune of 'Hush, Little Baby' to carry her away.

Holding her breath, she submerged herself under the water. She was there in an instant. A reset button flicked in her brain, and she opened her eyes, allowing her fantasies of Emily Edmonds to wash away. She was not Lucy Edmonds. She had another Mummy with a different surname, and soon she would be knocking on her door.

Steam haloed around her head as she emerged, giving in to the instinctive need for air. She closed her eyes as the scene played out, vivid in her imagination. It was warm, comforting, the perfect Christmas Day, back in a time where nobody could hurt her. Her hands caressed the silkiness of her skin, until the scene dissolved and the transformation was complete. She was no longer a child at Christmas but a woman, and she had housework to do and a mess to clean up in the basement. She examined her hands and thought of the blood, the life she had extinguished. Emily's muffled pleas had not gained her empathy, but fed her sense of power. Emily was merely a representative of all the people who turned their back on her pain. Lucy allowed the blood-tinged foam to wash over her as she dipped her chin into the water; her hands stroking now, gaining in rhythm. 'Yes,' she moaned. That felt good. There was nothing to regret. Soon she could start again.

She re-enacted the basement scene: the blood dripping from the corners of Emily's mouth; staining Lucy's gloves as she gripped her throat. The metal chair, tilting and collapsing beneath them as she straddled Emily's limp frame. Finally, the thrill of feeling Emily's pulse fade beneath her fingers as her pathetic life ebbed away. Lucy's eyes rolled back into her head as pleasure rippled through her body. Gradually, the water turned cold and the sound of the music box stilled.

Tomorrow she would begin again. And again. And again.

She would do what it took to find her mother. Somebody worthy of her love.

CHAPTER FOUR

Ruby nodded at staff through the reception window as she scrawled her signature across the visitor's book. Just being in Oakwood helped settle her, at least for a little while. Pressing the code on the keypad, she pushed through the double doors. She knew it off by heart and didn't need the staff to let her in anymore. She was as much a part of the furniture as they were and they often joked they should give her a job there. She inhaled the sweet smell of wild flowers picked from the fields to the rear of the building, which was built on five acres of land. The private nursing homes were a far cry from the acrid council-run buildings, stinking of piss and bleach: the stuff of nightmares – the residents staring with empty eyes like cattle in a holding pen waiting to die. Ruby had attended one such home when she was in uniform, investigating a series of sudden deaths where neglected patients were left to choke on their food. Seeing her mother here, in Oakwood, with a healthy flush in her cheeks and comfortable, pleasant surroundings, made living in her own shoddy flat worthwhile.

Joy was sitting next to Brian, an old boy in a wheelchair who spent every day reliving his job at his hardware store. Ruby sometimes chatted to him about screws and lug nuts, whatever he dreamt was on sale that day. But today she didn't want to chat to anyone else. Today she wanted to immerse herself in her mother's presence. The light scent of lily of the valley caressed her senses as she leaned over to kiss her. Her silvery white hair shimmered with a tint of blue, and she wanted to hug her tightly, to draw her close and never let go.

'Hello Mum,' Ruby said as she kissed her mother's cheek. Her mother frowned slightly, her mind emerging from a cloud, and Ruby guessed she was trying to place her face.

'It's me, Ruby. Your daughter.'

'Of course you're my daughter; who else would you be?' Joy said, her voice edged with irritation.

Ruby nodded, allowing her to save face. It made her happy to know her mother still possessed her pride and the stubborn streak that passed with it. A Preston trait that Ruby also bore. But the truth was, Ruby could be anyone. Some days her mother called her Gertie, after her deceased sister, or Alice, after a girl she went to school with. All shadows from the past, more alive than the people that infiltrated her presence today. The present had little room in Joy's clouded mind. Ruby glanced down at her mother's sparkly red pumps and smiled. She had never given in to uniformity, not even here, and always had something red about her person. A flower, a hair clip, a scarf with poppies, or a narrow red belt to hug her waist. Her father used to call her his little Robin Redbreast, and it was a memory she treasured. Ruby dreaded the day she would forget to wear it. Most days Ruby wore something red too: a dash of a red lipstick, or a cherry red brooch on her blazer lapel. It was a silly game, she had told herself, but she found it hard to let her solidarity go.

'So Mum, how have you been?' Ruby asked, preparing for a journey back into her childhood. There was no point in trying to discuss current affairs or her own life. It confused Joy, and the only safe place was firmly in the past. It didn't matter to Ruby, as all she wanted to hear was her mother's voice. Each visit was being transported back in time to when Joy felt most useful in the world.

'I've just mopped that,' Joy said, pointing to the lino with her shoe. 'Don't you go getting it dirty now.'

It was spotlessly clean and had a criss-cross pattern which was similar to the one in their kitchen where her mother had spent most of her time. Ruby's early memories were of that lino, as she played racing cars with Nathan, the next door neighbour's son. Their games were played to the backdrop of their mothers chatting at the kitchen table.

As Joy spoke of those days, Ruby indulged herself in the memory, becoming five years old all over again.

She remembered how the wheels of her favourite toy car used to squeak as she pressed them against the bumpy linoleum. Back then, she liked the octagonal brown patterns. In her five-year-old mind it was Brands Hatch, and she was winning in a two car race against her best friend, Nathan. He used to make her wince, vocalising his pretend brakes, screeching as he took the corners. Ruby smiled at the memory; the way Nathan called her Wuby, and how she'd screw up her face as she elongated her words, saying Ruuubbby, over and over, until he pronounced it properly.

Ruby listened as her mother spoke of those days, caught up in a dream of yesteryear. 'I told your dad to bring him into the living room,' she said, keeping her voice low. 'How he survived after losing all that blood is anyone's guess.'

Ruby nodded, remembering how she and Nathan had both dropped their cars and ran after their mothers, hanging around the open living room doorway as his father was dragged inside. There was blood, alright. Lots of it: trailing from the hall into the living room, where Jimmy Crosby lay. Nathan had tried to step inside, and Ruby shot out an arm, pulling him back by his knitted tank top until he was back in line with her. She gave him a stern look, pressing a finger to her mouth. The doorway was like an invisible barrier to her mother. Whenever anything was going on, she never noticed Ruby until she put a foot over the threshold, then she was banished to her room, or told to leave and close the door behind her. Even back then, Ruby thought like a detective, her eyes growing wide as she located the source of the blood. Jimmy Crosby's smart black suit was soaked with it, and Nathan's mother barged in, pushing people aside like skittles as she searched for the injury. 'Oh Gawd, what's happened now?' she squealed, her East End accent filling the room. 'Who's done this to you, Jimmy?'

The words echoed in Ruby's memory, and she flinched as her mother grasped her forearm. Joy was too wrapped up in the past to understand it was a flashback, and the anxiety in her eyes was the same now as it had been in their little East London terrace house all those years ago. 'I've got to call the doctor,' she said. 'Dr Tanner. Nobody else but Dr Tanner. He doesn't ask questions, you see.'

'It's OK, Mum,' Ruby reassured her. 'Everything's OK.'

'Best you get some towels all the same,' Joy said.

Ruby nodded, taking her mother's hand. She remembered how she had taken Nathan's dimpled hand and pressed it against the flock wallpaper in the hall, telling him not to move, while panic ensued in the living room.

Joy had stopped talking now, but the memory burned like a branding iron in the back of Ruby's mind. She only had to touch upon it and she was back there: her father sweating through his shirt as he pressed the towels down on the knife wound, the cotton almost immediately turning from white to bright red. She heard Mrs Crosby's high-pitched shrieking as she asked her husband over and over who was responsible. And Nathan, his blue eyes as deep as the sea, still standing with his hand pressed against the wallpaper because Ruby had told him not to move.

Ruby threaded her fingers around her mother's hand. Her skin was so soft it was almost translucent, and she felt a lump rise to her throat. Her eyes roamed over the network of blue veins growing ever more visible. She didn't want to think of her mother getting old and dying because then she would truly be all alone.

'It's dinner time now,' the nurse gently spoke. Harmony was a larger-than-life Jamaican lady with a springy black weave and a smile that lit up the room. She spoke in a happy sing-song voice which suited her title perfectly. 'Would you like to bring your mother to the dining room?'

Ruby turned over her left hand and checked the time. It had gone seven, and as usual the carers had allowed her to stay beyond the allocated visiting time.

'I want you to bring me,' Joy said, pointing at Harmony. 'Not *her*.' She jabbed a thumb back at her daughter.

'Now, Mrs Preston, is dat any way to treat your flesh and blood?' Harmony said, but Ruby waved the words away.

'It's OK, really. I'll walk with you. I've got to get back to work now anyway.' The first time her mother stopped recognising her was devastating, but Ruby had learned to cope with it as Joy's lucidity floated in and out.

'You've got fat,' Joy said as she curled her hand around Harmony's arm.

Harmony laughed, a lovely tinkly sound, and Ruby shook her head. Her mother's inner filter had disintegrated along with her short-term memory, but staff at the care home took it in their stride.

'More of me to love, sista. How about we get some flesh on those skinny bones of yours? It's shepherd's pie, and homemade apple pie and custard.'

'Bye Mum,' Ruby said as Joy escorted her mother through the dining room. With a murder on the go it could be another couple of days before a return visit. Joy kept walking without a backward glance. Harmony gave a quick wink over her shoulder. 'You take care now, Ruby, stay safe.'

Ruby swallowed hard, feeling as if she was leaving a piece of herself behind as she walked away.

CHAPTER FIVE

Lucy sat on the steps of the basement thinking through the last few days. Was she cursed? She had gone to such pains to get things just right: why weren't things turning out as they should? It all went downhill after she admitted to killing Harry Edmonds. But she had no choice. He would have found them. Men like that always did. And Emily had been so noncommittal about leaving; it was just a matter of time before she went crawling back. That was why it had to be just the two of them, without the distraction of other family members draining her affections. Not that Harry was that affectionate a spouse. From what Emily had told her, Lucy had done her a favour. It was why she paid Harry a visit after taking Emily to her special place.

She had left her finger on the doorbell longer than she should, as if she was injecting every bit of frustration into the stiff plastic buzzer. The door – which should have been her door – was opened before her. A gruff-faced man stood there wiping some crumbs from his shirt before giving her the once-over.

'Hello, can I speak to the lady of the house, please?' Lucy had said. 'I have some good news I'd like to share with her.'

'There's no lady living here; you must have the wrong address,' Harry had said, before attempting to shove the door closed.

But Lucy had come too far to take no for an answer. Shoving her foot in the gap, she raised her voice. 'I believe you're mistaken.

Your wife entered our prize draw and won a necklace,' she said, rattling the bag which contained a long smooth box.

Harry extended his hand. 'She's out. Give it to me and I'll pass it on.'

'I'm afraid I need a little bit of paperwork completed to say I've handed it over. Can I come in? It won't take a minute.'

'She's visiting her mother. I don't know when she'll be back. Leave your card and I'll get her to give you a call.'

Lucy paused. It was the pause, the flicker of anxiety in her blue eyes that gave Harry the edge, the recognition. She knew that now. Because he had seen that look before.

'On second thoughts, why don't you come in?' he said. 'I've got a phone number here somewhere.'

Lucy smiled, allowing herself into the hall. A fresh bouquet of lilies carried a welcoming scent. She brushed past them into the living room.

'It's not often she has visitors. I'm sure she'll be disappointed she's missed you. Why don't you have a seat?'

'Thank you,' Lucy said, but chose to stand. She had been here once before: when Harry was out. Emily had been tense, begging her to leave before her husband returned.

Harry folded his arms. 'Now how about you tell me where your mum really is?'

Lucy gasped as he turned and locked the door. 'How did you know?'

'She told me you were pestering her. What do you want? Clothes? Money? Take them; I'm glad to see the back of her.'

That explained a lot. 'So you knew about us?'

Harry gave a bitter laugh. 'You should never have come back. She was happy until you turned up.'

'No she wasn't! You made her life hell; she told me.'

'The best thing she did was get rid of you,' Harry sneered. 'I gave her some order in her life, pulled her out of the gutter, despite her being used goods. Still, I don't expect you would understand that, with your background.'

'You know nothing about me,' Lucy spat. 'If it weren't for you, Mum and I would be happy. We could have had a good life, but you forced her to give me up.'

Harry threw back his head and laughed. 'I know that you're poison. Evil in its purest form. I was protecting your mother by insisting she get rid of you. But here you are back again like shit on a shoe. This is all your fault.'

'You stand there and call me evil? You beat my mother. You need to be taught a lesson.'

'And you're gonna teach it, are ya?' Harry said, pushing her backwards.

Lucy gasped, enraged by the contact. Anger bubbled up inside her: the powerful rumbling thunder of hate. She flashed him a smile, catching Harry's astonishment as the persona of the unsure, nervous woman evaporated before him. Launching herself onto his bulk, she screamed a string of garbled words as her fists flew, punching his chest. 'C'mon then,' she said, sending him stumbling backwards. 'Or do you only hit women that don't fight back?'

Gritting his teeth, Harry fought to maintain his balance, pushing his attacker back on the floor. Groaning with the exertion, he straddled her, his face ashen, beads of sweat breaking out on his brow. He grabbed her wrists, fighting to control her flailing fists. 'You think you can come to my home and call me a wife beater? Well, let me tell you what you are. You're a rape baby. Born from rape. How do you feel now, you dirty bitch?'

Lucy's body went limp as shock invaded her being. 'What? No, it's not true, you're lying.'

'It's no wonder you're screwed in the head,' Harry panted. 'Your uncle is your father. How about that? Your mum's spent all these years trying to forget what he did, and then you turn up on her door to remind her.' Another bead of sweat dripped from his forehead, landing on Lucy's neck. 'Can you imagine how she felt when you wrote those letters? Sick to the stomach, she told me.'

Lucy turned her head away, the prickly carpet pressing into her face as angry tears streamed from her eyes. This was not supposed to happen. This was not part of her plan.

'I'm calling the police,' Harry grunted as he rose, his breaths jerky and laboured. He picked up the phone, rubbing his chest with his left hand.

Silently Lucy's fingers crept to the box containing the mock prize. It was long and narrow like a necklace box. Flicking off the lid, she grasped the contents.

At first he gasped in surprise, unaware of the foreign object tearing through the folds of his skin. Lucy pulled back the knife, triumphant and smiling, as he staggered forward on shaky legs. Adrenalin coursed through her body, making her strong, infallible. She could taste his blood from when it splattered against her lips, and her heartbeat pumped to accommodate the rush. Her senses heightened. She had entered the addictive phase of her predatory nature.

Harry dropped to his knees; his breath laboured and whistling as a stream of blood poured down his back. After one sudden wheeze, he lunged forward, his nose cracking as it made contact with the carpet. The clock ticked away the final seconds of his life, and waves of euphoria shuddered through Lucy's body.

Lucy's eyes snapped open as she emerged from the memory. She stroked the blood-encrusted blade, wondering: if she took a bath, would the water turn pink? Another opportunity to revisit that heightened state of pleasure. Rising from the stairs, she welcomed the thought of another bath. But she had things to do. The black-bordered envelope lay propped on the kitchen table, and she had preparations to make. Emily may not have been her mother, but she would give her the farewell she deserved.

CHAPTER SIX

The soft whirr of the hand drier made a soothing backdrop to Ruby's thoughts. Like the rest of Shoreditch police station, it was old but held an antiquated charm. The cracked floor tiles, the wonky tap, she didn't want to change a thing. But there were changes underway, whether she liked it or not.

A man's cough shook her from her thoughts, and she realised Luddy was waiting for her on the other side of the door.

'Luddy,' she said, wiping her damp hands on the back of her black trousers as she greeted her colleague in the corridor. 'What's so important that you have to stalk the ladies' toilets?'

'Sorry, Sarge,' Luddy said, a crooked smile on his face. 'The tannoy's broken. It's a phone call from the women's refuge. A woman named Charlie. She insists on speaking to a senior officer and Jack... I mean, DI Downes, has asked that you take the call.'

'Oh did he now?' Ruby said, marching towards the office. 'Has Worrow left yet?' she said, referring to DCI Worrow. As the Senior Investigating Officer, she had just led the briefing, delegating duties with regards to the initial enquiries.

'She's gone. She wasn't happy, was she?' Luddy ruefully replied.

'If she were any different I'd be worried,' Ruby said as Luddy held the office door open for her.

'She's worried the press are going to hang us out to dry again,' Luddy said, pointing to the phone which was off the hook on his desk. As with all phone calls, it had been placed on mute.

'Ah well,' Ruby grinned as she scooped up the handset. 'We don't join the police to be loved, now, do we?'

'Just as bloody well,' Luddy murmured, heading for the kettle to put on a brew.

Ruby's response was curt and to the point. 'DS Preston; what can I do for you?'

The woman's softly spoken whispers on the other line could not have been any more of a contrast to Ruby's strident tones. 'H— hello? Are you in charge of the Emily Edmonds's case?'

Ruby pressed the phone to her ear, and jabbed the volume control as high as it would go. 'You could say that. With whom am I speaking?'

'I'm a worker at a women's refuge. I need to speak to you about Emily.'

Ruby frowned. As far as she knew, all the refuges had been spoken to, and they had no knowledge of Emily Edmonds. 'Go ahead,' she said, grabbing a scrap of paper and pen from Luddy's overflowing desk drawer.

'Well, Emily was due to come to the refuge. I was working out an escape plan with her. But then her daughter, Lucy, got involved and said she would take it from there.'

Ruby's heart accelerated, delivering an extra beat. Lucy. The name invoked a memory she did not want to recall. 'Which refuge are you calling from?' she said, writing the words 'daughter Lucy' and underlining it twice with a question mark.

'I don't work in the refuge anymore. Look, I'm only ringing because I'm worried. Emily was all set to leave. Then one day she said she didn't need my help anymore because her daughter turned up out of the blue. Our friendship was ended, just like that, because this stranger turns up saying she's her daughter.'

'I thought Emily didn't have children,' Ruby said, leaning against the desk.

'She gave her baby up for adoption when she was sixteen. She's been through a traumatic time. I just wanted to help.'

'We're very keen to speak to Emily; so if you know where she is…'

'She sent me a text. She wants us to meet, and I've told her I will.'

'Where? Where's Emily staying?' Ruby said, her voice growing louder.

Fingers stopped typing, phone calls were ended, and the office fell into a hush.

'I don't know. She's texting me the details later. I'll bring her straight to you tomorrow when we've had the chance to talk. I know about Harry. Whatever's happened… it's not Emily's fault.'

'I'll come with you; keep my head down. She won't know I'm there,' Ruby said insistently.

'No. She trusts me. I'll bring her to you – tomorrow.'

'I don't understand your reluctance. What's your full name, Charlie?'

The woman's voice sharpened. 'That doesn't matter. I'm not with the refuge anymore. Look, if Emily's killed her husband it's not her fault. That man gave her a dog's life. I'll call in tomorrow; we can sort this out together.'

Ruby could feel her caller slipping away. 'Wait. What about Lucy? What can you tell me about her?'

Charlie gave an exasperated sigh. 'I saw her briefly when I arranged to meet Emily. She turned up and took her away. She was very rude.'

'What did she look like?'

'Slim, dark hair, lots of make-up. She had those big sunglasses on like the ones celebrities wear.'

'Could you identify her if you see her again?'

'Possibly. Look, I've got to go. We'll sort all this mess out tomorrow. Emily needs refuge. *Without* her daughter.'

She needs to be arrested, Ruby thought, wondering if the woman on the other end of the phone was making it all up. It wouldn't be the first time. 'Why don't we… ' Ruby realised she was talking to a dead line. She hung up and jabbed 1471. Damn. The number was blocked.

Only then did she notice the office had turned silent. Keyboards rapidly began working as she looked around; the colour flushed in her usually pale cheeks.

Ruby was shattered by the time she got home. Charlie's phone call had shed new light on the investigation, and thoughts of Lucy were gnawing at the back of her mind. But she didn't want to think of that now. Tomorrow would be a full day, and she wanted to put the whole sorry mess behind her, at least for a few hours. She sighed as she glanced around her flat; the cold laminate flooring chilling the soles of her bare feet. The occupants next door were arguing as usual, and on the other side of the wall the thump, thump, thump, of drum and bass vibrated in time with her headache. She turned on her old-fashioned turntable, expecting to drown out the noise with Coldplay. But instead, the sounds of Human League's 'Don't You Want Me' filled the air. Ruby frowned. She didn't remember putting that on. Fingering through her collection of vinyl records, she pulled out the Human League sleeve… to find the Coldplay album inside. Weird. But there was no time to ponder as she swapped them around. She slid across the thin orange curtains, barely hanging on the cheap plastic loops designed to keep them in place. The view of the high-rise estate didn't bother her, but her forthcoming guest valued his privacy, and as much as he hated her flat they had less chance of being seen than if they went to his.

Red wine was her drink of choice when it came to the art of seduction. Decanting the mulberry-coloured liquid into two glasses, she pushed away any lingering doubts to the back of her mind. Sure it was a bad idea, but it had been a bad idea for the last six months; a couple of times a month, preceded by the usual text:

'Fancy some company tonight?'

The nicotine patch had been thrown in the bin when the text came through. A post-coital cigarette was a joy like no other, particularly when she was in the company of such a satisfying lover. As a relationship it would never work out, and they both knew the score. She dimmed the lights and listened for his footsteps; hoping, for once, that the lifts were working. A smile graced her lips as she reapplied her lipstick. She wanted him to keep every ounce of energy for her.

She threw her shirt on the chair as she entered her bedroom, then undid her bra, rubbing the redness from the underwire in its wake. Later they would bathe together in her old-fashioned tub, and she would lay back into his chest as he gently soaped them in candle-flickered light. She eased her feet into a pair of black heels and threw on a silk dressing gown. A flutter rose in her stomach as the doorbell rang. She straightened the bed sheets before returning to the hallway and answering the door.

'Well, hello there,' she purred, arching her eyebrow at the man before her.

'Aren't you a sight for sore eyes,' DI Downes said huskily, closing the door behind him before taking her in his arms.

CHAPTER SEVEN

Lucy stared at the text. Not that she needed to because it was burned into her memory. She could close her eyes and the words would flash on the back of her eyelids as anger, hot and frothy, rose inside her.

'I saw the news. Please let me help. Refuge still an option. Is Lucy still with you? I don't trust her. XXX Charlotte.'

She had been just about to discard Emily's phone when it came through, which was convenient given Charlotte had been playing on her mind. Lucy took it as a sign. Seeing Charlotte was enough to keep her awake at night. She jabbed at the delete key, wishing she *had* let Emily go to the refuge now. All the time and effort she had put into her, then she just threw it all back in her face: calling her names and going berserk. What sort of a mother was that? Lucy grimaced. No mother at all. But she had taken care of her, and there was just one loose end to tie up before she could start afresh.

Lucy replied to the text in the same simpering tone.

'Meet me back of Mentmore Terrace, Lamb Lane. Cut through London Fields park. Under railway bridge at nine tonight. Lucy gone. Come alone. Need you. XXX Emily.'

Lucy shoved her hands into her coat pockets. She knew Charlotte would not be able to resist the text. She had read the newspaper articles as she searched her identity online. So kind, so giving. If only they knew. Lucy's mouth jerked upwards in a macabre half smile. Whatever romantic notions the silly woman held of rescuing Emily, they would prove to be her downfall.

The rusted blue gates of the scrap metal firm creaked in the evening breeze. Behind them, a metal chain clanged against a pole, as if announcing Lucy's arrival. She had parked at the back of an old industrial site, but the music playing in the distance told her that people weren't far away. She sidestepped the bulging black bin bags spilling their contents on the street. Something rustled inside, but Lucy's mind was on what awaited her around the corner, under the railway bridge, where they had arranged to meet. She had picked a secluded location, but Lucy didn't trust her not to bring the police.

Pulling the baggy grey hoody over her head, she slowly sauntered past the graffiti daubed walls. Lucy knew she shouldn't have come, but she could not let it lie. Turning the corner to the right, she kept out of sight until she saw a thin shadow of a woman under the railway bridge. Charlotte sneezed, and the high-pitched sound echoed down the lone street. Posh bitch. Lucy dipped her hand in her jacket pocket, stroking the handle of the flick knife. But stabbing was such a messy affair. She should have given it more thought. She glanced to the right at the old rusty Toyota parked on the kerb. The keys were hanging in the ignition. Another sign that it was meant to be. A dark thought entered her head, wet and rasping. *She doesn't deserve to live.* Lucy swivelled her head up and down the road. No CCTV and nobody in sight. It was too good an opportunity to miss.

Do it. Do it. Do it, a small voice drummed in her head. *She thinks she's so great. Run the bitch over.* Lucy glared at the woman pacing the kerb, and the voice grew louder in her head. *What are you waiting for?* Lifting the rusting handle, she grabbed the keys dangling from the ignition. The car may have been old, but the engine was souped-up, and Lucy grinned as she floored the accelerator. The sound of screeching tyres filled the air as she sped down the street. Charlotte stepped back, waiting for the car to pass. Lucy pulled down sharply on the steering wheel – jolted in her seat as the car mounted the kerb. Charlotte froze like a rabbit caught in the headlights, and a wicked laugh escaped Lucy's lips. On she drove until Charlotte's form grew; filling the windscreen. She bounced on the hood – a loud wallop of body mass on metal. Now you see her, now you don't, Lucy thought, as she was launched in the air before her.

Rolling onto the street, Charlotte hit the road, arms flailing like a limp crash test dummy. Lucy slammed on the brakes, watching the broken body in her rear-view mirror. The low rumble of the engine ticked over, and she licked her lips as a slow grin spread on her face. Charlotte's fingers clawed the pavement, her blonde head bobbing like a nodding dog. Down but not out, Lucy thought, adrenalin pumping through her body. Scanning the dimly lit streets, she gripped the gearstick and shoved the rusted Toyota into reverse. Another burst of laughter escaped her lips as her excitement climaxed.

Ker-thunk

Ker-thunk

The car rose and fell over Charlotte's body.

Heart thumping, Lucy checked for movement. She clamped the gearstick forward and sent it thudding forwards one last time. *Just to be sure.* This time it didn't make as much of a thunk, but lots of little cracks as the car crushed and splintered what was left of her bones. Lucy smiled. No chance of identifying her now. All that was left was a pool of blood and clothes.

She sped into the night, abandoning the car a couple of miles down the road. Pulling off the worn tracksuit top, she dipped the arm into the petrol tank before setting it alight. The blast singed the hairs on the back of her neck as she ran. Inside, she felt invincible. Untouchable.

She enjoyed the hunt. It gave her a special kind of joy. But there was no time to waste, and tomorrow, she would get back to the serious task of finding her mother.

CHAPTER EIGHT

'Alright? Manage to sort yourself out with a place?' DI Downes said, his expression harried.

'No... What's going on?' Ruby replied, all thoughts of her flat hunting dismissed from her mind. There was an energy in the office, a worker hive mentality: heads down, fingers pointing at screens, loud phone calls. 'Have you found Emily?' she said, hopefully.

'We've found *someone*,' Downes replied. 'A hit-and-run was reported in the early hours. Her name is Charlotte Lockwood. Looks like she's been murdered.'

'Shit,' Ruby said. 'Not our refuge lady Charlie, is it?'

'It's possible. She was known for her charity work. The night shift dealt with it; the handover package is on my desk.'

'Any family?'

'Aye. Just a husband mind, they both lived in Cornwall. She had ID on her person... what's left of it.'

Ruby nodded, guessing he had already been to the scene. 'Where?'

'Under the railway bridge in Lamb Lane: at the back of Mentmore Terrace.'

'Around the corner from a scrap yard? Yeah I know it,' Ruby said. 'I used to patrol there when I was on the beat. Doesn't strike me as the sort of place you'd have a lot of witnesses.'

'Uniform's on the street making enquiries now.'

'Has anyone tried ringing the refuge in Penzance?' Ruby said, her throat dry for the want of a good cup of tea.

'Office staff don't come in until eight. I thought you might like to—' The Dubliners' 'Dirty Old Town' blared from his pocket, notifying him of a phone call. 'Worrow,' he muttered, taking big steps as he left without ceremony.

Ruby clapped her hands together to grab her team's focus. 'Guys, can I have your attention for a minute, please? I know you're all up to your eyes in it but the powers from above are breathing down our necks, and I don't want to give them any excuse to have a go. Briefing's at eight, and I need a clean desk policy for when our DCI returns.'

A series of moans echoed around the room, and Ruby threw her colleagues a hard stare. 'I know it's a shock, but shovel your shit into a bin bag or a drawer until Worrow has been and gone. And smarten up a bit guys: we need ties and clean shirts. Eve you look just fine; if you could run out and get a pack of shortbread biscuits and some soya milk for her majesty that would be great. Take it from the tea club.'

Eve glowed at the compliment, but her smile fell when she realised all that was in the tea club tin was a button and five cent piece. 'I would, but it's empty.'

'Thieving little… who's had the tea club money away? Bloody police!' Ruby said, pulling a five pound note from her wallet and handing it over. 'Here. I'll be in my office. If any of my loyal subjects would care to make me a hot beverage, I'd be deeply grateful.'

Luddy stood up from his computer and began collecting empty mugs from his colleagues' desks. 'Alright, Sarge, message received. I'll boil the kettle.'

Ruby smiled. 'Cheers, Luddy, extra strong, three sugars, and a tiny drop of milk.'

'And stirred anticlockwise by the hand of a blonde-haired, blue-eyed virgin?' Luddy said, carrying the tray of coffee-stained cups out to their kitchen.

'Shame you don't have blonde hair, mate,' Ash snickered. 'You would have done just fine.'

Ruby recognised the scrawl on the yellow Post-it-note as DI Downes's handwriting. It was the number of the refuge in Devon, and a note asking her to call back. She peeled it from her computer monitor and tapped out the numbers on her phone. It was picked up after two rings, and the sound of Tracey Greenwood's voice was music to her ears. She had spoken to Tracey before with regards a previous incident, and she was one of those lovely helpful souls. Ruby ran through the scant details of Emily's case that they knew and the phone call from Charlie in the hope Tracey could come up with some answers.

'I was actually going to ring you,' Tracey said. 'I've just come back from holidays, so I wasn't here when the police called.'

'So you know of Emily?' Ruby said hopefully.

'No, I'm afraid not, but I do know Charlotte Lockwood... or rather I did. She came here to do some volunteer work last year. She was vetted, seemed like a nice lady, quite well-to-do. But after a few months we had to let her go.'

'Why?' Ruby said, giving Luddy a thumbs-up as he placed a strong mug of tea on her desk.

'Personal involvement with the clients. Giving them her mobile number, chatting out of hours. Not a big fan of policy, although it was there for her own good.'

'Do you think it's possible that she dealt with Emily Edmonds? She seemed adamant that she did.'

Tracey sighed. 'We've no paperwork on Emily, but we do have a record of Charlotte dealing with some anonymous calls from your area. She might have given out her number and started communicating privately.'

'Is that why you let her go?'

'We quizzed some of her clients and they backed up our suspicions. She even met a couple of them for coffee. All without making the refuge aware. We dismissed her that day.'

Ruby took a mouthful of tea, making a loud slurping noise as it burned the roof of her mouth. 'Sorry, hot tea. How did Charlotte take it?'

'I'm a milky coffee girl myself,' Tracey laughed. 'Charlotte was fine, but I wonder if that's because she was already meeting up with Emily by then.'

'What do you think her motives were? Was it sexual?'

'No… I think she had… issues. But don't ask me what.'

'OK. Thanks, Tracey, you've been more than helpful. Someone may be in touch at some point; meantime, if you hear from Emily, please let us know.'

'Good luck.'

Ruby opened her office window, wrinkling her nose at the stench of rotting garbage wafting in. The smell was stronger than ever as it baked under the sun which promised another sweltering day. She switched on her desk fan, placing empty mugs on piles of paperwork to stop them blowing away. Groaning, she caught sight of Downes's hulking frame from the corner of her eye. It wasn't that she disliked Jack, that was clearly evident given the number of times she had taken him to bed; he just was not equipped to deal with stress very well, and every emotion was laid bare for all to see. He never used to be like that, at least, not before his wife died. She wondered if his missus had been his sounding board. Ruby shuddered at the thought of becoming her replacement. Closing her eyes she removed her designer glasses and rubbed the bridge of her nose.

'Got anything yet?' Jack said, throwing open the door.

He was obviously still sore from his reprimanding from the Chief. That was how things worked in the police. Things had a nasty way of filtering down. Worrow gave Jack a dressing-down because of pressure from above. Jack in turn took it out on Ruby, which was her cue to bollock her team. But that wasn't how it worked with her. If she had a bone to pick with her team it would be for a good reason and not because her ego had been bruised.

She recounted her conversation with Tracey, in between sips of tea, as Downes perched on the edge of her desk. He nodded as she spoke, but his eyes were far away.

'Let's not complicate this,' he said, 'because it makes perfect sense to me. Harry Edmonds was stabbed during a domestic dispute with his missus because he warned her against seeing her daughter. She's then got the same advice from some overbearing woman named Charlotte, who's been mown down in the street. Looks like the finger of suspicion points to Emily.'

Ruby took another mouthful of tea, and a teabag rose up to greet her. She gave it a squeeze before firing it into the bin. 'But now we've got Lucy thrown in the mix for good measure. According to Charlotte, Lucy was rude to her.'

'Sure, but wouldn't yous? She just met her mother. It's only natural she'd want her to herself,' Downes said, his Northern Irish accent sounding stronger than ever.

'Yes,' Ruby said. 'But where is she? Lucy's had ample opportunity to respond to police appeals for information. So far we've had zilch.'

'Have you got any contacts in the adoption agency?' Downes leaned over to shut the door. 'We need the identity of Emily's adopted daughter so we can bring her in for questioning.' He rubbed his chin. It was his tell, something he did when he was dipping a toe over the thin blue line. 'It takes too long through the courts.'

Silence passed between them as Ruby absorbed his words. She knew what he wanted, but was not going to make it easy.

'So if you know of anyone… ' Another rub of the chin.

Ruby raised an eyebrow. 'Just what are you asking me, gov?'

'I'm asking… well, do you need me to spell it out?'

Ruby's lip tweaked to the left. 'Yes. Yes, I do.'

'You've got… contacts. People who can get that sort of information overnight.'

Ruby tutted. 'Jack. Why, if I didn't know better I'd think you were asking me to break the law.'

Downes's jaw tightened, his voice low. 'Can you get it or not?'

'Not. I don't mix in those circles anymore.'

'Fine,' he said, straightening himself to leave. 'We'll have to go the long way round.' Downes's words trailed behind him as he left, leaving her door gaping open, as he always did. The open door policy was Worrow's idea. Apparently it helped office morale.

Ruby pulled her e cigarette from her pocket, cursing the flat battery as she sucked the plastic tip. She rolled the vaporiser between her fingers, loath to scrounge yet another cigarette from one of her team. It was bad enough she had overloaded them with tasks. The problem being a sergeant was that she was forced to delegate work when she wanted to do it all herself. It was the same when she was young: she hated sharing her toys. It wouldn't have been too bad if she liked Barbie dolls and Tiny Tears, but Ruby was only ever interested in Action Man and roller skates.

She poked her head through her open office door, grateful that the most helpful member of the team was only a couple of feet away. 'Luddy?'

'Yes, Sarge,' he said, glancing up from his computer.

'I want you to go down to Harry's local with Eve. Use your charms on the barmaid; they're usually good for a bit of gossip. Find out if either of the Edmonds was having an affair. Did he gamble?

Owe money to dodgy people? Someone must know something. Start closest to the scene and work your way outwards.'

'Will do,' he said, shuffling his paperwork back into its folder.

Ruby linked her fingers, stretching her knuckles until the bones in her shoulders cracked. She couldn't remember the last time she'd had a good night's sleep. Her thoughts returned to Nathan, and their looming anniversary . The fact Downes knew about her association made her nervous, but he had never disclosed it to a soul. As for asking for information… bloody cheek. But he wasn't far wrong. Nathan was a powerful man, and if he didn't have a contact in the adoption agency, he would most likely ask his resident computer hacker, Tweedy Steve, to get it for him. But contacting her old flame was the last thing Ruby wanted.

Downes returned minutes later to throw her the car keys. It was her signal to move, and she sprang from her chair, cursing her police radio. How was she supposed to get any updates if the damned thing wasn't turned on? She slapped in a fresh battery from the charger on the desk before sliding it onto the clip on her belt.

'We've had an update,' Jack said, looping his arms through his shoulder harness before throwing on his jacket. 'They've found Emily Edmonds.'

CHAPTER NINE

Lucy slid her hand across the crumpled paper, smoothing it flat against the Formica kitchen table. It was silly to think she had found her new mother in Emily Edmonds. What a little mouse she was. She took a deep breath and exhaled. Time to forget all about her now. All traces of Emily had been eradicated from her life, including her sidekick, Charlotte. Another waste of space that did not deserve to live.

Lucy scratched off her name with the blunt end of a pencil, counting down the rest of the list. She knew she had been born to a strong, loving, independent woman. Someone who would take her in and love her for ever. They would go on shopping trips together, and when Christmas came... the child inside her giggled with delight. When Christmas came it would be the best day of all.

The tree in the basement had been lovingly prepared, and the new set of lights dappled the walls with a green and yellow hue. Candles were more authentic when mirroring the customs of Victorian times, but some small deviations could be forgiven. She had replaced the broken chair with a stronger one, and cut lengths of washing line instead of rope. Better for restraining, Lucy thought. At least, until they came to an understanding. This time she would try harder; keep her temper in check. She had to, if she had any hope of making it work. But there was no remorse for the others that failed. How else would she find her true mother unless she worked her way down the list? But time was running out. It was only a few months to Christmas, and Lucy would not spend it alone. The thoughts cast a shadow over her soul. She scribbled asterisks beside her potentials: *Monica Clarke, Anita Devine,* and another, who she barely dared to look at. The biggest challenge of all.

The kettle clicked off as it boiled, reminding her that she had things to do. She afforded herself a few minutes to recollect last night. It was fun creating new memories of her mother rather than the childhood recollections that lay rotten and festering in her brain. Monica had been careless: leaving her back door unlocked. Her house keys sat on the kitchen counter, just asking to be duplicated, which Lucy dutifully did, before returning under the protection of darkness. She had become adept at sneaking around, and Monica's four-bedroom detached property had lots of hiding places.

She'd imagined herself growing up there as a child: going to private school, attending barbecues and having playdates with the local children. *If only mother had not let her go…* but she shook the thought away. She was bound to have a good excuse, and Lucy was willing to forgive. She had glided around the home, careful not to leave any traces of her visit. Cold, impersonal, sharp, it featured a minimalist design. Spotlights against gloss, polished floorboards, gadgets that closed the curtains, all the latest technology at the touch of a button. Lucy was happy to see an absence of family photos. Disposing of family members was a messy business, but had to be done if they were to be together. The obligatory wedding picture hung in a framed canvas on the wall. A balding man with a chubby face, Monica's husband, appeared the product of too many gourmet dinners and fine wines. He did not look like he would present too much of a challenge. Monica, on the other hand, was a vision in an understated cream lace dress. Lucy had noted the colour of her hair, capturing the photo on her iPhone. Picking up a hairbrush, she unravelled some of the strands. A natural brunette with a soft bounce to the end of her locks: Lucy had a matching wig at home. She peered closer at the photo. Brown eyes. But that was easily fixed too.

Standing in the bedroom doorway, she had watched her new mother sleeping. She had barely remembered picking up the scissors, and they twitched in her gloved hand. The urge to crawl in beside her and wrap her arms around the sleeping woman was strong. But she had appeared too peaceful to disturb so she slipped out the back door; the reassuring curve of the scissor handle still nestled in her palm. An effective weapon, should anyone try to disturb her.

She smiled. Soon they would be together. Lucy would have her fairy-tale ending after all.

CHAPTER TEN

Ruby undid the top button of her shirt, sticky from the heat that showed no signs of abating. If it was this hot in the car, she couldn't imagine what the crime scene was like, and she wondered how long the body had been left to ferment. She had a reasonably strong stomach for such things, which was just as well given she mostly ate on the go. But, at night, the faces of the dead came back to haunt her, and a stiff drink was the only thing capable of quieting their pleas for justice. Ruby didn't believe in the supernatural, but she did believe in torment: each brutal act locked in time until answers were found. Who needed ghosts when the family of the dead begged for answers, unable to move on from their loss?

Downes had marched on ahead, leaving her to speak to the force press office who had called to speak to him with some enquiries about the case. The king of delegation, he was always passing on his little jobs, knowing she respected him too much to refuse. She turned the corner, impressed to see so many uniformed officers knocking on doors. The five-bedroom semi in Canonbury was situated on a nice leafy suburb unaccustomed to police officers and CSI. Ducking underneath the police tape, Ruby flashed her badge and joined her colleagues, gowning up under the watchful eye of Bones. She recognised Detective Chief Inspector Worrow underneath the suit: rigid, stiff, and stick thin. Her black bob was cut with precision, too severe for her youthful face. She was chatting to Chris Douglas, a trim, effeminate-looking man, with sandy blonde hair. She liked Chris, he had a dry sense of humour that took the darkness from his role. Forensic pathologists often attended murder scenes to gather evidence and examine the body in situ before it was transferred to the mortuary.

'Morning, Ma'am, Chris,' Ruby nodded, realising they were both leaving the scene rather than going in. 'I heard the owners called it in?' Traffic was good and the drive had been short, depriving her of a full briefing of events.

'They got back from holiday today,' Chris said. 'Bit of a shock to find Emily Edmonds helping herself to cucumber sandwiches, draped on their chaise longue.'

Ruby frowned, wondering if she had heard right. Chris touched her arm to rescue her from her confusion. 'You'll see when you go in there. Lovely property; although I think it'll be a while before they get the smell out of their chintz furnishings. Will we see you at the post-mortem later?'

Ruby caught the wicked gleam in his eye. He knew how much she hated PMs, and took great delight in her discomfort. It wasn't the smell that bothered her, although that was bad enough. It was the bone saw; the high-pitched drilling sound that reverberated through her brain. Her last attendance had given her a phobia of the dentist and now she brushed her teeth three times a day rather than face the sound of a drill again. She turned her eyes on Worrow who was daintily stepping out of her oversized suit.

'I was going to ask Jack, but he's got a lot on.' She nodded her head in agreement with herself. 'Yes. It would be good to have you present.'

'See you at the mortuary around six,' Chris said, looking amused.

Ruby forced a smile before turning to leave. She approached the house, her temperature rising as she re-evaluated her fondness for the pathologist.

It was an impressive semi; another building the likes of which Ruby could only aspire to own. Dream on, she thought, her eyes creeping over the length of black ribbon tied to the door knocker. The hall was wide and airy, but not airy enough to dispel the stench that greeted her as she passed through the front door. Her footsteps echoed on the gloss timber floor. She took in the family photographs, peering at the private school uniforms. She imagined their names as Rufus and Hermione. Ruby liked her own name. It was down to earth. Stoic.

She did not need the stepping plates or the sound of Downes's voice to guide her to the body. All she had to do was follow the smell. She fixed the mask over her nose: an instinctive measure which did little to block the stench assaulting her nostrils. Downes was standing in the living room, hands on hips as he spoke to Katie, an attractive young crime scene investigator who was new to the role.

'Ah, Ruby,' he said, tearing his eyes away. 'What took you so long?'

'I got cornered by Ma'am Worrow. She wants me to attend the PM this evening. Looks like you're off the hook.'

Downes clapped her on the back. 'Well, that's super so it is, just super. Sure you'll have a grand old time cosying up to the boss.'

'Thanks,' Ruby said flatly, trying to make sense of the scene before her.

The corpse of Emily Edmonds was seized by rigor; her knees drawn up to her chest in a foetal position on a very expensive-looking chaise longue. Her head lolled to one side, and her skin had taken on a mottled grey hue. Her long brown hair was tied in a ponytail, eyes open, an expression of terror relaying her final moments. The pretty floral dress she was wearing was too big for her body, and Ruby frowned, wondering at what point she had been changed. On the coffee table lay a teapot, sugar cubes, a jug of milk, a teacup and saucer, and an uneaten cucumber sandwich on one side.

'I take it that's Emily then,' Ruby said, feeling a surge of pity for the remains of the woman before her. But she did not feel surprise. Emily's death was something her gut had forecast from the first day she saw Harry Edmonds's body; although she was yet to ascertain why.

'Afraid so,' Jack said, his suit rustling as he folded his arms.

She took in the room, which was the same size as her whole flat. She doubted they would ever get rid of the smell. Even when the cleaners had removed all traces of the body, its presence would still be felt, and nobody would want to sit in the room alone. 'Who found her?' she asked, taking another step towards the body. Even without the facial bruising and cuts to her lips, Ruby could tell by the tortured expression that death had not come peacefully.

'The man of the house. Him and his missus came back from their holidays with the kids to find some black ribbon tied to the front door. There was no sign of forced entry, but he told them to wait in the hall while he checked the house.'

'I saw the ribbon on the way in. The children. What's their names?'

'Why?'

'No reason.'

'Felicity and Jasper.'

'Oh. He looked more like a Rufus,' Ruby said, stepping back to allow the CSIs to continue their work. She could see why the pathologist had come to the conclusion the body had been moved. Apart from the lack of evidence at the scene, the position of the body suggested it had been stored in a cramped space. The boot of a car, a large kitchen cupboard, or even a suitcase would produce that boxed-off shape. 'Very mumsy,' she said, pointing to the old-fashioned floral tunic dress. 'You know what I think?' she continued, not bothering to wait for a response. 'Lucy's turned up at Emily's door to confront her. There's been a set-to because Harry's a controlling sod and didn't want to know. Either Emily or Lucy decides to answer back. Harry ends up dead. Both women do a

Thelma and Louise and run for the hills. But the reunion doesn't go as planned, and Emily is murdered. Charlotte sticks her beak in, and she gets killed too. Lucy regrets her actions. She dresses her, does her hair, and lays her to rest in the nicest place she can find.'

'So we're dealing with a hot-headed individual who will stop at nothing to get what she wants,' Downes said, stepping back to allow the crime scene investigators to finish their work. 'It looks like whoever dumped the body closed the curtains and stopped all the clocks.'

'Mourning traditions,' Ruby said, remembering her mother doing the same thing after her father died.

'Indeed, although they're dying out now… no pun intended.' He nodded to Ruby. 'Seen enough?'

'More than,' she said, wondering how long she would smell the dead body on her skin, in her hair, her clothes. The fresh air was a gift as she stepped out of the house. Funny how she had never valued it until she was forced to inhale that rotting corpse smell.

Ruby rested her blazer on her chair, giving it a final sniff. It was no use. It would have to be dry-cleaned before she could wear it again. An expense she could barely afford. The home was due to put its prices up soon, and it was hard enough getting her brother to contribute at all. She thought of her mum and wondered what the chances were of getting in to see her for a visit. Minimal, given briefing was due in five and she had just been passed some vital information. Information that changed everything she knew about the case. The lunchtime special wafted through her window from The Eagle pub next door. Today it was curry. Ruby's stomach rumbled.

'I got you a sandwich, Sarge: chicken mayo,' Luddy said, dropping a Tesco bag between the piles of paperwork on her desk.

'Cheers, mate, and call me Ruby, for God's sake? Everyone else does,' she said, taking a peek inside the bag. 'Ooh, and Coke too; how much do I owe you?'

'My treat,' Luddy flashed a smile, his hand resting on the back of her chair. He had nice teeth, Luddy. Clean, even and minty fresh. Bit of a mummy's boy. He had a habit of lingering a bit too long, but Ruby was too indebted by his sandwich to ask him to leave.

She cracked open the can of Coke and took a swig. Then taking the sandwich in her left hand, she bit off a chunk of wholemeal bread. 'We've just located Emily's daughter,' she said, quickly chewing half her sandwich.

'Seriously?' Luddy said, his eyes widening at the prospect. 'Are we bringing her in then?'

'All will be revealed in briefing. But first, there's somewhere I've got to be.'

CHAPTER ELEVEN

Ruby shrugged on her shoulder harness. Her handcuffs and baton lay nestled next to her ribs on one side and a small can of incapacitant spray snapped into a pouch on the other. The weight was unevenly distributed because she preferred to keep a radio clipped onto the waistband of her belt. But she was willing to sacrifice a lopsided harness for the reassurance it provided. It would be even better if she was allowed to carry a firearm, but her ability to handle a gun was not widely known. She palmed the keys she had booked out from Ash, the designated exhibits officer. The four leaf clover keyring hadn't brought Harry Edmonds much luck, Ruby thought, as she strode to her car. The keys were due to be returned to his relatives this afternoon, and she had promised Ash that she would be back within the hour. Given that the house had been thoroughly searched, she did not intend on staying very long.

Ruby pushed the police card onto the dashboard of her car, hoping it would save her yet another ticket. Advertising her vocation was an invitation to having her tyres slashed, but she was tight on time and had enough confidence in Tresham Walk to take the chance.

Slowly turning the key in the front door, she silently slipped into the hall. It would not be the first time she had returned to a scene to find a perpetrator present, and such an experience kept her nerves tightly bound. She glanced around. The air was rich with the scent of death, and the lilies that once bloomed brightly were now drooping gracefully in their vase. Cast in gloom, the living room took on a menacing hue as the tightly drawn curtains absorbed all natural light. Ruby flicked on the light switch, her eyes falling on the blood-encrusted carpet, now stained in a deep burgundy red. The aftermath of the police investigation was plain to see. Cupboard doors yawned open and upturned furniture lay next to piles of paperwork and books stacked on the floor. Violent red blood splatters patterned the wall, having being analysed, photographed and recorded in detail. Ruby followed a pitter-patter of red-stained paw prints from the living room, tracing them to the cat flap embedded in the back door. Searching in the cupboards, she drew back the lid on a tin of cat food, emptying its contents into a plastic bowl. Hopefully someone was looking after the cat who had come in search of food. The kitchen drawers were grimy with fingerprint dust, but the answers she sought did not lie here. It was far too busy a room to keep secrets. The answers lay somewhere more private, somewhere hidden.

Tap… tap… tap… a knocking noise from upstairs reignited the feeling of foreboding that had shadowed her entry. She stiffened, casting her eyes to the ceiling. Sliding her hand under her blazer, she popped the clasp holding her baton in place, gripping it tightly in her palm. There was no need to extend it. Not yet. Most officers would have plodded into the house and slammed the door behind them, but past experience had left Ruby wary.

And now she found herself creeping up the stairs towards the source of the noise. Shadows danced on the landing, but she did not want to alert any possible intruder by turning on the light. *Tap… tap… tap.* The noise grew louder, and Ruby cocked her head to one side. It was coming from inside the walls rather than footsteps on the floorboards above. Pressing her hand to the radiator, she heaved a sigh of relief. It was just the heating on a timer, although why they needed it during an Indian summer was beyond her. But she wanted to leave just the same and clipped her baton back in place before finishing what she came here to do. Intuition drove her into the bedroom, and she searched every inch of floor space for a weakness. The thin bedroom carpet revealed sturdy wooden flooring with well-driven nails to negate any hiding places underneath. Regular hiding places had been well searched. She needed to delve deeper. Emily was a victim of domestic abuse, and such contact with her daughter would have been unwelcome by her jealous abuser. After half an hour of searching the bedroom, Ruby pushed her hair back from her face and got to her feet.

The bathroom still held a fresh lemony smell, and she examined the air freshener before placing it back on the shelf. The small sterile space was the one place Emily would have been granted some privacy, at least for a little while. She ran a hand along the paintwork on the outside of the door until she found the curve of an indentation. It was foot height, and a double layer of paint had been applied to the cracks in the wood. Someone had tried to kick it in. Gliding her hands over the lock on the door, she could see it had recently been fixed. Each clue painted a chilling picture of Emily Edmonds's life. Unlike Ruby's bathroom the grout in between the floor tiles was a perfect shade of white. She pressed down on each one, searching for a weakness, but there was none. After checking the cistern, she opened the cabinet. Shaving foam, mouthwash, a razor and some paracetamol. Emily would not hide anything here: not when it was filled with her Harry's things. It was just a regular family home. And yet Ruby could not shake off the feeling that somewhere in this house lay clues. Putting herself in Emily's shoes, she imagined she had received news from her daughter, but was reluctant to share it with the world. Her head tilted to the right, and she narrowed her eyes at the bath. Police should have removed the panel and checked inside.

Couldn't do any harm to check again. She cupped her fingers under the lips of the cheap plastic panel, driven by her intuition.

Like a game of hot and cold, she knew all at once that this was Emily Edmonds's hiding place. With the slightest pressure the corner popped free. Activating her phone torch she peered inside. Nothing but cobwebs and a layer of dust. Tilting her iPhone she illuminated the panel. 'Gotcha,' she whispered, reaching in her gloved hand. Taped to the inside was a small plastic bag. At last. Now she could leave. She would return the keys and update the search officers in case they wanted to return. Fixing the bath panel, she got to her feet. She had found what she was looking for, and it was time to share it with her team.

CHAPTER TWELVE

The incident room was an airless, soulless place. The steel framed window had been sealed shut for the last three years since a listening device was implanted from outside. Three floors up, they had expected privacy, and now they were paying the price as they filed into what Ruby lovingly referred to as hell. She prayed for rain. It was not that she hated the sun; Ibiza, Malaga, such places brought memories of glorious clubbing and sun-soaked days. Shoreditch briefing room in a heatwave did not invoke the same blissful feelings. With the door shut, and sweaty bodies lined up against the walls, it was a special kind of hell indeed.

Downes led the briefing, swapping intelligence and bringing everyone up to speed. He was leaving the best until last as always, and Ruby stood when prompted, ready to deliver the news.

'I've got two important updates which have just come in. Firstly, I want to read you some letters,' Ruby said, holding up two sheets of paper. 'These are copies of exhibits which I seized from Emily Edmonds's address this afternoon. They were discovered taped inside a bath panel in her home.' She handed Luddy copies to distribute. Clearing her throat, she prepared to read the first page.

'Dearest Mother.

Yes, you read right. I'm your daughter. I've come to find you. I know that this will come as a shock to you, or perhaps you've always known that this day would come – that the daughter you gave away would come looking for answers. But there's

*no need to worry. I don't care about the past. I just want
us to be a family. Writing this letter has not been easy, but
I want us to be together. I hope this advance warning will
make things easier when we meet. I'm so looking forward to
being a part of your family again.*

Lots of love, Lucy x'

Ruby lowered the paper and glanced around the room. Her
eyes rested on Ash as she wondered which second-hand shop he'd
bought his crumpled blue tie from. At least it proved someone had
listened to her request to smarten up.

'Right, I'm opening this up for discussion: what do you think?'

'Creepy psycho,' Ash said.

'Why?' Ruby replied.

He ran his hand over his thinning hair. 'Reading between the
lines. I've come to find you… I'm looking forward to being a
member of your family, then signing it lots of love. She doesn't
know this woman. It sounds desperate.'

'Maybe,' Ruby said, 'but are you making this judgement with
the beauty of hindsight?'

Eve fanned her face with her paper, her voice reminding Ruby
of a small chirping bird. 'I don't think she's crazy. She sounds sad,
lonely. It's not been easy for her, but she's writing the letter to
protect herself from rejection. She's hoping that by introducing
herself gradually she'll spare herself the embarrassment of being
turned away.'

'Fair point,' Ruby nodded. 'Anyone else?'

'I think the person behind this letter is very bitter but trying
to hide it. "The daughter you gave away", it doesn't sit easy with
me,' Luddy said.

Ruby nodded, giving him a knowing look. She had yet to inform
the team that they had located Emily's daughter, and wanted them to
view the letters with an open mind. 'We don't have Emily's response,

but I think we can guess given the tone of the second letter.' She fixed her glasses back on the bridge of her nose before continuing.

'Mother.

I was surprised to receive a reply so soon. At first I thought it was an indicator of your enthusiasm, until I read it through. I understand that you are concerned about how your husband will react, particularly given that you never saw fit to tell him of my existence. However, I would like to reassure you that I am not here to cause trouble. I have been able to put my childhood behind me. All I want now is for us to be a family and have a future together. I am sorry you have reservations, but our meeting is a necessity. The only thing that has kept me going all of these years is the thought of being reunited with my true mother. I look forward to seeing you very soon.

Lucy XX'

'Told you she was psycho,' Ash said as he nudged Eve.

'Well, I think it's sad,' Eve said. 'She's built up an idea of her mother in her head, and Emily has basically told her she's not interested. Granted, she's forthright, but perhaps that's because she's always had to be that way. What she said about putting her childhood behind her, it doesn't sound like she's had things easy.'

Ruby slid the paperwork back into the folder. 'I think we can all agree that Lucy has become forceful in her suggestions that they meet. This is someone who is not going to take no for an answer. We can only imagine that when Emily replied she was perhaps apologetic and pleading by nature, refusing to meet Lucy on the grounds that her husband knew nothing about her. Intelligence now suggests that Emily was a victim of domestic abuse.'

'Surely the question is: where's Emily's daughter? If you find her, you have our murderer,' Ash said.

'Not quite,' Ruby replied. 'We've already located Emily Edmonds's daughter.' She paused for effect, allowing the rumble of voices to echo around the room. 'Unfortunately, she's deceased. Emma Wilson died in a car accident two years ago, when she was twenty years old. So whoever wrote these letters is not Emily's real daughter. Which leads us to ask: who is responsible for writing these letters? And also: what's the connection with the ribbon tied to the door?'

Eve raised her hand. 'I've checked with Bones – it's crepe. It's a tradition which stems from the Victorian era. It means there's been a death in the family when it's tied on the door. It's usually tied around the door knocker or bell so callers don't knock loudly and disturb the grieving people inside. Black crepe looped with white ribbon signifies the death of a child.'

'Right,' Ruby said, feeling very tired. She should be thrilled to have so many clues, but with nothing to link them to they were being made to look like fools. 'Make a list of these traditions and pin them on the board. See if you can find any connections, past cases, anything of value. But don't spend too much time on it. We've got a lot to get through.'

Ruby knew that when the post-mortem was over she would need a stiff drink. Which is why she had arranged to meet Luddy at the Well and Bucket at eight. She loved the vibe of this pub, with its distressed tile-work and shiny copper bar. Pictures of creepy Victorians graced the walls, giving it an eccentric feel. She sipped on her luminous cocktail as Luddy tucked into a burger and chips. Ruby didn't want food. It interfered with the absorption of the alcohol which was nicely numbing the guilt she felt for not visiting her mother that day.

'That bone saw… I can still hear it now. I mean, Chris Douglas seems like a nice guy, right? But how can any normal young man want to work in a job where you saw through someone's skull and crack it open like a boiled egg? And don't get me started on the smell… '

Luddy gently laid his knife and fork to one side.

'Are you not having that?' Ruby asked, oblivious to the effect of her words.

'Funnily enough, I've lost my appetite. But do carry on with your vivid descriptions.'

'Oh yeah… sorry,' Ruby chortled, stealing a chip from his plate. 'Anyway, I managed to keep my lunch down long enough for him to examine the contents of her stomach. And do you know what he found?'

Luddy sighed. 'The remains of a cucumber sandwich?'

'No; good guess though.' She swivelled her head left to right before dropping her voice. 'Christmas decorations. In her stomach. At least that's what we think they were. She had lacerations inside her mouth. Apparently she was force-fed baubles. You know, the ones you hang on a tree?' Ruby knew that Ash would retort with a dirty joke but Luddy just nodded, allowing her to babble on until he suppressed a yawn with the back of his hand. It was then that Ruby realised she was rambling, which was usually a sign that she was drunk. 'Sorry mate,' she said, 'I've been going on a bit, haven't I?'

'No, I'm just a bit tired, that's all,' Luddy said, crunching his ice cubes with his back teeth. 'Can I get you another drink?'

Ruby shook her head. 'Best I be off. Early start and all that. Sorry for ruining your dinner.'

Luddy rose, his hand on her forearm. 'Would you like me to walk you home?' He flushed, probably realising how lame it sounded. 'I mean, you've had quite a few. Do you want me to see you to your door?'

'Nah, I'm only around the corner. Thanks for keeping me company though; there's nothing sadder than drinking alone.'

Ruby bent down to pick up her bag from where it had fallen on the floor. 'See ya tomorrow!' she said, cheerily, before disappearing onto the streets of London.

A lungful of night air brought her back to her senses, and she mentally admonished herself. Drinking on a work night was hardly setting a good example, particularly with a murder case on the go. She strode down the narrow streets, taking the shortcuts that would lead her to her flat. It was good to walk things off. She passed the smokers, the revellers, and the toothless drunk on the corner arguing with a scantily clad woman about his dog.

Ten minutes later, Ruby was wishing she had stayed on the main drag rather than the dark allies which cut time off her journey. The footsteps that had been echoing behind her halted as she swivelled her head, and a shadow darted from her vision. She briefly considered a confrontation, but she was too unsteady on her feet to guarantee she would come out of it unharmed. She straightened her posture, focusing hard on walking with more confidence than she felt. Whoever was behind her obviously did not want to be seen, which was just as well as Ruby was in no hurry to meet them.

She slid her hand to the light switch as she opened the door, unable to shake off the creeping sensation clinging to her spine. Under the gloom of the forty-watt lightbulb, she slipped off her shoes and padded around her flat. Something wasn't right. She picked up the framed photo of her with her mum that now lay face down on top of her television. Wandering into her bedroom, her gaze fell on the open wardrobe doors. Had she left them open? And her clothes – they were now neatly folded on the chair. A frown burrowed into her forehead. Was she being paranoid or had someone been here? After checking the rest of the flat, she reluctantly slipped into bed. But sleep did not come easy, carrying nightmares fuelled with fear and regret.

CHAPTER THIRTEEN

Ruby yawned. A restless night had left her with four hours' sleep, and yet, here she was viewing a property at seven in the morning. But she had to get away. She was feeling increasingly uneasy in her flat, and this was too good an opportunity to miss. She pushed open the door, and her first thought as she gazed around the beautifully designed surroundings was that she had come to the wrong address. Situated in Dalston, it was far more upmarket than anything she could afford, yet the letting agent had claimed it was within her price range. It had that fresh new carpet smell, which was an improvement on the scent of cannabis wafting from the neighbouring flats in her current abode.

'Hello,' she called out, 'anyone here?' Her voice echoed as she entered the room. She slipped off her heels and enjoyed the luxurious deep pile carpet underfoot. Rays of soft morning light flooded in through the window, and she admired the view of the city until the scent of a familiar aftershave brought her the identity of the man standing behind her. 'I should have known it was you,' her voice was silky as it betrayed her. Her body always did that when it came to Nathan, and the only way to resist him was never to be in his presence.

'Hello, Ruby,' he said, pulling back the strands of her hair and stroking the nape of her neck.

He'd always loved her neck. He said it was like a swan, elegant and graceful, stark white against the darkness of her hair. A million shivers ran down her spine as he breathed into her earlobe. His hands were on her forearms now, laying claim, as he always did. She stood her ground as she tried to contain her arousal. What was it about this man that made her brain turn to mush? It had always been that way, for as long as she could remember.

She closed her eyes and pulled away. Her hand found her throat, and she made space between them before turning to face him. He looked well. More than well. His muscles were defined; his face tanned, with a light stubble. He regarded her, unsmiling.

She cleared her throat. 'Why have you brought me here?'

'You weren't answering my calls.'

'I threw away the phone.'

'Hmm,' he said in a deep voice.' It was his signal of displeasure. Ruby had recognised it in his father, whose hardened frown was always followed with silence. 'What happened to your face?' he said, touching her cheekbone.

'I ran into someone's fist.' She pulled away.

Nathan's scowl deepened; Ruby's attempt at humour falling flat. 'You know what date it is today?'

'Of course I do.' She was not likely to forget. It was ingrained on her brain, and kept her and Nathan together, no matter how hard she tried to keep away. She had known that when the date came around he would be back to see her. Why? What was the point? It wasn't going to change anything. It was time to move on – walk away from the ghosts of their past and begin again.

'I should go,' she said, her brief glance turning into a lingering gaze. His presence was hypnotic. She found herself stepping towards him as if she was in a trance, her body calling out for his touch. Nobody gave her as much pleasure as he did. Yet nobody caused her as much pain.

'So, you're growing a beard?' she said, wondering why she was engaging in conversation when she'd said she was leaving just seconds before.

Nathan ran his fingers over his chin. 'And your hair has got long,' he said.

Ruby had considered cutting it short, but she couldn't. Even now he had a strong hold over her, and she found herself wearing clothes he liked, his favourite perfume. She had given into it a long time ago, unable to completely let him go. 'You're still a criminal then?'

'I'm still in the business of making money. You still in the filth?'

Ruby nodded, killing the smile as soon as she realised it had crossed her lips. 'Why have you brought me here?'

'You needed a flat; I've got you one.'

'Why? Your last floozy move out, did she?'

Nathan folded his arms, his biceps straining against the constraints of his shirt. His eyes darkened and he gave her the look. It was the look which told her he knew everything that had been going on in her life since she left him the year before. Such was his power. But she never promised to be celibate, and she knew it wasn't fair of her to expect him to be either.

'There's only ever been you,' he said, his words thick with emotion.

In that second she saw the young man she had fallen in love with all those years ago. Running through the night, their laughter echoing down the rain-streaked alley as police sirens cut through the air, then later, sitting on the bare floorboards of a derelict building as they got stoned in each other's arms; the curls of smoke carrying their words as they dreamt of future plans.

Ruby blinked, bringing herself back to reality. To the present day. She wasn't that girl anymore. And he was not that boy. Yet she knew that even if fate had not intertwined them, one with the other, she would never have forgotten him. 'It's too much; I can't live in this place.'

'I'll let you pay, if that's what you want.'

'Yeah, at half the market value.' Ruby would have loved nothing better than to leave her grotty little flat. But she knew where the money came from and her pride would not allow it, much less risk the implications if her superiors found her accepting gifts from criminals.

'They won't trace it back to me,' Nathan said. 'Besides, you don't have much choice. The lease on your flat is expiring soon.'

'How do you—?' Ruby said, stopping herself before she finished the sentence because she knew the answer. Nathan could find out whatever he wanted. 'I'll just lease it again for another year.'

'Nope, no can do. I'm selling it to the council.'

'*You're* selling it? You're not my landlord.'

'I am now.'

'No… you can't be.' Ruby paused, knowing that if Nathan wanted to buy her dingy flat he would have no problem in doing so. 'Well, that's fine, I'll just rent somewhere even shittier. Is that what you want?'

'You won't.' The words were firm.

Ruby should have treated him with disdain, but she couldn't. In her heart she knew that Nathan was a good man who took the wrong path. He could have been anything, but his upbringing dictated his direction. She had turned her back on him to go her own way, but, despite it all, they kept finding themselves thrust together. 'How have you been keeping? You okay?'

'Good.'

Another step closer. She could see the hurt in his eyes. He thought she was moving on, away from him. He couldn't have been more wrong. 'I don't love him, you know. I've just been so lonely.'

Nathan reached out and touched her cheek, and she gave in to the moment, closing her eyes as she leaned her face into the warmth of his palm. His lips brushed against hers, and she welcomed it. She could so easily melt into him – forget her job and the world outside.

Her arm reached around his waist, but he broke away, leaning his forehead against hers as he clasped her jaw in his hand. His breath had become heavy, and he closed his eyes before stepping away.

'What's wrong?'

'That was goodbye, babe.'

Ruby frowned. 'Goodbye? Are you playing games with me?'

'No… I… '

Ruby shrugged off his touch. 'You got me here on false pretences and now you're saying goodbye? Are you getting off on being cruel? Is that what it is?'

'I can't keep going like this… watching you… I gotta move on with my life. You're not gonna change, any more than I am. So I'm letting you go.'

'You don't get to do that. *I* let *you* go a year ago.'

'You didn't. Not really. We've both been holding onto the past. This is the last time you'll see me. But I want you to take two things.' He shoved a phone into her bag. 'This mobile is untraceable. If you get into trouble just leave a message and I'll be there. Secondly, you're taking this flat. I used to lie low here sometimes but I'm moving on. I don't need it anymore. I've never brought a woman around here, Ruby. I wouldn't do that and expect you to move in afterwards. But you're free to do with it what you will.'

Ruby stared at the key he pushed into the palm of her hand. It was blurred from the tears forming in her eyes. 'I can't.'

'Yes you can. As far as anyone else is concerned you were left it as an inheritance from that aunt of yours that died last year. The legal documents are in the bedside dresser.'

'Why? Where are you going? Are you in some kind of trouble?'

'No, but I need you to know I won't be there to look out for you anymore. You're on your own now.'

'I'm on my own? How dare you! You call me around here then talk to me like I'm some fucking kid trying to find my way in the world?' Ruby flared. 'I'm not the sixteen-year-old you shacked up with, Nathan; I'm thirty-eight years old. I have a good job and I run a tight team. Don't talk to me like you're some cocaine dealing superhero who watches from the shadows every night. I can get by just fine without you.'

Nathan grabbed her wrist as she tried to fling the key across the floor. 'I'm not some low life street dealer and you know that. So have a bit of respect.'

Ruby saw the flash of anger in his eyes but she didn't care. It was a trait he inherited from his father. A trait that served him a brutal childhood and gave him the respect of his peers. His cold, hard face pressed close to hers. Pulling her wrists away, she turned to leave.

'Wait. Don't leave it like this.' His words were filled with instant regret. She was the only person that was ever afforded such a luxury. His temper was quick, and she knew violence was just one of the tools he was forced to use to keep ahead of the game. But it was something he rarely allowed her to witness. The most he had ever afforded her was a flash of anger, some hurtful words, but he had never raised a hand.

Ruby sighed. She didn't want it to end like this either. Her voice softened. 'I hoped that the break would make you come around, leave it all behind and start a clean slate. But you can't, can you? You thrive on the power, the control. Your dad is controlling you now, even from beyond the grave.'

'I told you before: don't mention that bastard to me again.'

Ruby turned to look out the window. The streets of London were once their playground, but they'd been on different sides of the fence for a long time now. She turned to face him, wishing she could change his mind. 'Don't you see? We have history. I'll never have that with anyone else in my lifetime and neither will you. We could be so good together… but it's never going to work. Because we're always looking over our shoulder. The only way we can do it is if you turn your back on everything and start again. And I know you're not ready to do that.'

Nathan shook his head. 'You don't just walk away from this way of life. I know too much. I wouldn't last a week out there.'

Ruby took a step towards him, her eyes searching his face. 'Then why don't we both leave? Just run away somewhere, disappear from the landscape.'

'You'd do that for me? Give up everything?'

'Yes,' she said. 'As long as you did the same.'

'I know you. You'd resent having to leave your job, and you'd never abandon your mum.'

Mum. Ruby imagined Joy sitting alone, with nobody to visit her. She sighed. Nathan was right. 'Then I guess we should call it a day.'

Ruby's hand fell away from his, and her heart broke all over again as she realised he was not going to stop her.

'It's not that I don't... I mean, I do... ' Nathan swallowed hard, the words backed up in his throat. Declarations of love did not come easy for him, and right now, Ruby was fine with that because it hurt too much to hear them.

'I know,' she said, inhaling a deep breath. 'Shame it's not enough to keep us together.' Swiping away her tears, she turned and walked away.

CHAPTER FOURTEEN

Lucy was feeling as light as a breeze today. She giggled, pressing her hand to her mouth as the sound echoed around the confines of her car. The basement was waiting, all ready to welcome her next guest. Her dress, boots and white cotton smock were washed, pressed and laid out on her bed. She cast her eyes over her gloves; they were especially made, just like the rest of her outfit, and she could not wait to put them on. Everything was ready for when she could go to her special place, and what a relief that would be. She shrank back in her seat as the professional-looking woman shoved a key in the lock of the house across the road.

It was a lovely house, far nicer than the last place she had been to, and had encouraged her to dress in a style more fitting to her new mother. Monica had a well-paid job, drove a nice car, and liked to wear designer clothes. So Lucy had bought herself a Karen Millen suit, with designer heels to match. Monica was tall, about five foot ten, but Lucy's heels afforded her a generous enough height to convince her mother that she really was her adopted daughter. After all, if you gave up a child for adoption all those years ago and she came knocking on your door, would you really doubt what she had to say?

Lucy touched her long dark locks, checking them in the mirror. It was real hair, not that cheap synthetic stuff. The cap itched like hell though, and the warm weather made her scalp sweat. She took a deep breath before opening the car door. The most important thing was to appear confident. Just be the daughter she wants you to be, Lucy thought as she walked towards the townhouse. Monica's husband had a well-paid job in the city. But there was no room for men in the happy ever after that Lucy had planned. Her father figures had caused Lucy nothing but pain. Such a beautiful house, Lucy thought – certainly no shortage of money there. So why hadn't her mother got in touch? She clenched her jaw, forcing herself to relax as she pressed the doorbell. There was no point in getting upset about it now. Monica would have lots of time to explain.

Lucy did not expect the clamour of a dog from inside the hall. It must be a new addition. She hated dogs. They got in the way and nipped at your heels. She was never allowed any dogs in the foster homes she stayed in, which was just as well, or they would have been beaten to a pulp. But the one in the hallway of Monica's home sounded like one of these spoilt little designer dogs, which were probably treated far better than she ever had been. Lucy managed to keep calm as a shadow filled the doorway.

Monica looked even more glamorous up close. Her wavy brown hair had been perfectly styled, and she had definitely had her teeth fixed, maybe even a little Botox around the eyes. The soft ivory blouse clung to her curves, and the pencil skirt accentuated her hips. She was wearing just enough make-up to complement her flawless skin, but not too much that it aged her. The woman looked Lucy up and down, returning her gaze as she spoke. 'Yes?'

Lucy realised that she had been staring. But given this was the first time she was about to speak to her mother she felt it acceptable. 'Are you Monica Sherwood?' Lucy said, trying to sound nervous. People generally preferred if you were meek, subservient. She had learned from experience that it helped keep the situation calm.

'Yes, what can I do for you?' she said, perhaps affording Lucy a little more respect because she was so well-dressed.

'My name is Lucy. I'm your daughter.'

It was Monica's turn to stare open-mouthed now, and Lucy was ready to take the helm. 'Can I come in? We need to talk.' That was the understatement of the century, Lucy thought, as Monica cautiously allowed her inside.

She glanced past Lucy at the neighbouring houses: probably checking to see if they had noticed her arrival.

'I… I don't know what to say,' Monica said, her hand touching her bottom lip. 'I've thought about this moment since you turned eighteen,' she gave a small gasp as if somebody had punched her in the stomach, 'but I… I never imagined it like this… '

She seemed to go weak at the knees, and Lucy caught her arm and led her into a room on the right. It was tastefully decorated with cream furnishings and tasteful prints embellished the walls. Lucy scanned the fireplace for family photos, reassured there were no additions since her last visit. A surge of happiness grew inside her. If she had no brats to contend with, then it was all the more attention for her.

I've come home, Lucy thought. At last, I'm home.

CHAPTER FIFTEEN

It took every ounce of Nathan's strength not to stop Ruby as she walked away. Coming to this decision had not been easy, and he could not back out now. Giving her the flat was meant to be a final gift; a gesture of thanks for everything her family had done for his. But there was much more to it than that, and he was kidding himself if he thought otherwise.

Ruby was his biggest addiction, and in his fantasy world, where everything was black and white, they could be together without holding back. But as long as she was in the police then it wasn't going to happen. Their relationship veered from painful separations to brief lust fuelled reunions, when all he wanted was for them to settle down. His father would turn in his grave if he knew. The thought gave Nathan a certain satisfaction. He had come across some nasty fuckers in his lifetime, but nobody matched up to his old man, and he hated him with a passion. He couldn't believe it when his mother cried at his funeral. Not just crocodile tears, either. She was inconsolable. His brother, Lenny, was seventeen then and refused to attend. Nathan went for two reasons: firstly, to support his mother, and secondly so he could make sure the bastard really was dead. He had waited a long time for that day, and volunteered to help fill the grave afterwards. Injecting his anger into each shovelful of clay, he had enjoyed the satisfying thump as soil hit the expensive oak coffin. Not that Jimmy Crosby had the common decency to stay in the ground. Even now he haunted his son's thoughts, orchestrating his lifestyle, calling him weak as he spat in his face.

His father's words echoed in his mind as he watched Ruby leave. 'She's only a bird. Plenty more where that came from.'

It felt like the sky had fallen – the day his father died. He should have been relieved, but Nathan spent the day in shock. Jimmy was untouchable, and even in prison he had carried on his regime of terror. Nathan had learned to overpower his larger-than-life memory by claiming the family business for his own. Nobody liked his father, but they respected him, and after he died it was all up for grabs. Under the guidance of his mother he learned the ropes, modernising it until it was a sleek money-making machine. Gone were the drug-addled Toms, porno movies and seedy massage parlours. In their place were top class online escorts and a personal delivery service of class A cocaine. Racketeering was old and outdated, and there was no need to rob banks when you could get your hands on exceptional quality coke. Nathan was making too much money to need the protection racket and sold it on to a smaller firm. Nathan was a businessman; his only interest in organising the shifting of the product from A to B and making a healthy profit in return.

Lenny had had to pull some nasty stunts to keep them on top of the food chain, but their future was secured, and there was no need for any of that gangland shit anymore. They had made enough money now to buy themselves anonymity. But there was something about the violence that Lenny craved, and in the two weeks since his release from prison, he had lost his head. It didn't matter how many times Nathan told him to keep a low profile, he didn't seem to care. It wasn't that Lenny was a big bloke either, but it was that look in his eye – a twinkle of madness, his confident swagger – that told people he wasn't to be messed with. His mates would laugh and joke with him, but never stopped being on their guard. Lenny could turn in a second, and he was always tooled up. One minute he'd be laughing, and the next he'd be holding a knife to your face.

It was another reason he and Ruby were better off apart. As much as they were indebted to her and her family, Lenny had always looked at her with an intensity that was cause for concern. A mixture of lust and hatred was not a good cocktail. But Nathan couldn't just let her go.

CHAPTER SIXTEEN

'Detective Preston, hold on there a minute, I need to speak to you,'

The wind whipped away the voice but Ruby knew it belonged to Helen Phifer, the young journalist fresh to their patch. She sped up, painfully aware of the blister which was now forming, thanks to those bloody heels she wore last night. Why she thought it was a good idea to slip her feet into them today was anyone's guess. Ruby grappled with her door tag, pretending not to hear the young woman calling her name. Stumbling in her haste, she dropped the lanyard on the path. A small hand with red painted nails stretched forward to pick it up.

'Here,' Helen panted, 'I was calling; you mustn't have heard me.'

Ruby smiled at her optimism. She reminded herself that the girl was young enough to be her daughter and decided to give her a break. She was usually pleasant, a bit ferrety-looking, shiny brown hair, dark beady eyes set too close together.

'Thank you,' Ruby replied, as Helen pressed the fob into her palm. 'Now if you don't mind I need to get into work and take these awful shoes off, they're killing me.'

'Can you spare me five minutes? There's something important I need to talk to you about.'

Ruby hesitated, but Helen's next words won her over.

'It's to do with the case you're investigating.'

'OK, five minutes. But not here.'

The Shepherdess Café on City Road was Ruby's favourite greasy spoon. Strip lighting, shiny tables and old-fashioned sauce bottles made her feel at home, while the smell of freshly cooked bacon and sausages made her stomach rumble. She winced as she eased off her shoes from under the table.

'I'm never wearing those torture devices again. From now on it's loafers all the way.'

Helen smiled, stirring her coffee. 'I can't imagine you in loafers.'

'Oh yeah, I have a whole wardrobe of them,' Ruby lied. 'Beige ones, with little tassels on the front. They go with my twin set and pearls.' Ruby remembered who she was speaking to and checked her watch. 'Anyway, you've got four minutes left so make it quick.'

Helen raised her bottom from the seat to take a piece of paper from the back pocket of her jeans. 'I printed off this email. I wasn't sure what to make of it at first, but then I thought of your case and wondered if there was a connection.'

Forgetting all about her sore feet, Ruby unfolded the copier paper and smoothed it on the table.

'Dear Helen.

Detective Ruby Preston (RIP) is sleeping with gangster Nathan Crosby and DI Jack Downes. Disgusting behaviour from a MET police officer. The public needs to know.

Lucy'

Ruby paled with each word she read, and a sick feeling overcame her. Steadying her breath, she returned her gaze. 'Utter rubbish,' she said, the break in her voice denying the strength of her conviction. She was rattled and she could not hide it.

'Of course, that's what I thought. I mean, what's with that whole "RIP" business? It's obviously someone you've rubbed up the wrong way.' Helen looked at her watch and her forehead creased. 'I'd love to chat, but I think our four minutes are up.'

Ruby shot her hand across the table and dug her nails into Helen's wrist. 'Don't play games with me, girl. What do you want?'

Helen shrank back, looking every inch of her twenty years. 'Oh, I... I'm sorry. I just wanted your attention.'

Ruby released her grip. 'Why? We both know you can't print that information. It's slander.'

'I thought we could work together. See what else this Lucy has to say.'

Ruby inhaled a long, deep sigh. 'What do you know about Lucy?'

'Word is that she's your prime suspect for the murder of Harry Edmonds and his wife,' Helen said, her eyes wide with excitement. 'If I could open a line of communication, maybe I could get a scoop after you catch her. What about that?'

So this was what it was all about. Their meeting was not a ploy to blackmail, but a young girl under pressure to produce a news story. Ruby felt a pang of sympathy.

'Honey, if we arrest her and have enough evidence to charge then you're definitely getting your scoop.'

Helen beamed. 'Good. Then I'll keep my ear to the ground. Do you have anything you can give me in the meantime?'

Ruby pushed her hand into her pocket and slid out a business card. 'Give me a ring at nine tonight, and I'll see if I can give you the official line on it. That should keep you going.'

'Really? Cool. Maybe we could do this all the time.'

Ruby rose from the table. Plucking a pen from her breast pocket, she began to scribble on the back of the card. 'This is my personal email address. Forward the email and any others you receive to me. Then delete them from your email account, your sent box and your deleted items. Don't attempt to communicate with this individual. Most likely it's some nut. We can't take any chances. Oh and Helen? We didn't have this conversation. You get me?'

'But... ' Helen said, following her onto the street.

'No buts. Leave it in the hands of the police.' Except Ruby had no intention of reporting it to the police. At least, not yet.

The folded paper burned a hole in her pocket as she sat through briefing justifying her reasons for staying quiet. *It's a random accusation by some nutter, that's all. Happens every time a high profile case hits the press.* And as for signing it 'Lucy'? People talked. Emily could have confided in a neighbour. But it was the full stop after the salutation that got her. The same full stop that drew her in on the original letters to the murder victim, Emily Edmonds. Was it a grammatical error or set up to grab her attention? If it was the latter, it meant there was more to come. Ruby did not hop from Nathan's bed into Jack's as the email implied, but her relationship with the two men was the last thing she wanted publicised to the world.

And the 'RIP'? Ruby shuddered. Lucy was watching her. And she wanted her attention. By the end of briefing she had it all figured out. She would follow up on the email privately, using a computer techy to investigate its origin. In the end, it came down to a choice of two people: Nathan or Luddy. Neither were ideal, but both were trustworthy.

Yet still… the name prickled her senses. Surely it could not be the Lucy she knew. Not after all these years.

The press appeal was held that afternoon. Jack sat next to DCI Worrow as she appealed directly to the woman who had identified herself as 'Lucy' to come forward. She widened her appeal to friends, family, and members of the public to get in touch with any concerns they may have. Ruby sighed. Soon they would go from having minimal information to being deluged with it. Their caseloads were at breaking point as it was. But it was the same story across the board, and nobody could spare the extra resources to give them a dig out.

They failed to mention the possibility of an adopted daughter. It would have made a great human interest story, but it was too early to say just what was going on with this case.

Hunched under the glare of the cameras, Jack looked exhausted, his suit creased, the knot on his burgundy tie bunched to one side. Ruby had surprised herself by getting a decent night's sleep, but as she was drifting off she thought of the meeting with Nathan earlier in the day. She loved the new flat. It was perfect for her: close to work, in a nice, safe area, and very secure. But she could not be indebted to him. She had thought about returning the keys when something stopped her. She pushed them deep in her handbag, just in case the time arose when she needed a safe haven.

She was wading through her paperwork when Jack lumbered in, hands deep in trouser pockets, his broad frame filling her tiny office.

'What about ye?' he said, grabbing a ginger snap from the pack on her desk.

Ruby wanted to tell him about the email, and the young journalist that was sniffing around, but the words would not come. Mentioning their relationship – if she could even call it that – in the same sentence as Nathan was mortifying. Whatever the future held, Ruby could sort it out on her own.

CHAPTER SEVENTEEN

To say Monica was overjoyed to see her might have been taking it a bit far. As disappointing as it was, Lucy had to exercise patience. But the clock was ticking. Now the news of Emily's death had been broadcast the police would be on her trail. But they could search all they wanted; they would never find her. She had made sure of that.

'Please, take a seat,' Monica said, gesturing to the sofa as she invited her inside. A chemical smell assaulted her nostrils, and Lucy's eyes fell on the bottle of pillar box red varnish on the glass coffee table. How slutty, she mused, then dismissed the unkind thought. It rose like a blackbird along with her annoyance, and she took a slow breath to calm herself down. She perched on the edge of the sofa. She was still waiting for her homecoming welcome, but Monica was yet to open her arms for a hug.

'How did you find me?' Monica said, sitting in the furthest chair from the sofa.

'The records became available when I was eighteen,' Lucy replied. 'Although it took a while to find you with your married name. Aren't you pleased to see me?'

'I don't know how to feel,' Monica said, her face devoid of emotion.

Lucy folded her manicured fingers into the palm of her hands. Her palms itched, and a thin sweat had broken out on her upper lip. 'Of course, you're bound to be in shock. But it took a lot of guts for me to come here. I'm beginning to wish I hadn't.' She sighed sadly, hoping to shame Monica into a better reaction.

But Monica just stared at the deep pile carpet, dry-washing her hands.

It was early days, Lucy told herself; her new mother needed some time to process the information. But disappointment was already setting in.

'Can I get you a drink? Tea, coffee, a glass of wine? I don't know about you but I could do with a stiff drink.'

'I don't drink,' Lucy said, flatly.

Silence fell between them. Monica fidgeted with the cuff of her blouse, clearing her throat for words that did not come. A car drove past outside, blaring a drum and bass song. It was one of those days that was too nice to spend inside, and the window blinds trembled as a light breeze filtered in. Lucy blurted out the words balled up in her throat: 'Why did you give me up?'

Monica's eyebrows shot up, but she did not meet Lucy's gaze. 'It was such a long time ago… I didn't find out I was pregnant until I was too far gone.' Her fingers rose to her lips as she inhaled a sudden intake of breath. 'Oh, I'm sorry, I didn't mean… '

Lucy raised her hands, deflecting her apology. She had hoped that Monica stayed childless because she had been waiting for her daughter to find her. But she had been wrong. Monica was just a selfish bitch, with no time for anyone but herself. Lucy rose from the sofa, trying hard to suppress her anger.

'This was a mistake. I shouldn't have come.'

Monica flushed. 'I'm sorry. I know you're saying you're my daughter, and I believe you, but I don't know what to say.'

'Am I not pretty enough, is that it?' Lucy said, bitterness lacing her voice. 'I mean, look at you. Why would you want to be seen with someone like me?'

'No,' Monica said, rising from her seat. 'Of course not. Looks don't come into it.' She frowned, as if searching her brain for a better choice of words. 'I'm just not cut out to be a mother. The best thing you can do is forget all about me.'

'I think it's best I leave,' Lucy said.

Monica opened the living room door to show her out.

Lucy followed her into the hall, her heart sinking. This was not how she imagined it. This was wrong, all wrong. She allowed her fingers to slide over the brass owl ornament on the table. Surely Monica didn't really mean what she said? She was probably scared that she wasn't up to the job. But that was natural. All new mothers felt that way, and it was too early to write off their relationship just yet.

A sly smile crossed Lucy's face as she wrapped her fingers around the legs of the ornament. Swinging back her arm, it cut through the air as she brought it down on the back of Monica's head.

Confidence was the key when removing a body from a property, and Lucy dragged her through the adjoining garage into the back of the sports car without much effort. The yappy dog had been dumped in the boot, to be released on a housing estate a few miles up the road. Lucy didn't kill animals. She wasn't a monster, after all. It had been a few years since Lucy had driven an automatic but after a couple of jerky movements she got away.

It was a shame that she'd had to get blood all over Monica's expensive cream blouse, Lucy thought, as she finished securing her into the basement chair. She stood back and surveyed her work. Perfect. You could barely see the washing line wrapped around her wrists, and it looked so much better than that ungainly rope. Monica's head lolled to one side, her long wavy hair cloaking her face. Even unconscious, she looked pretty. Lucy leaned in and inhaled the scent of her hair. It smelt of flowers. She drew back, wishing she had been prettier, brighter, or charismatic enough to win her around first time.

Never mind, she's here now, the voice in her head whispered. Monica would be fine once she got over the shock of having Lucy in her life. She smiled. It was time to prepare for the perfect moment. One that would seal their relationship for ever.

CHAPTER EIGHTEEN

'He's a brute of a man when he's drunk,' Joy said. She was sitting in a chair next to the window, with a small glittery red hair clip pinned in her hair.

Ruby tried to disentangle herself from thoughts of her meeting with Helen. 'John doesn't drink,' she said, talking about her brother. At least, that's who she thought her mother had been referring to moments before. John was several years older than Ruby, and had emigrated to America when he was still in his teens, lured by the prospect of working for a building firm, of which he now owned a large share.

'No, not John. That Mr Crosby. I saw him. Kicking that boy up and down the garden like a football.' It became clear who her mother was talking about; although it was a memory Ruby did not want to revisit today. Meeting Nathan had brought back a pang of longing she had worked hard to shake off.

'He's evil, that man, he never lets up on those boys,' Joy said, her eyes twinkling with conviction.

'I know,' Ruby said, taking her hand and giving it a squeeze. Nathan could have done anything with his life. But he had ended up running the family business out of a sense of loyalty to a mother who had failed to protect him.

'Him and his brother are asleep, upstairs. Proper smashed her face in, he has.'

She was talking about the day Nathan's father almost killed his mother, Frances. Ruby allowed Joy to rake through the various embers of her memories, wondering why the most traumatic days were the ones that stuck the firmest. They'd had their fair share of happy days, too, and she looked back at her childhood with fondness. So why was her mum so caught up with reliving Nathan's past? Perhaps she still carried guilt for not calling the police when she had her chance. But it was too late for that now, and Ruby wished she could release her mother from the torment of reliving it over and over again. It was worse for Ruby, because each memory was painfully clear for her too.

It had been a Friday night. Fish and chip night. Her favourite day of the week. Since her father's death, her mother had done everything she could to maintain a semblance of normality. Ruby had just got to sleep when she was awoken by screaming and yelling next door. She crept downstairs as the crashing continued through the thin walls, and she and John pleaded with her mother to call the police. But her mother refused: not because she didn't care but because, if she did, it would cut off all ties. They had worked out a code. If things got bad then Mrs Crosby would call out a secret word, 'Never mind'. Ruby had pressed her ear against the wall to listen, willing her to shout the words. It was when the shouting subsided that she got frightened.

Joy's lower lip trembled as she spoke, looking deep into Ruby's eyes. 'As soon as he left, I ran next door. She was lying on the floor, blood in her hair, up the walls: she was a right mess. When I think of your dad... he never raised his voice to me. How is it that good men like him die when people like Crosby live?'

'I don't know, Mum,' Ruby said, enjoying the first lucid conversation with her mother in weeks. She remembered her mum shouting at her to grab the boys while she hoisted Mrs Crosby's arm over her shoulder like an old battered drunk. John was holding the door open, keeping watch in case Mr Crosby returned. Ruby had found Nathan and Lenny on the stairs, shaking like leaves in an October wind. But even as she brought them to her room she knew the brute would be back, and three hours later he was hammering at their door.

Joy shouted at him to go home, and Ruby caught the quiver in her voice. The safety chain was weakening as Mr Crosby's giant fists forced their way through, the white cuff of his shirt stained with blood. He may have been her older brother, but John was of no use when it came to confrontation, and quickly locked himself into his bedroom upstairs. It had been that way for as long as she remembered. Ruby had established herself as the stronger of the two from an early age. Her heart pumping, she ran to the kitchen, and returned to the hall just as Mr Crosby slammed his shoulder against the brittle wood. The chain vibrated; one of the screws fell to the ground: the chink chink sound deafening to Ruby's twelve-year-old ears. Her mother pressed her frame against the other side, but it was no match for Mr Crosby, who was out of his mind with rage.

'She thinks she can hide from me?' he spat. 'I'll teach her a lesson... I'll teach the lot of ya.'

Ruby rushed towards the gap and raised her hand, plunging a fork into the back of Mr Crosby's hand. He screamed in surprise, pulling back his fist. 'You little bitch!' he bellowed, but it afforded them enough time to shut the door and pull across the deadbolts.

The sudden sting of pain as the prongs entered his flesh stalled his momentum, making him stagger back onto the pavement. Neighbours had begun to gather outside, and two men from nearby gently approached him, guiding him by the elbow. 'Jimmy, she's had enough for one night. C'mon, let's get you inside.'

'Tomorrow,' Jimmy said, clasping his head in his hands, as if to fight the torment in his mind. 'She's coming home tomorrow.'

Ruby knew that was how it would be. Because that was how it had always been.

The next day, Mr Crosby had the decency to look sheepish as he gently knocked on the door, holding the biggest bunch of flowers Ruby had ever seen. A present for his wife to make up for the beating he had given her the night before.

'What do you want?' Ruby said, gaining some satisfaction at the four pinprick scars on the back of his fist. Narrow-eyed, she stood aside as her mother pushed past.

'Ruby, go to your room; this is for grown-ups.'

But Ruby refused, her lean frame merging into the corner of the living room as Mr Crosby was allowed inside. He was wearing his suit, the silver tiepin matching his cufflinks. His fingers were layered with rings. Everything about him shone. Everything except the grazes on his knuckles: a reminder of his brutality. He was a handsome man, but he had a coldness about him. A hardness that was not to be reckoned with. Ruby's heart burst with pride that she had stood up to this giant, and she couldn't understand why her mother let him in. 'Sometimes you have to do a deal with the devil to keep the peace,' Joy had once said, but it did not make sense with Ruby. Not then.

Ruby screamed at her mother after they left. 'How could you, Mum? You should have been calling the police, not letting them go back.'

'Oh Ruby, one day you'll see that life isn't black and white. She's not ready to leave him, not yet. But when she is I'll be the one she turns to. If I call the police now she'll just clam up and Jimmy will never let them around here again.'

Ruby sat beside her and took her hand. 'Mum, I don't understand, why is everyone so scared of him?'

'Because he's a very powerful man, Ruby, and it doesn't pay to cross him. I know you were trying to help, but you mustn't get involved again.'

'But the police…'

Joy turned, speaking in a harsh whisper. 'You're never, ever to mention the police in this house again, do you hear me? And certainly not in the presence of Mr Crosby.'

Ruby nodded sullenly, although she didn't understand. And now, as her mother recounted the story, she wondered how life would have turned out for Nathan had her mother done the right thing. For Ruby, joining the police felt like she was righting a wrong because she could not bear to spend the rest of her life believing she was powerless against the likes of Jimmy Crosby. She did not expect her mum to be proud of her, but some acknowledgement would have been nice. Joy fell into silence, and Ruby checked her watch. With a full shift ahead, it was time for her to return to work.

Harmony Williams led the visitor to where Joy Preston was sitting. 'You are one lucky lady,' she said to Joy, fixing her cushion as her guest sat beside her. 'Your daughter only left, and now you have another visitor. Have you won de lottery or something?' She chortled.

Joy stared blankly, barely registering her visitor's presence.

'I think she has,' the guest said. 'With people like you looking after her.'

Harmony beamed. 'Honey, I'm the lucky one, working with all these fine folks. We have a saying where I come from: de older de moon, de brighter it shines. Now you have a good day.'

The visitor leaned forward and patted Joy's hand. 'We will. This visit is long overdue.'

'Close the door behind you,' Ruby said, catching a few inquisitive glances as she beckoned Luddy inside. He was wearing a new tie.

A pink number, for which he had received merciless teasing after he admitted it was a present from his mum.

'I was just going to offer you a doughnut,' Luddy said, placing the open bag on the table. Eve had been late to work for the second time this week, and the old police rule of buying doughnuts for bad timekeeping still held.

'Cheers,' Ruby said, plucking out a sugary pastry. 'I need you to do something for me, but it's got to remain between us for now. Are you OK with that?'

Luddy nodded, a smile rising to his lips. 'Sure, what is it?'

'I'm asking you because I trust you. I don't want this blabbed all over the station.' She sucked the sugar from her fingers and handed him a copy of the email Helen had given her earlier in the day.

Luddy's lips moved as he read the print accusing Ruby of sleeping with Nathan and Downes.

'It's slander,' Ruby said, watching his eyes widen. 'So I want you to see if you can trace the sender. Put your enquiries through the system as intel received from an anonymous source. If anyone asks, refer them to me.'

'Sure thing, Sarge… Ruby. But shouldn't you report this? "RIP"? It sounds like a death threat to me.'

'It's not a death threat,' Ruby said, unwilling to elaborate. 'But if you find the source I want you to report back to me alone. How're your enquiries going? Any joy?'

'I've got an appointment to speak to Charlotte's husband. He's given us a solid alibi, and she didn't have any enemies.'

'Apart from Lucy,' Ruby muttered. 'No sign of the murder weapon that killed Harry Edmonds?'

Luddy shook his head, his glance returning to the paperwork. 'You're not in any trouble, are you? It's just that I've heard of the Crosbys, and they're a pretty nasty bunch.'

'Which is why I want to keep this between us. And no, you don't need to worry about me.' She picked at the remains of her doughnut. 'Do you know what would go nice with this?'

'A cuppa tea,' Luddy said ruefully, shoving the paper in his back pocket before taking her empty mug.

But there was more to the email than Ruby was letting on. As much as she tried to deny it, her past was catching up with her, and it was only a matter of time before the truth was revealed.

CHAPTER NINETEEN

Mr Lockwood looked every inch the grieving husband. Flabby bags hung under his eyes, and his bald patch shone underneath the spotlight in the hotel bar. Leather furnishings, soft music, and a relaxed atmosphere. A soothing location to meet a grieving widower. It was late evening, and having sent Luddy and the rest of the shift home, Ruby was happy to take the enquiry. She introduced herself and hoped that their meeting would be fruitful. She had vowed to leave no stone unturned. Sometimes, revisiting the past was better than trying to siphon through the myriad of information and phone calls to date.

'Thanks for meeting me at such short notice. Are you staying long?' Ruby said, shaking his hand in a firm grip. It was something her tutor had taught her when she joined the police. A weak handshake did not inspire confidence.

'I've no definite plans. But I hope to stay a few more days… ' His voice tailed away as he stared at his glass of overpriced water.

He looked like a man defeated, and Ruby wished there was something she could say to ease his grief. She knew from losing her father during her childhood that time was the only healer. But he had died of natural causes; she couldn't imagine how it felt to lose a loved one to such a brutal attack.

Ruby lowered her head, embarrassed at her own impetuousness. She hadn't even asked how he was doing since the loss of his wife. 'I'm very sorry for your loss. We're doing everything we can to catch the person responsible.'

Mr Lockwood touched the glass, his finger tracing the trailing drop of condensation. 'They said she didn't suffer because it was so quick. I wasn't able to identify the body. It was too badly—' He choked on the words, replacing them with a deep, shuddering sigh.

Ruby nodded sympathetically. 'Are you sure your wife never gave a child up for adoption? Maybe before you met? Her charity work… sometimes people get involved because they're trying to put things right.'

Mr Lockwood paled and began to rub his chest in a slow circular motion.

Ruby could see that he was holding back something that had pained him for some time. She realised her fingernails were digging into the leather seat, and clasped her hands over her folded legs instead. 'Are you OK?' she said, hoping the answers did not live far away.

Mr Lockwood nodded, his face returning to a pink hue. He plucked a small brown pill bottle from his jacket pocket before knocking back a tablet with a mouthful of water. 'For my blood pressure,' he said by way of explanation. 'You asked about children, didn't you?'

Ruby replied with a nod.

'Charlotte never wanted them,' he said. 'Her mother suffered with her nerves; she didn't have an easy childhood.'

'You're her second husband, aren't you?' Ruby said.

'Yes. She got married in Gretna Green when she was just sixteen. I think she saw it as a way out of her chaotic home life. Out of the frying pan into the fire, as they say.'

'So her first husband was abusive?'

Mr Lockwood took a sip of water before giving a short grim nod. 'When her mother died, she took her inheritance and left. Her family, the marriage, she left it all behind and started again in Cornwall. Her sisters have come crawling to me, looking for money. I sent them away with a flea in their ear. They weren't very supportive when she was alive. She doesn't owe them anything now she's gone.'

'I'm sorry to hear that. I can't imagine it's been easy for you.'

'They know where they stand. It's all water under the bridge now. I've passed on their details to the police, should you wish to speak to them. But I doubt they've anything to do with Charlotte's murder. They didn't even know where she lived, until now.'

Ruby's mind worked double time as it searched for answers. At least it explained Charlotte's behaviour. The endless hours of charity work, her need to befriend victims; it was an urge born from her past, trying to help women just like her. 'I don't suppose you have her sister's details on you… '

'I've already given them to the police,' Mr Lockwood said.

Ruby nodded. 'Of course. Sorry, we've hundreds of lines of enquiries. I'll follow it up when I get back to the station.'

'Charlotte wanted me to retire early, take a cruise around the world. I wish I'd listened. But it's too late now.'

Ruby nodded in agreement. She had also suffered loss, and was an expert on regret.

By the time Ruby got to the lift for her flat, she cursed herself for wearing her heels again. The tight black leather had pinched her toes into submission, and she limped inside, praying that it would get to the top floor without breaking down. She slipped off her shoes as she pressed the button for the top floor, risking the dirt-stained floor to ease her chafed skin. But her relief did not last for long, as a pair of hands parted the doors before slipping in beside her. Ruby swallowed, her heart lurching at the sight of the very last person she wanted to see. How on earth had they found her?

Ruby inhaled a sharp intake of breath as she recognised the thin pallid face of the man before her. He had the height of his brother, but none of his looks. It was Lenny Crosby, Nathan's older brother. Ruby cast her eye over his long woollen coat, worn over his customary designer shirt and black jeans. She wondered how many weapons were concealed in its pockets, and reminded herself to keep a brave stance. Lenny could smell fear. Lenny had weaklings for breakfast.

'Hello, Ruby,' he said, his dark eyes locked in a menacing stare. 'Why don't you and me have a little chat?'

'Why don't you fuck off and phone me like everyone else,' Ruby said, taking a step forward to leave.

Lenny's hand shot out, grabbing Ruby's arm and bending it behind her back. 'A feisty little bitch, aren't you? Do you know what happened to the last person who spoke to me like that?'

Ruby didn't ask because she didn't want to know. She gritted her teeth as a slice of pain shot up her arm, but she would not cry out. Fists clenched, she was ready to fight her corner.

'Shhh, shhh, calm yourself now,' Lenny said, his left hand reaching forward, and in one fluid movement cold hard steel was laid against her throat. He pressed himself tightly against her back, pushing her into the lift wall. She could smell the tobacco on his breath, and the sweat lacing his skin.

Ruby froze, keeping her voice level. 'What do you want, Lenny?'

'I felt it was time we had a catch up. It's been a while, hasn't it?' Lenny's lips brushed against her ear and he inhaled the fragrance of her hair.

She needed to extricate herself from this situation. Even if someone tried to use the lift, the Crosby family were too well known for her to expect anyone to help. Despite Nathan's efforts to stay below the radar, Lenny had ensured their reputation for violence was well-known.

'Just let go of me, will you?' Ruby said, trying to wriggle free. But the blade scratched against her neck in her attempts to resist it.

Lenny released her right arm, keeping the knife firmly pressed to her jugular. 'Play me up and I'll slit your throat.' He pressed the button for the top floor, and Ruby watched as the lift doors sealed them inside.

She fought to regulate her breath, softening her words so they did not sound like an accusation. 'Why are you being like this? We grew up together.'

'Don't give me all that family loyalty bollocks. You lost your right to that when you joined the filth. Now shut up and listen. What are the old bill doing sniffing around our family?'

Ruby frowned. It was news to her. 'I don't know. I'm not privy to that sort of information.'

'You're a copper, aren't you? You go to briefings.'

'It doesn't work like that anymore. We're only privy to the cases we're working on. What's this really about? The police have been on your tail plenty of times before and you didn't follow me around.'

'I don't sneak around,' Lenny said. 'I'm here to pass on a warning. Leave Nathan alone. You're fucking with his head.'

Ruby wanted to say that Nathan was old enough to make his own decisions, but as the knife caressed her skin she knew she had to pick her battles.

'I'm not with Nathan.' Wide-eyed, Ruby watched the numbers roll past on the digital display, until they came to her floor.

'Stay where you are.' Lenny's breath felt hot on her cheek. 'You know better than to start a fight with me. I'll tell you only once. Leave Nathan alone. I won't come for you; I'll come for your mother. Don't think I won't find a way, because you know I have the capability.'

Ruby wanted to remind him who he was talking to, but mention of the police so soon after his prison release could be the one thing to tip him over the edge. 'Have you been in my flat?'

Lenny laughed. 'Now why would I be in your shithole flat?'

'Why would you be sticking a blade to my throat? To get your point across I guess!'

Lenny drew himself closer; every inch of his body was pressed against hers. 'Look, babe. If I have anything to say to you I'll say it to your face. Have I made myself clear?'

'Perfectly. I just don't get why it warranted you pulling a knife on me.'

'Because sometimes it's the only way of getting the message across.'

Ruby swallowed, her eyes rolling down to the knife which was pressed against her quivering flesh. She gathered all her bravado, forcing the words between her clenched teeth. 'Tell Nathan to keep out of my way, and I'll keep out of his. Conversation over. Now drop the blade and open the door.'

Slowly, his right hand snaked around her waist. 'Shame really. You always were a nice bit of stuff.'

A wave of revulsion passed over Ruby while Lenny's fingers slipped under her shirt, his breath growing heavier as he caressed the contours of her skin.

'Don't fucking think about it,' Ruby growled, prepared to take her chances with the knife. 'If you want me to stay away from Nathan, don't give him a reason to turn against you.' She knew Lenny wouldn't kill her. Hurt her, yes, maybe even worse. But he would not kill her while his mother was alive.

'Just remember what I said, or next time I won't stop,' Lenny said, releasing the knife from her throat.

Ruby jabbed the button as the lift reached her floor, biting back the words on her tongue. She wanted to tell him to go to hell, but now was not the time. She left without looking back; but instead of entering her flat she darted into the stairwell.

Lenny knew where she lived. He could easily break in and finish what he started. He was known for it; although his victims sometimes confided in police, they never got as far as attending court. Lenny relished in torturing his victims then letting them go – only to catch them again, like a cat toying with a mouse. He'd allow them to smell freedom, gasp in a breath of relief, before discovering he had never really released them at all. It was the worst kind of torture.

She couldn't go back to the flat. It wasn't safe there anymore. At least, not tonight. She thought about Downes, but he would ask too many questions: questions that she was not ready to face up to herself. She needed to get her head down somewhere safe, but she could not afford a hotel. She thought of the flat Nathan had bought her and the keys buried in the bottom of her bag. She could be there in twenty minutes if she took the Tube. If what he said was true, nobody else knew about it, especially not Lenny.

She bit down on her bottom lip, toying with the idea of staying the night. It was not as if she was contacting Nathan; nobody needed to know. Just one night she told herself. Tomorrow she could figure out what she was going to do. It didn't mean that she was accepting anything, and it was all Nathan's fault this had happened anyway. She wondered what he had done to make Lenny blame her. A flutter arose in her chest.

Could Nathan have been talking about leaving the family business? She told herself not to get her hopes up. She had made her decision. It was too late now. Tomorrow she would ring the care home and tell the staff to call her if anyone tried to visit her mum. But deep down Ruby knew it was an empty threat. If Lenny was going to hurt anyone, it would be her.

CHAPTER TWENTY

Nathan enjoyed the sound of the ice as it clinked in the glass. It reminded him of the times he had with Ruby. He only drank rum because she liked it. In truth he preferred a fine malt. But it reminded him of the taste of her lips after she'd had a drink or two. He lay back in the leather chair as the fire crackled, indulging himself in the memory of their times together.

Annoyance washed over him as the door handle pressed down. He sat up sharply, ready to admonish Tweedy for the interruption because he'd told him he did not want to be disturbed. Tweedy Steve was a six foot seven bearded hulk. From his tweed jacket to his tweed-covered hip flask, it was not difficult to see where he obtained his nickname. Tweedy, Nathan and Ruby had known each other since school, when he had started a mini-fashion trend by stealing his dad's tweed jacket to wear on a night out. Tweedy was not intimidated by many people, but he waved his hands in an act of apology as he entered the room. 'Sorry, boss, but I thought you might like to see this.'

Nathan followed him down the stairs into the belly of the house. It was not a damp or dark basement, but a luxurious cave which contained a games room and several large CCTV screens around a circular table. It was made to be comfortable because security meant everything to Nathan, and his residence was watched twenty-four hours a day.

No expense had been spared in setting it up. Italian leather swivel chairs nestled into the mahogany tables, and in the corner, a stainless steel fridge was stocked with soft drinks, snacks, and bottled water. No alcohol was allowed. People had to keep a clear head in this room. If something happened on their watch there would be hell to pay. It also acted as a panic room. Behind a panelled wall were enough provisions to feed a family for a month, as well as an array of weapons for when times got tough. Nathan called it his bunker, and he'd slept a little bit easier after it was built.

Steve pointed at CCTV camera number five, which gave views of the flat Nathan had gifted to Ruby. He had them fitted when he bought the place, so Steve could keep a watchful eye when Nathan needed a hideout away from home. He and Steve were the only people to know of the address.

'It's Ruby,' Tweedy said. 'She got in about five minutes ago.'

Nathan's eyebrows shot up in surprise. He had not expected her to take him up on his offer so quickly, and he leaned into the screen for a better view. He was yet to admit to himself that he left the cameras running because he hoped to see her again. He watched her kick off her shoes and fill the kettle, locating the long-life milk in the fridge. His finger clicking against the mouse, he checked the other rooms and noticed the absence of an overnight bag. Her expression told him everything he needed to know. She was there because she did not feel safe at home. His first instincts were to go there and find out what was wrong. But he paused as he rose from his seat and forced himself to sit back down. If Ruby found out she was being monitored, she would never go there again. At least here he could watch her, keep her safe. Nathan turned to Steve, who was viewing with interest. He had a soft spot for Ruby, although he'd never admit it while she was in the police. 'Thanks for letting me know; you can take a break now if you like.'

Steve smiled. 'Cheers, boss, I'll go grab a sandwich, if that's okay.'

Nathan nodded in agreement, and turned his attention back to the screen. Ruby was tentatively going from room to room, checking the windows and blinds were tightly shut. She returned to the front door and checked it was locked. Once this was complete, she leaned against the door, taking a few deep breaths. Nathan clenched his jaw as he tried to exercise some self-control. Just what had happened to her? He thought about ringing, but what would he say? She knew where he was if she needed him, and there was a phone in the house if she needed to call. The fact she had gone there was a step towards accepting help, and he wondered if that was a step in his direction too. But how would that be possible? She would never fully accept his lifestyle, or the people he did business with, and he certainly didn't fit into her world of law and order.

She continued to wander around the flat, touching the soft furnishings, and entering the bedroom. Nathan watched, transfixed, as she picked through the drawers. He still kept some of his stuff there: a change of clothes, socks and jeans. She pulled out one of his T-shirts and pressed it to her face, inhaling his scent. The cold front he had fought so hard to build began to thaw. Ruby folded the T-shirt back the way she had found it, and gently shut the drawer. She walked to the other side of the room to find the walk-in wardrobe, in which he had left a variety of new clothes for her. The tags had been left on so she knew that they were hers alone. Nathan realised he was barely breathing as he watched the woman he loved shake her head. She was fighting it too. If she was going to walk out of the house, she would go now.

But instead, she picked out a pair of silk pyjamas and laid them on the bed. She slid open some more drawers and found some underwear. Nathan's heart began to pound as he realised she was getting undressed. His eyes roamed over the tattoo trailing down her back – a feminine version of his own. At least that was a part of him she would always carry. His arousal grew as she unbuttoned her slim-fitting trousers. It took every ounce of his self-control to switch the camera view to the living room. It was like tearing his eyes away from a work of art, but there was also something sleazy about watching without her permission. He had dated other women, stunners, who were the envy of all his mates. But the whole time they were together he compared them to Ruby. He longed for the curves of her soft stomach, her full breasts and firm shoulders. Most of the women he dated were stick thin and tanned within an inch of their lives. He did not settle for lookalikes. It was all or nothing with Ruby, and for the first time he realised that she had done the same with Jack Downes. He must be ten years older than Nathan – not a bad-looking man, but he bore no resemblance to him. Perhaps it was better that way. The thought of Ruby with anyone else pained him, and he knew he would not be able to control himself if she ended up being hurt. But people knew of their association, and would be too scared to cause her harm for fear of pissing him off. That was, anyone except his brother, Lenny.

He watched as Ruby padded into the living room, brushing her long black hair which trailed down the back of her white towelling robe. His mind ticked over, recalling the last conversation he'd had with his brother. The subject of his early retirement from the family business was met with outrage, and it had taken his mum coming between them to stop it coming to blows. Good old Mum. Living with Lenny must have brought its own set of challenges. Did he blame Ruby for his change of heart?

Nathan ached to join her, but he knew he was better off trying to find out what his brother was up to. He watched as she restlessly paced back and forth, checking the doors and windows one more time. At twelve o'clock, he watched her enter the kitchen and pull a knife with a ten-inch blade from the wooden block on the counter. Nathan frowned as she draped a tea towel over it and carried it into the bedroom. Pulling back the duvet, she calmly slipped it under the pillow beside hers. Then without warning she stripped off her pyjama top and threw it on the floor. Nathan touched the screen as she pulled his T-shirt from the drawer and slipped it over her head. He knew it was her way of keeping him close. He wanted to call her, to tell her that he would keep her safe, but he would have to content himself watching from a distance. She switched off the lamp, and the cameras flicked to night vision. She would be safe for tonight. But he would have to work hard to guarantee her future safety.

CHAPTER TWENTY-ONE

Monica's head jerked upwards as she inhaled a sudden breath. A wave of revulsion passed over her as she gagged on the rag tied over her mouth. Her eyelashes were clotted together with the mascara she had applied that morning, and she blinked hard to separate them. A sudden searing pain jackhammered from the back of her skull. She tried to touch her head, but her limbs were immobile. Were they numb? She jerked her wrists, but they were bound so tightly her fingers felt frozen. Panic and confusion flooded through her. She wriggled her toes, but they were bound at the ankles. A muffled whine escaped her lips. The lights of a Christmas tree blinked in the gloom, and the smell of ammonia rose from the floor and wrapped itself around her. The pain in her head, the stomach-churning smell, it was some kind of nightmare. It had to be.

She willed herself to awaken and find herself in bed with her husband, their limbs entangled under her crisp white duvet. He would bring her coffee and croissants hot from the oven, and tell her about his conference. But each inhalation defied the dream, bringing her deeper into the bowels of a nightmare. Instinct drove Monica to scream for help, but the sudden intake of stale air through her nostrils made her gag even more. Just what had she been doing to end up in this place? An image flashed before her mind; she was painting her nails because her husband was due home that night. Then the doorbell rang. What was that woman's name? *Lucy*. She knew there was something weird about her, and yet she allowed her inside. Of all the stupid… why had she let her in? The last thing she remembered was showing her out in the hall… A pang of fear stabbed her heart. Had Lucy taken her captive because she rejected her? Wherever she was, Monica knew this was bad. Very bad.

Her wrists chafed against the binding, and her whole body ached. She was barefoot: her feet tied to the base of the chair with some kind of plastic rope. Wriggling her ankles, she loosened them enough to dig her toes into the soft black soil underfoot. Why had the makeshift floorboards been pulled up? Just what lay in the dirt underneath? She peered around the room, disorientated by the flashing lights. A grimy steel tap dripped water into a porcelain sink; on the walls – she squinted – were they tools? Was she in a workshop of some kind? Or was it something far worse? As the lights flashed on she made out the outlines of a hammer and a hacksaw. Her breath was coming faster now, wetting the gag bound hard around her parted mouth. Her saliva intermingled with the crusty fabric, and a sickly rusty tang filled her mouth. The same taste you got when you bit your lip when it was bleeding.

Realisation dawned on Monica. It *was* blood. But was it hers or someone else's? She groaned, and the sound echoed around the dank room, making the hairs on the back of her neck stand to attention. Was she alone in this place? Her eyes rolled upwards to the single light bulb encased in a netting of cobwebs. Focus, she thought, trying to listen out for sound. She could not afford to panic; this was about survival. She pushed away the thoughts too terrifying to comprehend, grasping at her most recent memory instead. Just who *was* Lucy? She didn't even know her surname. She replayed their conversation, closing her eyes to ease the throbbing pain in her skull. With hindsight, her reaction could not have been worse. Confessing that she had not enough time for an abortion was not the appropriate response to the daughter she gave up for adoption. But she was only being truthful, and she had presumed that, at her age, the woman would have got over it by now. Obviously not.

Tears rolled down Monica's face as she thought about the life she had worked so hard to build. Her career, her home, her marriage: they had not come easy, and things were finally getting on track. The last argument she'd had with her husband was about them having a child together. He was unaware of Lucy, and she had not given her a moment's thought. She was far from the maternal type, and never imagined her past would come back to haunt her in this way. Monica drew back in horror as the fairy lights illuminated the stains on the wooden floor. Whatever this place was, Lucy had no intention of letting her go. Her heart hammered in her chest as hysteria took control. She bit down hard on the gag and screamed.

CHAPTER TWENTY-TWO

Ruby ground her teeth as she approached the Crosby family residence. She could never afford anything like this. Even with her pension pay-out she would have to be frugal. It just didn't seem fair.

Winding down her car window, she pressed her finger on the buzzer on the intercom buzzer, watching the cameras crane their necks in her direction. Ruby ran her tongue across her teeth. Her mouth felt barren. If there was ever a time she needed a strong mug of tea it was now.

'Yes?' a deep voice drawled from the intercom. It wasn't one of those cheap scratchy jobs either. It boomed loud and clear.

Ruby flashed her badge to the camera. 'I'm DS Ruby Preston. I'd like to speak to Mr Lenny Crosby. It's urgent. *Unofficial* business.'

She hoped the emphasis on unofficial would gain her access. As the gates rolled open, she cursed her accelerating heartbeat. This was the last place she wanted to find herself given her run-in with Lenny in the lift. But she had to clear the air between them, otherwise she would lose sleep for fear he may return.

Besides, she had a favour to ask. But favours from the Crosby family did not come cheap. Although Jimmy Crosby had died in prison, his legend lived on. Even up until his death, Crosby still earned his reputation as a hard man. She had heard the stories of how the family made people disappear, and of the cops and high-powered politicians nestling in their back pocket. And when it came to blackmail… if anyone could dig up dirt it was the Crosbys, and they weren't afraid to use it. She began to regret her decision not to tell anyone where she was going. For all she knew, undercover police could be watching the address, making a note of her presence. It was doubtful though; everybody knew the Crosbys were too clever to shit on their own doorstep. It was unlikely they'd hurt her, but then again, if she stumbled upon something she shouldn't… and Lenny had been on a knife edge since he came out of the big house.

Ruby glanced at her phone on the passenger seat. It was too late to text anyone now. She knew they'd be watching every movement she made on the video intercom. The gates closed behind her with finality as she drove up the gravel drive.

The Chigwell house was a grand affair worth several million: one of their many properties. Nathan had long since moved out of the family residence, having built his own fort in an up-and-coming part of Hackney. The front door opened and a dour-looking man appeared. Tall, stocky, dressed in black. The Rottweilers were given instructions to sit, which they did, flanking him either side. A low growl rumbled in their bellies, and it gave her the creeps to know they could make pieces of her in minutes. If they were there to intimidate, they were doing a good job. And so was their master. His name was Logan, but everyone knew him as Fingers. Ruby recognised him from old intelligence photos and checked the absence of digits on his right hand. Two were missing from the joint down after a gun backfired during an armed raid. It was common, back in the old days, before quality firearms infiltrated the country. It wasn't difficult to get a decent piece now, and there were plenty of people willing to rent them out, if the need occurred. Not that it mattered now. Ruby concentrated her efforts on getting safely inside. She was no threat to the Crosby family. She would be fine. She just wished her legs didn't feel like rubber as the door slammed shut behind her.

Fingers led her through the long wide hall into an expansive living room. Yucca plants dotted each corner, and Ruby glanced at the designer furnishings and luxury rug, trying to imagine them in her poky flat. She waited as told, knowing it was all for show. Planting herself firmly in a confident stance, she stood next to the fireplace with her head held high. But still the niggling thoughts came back to haunt her. *What are you doing getting mixed up with the Crosbys again?*

It seemed like an eternity before the door finally swung open and Lenny Crosby was standing before her. His eyes were dark, his expression guarded. He strode forward, dressed casually in a shirt and jeans: so different to his father, who wore only the finest tailored suits. DI Downes once told Ruby that he had met many dubious men in his career, but old man Crosby was the only one that ever frightened him.

'I didn't expect to see you so soon,' Lenny said, his eyes narrowed in disdain.

Ruby took a deep breath. 'I need your help.'

The left side of his mouth jerked upwards in a sneer. 'Do you now? This better be no wind up, 'cos if you're trying to set me up for something… '

'Then why the hell would I come? I knew your father. I wouldn't be here unless I was desperate.' Ruby sighed before shaking her head. 'I don't know… this was a bad idea.'

Lenny took a step forward. 'You're not leaving until you tell me what's going on.'

It was an order, and she knew he could overpower her if he wanted to, although she would make sure that he wouldn't come out of it unscathed.

'Well, chill then, will you? I'm not talking to you standing over me like this,' Ruby retorted, asserting her position.

'Give me your phone.' Lenny snapped his fingers.

'Why?'

'Because I asked nicely. Now hand it over.'

Ruby passed it over and watched him scroll through her texts and calls. 'This is ridiculous. If you're not interested in helping, then I'll have my phone back and be on my way.'

'Sit down,' Lenny ordered, returnning her phone. He called for Fingers, and the door opened.

Ruby swallowed, her throat feeling incredibly dry. For the hundredth time she wondered what she was doing there.

Fingers poked his bristled head through the door: 'Yes, boss?'

'Get us some coffees, will you?' Lenny said, taking a seat in the wide leather armchair.

'Tea for me, please,' Ruby said, heat rising to her face.

The man nodded before closing the door.

Ruby took a seat, feeling slightly foolish, but relieved to be back on an even keel. When Fingers returned, she was reassured to see it was actually a pot of tea and not a code word for something more underhand. She poured herself a cup, trying to keep her hand steady.

'You've got some balls coming here,' Lenny said, staring at her from over his cup. The tone of his voice, the coldness of his eyes… it was like watching his father all over again.

'I've kept my side of the bargain,' Ruby said, although it was not strictly true. She had kept away from his brother, Nathan, but *had* been to the flat. 'But now I need your help.'

Lenny's smirk grew wider. 'You're not the first copper to come here asking for favours. But you know what it means, don't you?'

Ruby slowly nodded. It was why she had put it off for so long. It meant she would be indebted to him in return, and as a police officer that was a very bad situation to be in. 'Are you going to help me or not?'

'Sure I'll help, what do you want?'

'I want you to find my daughter. I want you to find Lucy.'

CHAPTER TWENTY-THREE

Lenny crossed his legs, his teeth flashing in a predatory smile. It reminded Ruby of a documentary she once watched about crocodiles ensnaring their prey. 'Does Nathan know you're setting up house?'

Ruby shook her head. 'No. And I've got no intention of making contact. I just need to know where she is.'

'You're opening a whole can of worms here; there must be a good reason for it, if you don't wanna have a family reunion. I'm sure Mum would love to know about the secret little love child you gave away.'

Ruby leaned forward, her voice low. 'You can't let anyone know. Not Nathan, not your mum, nobody.'

Lenny's eyes glinted in amusement. 'Oh, I'll do it. But first, I want to know why.'

'I'm investigating a string of murders. I have reason to believe the suspect is a young woman who was given up for adoption.'

'There's lots of kids in London who were dumped by their parents. You must have more than that to suspect your own.'

Ruby inwardly cringed. She hated the term 'dumped' but was not about to justify her reasons to Lenny. 'I've had indirect contact.'

'And you want to nick her and solve the crime? Ohh that's low, even for you, nicking your own flesh and blood… '

Ruby stood, anger flaring through her. 'If I was going to arrest her I wouldn't be coming to you now, would I? Are you going to help me or not?'

The sly smile Lenny had been wearing dropped from his face, and he sprang from his chair, muscles tensing as he loomed down on her. She could smell the coffee on his breath, see the fire of fury in his eyes. 'Who do you think you are, coming into my manor and speaking to me like that?'

Ruby bit back her retort. He was right. This was his house, and she needed him more than he needed her. 'I'm sorry,' she said, dropping her gaze to the floor. 'Sometimes I forget how much things have changed.'

Silence passed between them. She would apologise, but she would not grovel. She stiffened as Lenny's hand reached into his trouser pocket.

'Cigarette?' he said, opening up the pack of Marlboro Lights.

'Don't mind if I do,' Ruby said, figuring she needed it.

Fingers brought in a notebook and pen as requested, and Lenny handed them over. 'Write down everything you know about your girl. I'll have the information in the next couple of days.'

'Thanks.' Ruby dragged on the cigarette, feeling the weight of the debt looming over her.

Her heart skipped a beat when the door opened, and she half expected to see Nathan stride in. But it was Frances Crosby, head of the family and mother of Nathan and Lenny. Her face broke out in a warm smile, and Ruby could not help but return her expression. She looked like she had hardly aged. Her ash blonde hair was cut into a shoulder-length bob, and she was wearing a beige dress that complemented her trim figure. But Ruby knew better than to be taken in by her soft smile. Behind the gentle looks was a powerhouse of a woman, with a deep hatred for the police.

'I thought I heard your voice,' she said – her East London accent had remained strong over the years. 'So good to see you again, darling. How's your mother?'

'She's much the same,' Ruby said, knowing that Frances still visited every now and again. 'They're keeping her comfortable.'

'I must pop in to see her. Take her some of those sweets she likes. What brings you here? Anything I need to be concerned about?'

'Nothing for you to worry about,' Lenny said, rising from his chair and pocketing the folded notepaper. 'Just business. Now if you don't mind I've got things to do.'

Frances nodded, her smile faltering only for a second before squeezing Ruby's hand. 'And how are you, my lovely? Are you happy? No sign of you leaving that job of yours?'

Ruby shook her head, 'I'm afraid not, bills to pay, you know…' Her voice trailed off because it was blatantly obvious she did not know, given she lived off the proceeds of crime.

'I remember when we didn't have a pot to piss in,' Frances said, her eyes falling on the expensive furnishings. 'And you know what? I'd give all this up just to have my Jimmy back in our two-up two-down in our little East London estate. But come, take a seat, I want to hear all about you.'

Once their small talk had been exhausted, Ruby took the opportunity to speak to the woman frankly. A question had played on her mind since speaking to her mum at Oakwood. Joy's memories revolved around the abuse Mr Crosby inflicted on his family, and she could not help but feel resentful of the intrusion of their time. 'Frances,' Ruby said, 'can I ask you a personal question?'

Frances patted Ruby's hand, her skin fleshy and warm. It was comforting, as Joy barely made any contact these days. Even her hugs were stiff and awkward, as if given by a stranger.

'You can ask me whatever you like, love, you know that.'

'Why did you put up with it all those years ago?' Ruby said, knowing that Frances would understand exactly what she meant.

Frances smiled, her eyes cast to the left as she recalled old memories. 'Your mother once asked me why didn't I marry someone like your father. Someone quiet and reliable, who wouldn't answer back. I turned to her and asked, "where would the fun be in that?" Being married to Jimmy was exciting, fresh. No two days were the same. When he met me he promised to take me places, and sure enough, he did.'

He took you down the hospital, Ruby thought, and nearly took you down the morgue.

But Frances didn't notice Ruby's misgiving glance; she was too busy reliving the past. 'Nowadays, if a couple have an argument the neighbours call the police. It's like you're not allowed to disagree.' She sniffed. 'Where's the passion, the excitement? If couples today sorted out their disagreements instead of holding them in, there wouldn't be so many divorces.'

Ruby nodded, knowing there was no point in disagreeing. 'I guess that's one way of looking at it.'

'Too right,' Frances said. 'Women today fight for equality. When I got pregnant, I stayed at home and raised the family. Nowadays, women have to work until they're old; they don't even get to enjoy their earnings because they're paying someone else to look after their children. Where's the sense in that?'

Ruby could not equate domestic violence with a happy marriage, no matter how much Frances tried to justify it. 'But we're not just talking about arguments, are we? I remember the day my mum took you and the boys in after Jimmy… Mr Crosby broke your nose and cracked your ribs. Nathan and Lenny were white with terror, too scared to move. How can that be love? And I'm not being nasty or judgemental, I'm just trying to understand.'

Frances sighed. 'Even if I had wanted to leave, there were no refuges back then, not like today. And my family wouldn't take me in. Jimmy had a reputation. People were scared of him, and there was no way anyone would've had me.'

'But Nathan… ' Ruby said, biting back her words, reluctant to cross the line.

Frances nodded in acknowledgement. 'Jimmy had a hard upbringing. He wanted the boys to be tough so nobody took advantage of them when they were older. I think he did a good job of that.'

Ruby nodded. She wanted to ask if she truly knew just how much Nathan and Lenny hated their father for the cruelty he inflicted upon them, and how she lived with herself, knowing she had failed to protect the children who viewed violence as a normal way of life. But instead Ruby just smiled and made her excuses to leave.

Frances walked her to the door, her voice echoing in the vast hall. 'You know, I'm sorry things turned out this way, Ruby. I think you and Nathan could've made each other happy. But I think it's time for you both to move on, you know? He's been dating a lovely young woman; Leona, her name is. She's very keen. But the minute she gets serious he runs a mile. He's still young. He can have children and get married and do all the normal things. And so can you. I don't think it's fair that you're both putting your lives on hold for something that's never going to happen.'

'Nathan's a free agent. We've been over for a very long time,' Ruby said, feeling a dig of pain in her chest.

'Time you made that clear then,' Frances said, imparting a gentle smile.

But Ruby did not miss the coldness behind her eyes. If only she had been that protective when they were young, she thought, waving goodbye as Frances closed the door.

CHAPTER TWENTY-FOUR

Ruby's fingers hovered over the email software on her phone. As confident as Lenny had appeared there was always a chance that he would come up blank. Luddy was yet to come up with something concrete, so she could not waste a second. She had to get in contact with her mystery email sender. Helen had not reported any further communications, but equipped with an email address it was too good an opportunity to miss. The plan was to attempt some direct communication just to test them out and see if it really was a hoax.

She typed in the address and in the subject box typed 'RUBY PRESTON' in capital letters.

> *'Dear Lucy,*
>
> *If you were trying to get my attention, you have succeeded. Although what you claim is untrue, I would be happy to discuss the matter with you further. I suggest we meet. I am guessing that you do not live far away.*
>
> *Ruby Preston'*

Ruby stared at the words on her phone. At least for now she would send it from her personal account. She did so in the hope that the original sender would believe they had some kind of secret communication going on. She pressed send before she changed her mind. Normally she would shrug off such communications, but three letters had played heavily on her mind.

'RIP.'

Written in brackets beside her name, Ruby knew this was no death threat. It was her middle name. Ruby Imogen Preston. A secret she had kept close to her chest. The only places it was recorded were on her birth certificate and that of her daughter's, Lucy Preston. It was a possibility that Lucy's name had been changed too. Her daughter could be anyone, but the meaning was clear. The use of 'RIP' was sending a message that only she and Lucy would understand. Ruby prayed she was wrong, but all the same she had to warn Downes. But the investigation was going at the pace of a steam train, and it was difficult to get him alone even for five minutes without interruption. Meeting for a drink after work was a definite no-no. For all she knew she was being watched. She certainly felt as if eyes were following her home. Could it really be her daughter trying to get in touch? And if so, was she responsible for the murders of Harry, Emily, and Charlotte?

As if on cue, Downes knocked on her door, making her jump in her chair.

'Briefing in ten. Are you alright?' he said.

Ruby signalled to him to close the door behind him. A fatal stabbing had come in overnight, a young man named Andy Hughes. He had been waiting for the bus when a gang of youths approached: picking a fight for no reason other than the fact he was there. He did not stand a chance.

'There's something I have to tell you,' Ruby said, pulling out the well-worn paper and laying it flat on her desk. He leaned over her shoulder, and she was pleased to find the absence of alcohol on his breath. She knew he had been trying, and it was probably why he had been looking so rough. The crumpled suit, his unshaven face; he was detoxing, and there was never a good time for that in the police.

'What the hell?' Downes said as he read and reread the email. 'Where did you get that?'

'From Helen. She's a journalist, but don't worry, I've sorted it, and it's not as if she can print it anyway.'

He frowned. 'Do you think it's the same person who sent the letters to Emily?'

'There are similarities.' Ruby pointed out the punctuation marks – the full stop that preceded the first line – 'But that could just be bad grammar.' She brought up the email she had just sent on her phone. 'I've emailed them. They're probably crapping themselves because I've responded. I don't suppose I'll hear anything back.'

'But the mention of "RIP". You realise I have to report this,' Downes said.

Ruby shook her head. 'Not yet, let's wait and see what she comes back with first. The punctuation could be just a coincidence, and the name Lucy is no secret. Helen knew about it long before the press release. You know what it's like around here: nothing stays hidden for very long.' Ruby knew that sharing her middle name would implicate her daughter. It was information she would keep to herself for now.

'Not as far as the press is concerned,' Jack murmured. 'What if there's more? It's not going to look very good: you and me together, along with the allegations that you're seeing a Crosby.'

'It's all lies,' Ruby said. 'I haven't been with Nathan in over a year, and even then it wasn't what you'd call dating. We were just…'

'Fuck buddies,' Jack muttered. 'It doesn't make it any better.' He paced from the window to the door. It took only two of his strides before he had to turn around. 'We're going to have to be discreet,' he paused, and seemed to consider his words. 'Unless you want things out in the open.'

'You're joking, aren't you?' Ruby said, the very thought of her colleagues knowing about their fling making a bolt of anxiety rise inside her.

This information had the potential to explode in her face. What had started off as a one-off domestic murder was now snowballing into something beyond their capabilities. But Ruby did not want to let it go. If this *was* her daughter she needed to know what was going on. She had lied to Lenny: if her adopted child was responsible for the murders she would have no choice but to turn her in.

Yet a small part of her refused to believe that the innocent child that she and Nathan had produced could commit such horrific acts. The plan was to find her, and then hopefully rule her out. But now she owed Lenny a favour, and soon she would be treading a very thin line. Her relationship with Frances was tenuous, but as long as her mother was still alive she would come to no harm. Frances was one of the few people Joy still recognised, and the women's friendship had survived many changes. Both families were intertwined in a complicated relationship not easily unbound. But now Lenny resented Ruby's influence over his brother as she tried to persuade him to go straight. Meddling in the Crosby family business was not a good idea. At least for now, their mother's closeness offered Ruby a degree of protection.

She refreshed her phone, waiting for a response. A notification pinged.

One new email.

CHAPTER TWENTY-FIVE

Lucy pushed her head through the open bedroom window and inhaled deeply. Wavy heat lines rose from the road below, bringing with them the whiff of melting tar. She wiped the sweat from her brow, feeling like an ant burning under a magnifying glass. Any second now, she may just combust into flames. Maybe it would be better if she did. It had been hard to shift her mindset away from what she was brought up to believe: that she was a worthless waste of space, only good for the benefits her foster parents earned from keeping a roof over her head. A voice crept into her memory. *C'mon, doesn't matter if we do it, because we're not really related after all.* It was the voice of her foster brother the day before Lucy was sent back to the home. Each time she was returned to care because of her disruptive influence on the family household. Nobody believed her side of the story. At the age of thirteen she was on the scrapheap of life, with one failed adoption and numerous foster parents. Nice people didn't want a troublesome child like her, and nobody stuck around long enough to ask her why she behaved the way she did.

How nice it must have been for them to carry on their lives without her. For years she endured the pain of watching other children get chosen for permanent homes. There had been one moment of hope. Mr and Mrs Mills, her third set of foster parents, had almost won her around, gifting her with the music box so alike the one from the movie she watched on a loop every day. Foolishly, Lucy had allowed herself to dream of them making a permanent commitment. But like a dog in the pound, she was destined for return. If she were an animal, she would have been put down.

But that was OK because now things would be different. She thought of Monica, with her beautiful features and manicured nails. She liked to sit on the basement step watching her as she slept. *She's not asleep, she's concussed.* The small voice spoke from the corner of her mind. Lucy's jaw tightened. She was done with listening to reason. Monica *was* sleeping and everything would be just fine. Besides, she didn't want to spoil things by waking her up. Having Monica look at her with fear in her eyes would only serve to dampen the warm spark of hope inside. *You're stupid if you think you can get away with it. Why would she want someone like you?* 'Shut up,' she growled.

The stiff timber frame rattled as she banged her head against it in a rush to get inside. She needed to sit at her dressing table to quieten her inner voice. She rubbed the back of her scalp, taking her place before the mirror. The row of wigs, the false eyelashes, and the coloured contact lenses: all props to make her forget who she was. Only then could she start again. She eased the brunette wig from the styrofoam head and dipped her chin as she set it in place. Soon she would be Monica's daughter for real. Her make-up may not be as eloquently applied, but her mother would love her just the same. Then later, when Mummy was feeling better, they would play her little game, and it would be Christmas all over again. Lucy checked her reflection against the photos sellotaped to the mirror before her. She liked the one of Monica sleeping the best. Lucy had made use of her special camera which could silently capture any image in the dimmest of light. Her eyes trailed over Monica's satin nightdress as she peacefully slept in her king-sized bed: even in sleep she looked beautiful – just like a movie star. Lucy applied a coat of pink lipstick. Rolling it over her mouth, it stained the edges, making it appear bigger than it was. She smacked her lips together, too lost in thought to notice the stains on her teeth. She would show them. With the help of her new mother she would turn things around.

After ten minutes she was almost ready. Her sweat-laced skin had absorbed the foundation pancaking her face, and she dabbed her face with the powder puff to mask the streaks. There. Perfect. Now she was ready to wake Monica up. Lucy felt a flutter in her belly as a sense of cautious hope returned. Emily was just a test run. This time it would be just right. And nobody would get in her way.

CHAPTER TWENTY-SIX

Ruby shoved the phone into her pocket. The last thing she wanted was Downes seeing the response before she'd had a chance to check what it said. It was not until she got into the toilet cubicle that she had the opportunity to read it. The stink of newly applied bleach made her wrinkle her nose, but she pulled down the toilet lid and sat to read the email.

> *'Ruby.*
>
> *Where were you last night? I waited, but you never came home. You say you want to see me, but we both know that's not true. Otherwise you would never have given me up in the first place. How did you feel when I was born at three a.m.? Some say it's the witching hour. Is that why you gave me up? Was I evil? Well I have news. I don't want you any more than you wanted me.*
>
> *See you around.*
>
> *Lucy'*

Ruby's heart sank because now she was left in no doubt. Lucy Joy Preston had been born at three a.m., and such information was imprinted on the original birth certificate, which Lucy, as an adoptee, could only have obtained when she turned eighteen. The anniversary Ruby and Nathan shared was their daughter's birthday. But she had passed her eighteenth birthday a couple of years ago – why was she coming after her now? Ruby swallowed, her mouth arid. She scanned the words a second time, trying to comprehend their meaning. 'I waited, but you never came home.' Had she been in her flat? And did that mean her daughter was the killer? Her mind bombarded by questions, she tried to plan her next move. But what was she supposed to do? Admit that, not only had she been sleeping with her DI, she had been involved with a member of the notorious Crosby family too? Then there was the revelation that she had given up their daughter for adoption when she was a teen. It was something she had omitted to declare when she joined the police. Had they known of her background, she would not have got a look in.

She knew she *should* think about what she was going to say. The email *should* be referred to a police negotiator, someone who would compose a reply where every word counted. But her fingers moved swiftly as instinct took over, reassuring the sender of the email and asking if they could meet up to talk. She had barely pressed 'send' when an error notification was returned as not recognised. It meant Lucy had instantly deleted the address. Ruby swore under her breath. That was what she meant by 'see you around'. She was toying with her, instigating revenge for a perceived betrayal years ago. Switching her phone to silent, Ruby shoved it into her pocket. It was time for briefing. She needed to absorb the investigation to date.

She was grateful to see the mug of strong tea awaiting her in her customary position near the head of the conference table. She nodded a thanks to Luddy, her mind still racing with recent events. Leaning over, she whispered in his ear. 'Any joy with that email address yet?'

People were still coming in, and she was satisfied they could not be heard. But Luddy looked furtive as he leaned in to reply. Ruby made a mental note not to put him up for any covert work.

'I'm trying to locate the IP address, but with all the other enquiries… '

'Do us a favour and make it a priority, will you?' Ruby said, forcing a reassuring smile.

She knew what her colleagues would think of her when the news came out. Downes would be deemed a stud, bedding a woman ten years his junior, but she would be viewed as some kind of trollop, sleeping with her DI to further her career. If only people knew. It had always been just her and Nathan. Even during the long gaps in their relationship, which could fall into months or even years, her dates with other men had never progressed past a heated kiss goodnight. It was only in the last year that she had begun to feel lonely, and after Jack's wife died they fell into each other's arms. He was safe, her rock, and she trusted him with her life. But the email made it all sound so sordid, and she could not bear for her colleagues to look at her in that way.

'Sorry,' Eve whispered, sliding in late under the watchful eye of DCI Worrow. Worrow was the Senior Investigating Officer for the case, and under pressure to produce results. As always, she was immaculately turned out, no make-up, but perfectly bobbed hair and a tailored grey skirt suit. Ruby's wardrobe consisted of several pairs of figure-hugging black fitted trousers and a few designer tops and shirts which she alternated on a daily basis. From the age of eight she had hated skirts and dresses with a passion.

'Right, let's get briefing underway,' Worrow said. 'Welcome to Operation Javelin to anyone who hasn't attended previously.' She pointed to the wall behind her, to the pictures of Harry Edmonds and his wife Emily. Underneath, Charlotte Lockwood's image stared back – her lips pursed as if she was about to say something – in a moment that was frozen in time. 'These are respected members of the community, and we're under a lot of pressure to get a quick result. Unfortunately, funding and manpower have been in short supply.' She glanced around the room, taking in their faces. 'So I'd like to begin by thanking you for your hard work and dedication. I know some of you in particular haven't been seeing a lot of your families.' Worrow paused, her glance landing on Eve. 'However, that's the nature of our job. Anyone that doesn't like it should put their name down in Sainsbury's, or B&Q. Now, on to the task in hand.'

Ruby contained her displeasure, turning it over like a bitter sweet in her mouth. Worrow was a terrible leader. It was just like her to say something positive then take it back, all in the same breath. Her phone itched in her blazer pocket with the need to check her emails again. She was sitting next to DI Downes, and blushed as he spread his long legs, his thigh touching hers.

Flicking through her paperwork, she joined in with delivering updates on the case. Intelligence was swapped; the recent appeal had brought forward some leads, a car hire company being one of them, who reported a woman behaving oddly as she rented a hire vehicle the day before Emily's disappearance. Enquiries had been made to trace the vehicle, but given the car had been rented several times since that forensics could be of limited value. All the same, Luddy had seized it, and CSI were checking over it for signs of blood, hair, fibres, anything which could provide valuable leads.

With definitive proof that Emily's real daughter had long since passed on, the possibility of mistaken identity was discussed. Ruby's stomach clenched. She could get into big trouble for withholding evidence. She was out of her depth, and Lucy had only just begun. Worrow's voice washed over her as she relayed her opinion that killers didn't just disappear into thin air. But Ruby knew that the biggest question of all waited to be answered.

Was this the end of the killing spree?

Given Lucy's recent taunting contact, it seemed she had only just begun. An image resurfaced from Ruby's memory, bringing with it a slice of pain. Even now it hurt to think of her little girl. With her cupid bow lips and tuft of soft black hair, giving up her baby was the hardest decision she ever had to make. She had not given birth to a murderer, Ruby told herself – it could not be true. But the evidence was mounting up, and she wondered if she was approaching this viewpoint as a detective, or a mother who could not face the truth.

CHAPTER TWENTY-SEVEN

A text beeped on Nathan's phone: '*MISSION COMPLETE*'. The product was loaded, concealed neatly into a lorry-load of furniture. Mission complete indeed. The corner of his mouth rose upwards in a smile. Who did Quinny think he was? Tom Cruise? Jerking his shirt sleeves down his wrists he checked the silver cufflinks. Give him his due: Quinny had done everything he asked despite the fact he had just got out of prison. Nathan shrugged on his Armani jacket, admiring its cut. He was in better shape now than when he was in his twenties. He ran his fingers through his hair, admiring his reflection in the mirror. Lenny's welcome home party was in full swing now, and big band music vibrated from below. They had spent a small fortune preparing the club – it had never looked so grand. It was the party of the year; the guest list would have been of great interest to the police. At least fifty per cent of his guests were packing heat. He just hoped his brother could stay out of trouble long enough to prevent the filth turning up.

After five years inside, it was hardly any wonder Lenny was as tense as a coiled spring. Nathan hoped that this morning's bit of business would go some way towards quenching his thirst for revenge. The guy he'd visited was a meathead, a twenty-five stone hulk with a pea for a brain. His fate had been sealed the second he grassed on his brother for the grievous bodily harm that had put him inside. Meathead survived his kicking after the verdict came through, but Lenny would not rest until he paid him a personal visit. Their victim had mistaken Nathan's aloofness for weakness, making his brutal reprisal all the more of a shock as he and Lenny pinned him to the floor. He could still remember fatso's expression as Lenny produced, not a knife or a shank, but a spoon. 'All the better for scooping, my dear.' Lenny's thirst for violence knew no bounds, and Nathan could still see fatso's freshly plucked eyes, white and viscous, like two plump boiled eggs. He was one of the lucky ones; Lenny had let him live. Nathan had managed to persuade him that such a savage act would serve as a living advertisement to any other players thinking of serving them up.

He exhaled a heavy sigh. He should re-join the party. Leona would be waiting, throwing a cautious eye over him when she thought he wasn't looking. He had come to accept his mother's interference in his life, and inviting Leona to Lenny's homecoming party seemed the acceptable thing to do. It was not as if he could ask Ruby. Leona had greeted him like an overexcited puppy. The girl had little substance and her behaviour was all for show.

Sliding his phone from his pocket, he deleted Quinny's text before dialling the number.

'Hello?' Quinny responded cautiously.

'It's me. Everything go as planned?'

A sigh of relief followed. 'Oh, hello boss; I wasn't expecting your call. Yeah, everything went smoothly. I start the ball rolling tomorrow.'

'Mmm,' Nathan said. 'Remember to get rid of the phone, then buy another pay as you go.'

'Are you sure?' Quinny said, sounding as if he was outside as the wind took his words. 'It's just that it seems like a waste of money, changing phones all the time.'

Nathan's voice sharpened. 'Are you questioning my judgement, Quinny?'

'What? Oh no, no, of course not. Sorry, boss, just trying to save you some money.'

Nathan snorted. 'I can afford it. But *you* can't afford to mess up. You don't want to end up back inside now do you?… a good-looking boy like you.' His tone was light as he delivered the threat, but the young lad knew the score.

Quinny's voice dropped: 'No, no I don't. I'll text you tomorrow from the new phone. When are you coming?'

'What did I tell you, shit for brains? Not over the phone. Stick to the plan.'

'Sure, sorry, boss, I—'

Nathan hung up, locking the door of his private office as he left. Since Lenny came out, all of his senses had been on high alert. Staying on top of the game was not easy with so many newcomers snapping at his heels.

The music had changed now: the live band playing a slow, melodic ballad, transporting them back in time. Lenny loved all the old stuff. The dress code was 'big band era' and their guests had not let them down. Nathan milled through the crowd, receiving numerous slaps on the back and ironclad handshakes. Even his more dubious friends had worn tuxedos; the women on their arms looking glam in their vintage swing dresses. Around him, people were laughing and joking, but business was still underway, with Lenny serving up tasters of his finest class A in the private booths. Their attractive young escorts were there too, to sweeten the deal. There was no need, not today. But Lenny couldn't help himself: that's just the way he was.

'Dance with me, babe,' Leona's hand snaked around his waist, and Nathan turned to greet her.

'I don't do dancing,' Nathan said, loosening himself from her grip. He had grown to dislike the thin sour odour of her perfume, her skin chemistry turning an expensive scent into something which smelt like urine.

Her smile slid from her face, but she still looked pretty despite her disappointment.

'You've got friends here, go and enjoy yourself, have some cocktails. I've got a bit of business to do.'

'OK then,' she said, stealing a kiss before joining her friends at the bar. Leona was no stranger to this life; her father was one of Lenny's oldest friends.

'You've done yourself proud, boss,' Fingers said, handing him a glass of champagne. 'This party will be the talk of the town.'

'It's good to see the old crowd again,' Nathan said. 'Just keep an eye on Lenny, will you? If anything starts, make sure you and the boys nip it in the bud. I don't want any bust ups. Not tonight.'

'He won't misbehave,' Fingers said. 'Not with yer mum about.'

Nathan nodded in agreement. As tough as he was, Lenny would never disrespect his mother by ruining the party she had spent months organising. 'Cheers,' Nathan said, knocking back the expensive Cristal. He surveyed his club, knowing he should be proud of his wealth and authority. But the better things went, the warier Nathan became. Underneath the veneer of success lay a greasy underbelly, and in this game, things had a habit of sharply turning on their head.

CHAPTER TWENTY-EIGHT

'What's dat smell, bitch?' The pasty-looking teenager sniffed the air. Ruby didn't recognise him, but she knew his mates who were hanging around in the stairwell of her block of flats. He dug his hands down the front of his tracksuit bottoms, dragging them even further down his torso. 'It's bacon, that's what, 'n' it stinks.'

'Leave her alone, man, that's Ruby. She's alright she is,' the tallest of the three said. At twenty years old, Darren was a young man who was respected on the estate, and Ruby figured the gobby one was most likely trying to impress him. Darren's mother was a heroin addict who shoplifted to fund her habit. Ruby had taken him under her wing a couple of years ago when she helped him to get an apprenticeship in a hotel kitchen. It was all thanks to Nathan, of course, who pulled in a favour to give the kid a chance to become a trainee chef. His mother was still shooting up most nights, but at least now he had his own money and a little bit of hope. Ruby figured that spending his evenings in the stairwell with his mates was better than watching his mum get high.

'Cheers, mate,' she said to Darren, offering him a cigarette. They were currency around here, and it was wise to have a pack handy, just in case. 'You've not seen anyone suspicious knocking around tonight, have you? It's just that I've been getting a bit of grief lately and I think they know where I live. Anyone come this way that you don't know?'

Darren took the cigarette and slid it behind his ear. 'Nah, we ain't seen nobody. Just the usual dropouts.'

'You gettin' grief, miss? You should call the police,' the youngest of the group sniggered.

'Miss?' Ruby said, stifling a laugh. 'You're not in school now, although by the looks of it, it's way past your bedtime.'

She disappeared into the lift to the sounds of their laughter. Sure they had their fair share of troublemakers on the estate, and gang culture was evident, but there were a lot of decent kids just trying to get by. Thoughts of Darren and his crew fell away as the lift ascended to her floor. She had been dreading going home all day and had left only when Downes had kicked her out of the station at just gone eleven.

It seemed to take for ever to get her key in the fob, and the first thing she did when she got into the living room was to reach her hand across the paint-blistered wall and turn on the light. The round paper lampshade cast the space in a gloomy yellow hue. She wondered what she was doing staying in a dump like this. She still had the keys to Nathan's flat in her bag, and it took all of her willpower not to turn on her heel and go there. Gently closing the door, she scoped out her flat. Apart from an old-fashioned dresser, a second-hand sofa and a ten-year-old TV, the living room was completely sparse. Her bedroom housed a small double bed and wardrobe, and the kitchen was no bigger than a cupboard, with basic amenities for cooking. But she preferred to eat at work, and despite the station kitchen not being much bigger, the food tasted better from there. Her flat had always given her the creeps. She had not been surprised to discover that the previous tenant was found overdosed on the sofa because a faint echo of his hopelessness still hung in the air. Still, it was as much as she could afford with her budget, and relatively close to work.

Satisfied the place was empty, she poured herself a drink. Had someone been in her flat? The truth was she did not *want* to know. For now, she was alone. But for how long? Cursing her paranoia, she knocked back the contents of her glass. A slug of whiskey hit the back of her throat, running like firewater into her belly and rewarding her with a warm glow. A gift from Downes before he discovered her penchant for rum. She kicked off her shoes and leaned back on the sofa, watching the door. To her right was the bottle of whiskey. To her left was a baseball bat. But she was plagued with thoughts, and even the alcohol coursing through her bloodstream could not make her feel any better.

By one a.m., all she could think about was Nathan, and she longed for his company. Drunk on whiskey and feeling insecure, calling him seemed like the best idea she'd had all week. She wiped her hand with the back of her mouth, slowly screwing the lid back on the bottle. I just want to hear his voice, she thought, then I'll go to bed. Her reservations muffled behind a drunken stupor, she dropped to her knees in the corner of the room and peeled back the stained red carpet. The smell of dried-in cigarette butts rose up to greet her but she continued until she found the loose wooden floorboard. Her secret hidey hole: one that even her fellow police officers would not locate. Pulling back the loose board she swore as her thumbnail ripped backwards, making her yelp.

Ruby shook her finger, the broken nail sending darts of pain up her thumb. She sucked it hard before examining the damage, feeling like a toddler that had been relegated to the naughty step.

'Shit,' she said, shaking her hand one more time before digging out the phone. It was turned off, and she didn't have the charger. Hesitating only seconds, she pressed the on button, deciding to leave it to the lap of the Gods. If the phone's battery was flat, then she would just go to bed. If it came alive she would make the call. The screen lit in a blue hue, and her heart gave a small leap in her chest. Fine. That was the way it was going to be. She called up the only number saved on the phone, filed under the letter 'N'.

Biting her lip, she listened to it ring out, her sensible thoughts drowned by the numbness of alcohol. An automated answering machine told her to leave a message. It was a shame. She would have liked to have heard him speaking. Inhaling a deep breath she realised she had dialled before rehearsing what she was going to say. 'It's me.' Long pause. 'I just want to ask what's going on? I mean, have you been in my flat because someone's been in my flat, more than once, and, well, I don't like it. If this is some kinda ploy to frighten me… well, I know you wouldn't do that, but if it's your brother… ' She rubbed her forehead, wishing her words would make sense instead of a jumbled mess. 'Oh, listen, it doesn't matter. I'm drunk… very drunk… forget I called.' She hung up the phone and turned it off, managing to place it under the flooring before going to bed.

Bringing the baseball bat for company, she stripped off her clothes and left them in a pile on the floor before climbing under her duvet.

It felt like coming out of a coma when she was woken by a figure standing over her, cast under the shadow of moonlight. Grasping the baseball bat between her hands, she drew back to swing in defence as her heart clattered out of her chest in horror.

'Babe, babe, it's me, take it easy.'

'What?' Ruby said, still half asleep, as her body had jumped to her defence before her mind caught up.

Nathan pulled off the black woollen hat and sat on the edge of her bed. 'Shit, Ruby, do you sleep with a baseball bat?'

'You're lucky it wasn't a knife.' She leaned her head back against the pink padded headboard as she allowed him to take it from her hands. Her broken thumbnail stung, reminding her she was not dreaming. Besides, her dreams of Nathan were happy and carefree.

On a beach, or in a cosy room with a crackling fire. Not sitting on the bed dressed in black like the Milk Tray man. 'You frightened the crap out of me,' she said as soon as she caught her breath. 'What are you doing here?'

'You called me.'

'No, I didn't.'

Nathan took the glass from the bedside table and gave it a sniff. 'Mr Jameson says you did.'

A vague recollection of a rambling message came back to her. What had she been thinking? 'Oh. Sorry. I didn't mean for you to drop everything.'

Nathan tore his eyes away from her skimpy camisole before rising from the bed and walking around the room. 'You said someone's been in here?'

'Yeah,' Ruby said, smoothing back her hair as she wondered how he gained access to her flat. 'It's a proper Piccadilly Circus in here.'

'You shouldn't be staying in this dive. It's not secure.'

'Obviously,' she said, and gave a wry grin. All the same, she didn't want to be left on her own. Not now she was sober. 'Have you time for a cuppa?'

Nathan took the chair at the end of the bed. 'Sure, it's not as if I was busy or anything.'

'Oh… sorry, do you need to go?'

Nathan waved her concerns aside. 'It was just a party. I was glad of the excuse to get away.'

With graceful ease Ruby slipped out of bed, clad in nothing but a white satin cami and mismatched knickers. She kept him talking as she made the drinks, worried he might slip away as effortlessly as he'd found his way in. One thing about Nathan: you never knew what was going on in his head. She decided on two hot chocolates instead, wondering what his tough nut cronies would think if they saw him sipping the drink covered in whipped cream and mini marshmallows. It was the least she could do given he had dropped everything to come to her.

'I thought I wasn't going to see you again,' she said, sprinkling the last of her marshmallows.

'You're a hard habit to break.'

'Yeah like nicotine, or something toxic.' She was going to say drugs, but she didn't want to spoil the moment. Handing him the mug, she grinned as he took a sip, resisting the urge to lick the whipped cream clinging to his top lip.

She climbed into bed and budged up, patting the space beside her. 'C'mon, come and sit beside me. I promise I won't pounce.'

Nathan joined her on the bed, sitting on top of the covers. 'Why don't you stay in your new flat? It's a lot safer. Look how easy I got in here. Anyone could have walked in, and you've got your fair share of enemies around here.'

Ruby shuddered. She had put enough people away in the last few years to know he was right. 'In case you hadn't noticed, I was ready for you. I only stopped because I recognised your voice.' It was true. Nathan's deep voice was one she could identify anywhere.

'I'm serious. I can't help you if you don't help yourself. Who have you pissed off now?'

'Have you spoken to your brother?'

'Yeah, I have and he's not been near the place. I know it's not been the same since you went to the other side, but my mum still has a lot of respect for you and your family. She wouldn't allow anything to happen to you.'

The other side? Ruby swallowed back the words on the edge of her tongue. Mentioning Frances, his apparent girlfriend Leona, or her meeting with Lenny would not go down well. She leaned her head on Nathan's shoulder. He was cold but smelt good. It was a safe smell. She wasn't about to shatter the misguided faith he held in his brother, and she certainly was not going to tell him about her communication from Lucy.

Giving their daughter up was something she knew pained Nathan no end. It brought them together each year on the day of her birthday. If he knew Ruby was directly in communication with her he would stop at nothing to have her back in his life. The only thing that had prevented him from finding her already was the hope that she was happy and settled with a family of her own.

'I'll go to the flat. But not tonight. Stay awhile, please?'

Nathan answered by leaning back on the bed and folding his arms.

Sleep overcame Ruby, and soon she was back in one of those dreams where she and Nathan had lit a fire in the squat. They were lying back on the blankets, staring up at the ceiling; her head on his chest as they dreamt of the future.

The shrill ring of the alarm pierced her brain into an abrupt awakening. She grasped the floor for the clock that was vibrating on its back as the key wound anticlockwise, sounding the only ring that was loud enough to wake her. Slowly she began to piece together the happenings of the night before, and she leaned up on her elbows, casting her eyes around the room for signs of Nathan. *Was he really here last night?* She lifted the pillow to her face and breathed in his familiar intoxicating smell. He must have fallen asleep for a while, then left at dawn. It didn't matter what time it was he always woke with the sun. Her mouth felt like sandpaper, and she smacked her tongue against the roof of her mouth; awaking with her usual regret for putting her weakness on display. Why did she drink when it made her so needy?

Rubbing the sleep from her eyes, she stepped out of bed and smiled at the empty cup on the table. She vaguely remembered making hot chocolate, and was pleased to see he had drunk it. She could cope with Nathan cutting himself out of her life as long as she knew he was there if she needed him. It was selfish but not something she was willing to give up just yet. A year without her lover had brought pain and loneliness she had never felt before, and as she picked up the empty bottle of whiskey and threw it in the bin a small part of her vowed never to return there. But it was not something she had the luxury of dwelling on – as she stepped out from under her dripping showerhead her phone rang to demand her presence at work.

CHAPTER TWENTY-NINE

Monica winced as light flooded the room, cutting into her brain and stinging her eyes. She had lost all track of time, falling in and out of consciousness, gratefully accepting the blackness as respite from the terror she was unwilling to comprehend. She realised that at some point she had wet herself, but it was a calm acceptance as her grasp on reality weakened. Somewhere deep within a voice was telling her to struggle free from her bindings, but every time she tried a wave of nausea passed over her, and the thought of choking on her own vomit terrified her more than being left in the basement to await her fate. And now, as bare feet descended the stairs Monica forced her eyes open in order to plead unblinkingly at the person who put her here.

'Hello, Mother,' Lucy said, brightly, as if she was meeting Monica in a coffee shop rather than having her tied to a chair in the basement of Lucy's home. 'Did you have a nice sleep?'

She was wearing a fluffy towelling robe, with blue and white striped pyjamas underneath. There was something about her hair... Her fringe was crooked. Monica peered, noticing for the first time that she was wearing a wig. The woman's make-up appeared hastily applied in the same style as Monica's usual look: dark kohl-lined eyes, arched eyebrows, and baby pink lipstick. But today, as the fairy lights blinked red and green, her face looked gaudy, like a freakish circus clown.

Monica's nostrils flared to accommodate her panicked breaths as Lucy dug her fingers into the side of her jaw.

Turning Monica's face to one side she surveyed the damage. 'Ouch,' she said, sucking sharply through her teeth. 'You're still bleeding. That's got to hurt. You should have been nicer to me, then I wouldn't have had to knock you out.' A small titter escaped her lips. 'I forgive you now, though. It was just the shock talking, wasn't it?'

Monica exhaled a muffled groan; her eyes rolling to the back of her head. The darkness was dragging her back down, deep into the abyss. Three sharp slaps stung her face, and Monica drew back her head to avoid the fourth.

'That's better,' her captor smiled, her teeth stained with bright pink lipstick. 'Don't you know it's rude to fall asleep in company?'

She's mad, Monica thought, snapping out of her stupor. Fresh tears blurred her vision as the words rebounded in her mind. *This person is insane.*

'That's more like it,' Lucy said, drawing back her hand. 'Are you listening? Or do I need to slap you harder?'

Monica whimpered from under the spit-drenched gag.

Lucy wrinkled her nose. 'You are a stinky mum. Have you wet yourself?' She tutted. 'That just won't do. You've got a very special visitor coming today. But I have to warn you: she likes everything just right. She's a lovely little girl, and she's so excited about seeing you.'

A visitor? Monica's heart accelerated with hope. If someone else was visiting, perhaps they could persuade this crazy woman to let her go.

Lucy pushed up her sleeve and checked her watch. 'I must get dressed. Things to do, people to see. Now, how about a hug?'

Monica stiffened as Lucy wrapped her bony arms around her. Her towelling robe smelt of fabric conditioner, and she closed her eyes as she inhaled the scent of everyday life.

Lucy pulled away. Her robe was stained with snot, tears, and a delicate dribble of blood. 'Aww don't look so worried. You'll be just fine. I really like you, Monica. I want you to be the one.'

Lucy cocked her head to one side like a bird examining a worm. Her voice fell into a conspiratorial whisper as she risked a glance upstairs. 'But you only get one chance. Don't mess it up.'

What was she talking about? Monica recalled the recent news broadcast of a woman who had been found murdered in the area. First her husband and then, days later, her body was found. She shuddered. It couldn't have anything to do with Lucy, could it? Was Lucy really her daughter? Monica looked at her, pleading with her eyes. If only she had been nicer to her when she knocked on her door, or better still, not answered it at all.

'Are you hungry?' Lucy said, standing back with her hands on her hips.

Monica slowly nodded, each movement delivering hammering blows of pain. Anything to remove the gag from her mouth, if only for a few precious seconds. She had to speak to her, to tell her whatever she wanted to hear. And as crazy as it sounded, she did not want to be left alone. If she could just get free and apologise, then perhaps she could persuade Lucy that this had all been a horrible mistake.

As if reading her thoughts Lucy shook her head. 'Later. You can have a drink later. I don't think it's a good thing that we talk to each other right now. I'm very cross with you, Mother, and I don't know what I might do. Besides, I've gone to all this trouble and I know this little girl is very excited about meeting you. So take my advice, and don't make the same mistake twice. Be kind and get the words right. I can't face any more disappointments.'

More disappointments? Monica trembled with fear. The stains on the floor. The pungent smell. Lucy wanting her to be 'the one'. As opposed to what? The others that had failed? *Where were they now?*

Lucy turned and climbed up the stairs. The light flicked off, plunging the room into darkness – the silence punctuated only by the sounds of Monica's sobs.

CHAPTER THIRTY

Three fish. That's all that were left in the tank, and two of them were guppies, so tiny that the elderly residents of Oakwood Care Home could barely see them. So much for being therapeutic. The Siamese fighting fish had looked beautiful when he bought it from the pet store. Who would have thought that such a handsome creature was capable of such destruction? It made him think of his own circumstances. Not for the first time, Mr Carter wondered if getting into bed with the Crosby family had been a good idea. Oakwood's focus had always been on high quality care, and without the Crosbys' substantial cash injection he would not have been able to progress to the next phase of development. Mr Carter knew all about the other homes that offered similar services, as advertised on their pamphlets. But their reality was far from the truth. Recently, one of his competitors had been exposed on *Watchdog*: shamed by hidden cameras as they highlighted the abhorrent treatment of pensioners who were left soiled, neglected, and were rough-handled on a daily basis. It was why he insisted everything had to be just right, and the response had been very encouraging. Funding the new wing was part of his dream, and having the capability to pay for decent staff who genuinely cared about their clients set them apart from other care homes in London that could barely afford to pay trustworthy, English-speaking, workers.

Of course, such things came at a price, and he had not been entirely comfortable with his new sleeping partner, but it was the lesser of two evils. The banks would have fleeced him, despite his early success.

Carter shook Nathan Crosby warmly by the hand as he rose to leave. His meeting had made him sick with nerves, although the figures he had prepared were looking good, and Nathan was already getting a return on his investment. But their encounters made him nervous. Carter had always been a God-fearing man and the closest he had come to breaking the law was eating a bar of shoplifted chocolate when he was fourteen. The handsome well-dressed man before him did not look like a criminal, but neither did the bankers who should be doing time in jail, as far as he was concerned. Given a choice, he would take the Crosby family any day of the week. Since getting involved with them, Oakwood Care Home had come on in leaps and bounds. He had been too scared to ask Nathan about his interest in their client, Joy Preston. It seemed odd, given that Joy's daughter was a police sergeant with the Metropolitan police. It had been made quite clear to him that Nathan Crosby's involvement was to be treated with the utmost discretion, and this was something Carter was more than happy to provide. 'Discreet is my middle name,' he had said, as they shook hands on their agreement. Curiously, also in the agreement it stated that Ruby Preston was to be charged just a fraction of the ongoing costs for her mother, and that her discovery of their arrangement would seriously jeopardise their future working relationship. Doing anything to upset the Crosby family was not on the agenda. It was not all that dissimilar to the hotel industry, of which Carter had been such a big part in his younger days. Relationships could be found in the strangest places. The meeting concluded, he opened the door of his office and saw Mr Crosby out.

Their most popular carer, Harmony, dealt with Joy, ensuring that she had something red upon her person at all times. A hair clip, a scarf, it didn't matter, as long as Nathan's wishes were upheld. Mr Carter could not really understand what all the fuss was about as it was inevitable that Joy would forget her old habits given her dementia. But it seemed to make Ms Preston happy to see these little touches, and it was only then, when he thought about it, that Mr Carter realised that Nathan was going out of his way not just to make Joy comfortable but to put her daughter at ease as well. It was something Mr Carter had mentioned to his wife previously, as he tried to make sense of it all. His wife had informed him that it was a romantic gesture, made all the more romantic by the fact the woman in question was unaware. All the same, she warned him, romance would not come into it should the general public be made aware of his benefactor, so it was best to leave it at that

'How are you doing today?' Nathan asked, pulling up a chair as he sat across from Joy Preston.

He hated care homes, although Oakwood was one of the better ones. It was flooded with light thanks to the floor-length windows which afforded views of the flourishing garden. Heat blasted from the radiators, and Nathan noticed that half the residents were asleep. Even Joy's eyes were drooping, and he shifted in his chair, feeling guilty for wanting to leave the woman who had saved his mother on more than one occasion. It had never been openly spoken about, but Joy's calming influence on his family's turbulent life was something they were all grateful for. Such debts would never be forgotten.

Joy often mistook Nathan for his father. In the beginning his visits were short because he could not bear to have such a flaw pointed out. Even hearing his father's name made his gut churn. But now he was older and had become accustomed to her ways. All the same, it was nice when she recognised him for who he really was, even if his place was always in the past.

'Nathan… ' Joy said, staring at him like she had lost something in his face.

He offered her a smile. 'Yes, it's me. How are you doing?'

'Killing the minutes and watching them die,' she said, faintly, before turning her gaze to the chaffinches darting on the hedgerow outside.

Nathan grew up wishing his mother was more like Joy. Frances's harsh upbringing gave her a warped sense of what was normal, confusing jealousy and control as signs of love. But as a boy, Nathan knew from watching Ruby and her parents that this was not the case. It was also why he and Ruby had believed that giving their baby up for adoption was the right thing to do. Back then, they were just kids. Things had seemed so bleak, and even Lenny agreed it was for the best when he confided in him about their plans. Nathan could never have known how much things would change after his father died. Shedding the old regime to work with upmarket clientele gave him the feeling that his work was socially acceptable, and with a brain like a calculator he discovered a talent for making money that he did not know he had possessed. He would be happy with his lot if it were not for Ruby and their child; he regretted the chances they had missed to make each other happy. He wondered what his daughter was doing now, and if she was happy.

'Lucy,' he exhaled the words in a sigh, not realising he had spoken his thoughts aloud.

'Lucy,' Joy repeated. 'She came to see me the other day. Such a nice young woman. I hope she comes again soon.'

CHAPTER THIRTY-ONE

Ruby's heart felt like it was going to pound its way out of her chest as she sidled into Worrow's office. Situated on the fourth floor, it was where all the higher ranking officers kept a safe distance from their minions. The 'ivory towers', as Downes called it, with primrose-scented tissues and a newly installed air-conditioning system. She swiped a jelly baby from the glass bowl on Worrow's clutter-free desk, casting her eyes over the expensive leather chair and top-of-the-range computer. In comparison, Ruby's office looked like it had been furnished from the remnants of a warehouse closing down sale. She brought her focus to the task in hand, trying not to look as guilty as she felt. She couldn't believe that she was doing this, but what choice did she have? It was for the greater good, she told herself, and Downes would be a hypocrite to criticise her. Lenny must have known something was going down on his patch. The Crosbys' ability to spot a plain clothes police officer had always amazed her, but she had not been privy to the information he sought. It had to be something to do with a drugs deal and a possible police raid.

As loath as she was to help him, she was left with little choice. Passing information on to Lenny might help her catch the murderer, or, at the very least, find Lucy. But getting caught was not an option. Ruby shuffled the mouse on the desk, her eyes flitting to the open office door. The password request box popped up, but there was no way she was going to leave a digital footprint by typing in her own. She had noted Worrow's keystrokes plenty of times during the conversations when she logged on, and quickly typed in 'Miss Marple': the name of Worrow's pug. Bingo. She was in. Her breath accelerated as she looked up the briefing online, her eyes darting from the open door to the screen.

Worrow was entitled to read the latest operational command, but it was not in Ruby's remit. And even if it was, she did not want a record made of her search. She quickly accessed the information she needed, scribbling down the date and time. She had been right. Intelligence stated that a furniture lorry was destined to enter the port of Harwich from Holland in two days' time – believed to be carrying class A drugs. Ruby bit her lip. This was big. Much bigger than she anticipated. A shipment like this could be worth a small fortune, and here she was about to pass on information, jeopardising any possible raid. Footsteps echoed in the hall, eliciting a flurry of panic inside her. Trying to exit the programmes all at once had caused an egg timer to pop up, and Ruby moaned under her breath as the footsteps approached. It was Worrow: she could tell by the tone of her pernickety voice. 'Hurry up, hurry up,' Ruby whispered, as the clip clop of Worrow's sensible shoes echoed in the corridor. A red flush spread across Ruby's chest as she clicked out of each site in turn.

The log off screen flashed up, but it was too late to leave the office now. Ruby grabbed her scrap of paper and pen just as Worrow walked in. Ducking down behind a filing cabinet, she wondered what the hell she was going to say when she was found. A lost contact lens? A missing earring? She slid her reading glasses into her breast pocket. Lame excuses, but ones she was willing to use. But as Ruby's DCI entered the office the phone on her desk rang. Ruby exhaled. Saved by the bell. Worrow was too engaged with her telephone call to notice her presence. Her voice was hushed now, and Ruby peeped out to see her close the door. So much for open door policy, Ruby thought.

'I've told you before, don't ring me at work,' Worrow said, her back to Ruby as she leaned against her desk, pausing as the buzz of a raised voice was returned. 'I know... no I... no, of course I don't want that... ' Worrow exhaled sharply as the voice on the line voiced their displeasure. 'I'm not answering my mobile because I'm busy.' Worrow ran her fingers through her hair, clasping a handful at the top of her scalp. 'You'll have to sort this out on your own.'

Ruby kept her breath soft and shallow, terrified that her superior would find her when the conversation ended.

Worrow took a deep breath, exhaling loudly. 'Because I value my job, that's why.'

Ruby's legs began to fizz with the onset of pins and needles as her blood supply was compromised from her cramped position behind the cabinet.

'There won't *be* any disrepute. What you do in your own time is your business. As for the rest of it... I'm not being tetchy. No, *you* listen to *me*, it's your mess, *you* sort it out.' The conversation ended and Worrow fell silent.

This is it, Ruby thought, waiting for her superior to turn her head. But luck was on Ruby's side. Worrow's mobile phone rang. It was a job call, and Worrow spoke for all of two seconds before hanging up and striding back out. Heaving a sigh of relief, Ruby straightened herself up. She had got more than she bargained for, in more ways than one. What was going on with Worrow to make her react that way? Ruby's fingers lingered over the phone keypad before dialling 1471. Noting down the phone number, she bit down on her bottom lip. It was one she recognised. Just what were they playing at, ringing Worrow for help? And how much trouble were they in if it would risk Worrow's job?

Ruby would think about it later. Right now she had to organise her meeting with Lenny. She descended the stairs, hating the sickly feeling of being on the wrong side of the law. She'd joined the police to protect people and to uphold order. There was never any intention for personal gain – even though she'd had plenty of opportunities to turn crooked and help the criminals she grew up with. Such endeavours would have given her a nice income, and she certainly would not have been the only one. But Ruby was not a dishonest person, and her team meant everything to her. She would have given up her life rather than turn bent like some of her predecessors.

But now she was forced to make this deal with Lenny because she could not bear to have another life lost. It was a trade-off; sacrificing a considerable drugs find in order to take a killer off the street. There would be other drug busts. She was going to find Lucy and she was going to take her in. At least she knew why Worrow had been so stressed lately. Ruby nibbled the skin around her thumbnail. For now she would hang tight and not make any rash decisions. The caller was yanking her chain, and brought with them a problem that Worrow was working hard to shake off. What did they mean 'disrepute'? And what had that got to do with risking Worrow's job?

Standing in the stairwell, Ruby slid out her phone and sent a quick text to Lenny, asking to arrange to meet. The thought of obtaining her daughter's details brought discord. It would be hard enough speaking to her, but what if she had to make an arrest? A ripple of anxiety rose up inside her. She had no choice. Contact would have to be made. Time was running out, and she could not afford to waste another second.

CHAPTER THIRTY-TWO

Monica jumped as a door slammed upstairs. Just how long had she been down here? Without any windows it was impossible to tell. The heady smell of stale urine clawed the back of her throat, and she squirmed in her chair, breathing in recycled air. Her mouth was bleeding now from her failed efforts to bite her way through the saliva-sodden gag. She wriggled her wrists and was rewarded with a slice of pain. The more she struggled, the deeper the thin strip of rope embedded in her flesh. Yet, she had to fight because there was no other way out of this scenario. Fear crushed Monica's soul as the reality hit her: she might never see daylight again. She hung her head as a whimper rose in the base of her throat. To die in this humid hole, where no one might find her, was too much to bear.

Monica's thoughts galloped on, each one more frightening than the one before. Would anybody actually care? For the last few years she had worked so hard in her career, walking over her friends to gain promotion. Had her well-paid job been worth abandoning them all for? Now, when death was near, the answer was loud and clear. No amount of designer jewellery or trendy clothes could comfort her. She thought of her husband, Adam. He would probably be relieved when she didn't come home. She had done nothing but nag him in the last few years, always pushing for a better promotion and a bigger house. Her sniffles echoed in the darkness. What was she doing, reflecting on her life when she should be trying to escape? She was used to thinking on her feet; surely she could work a way out of this? But without the power of speech, just how was she going to reason with her captor? If only she could persuade her that she had been wrong about turning her away; perhaps then she stood a chance. Maybe Lucy was just trying to frighten some sense into her. But somehow Monica doubted that very much. The muffled sounds of the television droned, chilling her senses.

She could smell her own sweat, brought on by the fear of her captor being so close. But without her she could be left to rot, starving to death in this blackened tomb. A feeling of dread bore down on her as footsteps clip clopped overhead. After what felt like a lifetime, the basement door opened, flooding the stairs with light. But the footsteps this time seemed lighter than before, and the voice several octaves higher. Monica's heart accelerated as the voice carried down to her. 'La la la…' it sang as the figure descended the stairs. This was not the little girl Lucy spoke about. Something was wrong. Very wrong. Monica clenched her fists in preparation for what lay ahead. The Christmas tree lights flicked on, and she strained her eyes to see the person before her – gasping in realisation.

There stood an adult-sized girl: a smiling blue-eyed monster with blonde ringlets in her hair. She was holding something square. A music box. The fairy lights flickered: off, on, off, on, casting her white teeth in an eerie green and red hue. Another wave of sickness claimed Monica as she tried to comprehend the situation. There was no little girl coming to save her; it was the same crazed woman, dressed as a child. Monica's eyes fell on the old fashioned dress, dark tights and lace up boots, and all hope fell away.

'Surprise! It's me!' Lucy exclaimed, placing the music box gently on the shelf.

Monica's stomach dry-heaved. She tried to respond, but all that came out was a series of grunts. Confusion overtook her. Just what was going on? Her throat felt dry and arid, and her stomach clenched in fear.

'It's okay, don't be scared,' Lucy said, in a childish voice. 'We haven't started yet. Do you know what you have to do?'

Monica responded by shrugging her shoulders. If only she could get off this damned gag.

Lucy giggled. It was an ugly laugh. 'You are a pretty mummy,' she said, making Monica flinch as she stopped to stroke her hair. 'I like you. I think you are the prettiest mummy of all.'

Monica's breath was coming fast. A wave of dizziness overcame her as the blackness called. She closed her eyes, praying for an end to her misery.

'No, no, no, Mummy, you mustn't fall asleep. We haven't started yet. Remember what I said about saying the right thing?'

Bony fingers pulled on the tightly wound knot at the back of her gag. Slowly she unwrapped the filthy material, allowing Monica to spit and cough while gulping in mouthfuls of air. Monica licked her dry crusted lips, turning her eyes mournfully up to her captor. 'Water,' she croaked. If she could distract her long enough to go and get a drink, then perhaps she could scream for help while the basement door was open. If nothing else, it would buy her some time.

But Lucy was not that easily convinced and simply shook her head. 'I'm not allowed to use the tap,' she said. 'Now, do you know what you have to do?'

'Please, I'm not well. I… I need a drink.' Monica swallowed back her spit, trying to ease her scratchy throat.

But Lucy was skipping round and round the chair, making her dizzy.

'What's your name? Your real name?' Monica croaked, trying to appease her.

Lucy frowned, halting mid skip, and Monica wished she could take back the words. Whatever she had said had clearly annoyed her. She grimaced as Lucy stepped forward and slapped her hard on the face. The sharp sting brought Monica back to her senses, and if nothing else, at least she was seeing straight now.

'I'm sorry,' she said. 'Please just tell me what I need to do. I just want to go home.'

'You should know my name if you're my mummy. So that's very naughty indeed. Do you like my tree?' she said, her mood changing in a split second. 'It's Christmas tomorrow; it's going to be the most wonderful day. There's going to be food and cake and lots of nice toys; we're going to play music together and dance… won't that be wonderful?'

'Yes.' Monica nodded her head. 'Wonderful.' The words fell like a stone from her lips.

'Tomorrow you can say the words and we can be together for ever because then you're my real mummy and we can have the most wonderful time and you will love me for ever and ever and nobody will ever hurt me again.' Lucy did not pause for breath as the words spilled from her lips. 'But now you must go to sleep because it's Christmas Eve and Santa will be here soon.'

The thoughts of the gag going back on her mouth struck another spear of fear into Monica's heart. She shook her head wildly, each movement returning intense pain to the base of her skull. 'Please no, not the gag, please. Tell me what I have to say and I'll do it now. Tell me. Please don't put that on me again, *please.*'

'If you're my real mummy you know just what to say. Now keep steady or I'll slap you,' Lucy said sharply, grappling to keep Monica's head still.

But Monica didn't want to keep still; she wanted to get away. Plunging her teeth into Lucy's wrist, she bit down hard. With one final twist of her sweat-laced wrists, she managed to twist the rope enough to pull her right hand free. Grasping Lucy's blonde ringlets she recoiled in horror as the wig came loose in her hand. Her pause cost her dearly. Lucy reached behind her and launched an object towards her head. With a terrifying finality, everything went black.

CHAPTER THIRTY-THREE

Ruby allowed the engine of the car to tick over as she parked up underneath the bridge. A quick text to Lenny Crosby had secured a meeting time and place. She had hoped that by meeting at Charlotte's murder site she would be gifted with a flash of insight. If the killer had been able to escape unseen after mowing the woman down in cold blood, then Ruby's liaison with Lenny should surely go unnoticed too. She watched as a well-fed rat scuttled under the bridge, disappearing around the corner. Just what had Charlotte been thinking, arranging to meet Emily here in the dark?

It had turned out that Charlotte Lockwood was no stranger to London. Despite the façade of rich living, police investigations had uncovered that she had come from modest means: originating not far from here, in an area of East London that had yet to benefit from restructure. They had managed to track down Charlotte's first husband, but he had an ample alibi for the night of her death. Her post-mortem results were disappointing; the only evidence on her ravaged body being the deep grooves of the tyres which had punctured her organs and shattered her bones. It was believed that the driver of the vehicle ran over her three times. What kind of anger and hatred would someone have to carry inside to do that to another human being? And why? But Ruby knew it was a question that would never grant a satisfactory answer. She didn't believe in evil before she joined the police. She thought by then that she had seen all that the darker side of human nature had to offer. But she had barely touched the surface, and evil was as plausible an explanation as anything else these days. Some people had villainy ground into the marrow of their bones.

Ruby checked her rear-view mirror as a black BMW pulled up behind. Tinted windows barely afforded her a view of Lenny Crosby's thick-necked driver. Waiting for him to show had made her nervous; not because of who he was, but because she was about to pass on precious information. Her stomach churned. If her colleagues knew what she was doing, they would call her a bent copper and turn their backs on her for good. She would lose her job, maybe even go to prison. She rested her fingers on the keys of the ignition before switching the engine off.

She had bent the rules before, but never like this. And the last thing she wanted was to be in Lenny Crosby's pocket. But at night when she closed her eyes she saw the final moments of terror ingrained on Emily Edmonds's face. Such a killer did not come from nowhere and return to nowhere. They were likely to strike again. And if it really was her daughter, Ruby had a personal responsibility to sort it out. She would turn her in if she had to, but she would do it her way.

Dressed in a black suit and shades, Lenny exited the vehicle behind her. Ruby froze as her passenger door was pulled open, allowing a blast of street air to invade her space. She gave him the once-over, checking his hands for weapons. His expression gave nothing away. Stony faced, he slid into the seat beside her.

'I've got something for you; a birthday card,' she said, keen to have their meeting disposed with. She dipped her hand into the door panel compartment. 'But before I pass it over I want to make it quite clear that I won't be remembering your birthday again.' She delivered an intense stare as the words left her mouth, watching Lenny's grin spread as she spoke behind guarded words. She did not trust him any more than he trusted her. Any verbal admission of wrongdoing could end her in a lot of trouble, if he were recording their meeting. 'Are we clear on that?' she said as he reached out to take it.

'Don't fret,' he said, his eyes roaming her body.

The spice of his aftershave rose between them. He was groomed to perfection; smart suit, shoes shined, and a crisp white shirt with two buttons opened at the neck. But, unlike his brother, he was a wolf in disguise, and it would take more than an expensive suit to hide the violence within. Ruby wanted to ask if he was going somewhere, but there was no point in trying to obtain information when she was handing over intelligence to the most vicious man she knew.

'Don't you have something for me in return?'

Lenny tutted, his eyes dancing as he revelled in the game. 'Hasn't anyone ever told you that you don't give to receive?'

He snatched the envelope from her grasp, tearing it open before her. Ruby watched his eyes dart from left to right as he greedily scanned the information. It seemed to confirm his suspicions, and he slowly nodded as he absorbed the text.

The heat of anger rose inside her. He was not going to have one over on her. She wouldn't allow it. Her fists clenched, ready to snatch the information from his hand.

Lenny glanced up to see her glowering next to him, and a laugh escaped his lips. 'For fuck's sake, relax will you? I haven't forgotten.'

Sliding his hand into his jacket pocket he pulled out a piece of folded notepaper, touching the palm of Ruby's hands as he handed it over. His fingertips were cold, and Ruby suppressed a shudder. She was making a deal with the devil and hoped it would be worth the inevitable repercussions. Ruby glanced at the writing. It simply gave an address and the name 'Goldie' and a time: 2.30 p.m. The name was familiar. It was someone Ruby had dealt with before.

'What's this?' Ruby said, forgetting her earlier caution.

Lenny curled his fingers around the door handle to leave. 'It's a lead. You're the detective, you work it out.'

'And if it doesn't pan out?' Ruby said, folding up the paper and shoving it in her breast pocket.

'I told you I'd find her and I will. Goldie's just a gesture of goodwill; something to keep you out of trouble. And thanks for this, by the way. If you ever want to do business again… '

Ruby shook her head, swallowing back the bile induced by her betrayal. 'We're both getting what we want. Let's just leave it at that,' she retorted.

She felt sick in Lenny's company, and there was no way there was going to be a repeat performance. Ruby pulled away from the kerb as Lenny returned to his car. But she could still smell his scent in the air. It clung to her senses, along with a growing sense of disloyalty. Her fingers tightened on the steering wheel as she drove to the police station. Back to the people she betrayed. But she knew she would get over it. It was collateral damage; the price she had to pay. She could live with her treachery, if it meant catching the killer before they struck again.

CHAPTER THIRTY-FOUR

After obtaining the IP address, Luddy had seized the CCTV from the internet café from where it was sent. At least now they had a description of Ruby's mystery emailer. A dark-haired young female, her features were partially obscured. Her image was firmly imprinted on Ruby's mind as they approached Goldie's address.

'Remember what I said.' Ruby turned to Luddy as they approached the door of the flat. 'Goldie may seem all sweetness and light, but she'd have you over in a heartbeat. Don't turn your back on her, and don't give her any money.'

'Money? Why would I give her money?' Luddy said, dropping his voice as the door opened.

It did not take much persuading for him to accompany Ruby to the address listed under the guise of the police investigation. Goldie was a bolshy twenty-two-year-old woman who worked for a pimp named Frenchie, known for his connections with dealers in France. Once a hive of intelligence, Goldie had stopped providing information for money after receiving a warning for which she ended up with internal bleeding and the loss of her thumb. Ruby had her suspicions that Lenny had been responsible and guessed that the woman had escaped execution only because she was worth more alive than dead.

On the streets from an early age, Goldie had become hardened to her way of life, and earned her pimp a decent income. Ruby did not want to keep such a valuable source of information waiting. Equipped with takeaway teas and a sandwich she brought the offerings along with her. Goldie's time was precious, and after a night on the streets she was probably yet to eat. As much as she needed her, Ruby did not want to attend that particular estate alone, and Luddy swallowed her lie about chasing information from an anonymous source.

Goldie flashed a smile as she welcomed them inside, revealing the gold-plated teeth which had earned her the nickname. That, and the blonde beehive hairstyle piled high on her head. It was not there just to look pretty. Ruby knew that Goldie's long silver hairpins acted as weapons, if the need occurred. She was battle-scarred from a life on the streets. A broken arm, cracked ribs, and now an amputated thumb. Just a few of the injuries she had experienced over the years.

'How's it going?' Ruby said, taking a seat across from her.

The flat was small and grubby, with one bedroom shared by six women who slept top to toe on a mattress on the floor. They worked the streets by rotation; their lives revolving around sex, sleep, and getting high. Ruby knew their life histories because she had tried to help them, but failed. They had all got there the same way: groomed from a young age by the charming man who would become their jailer. But Frenchie did not need bars on the windows as long as he fed their addiction.

'Cheers,' Goldie said, hastily unwrapping the tuna sandwich from its wrapper. 'I'm starving, that's how it's going. Frenchie barely gives me time to sleep, fucking knobhead.'

Ruby could submit an intelligence report: organise another raid to close Frenchie down. But it was a revolving door syndrome, and any loss in earnings would have to be paid back from him driving the women twice as hard. 'We can help, if you'll let us,' Ruby said, taking a sip of her tea. Even while she was saying it she knew Goldie would never leave Frenchie: not while she depended on him to supply the drugs that her body craved.

'I saw the press conference on the telly last night,' Goldie said, failing to acknowledge Ruby's offer of help. 'That geezer offering ten grand for information about the killer of that Charlotte woman. You know, the hit and run under the bridge.'

Ruby was aware of the reward. It had been sanctioned by the police. Charlotte's husband had offered it in the hope it would provide them with information on her murderer. They also made the newspaper aware of the name 'Lucy', although it already seemed common knowledge in the media. She knew who to thank for that. She leaned forward in a conspiratorial whisper. 'What have you got?' she said.

Goldie nodded, wiping the crumbs from her low-cut top. 'This Lucy, she's the same person mentioned in the press conference, isn't she? If you want to help me, the best way of doing it is to get me that reward money.'

'Want one?' Ruby asked, offering a Silk Cut up to Goldie. It was a new packet: bought to lower the barriers between them.

Goldie lit the cigarette, her words peppered with smoke. 'There's been this girl sniffing round, asking questions. Called herself Lucy; said she was looking for her mum.'

Luddy reached into his folder and Ruby caught his eye, giving a discreet shake of the head. There was no way Goldie would sign a statement, and even a police pocket notebook entry could be enough cause for her to clam up. They would have to commit her words to memory, or not at all.

'I'm telling you because you're the only one I trust to get me that reward. I don't want it getting out that I've been helping the police. Not after… ' Goldie rubbed the nub of her thumb. Her visit with Ruby may have been cleared, but she was left with a lifelong reminder of what happened to people who grassed.

Luddy placed his hands back on his lap, and Ruby relaxed into the conversation.

'You have my word. If your information leads to a charge, then you'll get your reward.' She dragged on her cigarette, enjoying the hit of tobacco as it reached the back of her throat. 'What can you tell me about Lucy? I need times, descriptions, anything you can give me.'

'She came to me a couple of nights ago,' Goldie said, 'She was new to the area, didn't know her way around. But she was street-smart, you know? Knew where to come for information.'

'Can you describe her?' Ruby topped her cigarette as Luddy coughed from under the cloud of smoke.

'White girl. Scruffy clothes, hungry face. I suppose she was about five foot five, black hair cropped short, big eyes.'

'Colour?'

Goldie shrugged. 'Oh God, I don't know; it was dark. She was wearing baggy clothes, but I'd say she was skinny. She didn't look like no junkie though. I asked what she wanted and she said she was looking for her mum. Get this, she said her mum's name was Ruby Preston.'

'Why did she say that?' Luddy said, seemingly forgetting his promise to leave the talking to Ruby.

Ruby inwardly groaned. She had not expected Lucy to give away any information about herself, much less have Goldie blurt it out.

Goldie seemed oblivious to the stir she had caused. 'She said she'd been given up for adoption when she was a kid, and now she was coming to even the score. I told her to go through the authorities. I know all about that. I've given up a kid myself.' Goldie cocked a head to one side. 'Is she yours? There ain't many Ruby Prestons around here that I know about.'

'Did she say where she was staying?' Ruby said.

Goldie looked from Luddy to Ruby and nodded her head in acknowledgement of her avoidance of the question. 'In the homeless shelter as far as I know. I don't think she was planning no happy reunion.'

'But you don't know where she is now?' Ruby asked.

'I have something better,' Goldie said, shoving her hand down her pink fluorescent bra and producing a piece of wrinkled paper. 'Her email address.'

'Didn't she give you a phone number?'

'Nah. Said her battery was flat. She told me to email her when I had news. I said she'd have to pay for it, and she said she'd get the money somewhere. She was looking for work: cash in hand.'

'Okay, call out the address and I'll make a note,' Ruby said, sliding a pen from the bun in her hair. She looked up to see Goldie smiling, her teeth looking like a carnival attraction.

'You're as bad as me, girl. What else you got tucked away in there?'

'Wouldn't you like to know,' Ruby said, pulling out her notebook to take down the information. 'I'm ready.'

Goldie blurted a laugh. 'You think I'm gonna hand over information just like that? Come on, girl, you know how this works.'

Ruby frowned. 'You said you were helping out for the reward. That's ten grand you could pocket. What more do you want?'

Goldie stubbed out her cigarette into an overflowing ashtray and rose from the sofa. The nub of her thumb looked angry and raw as she waved her hand in the air. 'Don't mug me off. There's fuck all chance of me getting that reward, and what I know is worth a lot more.'

'Goldie… ' Ruby stood, the air of friendliness dissipating fast.

'I'm in for a beating if I don't hit my quota. It's dog eat dog out there.'

Ruby exhaled loudly. Goldie was pulling a fast one. She had already been paid for her time: Lenny had seen to that. But she was canny enough to pick up that she had information Ruby did not want Luddy to know. 'Amazing. Even in your walk of life you have targets to meet,' Ruby mused, trying not to sound pissed off. 'Now what do you want? For all I know it's not even working.'

'A ton. I would ask for more, but I know you're skint.'

Ruby laughed at her audacity. 'A hundred quid? You're having a laugh. Do you know how much money I come out with after paying all my bills? A pittance. I could barely afford this pack of cigarettes.'

'I'm sorry to hear that love, but we all have our sob stories and believe me, I'd swap places with you in a heartbeat. Ask that boyfriend of yours. He's got plenty of spare cash lying around.'

Ruby frowned. Goldie was crossing the line.

'We're not… ' Luddy began to say, because Ruby guessed that somehow in his dream world he thought Goldie was talking about him. Ruby stood, nodding at the door. 'Do you mind waiting outside for a second, DC Ludgrove? I'll be right out behind you.'

Luddy frowned, opening his mouth to speak, then thinking better of it as he obeyed orders.

Satisfied he was out of earshot, Ruby faced Goldie head on. 'What the hell do you think you're playing at?'

'Oh, so your copper friend doesn't know about you and Mr Crosby then? I reckon this information is worth a bit more than a sandwich and a cold cuppa tea, don't you?' Goldie's eyes narrowed as she smiled.

In one swift movement Ruby grabbed Goldie's good thumb, bending it back as far as it would go. 'You want to keep this one intact? Then best not to piss me off. I've already paid for our meeting, so hand it over. Now.'

'Alright, Jeez,' Goldie said, shaking her hand as Ruby released it. 'I forgot what a fiery little bitch you were. Here, take it. I won't be contacting her. People like that bring nothing but trouble to my door.'

Ruby shoved the folded up notepaper into her pocket. 'You shouldn't push me, Goldie.' She turned to glance out the window to see the reassuring form of Luddy's silhouette. 'I've got the Crosbys breathing down my neck on one side and my boss on the other. I thought we were on the level.'

Goldie sniffed. 'Well, in that case, I'm sorry. You can't blame a girl for trying, can you?'

Ruby shrugged. 'Do you think this Lucy was involved in the murders? For all we know this might just be a coincidence.'

'She never mentioned any murders to me. She just seemed determined to find out where you lived. I offered her some work to see her through. Frenchie's always on the lookout for some fresh meat. And young girls are right up his alley.'

Ruby inwardly shuddered. If this *were* her daughter, then she would have to scoop her up off the streets before she came to any harm. Goldie worked on commission and would not think twice about destroying a young girl's life in return for smack. 'I don't think Nathan would be very happy with that,' Ruby said. 'He has a vested interest in this girl.'

Goldie's mouth gaped open. The last thing she would want to do would be to anger the Crosby family. 'She turned me down; said she had some bar work lined up. I will tell you one thing though, she had a look of you about her.'

It was not until Ruby was clear of Goldie's flat that she checked the notepaper she had handed over. She frowned, unsure how she should feel. It was the same email address that she had contacted earlier, which Ruby had presumed was defunct. But now she wondered if she was wrong. The 'no longer in use' email could have been faked to throw her off the scent. It seemed that Lucy had doubled her efforts; contacting both the journalist and Goldie while on her hunt. Ruby welcomed the contact. The thought of her daughter being connected to the case made her go cold inside. In her wildest dreams she had never envisaged such a reunion. But she had to be strong, and serve the public she vowed to protect.

'What was that all about?' Luddy said as he turned the ignition of the car.

'Ask me no questions and I'll tell you no lies,' Ruby said, staring at the notepaper.

'You always say that, Sarge. Was that an official line of enquiry or not? That stuff she said about Lucy being your daughter… '

'Is something you have to wipe from your mind. She's a smack-head, Luddy. She'll do anything for money. That's why you don't go around there alone. She used to give us some great intel, but she wasn't past blackmailing officers either. Remember DC McGuire?'

Luddy scratched his head. 'I remember. He was involved in a sexual assault.'

'Right,' Ruby said as he drove away from the block of flats. 'Who do you think made the allegation?'

'But the police seized DNA evidence.'

'So they did. And Goldie put it there. Shoved her fingers down her knickers and grabbed him by the hands. I told you. She's dangerous. You need to be on your toes with that one.'

Luddy frowned. 'So when she said Lucy was looking for you… '

'It's just more of the same. I don't want you giving that shit airtime, do you hear me?'

'And the email address?'

'Leave it to me. If anything comes of it, I'll update the investigation. Alright?'

Luddy braked sharply as the traffic lights turned red. 'I don't mean to speak out of turn, Sarge.'

'Ruby. Call me Ruby. I've told you a million times.'

'Ruby,' Luddy repeated. 'I'm worried. This is a big investigation. The last thing I want to see is you getting into hot water because you're not following police procedure.'

Ruby's jaw clenched as she tried to contain her annoyance. 'How many years have you got in the job?'

'Five next month,' Luddy said, giving her a sideways glance as the lights turned green.

'How about you come back to me in another five years, when you're a little more qualified to tell me how to do mine?' Ruby pushed up the ventilator flaps on the dashboard, allowing a gust of dust-coated air to blast its way out. It smelt of engine oil, takeaway food, and the recent shower of rain. She lived and breathed the streets, and would lay her neck on the line to protect its occupants. But how did she tell an idealist that the world was not black and white? Ruby had fought the war from both sides, and did not trust either of them.

CHAPTER THIRTY-FIVE

'We meet again,' Chris Douglas, the forensic pathologist said as he gowned up outside the address of the semi-detached property on Greenwood Road.

'It's becoming a bit of a habit, isn't it?' Ruby replied, ramming her foot through the paper suit. Her mood was steadily going downhill. After no response from the phone number, she was beginning to regret her meeting with Lenny. With the discovery of another body things were taking an ugly turn. She looked up to see Chris regarding her with some curiosity.

'Are you alright?' he said, handing her a paper mask as he followed her to the crime scene. The late afternoon sun beat down on Ruby's back, and she was growing more irritable by the minute.

'I'm fine.' Ruby pulled the elastic over the back of her head. 'They said the body appears staged?'

'Yes. Complete with crepe on the door. Given its connection to Emily Edmonds I thought I'd take a look.'

Ruby ducked under the flapping crime scene tape. She wanted more than anything for Chris to be wrong. At least the Emily Edmonds's case had been contained. Emily, Harry, and even Charlotte all belonged to the same story. But an unrelated victim meant the potential for future bloodshed was strong. The length of black crepe billowed on the front door, acting as a warning for those who entered.

She gazed around the property. A four floor Victorian home. It was currently vacant, having been placed up for sale the month before. Just like the last time, DI Downes had beaten Ruby to it, but on this occasion the body was situated in an upstairs bedroom. She craned her neck as she followed his voice, being careful not to touch the banisters while she climbed the narrow stairwell. Spread out over four floors, the rooms were small and box-like, but lavishly furnished. Once again, Ruby found herself comparing it to her poky little flat, but consoled herself that at least her flat did not currently house a corpse.

'There ye are,' Downes said. 'Any luck with your enquiries?'

Ruby shook her head. She'd barely had time to drop Luddy off at the station before being made aware of another body.

The team were working flat out, but here she was, concealing intelligence about a possible lead. A lead which could provide vital clues to the team. But questions would be asked about its origin, and after this afternoon's encounter she did not trust Goldie not to squeal. She wanted to believe that the person claiming to be her daughter was not the same Lucy responsible for the murders, but the email address suggested otherwise. And now there was a new victim to add to the list. The weight of responsibility never felt heavier.

'May I?' Ruby said, switching on the light with her gloved hand. The thin curtain fabric did little to blot out the strength of the late afternoon sun, but Ruby wanted the clearest picture possible of the crime scene before her. She gazed at the mirror which was shrouded in a thin veil of black gauze. On the dresser, a small quartz travel clock lay devoid of batteries like a creature with its internal organs removed. Ruby turned it over. 'One p.m.: the same time that was on the clock at Emily's dump site,' Ruby said. Somewhere in the corridors of her mind she felt a whisper of familiarity to this scene, yet it was faint: too faint to draw upon as she tried to drag it into her mind.

'They've unplugged the digital clock too,' Downes said. 'Did you catch the briefing on the victim?'

Ruby shook her head, having missed radio updates during her heated debate with Luddy.

'Her name's Monica Sherwood. Works in banking. Her husband reported her missing yesterday. He came back from a conference to find the house empty. Her phone, wallet, everything was at home, which is several miles from here, by the way.'

'No sign of forced entry?'

'Nope, neither here or at home. Like Emily, she gave a daughter up for adoption over twenty years ago.'

'Which means we've got a serial killer on our hands,' Ruby said solemnly, approaching the body.

Monica's hair was draped over the pillow; her lips coated in what looked like a fresh application of red lipstick. Her long brunette locks appeared recently brushed, but the clump of matted hair at the back of her skull suggested something more sinister. An application of ivory foundation masked the bruises darkening her skin. Her face lacked the terrified expression of her predecessor, Emily Edmonds, which still haunted Ruby's nightmares.

'Death was quicker for this one,' Ruby said, voicing her thoughts aloud. She cleared her throat, realising that the forensic pathologist was staring at her. 'Any idea of cause?'

Chris bent over the body, lightly moving Monica's head to one side. 'There's obvious trauma to the back of the skull. She has ligature marks to her wrists, and from the lesions around her mouth I'd say she was wearing a gag. She doesn't seem to have the same lacerations to the tongue as the previous victim. Body appears to have been washed and staged like before, which won't help with forensic recovery. I'll be able to tell you more after the post-mortem.'

'And there was no sign of forced entry here either? Just how are they getting in?' Ruby said, wracking her brain for a connection.

'Someone from Crosby's Estate Agents came upon her when he was showing potential buyers around. Not something you'd expect to see during a viewing,' he chuckled.

'Indeed,' Ruby said, although it was hardly the time to be cracking jokes. People like Chris seemed immune to the horrors of death, as it was thrust upon them day after day. Ruby strived to cling to that semblance of her humanity no matter how grim things became. Unease crept over her at the mention of the Crosby family name. Was it a coincidence that the victim had been dumped in one of their properties? Or was there something more sinister at play?

'Are we pulling this duvet back, or what?' Downes said, receiving the thumbs up from Emma, the crime scene investigator, as she turned to reload her camera. Taking a corner each, Downes and Ruby pulled the top half back, revealing Monica's torso. Despite the questionable smell the long white Victorian nightgown was spotlessly clean.

'Looks like Monica has been given a change of clothes too.' Ruby peeped under the bottom half of the duvet to see that her feet were bare.

'Well, they've gone to a lot of trouble,' Chris replied.

'This was the result of long-term planning,' Downes said. 'It wasn't an act of impulse.'

Chris turned to look at the mirror. 'Very curious. I'll do some rearranging, try to have this lady on the table this evening.

'Best I'd be off,' Ruby said, bemused, as she watched Emma walk DI Downes out to the front door. She was yet to finish photographing the scene, but as the young girl chatted happily about some pub she frequented, her mind appeared to be on other things.

'Oh and Ruby, count me in the next time you're organising a shift drinking session. All work and no play and all that,' Chris said.

'Will do,' Ruby replied, wishing there was something to celebrate.

CHAPTER THIRTY-SIX

'What's wrong with you?' Ruby said, watching Ash frantically poke at his phone. Too engrossed in his task, he did not hear her come in, and he continued swearing under his breath as he peered at the screen.

'He's deleting his tweets,' Eve said, striding past her with a wad of paperwork.

'Tweets? You do realise we're running a murder investigation here, don't you?'

'It's of life-and-death importance apparently.' Eve said, wearing a hint of a smile. 'DCI Worrow's following him on Twitter. It's part of her new initiative to get to know us all a bit better.'

'Not another one of her bloody initiatives,' Ruby said, rolling her eyes. 'It's not as if she's got anything better to do, is it?'

'Just be glad it's not Facebook,' Luddy said. 'Did you see that photo he posted last night?'

'I'm not on Facebook for exactly that reason,' Ruby said, stealing a boiled sweet from his desk. She had renewed her conviction to give up cigarettes yet again, figuring her bad habits would be her downfall one day. 'Has anyone spoken to Monica's husband, Adam Sherwood, yet?'

'I did, just before the body was found,' Eve said, raising her hand as if she was in school.

Ruby made a mental note to speak to her about being more assertive. 'Before they found the body? What are you, psychic?'

'Well, I do follow the horoscopes, as it happens,' Eve blushed under the strength of Ruby's withering gaze. 'Sorry. Erm… all missing person's reports are highlighted to us now, particularly if they've given up a child for adoption in the past.'

Ruby thought of the email address that she had used to contact Lucy. She would keep trying in case its owner activated it again. She had little choice. Not when there was a nutcase scooping up women from their homes. 'What's her husband got to say about it?'

'Adam, her other half, said that she didn't want children and never spoke about the adoption. I got the impression that she wasn't the maternal type.'

'So if someone came to her door purporting to be her daughter, she may not have given them a warm welcome,' Ruby said, removing Ash's phone from his grip and shoving it in the drawer.

Eve rose from her desk. 'I'm just popping out,' she said, picking up her jacket from the back of her chair.

'Can I have a quick word first?' Ruby said, nodding towards her office.

Eve faltered. 'Sure. Would you like me to bring in a cuppa?'

'Go on then, you've twisted my arm. Strong, three sugars… '

'And two teabags. Yes, I know.'

Ruby pulled her chair into her desk. She had five minutes to look into Worrow's agitated caller because of the workload threatening to engulf her whole. Something was going on with Miss Prissy Pants and she would make it her business to find out what. As Nathan used to say, there were two things in life that got people into the most trouble: money and sex. She clicked on the form to request a credit check. It was time to do a little digging.

'Sorry,' Eve said, mopping up the spillage from the mug of tea she had just placed on Ruby's desk.

'That's OK,' Ruby said, switching off her computer screen as she gratefully accepted the beverage. She blew the steam before taking a sip. 'Blimey, has the milk been rationed?'

'Sorry,' Eve said. 'Will I go and get some more?'

'Sit down,' Ruby said, 'and for God's sake, stop apologising.'

'Sor—' Eve stopped suddenly, swallowing the apology she was about to deliver. She took a sip of coffee, most likely to shut herself up. Placing the mug on the desk, she twiddled with her fingers.

'I just wanted to check you're okay,' Ruby said. 'You haven't seemed yourself lately. Not working you too hard, are we?'

'No, I'm fine.' Eve peered out the window in a manner that suggested she would like to be anywhere as long as it wasn't in Ruby's office.

'It's just that…' Ruby said, wishing she had rehearsed the words. Everything was so politically correct now; say the wrong thing and you would find yourself up in front of a tribunal. It was a far cry from when she joined, when she was patted on the bottom and told to stay out of trouble.

She brought her attention back to Eve. Their impromptu meeting was the last thing she needed with everything else going on, but she had watched her for some time now and her behaviour was beginning to grate. 'I know it's tough working in an office full of men, but is something wrong? Your confidence seems to have nosedived in the last few weeks.'

Eve's glance fell onto her lap, where she pulled at a loose thread from her knee-length skirt.

In the absence of a response, Ruby continued. 'You're a good detective, but if you want to progress up the career ladder, you need to be more assertive. Don't let them take the piss out of you. Even DI Downes treats you like a lapdog.' She sighed, wondering if her words were sinking in. 'He grew up in an age when sexism was accepted, but it's no excuse and shouldn't be tolerated now.

'Things will be a lot easier if you learn to stop apologising and grow thicker skin. Does that make sense?'

'It's not easy,' Eve replied, in a quiet voice.

Ruby strained to listen. 'And that's another thing: you've got to speak up. Talk with authority; say it loud. Don't apologise unless there's a very good reason for it. Banter is fine, but don't let them treat you like you're a second-class citizen. You can help them with their workloads as long as it works both ways.' Ruby sighed as she watched Eve withdraw into herself. 'I'm not having a go at you; I'm just trying to help, because sometimes I see you when nobody's looking and you don't seem very happy. Are you being bullied? Is that what it is?' Silence fell, and Ruby's gaze lingered on Eve as she waited for her response.

'No, but it's not easy for me. If people knew… ' Eve blinked twice, her blue doe-eyes filled with sadness.

'Knew what?'

'I can't say,' Eve sniffled.

'You can tell me to mind my own business, but if something's affecting your work then we need to discuss it. Is it something at home? Family problems? Finances?'

Eve bit her bottom lip, a scarlet hue rising up her cheeks. 'I told you. I can't say. I'll take on board everything you said; I'll try harder. Now can I go? My shift ended half an hour ago.'

Ruby frowned. Since the discovery of another body it was a given that the investigating team would be in for another late finish. But there was something about Eve's demeanour that made Ruby uneasy. Eve had changed from being calm and composed to someone ready to snap.

'OK. But my door is open if you want to talk.'

Eve stared at the floor, her eyes swimming with tears. Ruby got the feeling that the young woman had not listened to a word she had said.

'Just remember, you can't afford to be taking on other people's workloads as well as your own. If any of them lot give you grief, then just tell them where to go.'

Eve nodded vigorously as she rose. Pulling a tissue from under her sleeve, she made it past the door before bursting into tears and running out into the corridor. Ruby walked out of her office, and all eyes turned on her.

'What did you say to her?' Downes asked, biting off a chunk of Mars bar.

Ruby rolled her eyes before she turned to face him. He never had been blessed with a sense of discretion. 'Nothing. I think she's a bit stressed.' She turned to the rest of the team. 'So ease off on her, guys, okay?'

Heads nodded and murmurs rumbled in an acknowledgement of her request. Ruby was not going to chase after Eve. But she would be keeping a close eye on her.

Downes scrunched up the chocolate wrapper and threw it in the bin. 'Oh and Ruby? Briefing's in ten. Crime scene investigators have picked up specks of blood in Monica Sherwood's hallway, and DCI Worrow has made the decision to bring in her husband for questioning.'

'I thought our sights were on Lucy as a suspect for this case?' Luddy said. He stretched his arms in a yawn. Sweat patches dampened the underarms of his shirt. He looked tired. They were all being pushed to the limit.

'Think about it,' Ruby said, pre-empting her boss's reply. 'If you wanted to bump your missus off it's a pretty clever tactic to piggyback another killer's method. Just say you're going away, then come back early and set it up. There was no sign of struggle in her home which means either it was someone she knew, or was happy to allow inside.'

'Or someone that had a key,' Downes piped up, sucking the melted chocolate from his thumb.

'It's a leafy suburb and quite private. Most of the people that live in that area work during the day.'

'What about the property where the body was found?' Ruby asked Luddy. 'Have you picked up anything?'

'It was burgled last year, and they changed the locks straight after. It's a high value property worth in excess of two million.'

Ruby frowned as something clicked in the back of her brain. A high value property. The ones Nathan's estate agency dealt with. She shook the thought away. Why would Nathan, or any of the Crosbys, be involved in this? It was a ludicrous idea. She sighed, knowing police would check it out just the same. 'Early examination at the scene suggests Monica wasn't killed at the dump site,' Ruby said. 'She could have spent time elsewhere, possibly the same place as Emily. I know it's difficult, but we need to continue working with the adoption agency to obtain details of women who have given their children up for adoption in the area. Then we've got to offer safeguarding; at least until we get this person behind bars.'

'Getting information from the adoption agency is like pulling teeth,' Luddy said. 'They're insisting it goes through the courts.'

'And that will be fast-tracked now another body's turned up on our patch. Luddy, I want you to oversee all dealings with the adoption agency and report back to me. We need to delve deeper with them, find out how our suspect is getting this information so readily.'

'Will do,' Luddy said. 'I'll follow up with them today.'

'Good,' Ruby said. Not because she thought he would help solve the case, but because of what he had heard. If the courts authorised the police to view a list of local women who had given their children up for adoption, Ruby knew her name would be among them. And the fewer people who knew about that, the better.

CHAPTER THIRTY-SEVEN

Lucy swiped her cheekbones with the dampened cotton wool, removing the last layer of make-up. Staring at her pallid reflection she wondered where she had gone awry. Why did she keep picking the wrong mother? All she had ever wanted was somebody to love her, to say the magic words and bring her home. Tilting the bottle of toner, she dabbed it onto another cotton wool pad. Lucy dragged it across her skin, shedding her persona as she returned to real life. But she could not leave her troubles behind. Her potential mothers were selfish bitches. They screamed and whined about how they wanted to get home, without even a thought for her. Nobody ever apologised, or asked her how *she* was feeling. And when they begged… why weren't they pleading for forgiveness? Why weren't they saying what a terrible mistake they had made? Time and time again she overlooked their hurtful comments in an effort to make things right.

Picking up the paddle brush, she eased it through her hair, staring unblinkingly at the mirror. She didn't recognise the blank-faced person gazing back at her. She was a nobody, with no real identity or persona. Stepping out of real life had become a practice which made her feel real again. As if she mattered in the world. When she eased on her dress and wore her blonde curls a calmness spread over her. It was nice to be a child again, without boundaries or cares for the adult world. In the confines of the basement she was safe, and all attention was on her. And if pain was to be inflicted, she would be the one doing it. But all she wanted was to be graced with the life she deserved.

Barefooted, she hardly made a sound as she padded into the kitchen, pausing to gaze out the window to the streets below. She had truly believed Monica was the one, and she could have been had she not cracked her skull. She had not meant to hurt her, but a hysterical snapping woman would hardly qualify as the mother she had longed for all her life.

Her eyes strained against the daylight, and she wished she didn't have to go outside. Lucy loved her underground space and the feelings it invoked. Her Christmas tree, the twinkling lights. From the minute she forced her way through the cobwebs and decay she had seen potential in the dank space.

Finding her mother had become an addiction which absorbed the pain inflicted by her past. And as for Ruby Preston? Lucy was enjoying their little game. Somehow it made real life more bearable as she integrated with the outside world. She smiled as she picked up the black-edged envelope, running her fingers over the rim. She was looking forward to her next contact. She had lots more in store for her.

CHAPTER THIRTY-EIGHT

'Please, Mummy, can we have these ones? They're my favourites in the whole world,' Sophie said, jumping up and down in an effort to reach the chocolate-coated breakfast cereal on the top shelf.

'No, love, they're full of sugar. How about Rice Krispies instead?' her mother replied, placing the blue box into the shopping trolley.

As Lucy watched Anita placate her child in Tesco she realised where she had been going wrong all this time. She involved herself with women who did not know the value of nurturing. Selfish women, like Emily and Charlotte, who lacked the maternal instinct and therefore could not accept her as their own. Watching Anita with her daughter was a joy to behold, and immediately Lucy knew it was meant to be. With her plaited dark hair and pink summer dress, Sophie was obviously the focus of her mother's adoration. This was a child who was happy, secure and loved. Lucy smiled. This was her mother too. Her *true* mother, who would take her in without a moment's hesitation. Lucy imagined turning up at her doorstep. Anita would probably be overwhelmed that her first-born daughter had come home. Just like in the movies.

But what had been an advantage would also turn out to be something of an obstacle. She could not have her perfect family with another child in the way. A six-year-old would have to be disposed of, but she could not drop her off in a housing estate as she had done with Monica's dog. The murder of a child would bring a whole new side to the police investigation which was getting increasing media attention. They were already painting her as a monster. But it was simply not true.

Lucy told herself that sacrifices would have to be made. Of course there were other options; she knew people who would pay well for such a pretty little girl. But those sorts of people were ill-intentioned, and she could not have such a transaction on her conscience. No. It was kinder to end it: allow Sophie to die in peace with fond memories of her family, knowing that she was always loved. And Lucy would be there to take over in assisting Anita with her grief. But it would take serious planning, especially now that the police were on the lookout. Monica's death had raised their attention, but nobody understood.

She had gained a lot of satisfaction from wiping out the unworthy candidates: Harry, Charlotte, Emily, Monica – just thinking about their murders sent a delicious shiver down her spine. But she was not sure how she felt about taking such a young life and struggled to justify it in her mind. Yet she could not waste another moment. It would be Christmas in a few months and everything hinged on that perfect day. There would be no more rehearsals. Everything had to be perfect.

Lucy walked between the aisles of the shopping centre, staring at the products on display. She wanted this meeting to be special, comforting. Plucking some cleaning products from the shelves, she popped them in her basket. She had much stronger stuff at home, but the gentle-scented air fresheners and candles were kinder to inhale. She wondered what Anita liked the best. She would have to make a note of her favourites the next time she visited. She already knew that Sophie liked Coco Pops for breakfast, and Ribena instead of tea. She came to the end of the aisle, turning right for breakfast cereals. Her thoughts brought a frown. Just how long would Sophie be staying there? Lucy wasn't very good with children. Sophie seemed a bit like one of those exotic pets that she wasn't quite sure what to do with. A bitter voice rose from inside. It knew exactly what to do if she wanted to have Anita all to herself. But there was another side to Lucy: the side that did her food shopping in Tesco and checked the weather forecast for rain. She was the sensible one and was worth listening to because she didn't want to end up in prison. Her whole childhood had been a prison. No, there must be a way to compromise. But if Anita came, then Sophie was coming too. She would sort out the finer details later.

Lucy looked around, realising she had lost them. It didn't matter. She knew where they lived, their routes, where she went to school and where Anita spent her time. Flowers. She could buy some flowers and make the place look pretty. There were all sorts of things she could get to make it nice. She could even get a commode instead of a chair. One of those seats with a built-in potty. After all, Anita was a lady; she would not soil herself like the others. Lucy dismissed the thought. It was too messy. Besides, Anita was going to pass all the tests. And then she would be free.

A small doubtful voice spoke from inside. *Just how do you think you're going to get away with that? Everyone is looking for you.* Lucy smiled. She would get away with it because she was not Lucy in the real world. The person she was presenting now, as she walked down the aisle of the supermarket, was someone else entirely. Having a loving mother was her destiny, her happy ending. And every story deserved a happy ever after.

CHAPTER THIRTY-NINE

Nathan sighed as he took a seat across from the young woman who had introduced herself simply as 'Cathy'. Her make-up was gaudy, her eyes mistrustful, and her clothes smelt like she had lived in them for a month. He really didn't have time for this today. The clubs were Lenny's responsibility, and he had better things to do than interview some street rat looking for a job.

She wiped her nose with the back of her hand, her dark kohl-lined eyes peeping out from under her blunt fringe. 'I heard you're taking on girls. I need a job.'

Nathan shook his head. He was getting too old for this shit. 'I'm not running a crèche here, love. What age are you? Sixteen? Seventeen?'

She glared at him, eyes alight with a fire of indignation. 'I'm twenty.' Producing a bent-up passport, she slid it across the table. A sad, pale-faced girl stared out from the passport photo. Nathan examined the paperwork. He could spot a fake a mile off, mainly because they used to make good money from producing them. This was the real thing.

She reached out to snatch it back, and Nathan clamped down her arm, pushing up the sleeve of her jacket to examine her skin for puncture marks. Satisfied she was clean, he released his grip.

'Did he tell you what the job entails?'

'I'm not a kid. I've been living on the streets long enough to know how things work around here. Is there a job going or not?'

'Take your top off.'

Cathy's eyes darted left and right as she stood. 'Can't we go somewhere a bit more... private?'

Nathan screwed his face in disgust. 'Jesus, I'm not interested in that; I'm checking you for wires.' Like anyone who attended the club out of hours she had been searched on the way in. But there was something about the lack of fear behind her eyes that made Nathan uncomfortable. He had seen that defiance before, and it usually brought him nothing but trouble.

'Oh. It's just that I heard Lenny likes to... ' she said, pulling off her sweatshirt. She stood before him: her skinny frame encompassed in a black bra and jeans.

'Well, I'm not Lenny.' Nathan signalled at her to turn around. She was too young to carry the scars and bruises that mapped her body, and he dropped his gaze.

'Do you want me to take the rest of my clothes off?' Cathy said, reaching around to remove her bra.

'Get dressed,' Nathan said, in a voice that was not to be disobeyed.

Cathy sniffed in disgust as she pushed her head through her jumper. 'I fucking hate the cops; all they ever give me is grief.'

She was nothing more than a kid, and Nathan shuddered to think what Lenny would be doing with her now had he been the one interviewing. Nathan had moved the escorting service online, closing down the shoddy massage parlours and backstreet knocking stops. But he still had a long way to go in order to persuade Lenny to shut down that leg of the business completely. His brother enjoyed having girls on tap. 'You don't want to work for us,' Nathan said. 'Why don't you go home to your family?'

'My parents don't care about me,' Cathy said, sullenly. 'I'll do whatever you want. Please. I don't have nowhere to live. I've been sleeping under the bridge, but there's some weirdos hanging around and I don't feel safe there anymore.'

'There's weirdos everywhere,' Nathan said, drumming his fingers against the table. 'We just deal with rich ones.' Nathan rubbed his stubbled chin. Getting her into escorting would be like feeding her to the sharks. Sure the clientele had improved, but he could not assure her safety, and despite her bolshy attitude he could not shake off the feeling he was taking advantage of a vulnerable young girl.

'I'm not asking for a hand-out; I'm asking for a job. I've heard your girls make good money as escorts.'

'Sorry, babe, but it's not for you. You're too young for a start and way too skinny. Here,' he said, reaching into his trouser pocket and pulling a twenty-pound note. 'Go and sort yourself out with a hot meal. I can't help you.'

Cathy pushed the money away. 'Please, Mr Crosby. I just need somewhere I can wash and lay my head at night. I'm a good worker. I'll do as many hours as you want.'

Nathan frowned. She was not going to give up. He imagined her lying in the doorway of his club, making him look bad. It was only a matter of time before some scumbag took advantage of her. Someone like Frenchie, who fed his girls on a diet of smack and greasy STD-ridden punters.

'Oi, Jules,' Nathan waved at one of the barmaids, a mixed-race girl with an East London accent. Dressed in the uniform of black shirt and trousers, she sauntered over, frowning, as she clapped eyes on Cathy.

'Not you again. I told you to bugger off,' she said, her jaw mechanically working on a wad of chewing gum. 'Honestly, Mr Crosby, she's been bugging me all week. I've told her you don't take on street kids, but she wouldn't leave me alone.'

Nathan did not take kindly to being told what he did or did not do. 'You're short at the bar, aren't you?' he said, shoving the twenty pound note into Jules's hand, pulling another tenner from his pocket and laying it on top. 'Show her upstairs so she can have a wash, and buy her a change of clothes. She can have a trial behind the bar tonight; we'll see how she goes.'

'Cheers,' Cathy said, breaking into a smile.

Nathan grabbed Cathy's wrist. 'Don't you go stealing from me, mind. People that steal from me soon live to regret it.'

Nathan pulled the terse look he always did when Ruby's name flashed up on the screen. He had just got rid of one ball of grief and now, here she was, a reminder of a past he was trying hard to forget. 'Yes?' he said, his forehead creasing in a frown.

'Oh, nice. Hello to you too,' she said, the wind muffling her voice.

Was she on her way home from work? Out on a job? Was she safe? Nathan's jaw tightened as he tried to quell his concern. 'What do you want, Ruby?'

'I've something to ask you. Are you on your own?'

'Yes. Go on,' he said, trying not to be lured in by the sound of her voice. He thought of the scent of her skin, her lips, her teeth, her tongue.

'We're investigating a series of murders: women who have been gagged, bound and their bodies staged in expensive properties for the police to find. You wouldn't happen to know anything about them would you?'

'You've come to the wrong place if you're expecting me to help the police with their enquiries,' Nathan said drily. He did know about it. The last two bodies had turned up in properties which were on his books.

Despite his frostiness, Ruby breathed a good-natured laugh. 'Okay, okay you can't blame a girl for trying. We're on the lookout for a young woman, early twenties. White girl, not very tall, slim, either black or blonde hair, goes by the name of Lucy. She was in the homeless shelter but she's moved on. Apparently she's looking for work. If you see anyone suspicious in the area, can you let me know?'

'As I said… I'm no grass.'

'She could be a murderer.'

'I don't care if she's Myra fucking Hindley. I've told you, I—'

'Don't help police. Yeah. Innocent women have been killed, and it's not ending there. But don't you worry your head. You go back to whatever important work you're doing. I'm sure it's a wonderful contribution to society.'

Nathan stared in disbelief as the line went dead. She hung up on him. She actually hung up on him. Of all the bloody…

'She was in the homeless shelter, but she's moved on. Apparently she's looking for work… ' Ruby's description of her suspect echoed in his brain. It was a description that could fit anyone, yet… 'Lucy'. A name which invoked pain, past memories. He had seen Cathy's passport. It couldn't be her. It wasn't possible. He could ring Ruby now, ask her to come around unofficially to speak to the girl. But the thought was fleeting. Police were not welcome in his establishments, and if there was a problem to sort out he would see to it himself.

CHAPTER FORTY

'Thank you for coming,' DCI Worrow said, as Ruby pulled up a chair. 'I understand that you're very busy.'

Ruby crossed then uncrossed her legs, trying to contain her rising jitters as she wondered why Worrow had called her at such a late hour. It was nine p.m. and they were the only people on the floor of the so-called ivory towers. Unlike the minions in serious crime who were still working on the floor below, the rest of her superior officers had all gone home.

Worrow interlocked her fingers and rested them on the desk. Even at this late hour she was perfectly groomed; her black bobbed hair styled to perfection. Ruby patted her dishevelled bun to find the pen she had embedded in it earlier. Too late to worry about it now, she thought, as DCI Worrow spoke.

'I came in to see you this afternoon and I was disappointed to see that both yours and DI Downes's office doors were closed. This goes against my imposed open door policy, and I believe it could be contributing towards the low morale of your team.'

The woman spoke in such an officious tone it was as if she were reading the words. But that was her nature as far as Ruby could see: stilted, unnatural. Ruby wanted to say that the only time her team suffered from low morale was when Worrow came to visit. She refrained from rolling her eyes, as such behaviour would be unbecoming of a police sergeant. Her superior's attitude got on her nerves. Coming out with this crap when they were juggling with a serial killer? Fresh from a university business degree, Worrow was always coming up with ideas, strategies and discussions. While Ruby admired her, getting fast-tracked for promotion at such a young age, flying through the ranks had left Worrow with little time to experience life on the streets. It was hardly any wonder that officers could not identify with her. With a privileged upbringing, and a swish Hampstead pad, she was totally out of place in Ruby's world. And the thing was, she was never going to change. Shoreditch was a temporary stay for Worrow: a test of her resilience. But unlike Downes, Ruby did not want to set her up to fail. Instead of arguing, Ruby decided to give her a break and listen to what she had to say.

Ruby nodded as DCI Worrow spoke about open doors, social media and weekly team building meetings. She tried to look interested as she told her about the new spreadsheet she was introducing to the team to track their individual targets and detection rates.

'We're nearly finished,' she said, as Ruby's head snapped up from checking her watch. 'There's one more thing I need to speak to you about.'

Ruby tried to look interested. But it was past nine o'clock; she had not eaten since twelve and there was still lots to do.

'I've had an informal complaint from a member of your team. They've expressed some concerns with regards your style of management.'

'Style of management? Are you serious?' Ruby blurted in disbelief. As Worrow's eyebrows shot up, Ruby regained her composure. 'So you're saying someone from my team has complained about me.'

Worrow drew in a terse breath. 'It's not an official complaint, just an expression of concern.'

Ruby could feel her blood pressure rising. Why didn't Worrow just get to the point? 'Ma'am, with all due respect, I've no idea what you're talking about. Concern for what?'

'They wouldn't provide any details, only to say they had concerns with regards your background and the company you keep. They also had misgivings with regards your reluctance to adhere to procedure. While no formal complaint has been made, these are things I will be keeping a very close eye on for the welfare of my team.'

Welfare of *her* team? Since when had she done anything to contribute? The heat of her temper rose within and she fought back the urge to slap the smug smile from Worrow's face. How dare she, Ruby thought, lecturing *her* about the welfare of her team? To Worrow, they were just numbers to input on a spreadsheet: how many arrests; how many successful charges; making up pretty little pie charts to impress the bosses. She did not know that Ash's wife suffered from morbid depression and his mum had moved in to help with the kids. She wasn't aware that Luddy was struggling with his sergeant's exams because he was dyslexic and too embarrassed to admit it. And she sure didn't know that Eve was struggling to get past her insecurities. Worrow had not earned the right to call them her team when all she had ever paid them was lip service. 'I'm still not clear what the complaint is about. Can you at least elaborate?'

'A member of your team has issues with your reluctance about sticking to police policy.'

'And the company I keep?' Ruby asked, her heart picking up a beat. Worrow was new to her post and trying to make a name for herself. If she knew of her acquaintance with the Crosby family, it could spell serious trouble for Ruby's career.

'They wouldn't elaborate other than to say it was not befitting of a police sergeant, particularly a member of the serious crime team.'

'But I was double vetted prior to taking the post.'

'Something I'm well aware of, and there's nothing to say these claims are substantiated.' Worrow sighed and lowering her voice she leaned across the table. 'Ruby, I know you think I'm some sort of automaton, that I'm just here to step over people on my way to promotion.' Ruby opened her mouth to respond, and Worrow raised her hand. 'Let me finish. Believe it or not I'm on your side.

I appreciate how tough it is working in a male-dominated world, and I just wanted to say, you need to watch your back – I'd hate to lose you.' Worrow's gaze shifted towards the door as if she expected the professional standards department to jump out at any minute. Straightening her posture, her cool veneer regained a foothold.

'What do you suggest I do?' The heat of Ruby's anger visibly evaporated as the fear of losing her job took hold. 'This job is my life. I've worked hard to get where I am. I can't lose it all now.'

'I appreciate that, and nobody is questioning your dedication to the team. But you've got to be seen to be doing the right thing. You mix with unsavoury characters as part of your role and as long as you have a legitimate reason for doing so, then you've nothing to worry about.'

Ruby fell silent as she tried to figure out how much trouble she was in. Was Worrow holding back? Did she know more?

Worrow interlaced her fingers. 'I may have come down a bit hard. There's nothing official in motion and nobody's out to get you. I just wanted to make you aware so we can nip it in the bud.'

'I'm just trying to think of what I've done to warrant a complaint. I guess I'll have to document who I speak to in the future, in case I get pulled up for it.'

'That would be wise, even if it's a quick update in your pocket notebook. Just keep yourself covered, that's all I'm saying. This isn't like any other job. You don't get to leave it at home at the end of the day.'

Ruby smiled. 'You're not going to tell me to get a job in B&Q now, are you?'

Worrow could not help but smile in return. 'No, I think we'll keep you where you are. Besides, I've heard you're terrible at DIY.' She unclasped her hands and pushed back her chair. 'Yes, well… I believe this has been quite a productive meeting. Let's hear no more about it.'

Ruby nodded. Worrow had made it clear. The unofficial com-plaint was going away. She did not feel guilty, because her loyalty to her team should never have been called into question. But as Ruby left Worrow's office she wondered if she knew her boss at all. There was a lot more to Worrow than the unyielding senior officer she presented to the team. She had caught a spark of humanity behind those cool blue eyes, and given her recent phone call she was not as prim and proper as she pretended to be.

CHAPTER FORTY-ONE

'Glad you could make it,' Ruby said, as Eve rested her bag on the shiny copper-topped bar. 'How are you feeling now, any better?'

'Yes, much,' Eve shouted over the din of the crowd. After a shitty day's work, Ruby had suggested they attend The Blind Pig, in Soho, and the team seemed happy to follow suit. Every month she held a 'mystery pub' works night out. Her team were willing to travel the extra miles to see what sort of weird and wonderful place she would come up with. Even Eve had come from home, catching the Tube to join in on the fun. A work night out was much needed, and it was pay day after all. Cocktails were an expensive luxury that Ruby could barely afford, but every month the first round was on her.

'Well, drink up then, we've only got an hour until closing,' Ruby said, handing Eve her drink. 'I've ordered you a "Slap 'n' Pickle".'

'I shouldn't really be drinking, I'm on antibiotics.' Eve said. 'What's in it?'

'Gin, brandy and pickle brine,' Ruby said with a mischievous grin. 'Go on, I've bought it now. One won't do you any harm.'

Eve took a tentative sip, looking like she had swallowed a lemon.

'So what's this I hear about Facebook photos?' Ruby said, turning back to Ash and Luddy, who were drinking rum-infused milkshakes.

'You want to see?' Ash said, his cheeks pink from the alcohol infiltrating his system.

'I'm surprised Facebook let you post them,' Luddy said, a grin spreading across his face.

'Oh they've been removed, but I've got them on my phone. See?'

Ruby leaned over and stared at what looked like badly taken holiday snaps of various landscapes.

'I don't see anything…' she peered, 'apart from that round thing blotting the sun. What is it?' She brought the phone closer to her nose. 'Hmm, it's not a fly… hang on, are those…' she spluttered on her drink, 'are those hairs?'

Downes's hearty laugh exploded from behind her. 'Don't you know a bollock when you see one, Ruby?'

Ruby's expression turned into a mixture of horror and disbelief. 'In the name of all things holy… What? … Why?' She thrust the phone back to Ash, who was now wiping the tears erupting from the corner of his eyes.

'It's called nutscaping; it has its own website and everything.'

'How do you?…' Ruby said. 'On second thoughts, I don't want to know.' Her eyes widened. 'You didn't tweet that, did you?'

'Oh yeah,' Luddy said. 'Can you imagine Worrow's face when she saw that? Old Ash has been on holiday and dropped his kegs to bend over and take a photo of his nutsack!'

'Excuse me, it's very tastefully done,' Ash sniggered. 'I had to get the camera ready, then get me old man out of the way… not an easy task, I can tell you.'

Ruby's smile faded as Worrow's name returned the memory of their encounter earlier in the day. She was yet to come to terms with the fact that a member of her team had grassed her up. Most likely someone she had just bought a drink. 'Going for a ciggy,' she said, signalling towards the door. 'I'll be back in a minute. Time one of you tight sods got a round in.'

The faded gold lighter flickered into life, giving barely enough flame to light the Silk Cut in Ruby's mouth. It was one of her most treasured possessions, and all she had left of her dad. She sucked until a circular orange glow punctuated the night air. Closing her eyes, she inhaled, mulling over the troubling thoughts invading her brain.

'I thought you'd given them up?' A soft voice came from behind. It was Luddy.

'I have. This is just a social smoke,' Ruby said, lowering the cigarette, now imprinted with her signature red lipstick. 'What are you doing out here? You don't smoke.'

'Fresh air. I don't think the cocktails agreed with me,' he said, masking a burp into his closed fist.

Ruby smiled, taking another slow drag of her cigarette. 'Did you know that The Blind Pig is American underworld slang for den of iniquity?'

'No, I didn't,' Luddy said, shoving his hands in his trouser pockets. 'I've never been to this place before. I don't know how you found it.'

She stared into his eyes, slowly delivering her words. 'Do you think I'm corrupting you?'

'Corrupting me? No,' Luddy exhaled an awkward laugh.

'Then why did you report me to Worrow?' Luddy was the only person who had challenged her in the last few days, and it stuck in her gut to think that he went running to his DCI instead of having it out with her.

The smile slid from his face. 'For what? I haven't spoken to her.'

Ruby dragged hard on the remnants of her cigarette, locking the smoke in her lungs before letting it go. 'I thought we were a tight team. If my rule-bending worried you that much you should have spoken to me.'

'Is this about our visit to Goldie? Sarge, I… '

Ruby swivelled her head left and right, grateful that nobody had heard. 'It's Ruby for fuck's sake. I don't let you call me Sarge when I'm at work, much less draw attention to us when we're out on the piss.'

'Ruby then,' Luddy said. 'I didn't report you. Sure, I was worried about how you handled things, but only for you, not the job. You're the best sergeant I've ever had. The last thing I'd do is go telling tales.'

'Well, somebody did.'

'Actually, I'm quite offended that you thought it was me,' Luddy sniffed.

'Well, if you didn't,' Ruby said, ignoring his mild outrage, 'then who did?'

Ruby was relieved that she had clung on to her senses and decided to leave the pub early. It was a very rare occurrence. It was not a proper piss-up unless she had disgraced herself in some way, either by dancing on a club podium or waking up with Downes in her bed. But there was work to be done, jobs to oversee, and witnesses to interview. So they had all sensibly rolled home at closing time, their expensive cocktails warming their bellies. But the drinks outing had done little to quell her rising anxiety. Someone was out to cause her trouble and given her recent activity they might not be short of ammunition.

Ruby stiffened as she caught sight of a shadow in the stairwell of her flat. Clenching her fists, she prepared for confrontation. As they stepped forward, she exhaled a sigh of relief. It was Darren, the neighbour she had helped out in the past.

'Sorry,' he said, stepping into the light. 'I didn't mean to frighten you.'

'You didn't,' Ruby lied, wondering what he was doing on her floor. 'Everything alright? It's not your mum, is it?'

'Nah, she's alright,' Darren said, his hands nestled down the front of his tracksuit bottoms. 'It's Mr Crosby… Nathan. Have you heard? He's been stabbed.'

CHAPTER FORTY-TWO

Flashing her warrant card, Ruby smiled apologetically at the matron as she granted her access to the ward. At two a.m., it was way past visiting hours, and she was careful to shield her face as she passed the CCTV cameras on the way in. It was unlikely to be viewed, but if anything else was to happen that night, awkward questions would be asked in the morning. The last place she expected to find herself was at a hospital at two in the morning. But a stairwell chat with her neighbour Darren had given her information that temporarily stopped her heart. Nathan had been admitted to hospital after a ruck in his home. Little was known, apart from the fact they had tried to stab him as he slept. She had taken a chance coming to the hospital, but she knew the matron would have kicked his family out as soon as Nathan was bedded in.

The soft glow of a bedside lamp warmed his features, and she saw a peace that had not been present in years. She had no intention of waking him. A stabbing was recorded, but little explanation was offered. Ruby clenched her jaw. It was related to Lenny. It had to be. Since coming out of prison he had caused nothing but trouble, gaining back his territory from the dealers trying to muscle in.

Silently she sidled up to the bed, her heart sinking at the sight of Nathan's vulnerability. The private room offered comfort, but it was of poor consolation when he could have just as easily been lying in a hospital mortuary. The thought pierced her heart, and she swallowed back the bitterness rising up her throat.

Nathan's eyes opened as he inhaled, and he blinked a few times before focusing his gaze on her. 'Ruby,' he said, his throat dry, reaching out his hand over the waffle blankets.

Ruby glanced up at the closed door before pulling in her chair. Barely trusting herself to speak, she leaned in and kissed him tenderly on the lips.

Her tears betrayed her bravado as they silently spilled down her cheeks. She had come here to tell him off, to warn him against any dealings in his brother's business. But with a bellyful of alcohol lowering her defences, her emotions erupted and all the stresses of the last week came out. She steadied her breathing, taking his hand as it was offered.

Nathan's thumb rubbed against hers. 'Babe, don't cry. I'm okay. They're letting me out soon.'

Ruby drew back, pulling a tissue from her pocket and rubbing away the tears. She cleared her throat, composing herself. 'You could have been killed. I could be looking at your body on a slab right now. Why do you keep putting yourself in danger?'

'It was a misunderstanding, crossed wires.'

'Don't bullshit me, Nathan. Couldn't your brother have got his heavies elsewhere? Why did he have to involve you?'

'It wasn't like that. You know I don't get involved in his battles anymore. *They* came after *me*. I didn't go starting anything.'

'*They*? So who was it? And how did they break into your house?'

'It doesn't matter. It's all sorted now.' Nathan winced as he shifted position.

'So someone else has got it in return and the war rages on.'

Nathan didn't answer. He lay back in bed, tight-lipped.

Ruby felt a pang of guilt. He wasn't well enough for an interrogation, but she was so angry at him. 'I'm not here to question you, and I respect your decision to move on without me. But please, Nathan, leave it behind.'

'For Christ's sake, I've had it in my ear all day from me old mum, nag nag nag. Not you and all.'

Ruby knew his mother would not be nagging him for his involvement, but his carelessness in getting hurt. She could imagine Lenny standing grim-faced at the end of the bed with his fists in his pockets as their mother ranted about honour and protecting the family name.

Ruby sighed, a wave of tiredness overcoming her. 'Is it really sorted?'

'Yes.'

'Then get some rest. You look like shit.'

Nathan gave the faintest of smiles before his eyelids flickered into the depths of sleep.

Ruby set the alarm on her phone and sat back in the chair, watching his chest rise and fall. In sleep, his features relaxed into peace once more, and she wished nothing more for him than to have a normal life, being graced with the things everyone else took for granted. She wanted to crawl in beside him and bury her head in the crook of his neck. But that was behaviour definitely unbecoming of a police sergeant, and she didn't think the matron would approve. The least she could do was stay and repay him for being with her when she needed him. Lenny and his mum had gone for the night, and she would be left in peace in the private room. It was not unusual for police to stay with a victim of crime overnight, particularly when they were so well known. But in such cases, the officer wasn't usually in love with their subject.

Ruby was gently lured out of sleep by a familiar hand stroking her hair, gently waking her. She raised her head from the side of his bed wondering how she had deviated from her chair to leaning over the mattress, where she had fallen into slumber. 'What time is it?' she asked, hoping none of the nursing staff had seen her.

'Almost six. You shouldn't have stayed.'

'I know,' Ruby said, knowing he would have done the same for her. 'How are you feeling?'

'Honestly?'

'Yes, honestly,' she said, rubbing away the crick in her neck.

'Horny.'

Ruby laughed as she stood. 'You never cease to amaze me, you know that?'

'See for yourself. It's been a while since we… and you smell good.'

'I think you should reserve your strength for getting better,' Ruby said, not wanting to think about the last woman he had sex with. Was he really seeing another woman? It was a painful thought, and she had no right to be jealous given her casual fling with her DI.

But that was always the way it had been with them. One minute they were fighting, the next making up. Their bodies couldn't resist each other. The only way around it was to stay away. 'I'd best be off. I've got work in two hours.'

'Call in sick.'

'And what? Stay by your bedside? I'm sure my showdown with your brother would provide some light entertainment.'

'Don't piss him off, Ruby; he's not been in a good frame of mind since he came out.'

Ruby gave him a withered look. 'I know.'

Nathan narrowed his eyes, unspoken words passing between them.

'Anyway, take care of yourself. You know how I feel about all this. Just call if you need me.'

'Don't I get a kiss?'

Ruby leaned over and kissed him softly on the lips. 'Goodbye, Nathan.'

She turned and walked away. Goodbyes meant nothing in their world.

CHAPTER FORTY-THREE

'Ruby, fancy seeing you here,' Frances said, tottering up the newly cleaned corridor before opening hours. Ruby could barely hide her annoyance.

'I'm always here,' Ruby said nonchalantly. 'A lot of our victims end up in hospital.'

Frances's lips pursed in a taut little smile, her fingers tightly gripping the lip of her designer handbag. She looked too overdressed to be visiting hospital, and Ruby hoped she was going on holiday. Preferably somewhere very far away.

'Why don't you join me for a cuppa in the canteen?' Frances said. 'You're a tea drinker, aren't you? Although judging by your breath I'd say you'd had a drink or two.'

Ruby frowned. Had Frances paid someone to tail her, or just smelt it on her breath? Ignoring the barbed comment, she took a seat across from her in the small hospital canteen. She checked the clock on the wall. It was time she could ill afford. She needed to get home and have a shower before work. But you did not say no to Frances Crosby; things were tenuous between them as it was. Ruby stirred her tea, which was disappointingly weak. Masking a yawn, she waited for what was going to come next. Everything had an agenda with the Crosbys. There were no accidental meetings. She swivelled her head to look for Lenny and was relieved to see no sign. It was odd she had yet to mention Nathan's stabbing, but unless she brought it up Ruby was going to leave well alone. There was no fooling Frances. She would have known that Ruby had ignored her advice to stay away from her son.

'Have you heard the news?' Frances said, taking a dainty sip from her cup. 'Our Nathan's getting married.'

Ruby almost spat out her tea, and in an unladylike slurping manner just managed to swallow it back in time. Her throat burned from the insipid liquid, but Ruby barely noticed; she was too busy contemplating Frances's words. Surely she had been hearing things given what Nathan had just said to her? She raised her eyebrows, forcing a smile as she tried to regain her composure.

'No, I hadn't heard, but I don't really mix in those circles anymore.' She would not give Frances the satisfaction of enquiring about it. It was quite clear why she wanted to talk to Ruby on her own.

'Oh yes, he's been seeing this lovely girl called Leona for some time now. She's got a degree you know; she's very pretty as well. Of course, at twenty-eight years of age she would be.' Frances leaned her head to one side, speaking in a sickly sweet tone. 'They're completely head over heels. We're expecting him to pop the question any day now. They've even been out looking at rings.'

'That's nice,' Ruby said. 'You'll be able to have those grandchildren you've always wanted.' Ruby cursed herself for the bitterness lacing her words. Her stomach was churning with the news. Frances was lying. She had to be. Or was this why Nathan had bought her the flat? Was it a final farewell because he wanted to move on with someone else? He was never any good with break-ups; dealing with emotions was beyond his capabilities. But getting his mother to do his dirty work seemed out of character. And Ruby could not believe that he had any part in this meeting.

Frances pursed her lips in a smug smile. 'I'm going shopping soon to buy an outfit for the wedding. It'll be a lavish affair, of course; her family is very well-to-do.'

'I wish you all the best,' Ruby said, gathering her things to leave. 'But I really must be off now.' She bit back the words balled up in her throat. She wanted to tell Frances about the daughter she and Nathan gave up for adoption. That would wipe the smile from her smug face. She also wanted to say that if she hadn't been such an overbearing cow, she could have already had a place in her granddaughter's life.

Perhaps it would be for the best, Ruby told herself as she returned to the station. A new start for Nathan with his twenty-eight-year-old bride, who would give him all the children he wanted, or at least that his mother wanted. And she would be free to get on with her work and concentrate on the one thing left in her life that had any meaning: cleaning up the streets that she loved so much. But criminals are like weeds: you stamp one out and the next morning there's another two growing in its place.

Every time she closed her eyes she could see Frances grinning at her. The ferocity of her emotions took her by surprise. Why did she let that woman affect her this way? It was exactly what she wanted. And Ruby fell for it every time. She pushed her thoughts of Frances away and regained her focus. Women were in danger. She had to find the killer before they struck again.

Ruby sat at her desk with the door closed. Having sat through briefing in the stuffy conference room, she now had the unenviable task of working out the overtime figures for approval. Piles of paperwork were mounting on her desk, and as she shoved her overflowing 'in' tray to one side a black-edged envelope caught her eye. She picked through the rest of the unopened post, blowing out her cheeks at how much she had let things slide. There was not one but two of these envelopes, directed solely to her. 'DS Ruby Imogen Preston, C/O Shoreditch Police Station'. A shiver ran down her spine and she closed the window. But it was more than the outside breeze making her uneasy. She had seen these envelopes somewhere before. But she was yet to draw up the memory which would provide her with answers. Plucking a pair of scissors from her desk drawer she slid it through the top of the envelope, extracting the information within.

A slim white card, black lined, just like the envelope.

'In Memoriam:

EMILY EDMONDS

Died in her sleep

Rest in Peace'

'What the?' Ruby stammered, sliding her reading glasses from her pocket and reading the text again. Like the envelope it was printed in black ink, but these words drew her in. She glanced at the other envelope, itching to tear it open. But she had already tainted one; best to save the second in case of DNA evidence. What were the chances that it mentioned Charlotte's or Monica's names? Or was there a future victim declared?

Ruby stared at the postmark. The first one was stamped the day before Emily's body was discovered, so it would have been delivered the day her body was dumped. She glanced at the second envelope, dated the day Monica's body was found. Was it someone who had watched the TV appeal playing a sickening joke? But it had been addressed directly to her. Not Downes or Worrow, who led the appeal.

The emails, the letters, and the use of her middle name: it had to be her daughter, trying to gain her attention. With a heavy heart she picked up the phone and dialled a number. 'Bones?' she said, waiting for him to respond. 'I've got something for you. And I need it analysed right now.'

CHAPTER FORTY-FOUR

'Don't forget to tell the teacher that you're having school dinner today,' Anita said, releasing her daughter to the school gates. Sophie kissed her mum before running inside, her long dark pigtails slapping against her backpack. Funny how she had inherited her father's dark hair when her own was so light. Anita smiled as her daughter paused to blow a kiss. She dreaded the day when Sophie would become embarrassed by public displays of affection. She treasured their time together, and still held her hand as they walked to school, telling stories on the way. Anita would start the story with one line and Sophie would continue it with a couple more. Back and forward their stories would go, leading them to some inexplicable situation involving monsters, sticky sweets, animals that could talk, and of course, the moral of the story. It was like something out of a Roald Dahl book, and Anita was always up for cultivating her daughter's vivid imagination.

Today Sophie had swimming lessons and was slowly overcoming her fears. The leg braces she wore as a toddler had straightened her bowed limbs, but she still carried the stigma of being different to her friends. While they started school in knee-length skirts, Sophie begged to wear trousers. The thoughts of their swimming trips had struck her with fear. In the beginning, her teacher encouraged her to dabble her feet in the water as she watched the other children at play. Now she had gained enough courage to wade in.

Anita watched as the lollipop lady ushered the late arrivals across the road. The drooping socks, the unwashed hair – she could have overlooked the children's less than perfect appearance. But sending them to school on their own? She tutted under her breath. There was danger everywhere. How could their mums care so little to allow them to find their own way in? Anita stayed on the corner until she was sure the children had safely made their way inside the school gates; the same way she did every morning. Their mothers had most likely gone back to bed, if they got up at all. Each morning Anita told herself not to be so judgemental, that perhaps *she* was the one with the problem, not them. She had always been overprotective, but, as she said to her husband she had lost one daughter. She could not live through losing another.

She peered at the red sports car as it crawled past the school. Was this another instance of her paranoia? The concern was real enough to deliver a chill down her back. It was the fourth time she had seen it this week, and it always slowed as it passed. She had yet to see a child being dispatched from the passenger seat, and each time it drove past it turned around and returned the way it came. Anita could not help but be suspicious. Next time, she told herself. Next time she would bring a pen and paper and jot down the license plate. Perhaps she could pass it into the local police officers, who might check to see if it was known.

Sometimes she thought she would be better off living in blissful ignorance. But how could you protect your child if you were not aware of the monsters on the prowl?

CHAPTER FORTY-FIVE

Ruby dared to feel optimistic as she pushed through the doors of Oakwood Care Home at lunchtime. His face set in grim determination, Bones had taken the seized envelopes and promised a quick result. A forensic investigation would be launched on the gum sealing the envelopes as well as the usual fingerprints, paper, and printer ink analysis. It seemed a good opportunity to sneak out for a ten-minute visit. But she should have known that her good mood wouldn't last.

Harmony met her in the corridor and gently steered her to one side. She was the sweetest, most maternal person Ruby knew and she treated everyone as if they were her nearest and dearest, instead of just part of her job. But today her eyes were filled with concern, and Ruby felt her heart flutter in her chest.

'What's wrong?' Ruby said, looking past her shoulder. 'Is Mum OK?'

'Now don't you go worrying, gal, she be just fine. She's just a bit agitated. I wanted to let you know so you could both take things slow.'

'Agitated? Why, what happened?'

'She decided she didn't want to eat and threw her porridge against the wall. There's no reasoning with her I'm afraid, but come, sit awhile. She be a lot calmer now.'

'Mum?' Ruby said, feeling the old familiar tightness grab a tight hold of her chest. She had felt the same way when her mum had to be taken into the home: overwrought with guilt because she had not been able to care for her by herself. She had tried and failed, and they had both been miserable. After finding Oakwood the tightly bound anxiety had slowly released its hold. Mum was happier, which in turn helped Ruby relax. But she could not bear another reminder of her mother's crumbling mind. And now, seeing her with her unkempt hair and oddly coloured socks the old feelings of anxiety and guilt returned.

'It's just an off day,' Harmony said, no doubt sensing her discord.

'Thank you,' Ruby said. 'I won't stay too long because I've got work, but I'll ring a little later; see how she is around lunch time if that's OK.'

'You ring whenever you like, my love. I'm sure we'll persuade her to eat by then, even if I have to get Geoffrey over there to ask nicely. Isn't that right, Geoff?' she said, winking at the auburn-haired young man who was helping an elderly gent to his seat.

Ruby thought how there was something very attractive about selfless people. If only she didn't find herself chasing the wrong men.

Ruby leaned in to kiss her mother on the cheek; backing off when she received a hostile glare. 'I can't stay long,' she said, itching to fix the buttons on her mother's red cardigan. She had obviously dressed herself, batting away any offers of assistance. Perhaps her annoyance lay in the memory taking centre stage today. Her mother mumbled under her breath, her fingers tightly bound in two fists.

'What's wrong, Mum? You don't seem yourself today.'

'What's wrong? What's wrong you ask?' Joy said, shaking her head. 'It's Ruby. She's only gone and got herself pregnant. With none other than that young Crosby boy from next door.'

'Mum… ' Ruby said, trying to gently steer her mother into the present. But Joy was not listening.

'I should have known when she left to set up home with him. I've got a good mind to go around there right now. She thinks she knows everything, but she's just a child herself.'

'It's okay, Mum, I'm Ruby. I'm home. Everything's okay.'

Her mother looked at her as if she were mad. 'You're not Ruby; my daughter's barely eighteen. You're a long way from eighteen.' She folded her arms, her fists still tightly bunched. 'Dammit, if it were anyone but the Crosbys I'd be pleased for her.'

This piqued Ruby's interest, and not knowing whether it was the right thing to do or not she played along. 'What's wrong with the Crosbys?'

'Gertie, if you don't know what's wrong with the Crosbys you haven't been listening to me for the last ten years.'

Ruby sighed. Her mother's sister Gertie had passed away two years before. She had always said Ruby looked like her. 'Sorry. I thought you liked Nathan,' Ruby said.

'Of course I like him. That poor boy is like one of my own. But his father... meanness like that passes through the bloodstream. There's no avoiding it.'

Ruby knew what her mother meant. His father's cruelty had beat Nathan from a beautiful little boy that called her Wuby to a man too tortured to show his emotions, confusing love with weakness. His brother, Lenny, had taken the brunt of the physical punishments. But Nathan had not escaped his childhood untarnished. Years of mental abuse had taken its toll: watching his mother and brother get beaten, being swatted back when he tried to help. He hated his father with a passion, but had been powerless to stop him.

'I remember when he was seven years old,' Joy said, grim-faced. 'I found him hiding in the wardrobe, shaking like a leaf because his father had lost it, threatening to blow their brains out with a gun before he left. The poor child was so scared he vomited into his hands. Can you imagine what that does to a person? And now they think they can bring a child of their own into the world. It's unthinkable, that's what it is.'

Ruby knew all about it. Years of abuse had come out as Nathan and Ruby lay in their squat, stoned. She knew at the time it was therapy, but it pained her to relive each stinging blow, each cruel word. It was those dark confessions that got Ruby through the hard times in their relationship; when Nathan wouldn't speak, or became bad tempered because she spoke to another boy. She was the only solid thing he had in life. The only person that could make him feel that there was still some good in him. But as Nathan grew, so did his independence. Their year of living recklessly ran out of steam, and Ruby grew tired of getting wasted on cannabis when she should be doing something with her life. Finding out she was pregnant was a game changer. It was why Ruby had agreed with her mother when she suggested they give the baby up for adoption.

Joy had gone quiet now; her energy sapped by the anger she had awoken with that morning. Nathan would never have a bad word said against his own mother. But he must have known she could not be relied upon to put their daughter's welfare first. To her, children were possessions, part of a family unit that could never be torn apart. She would have insisted both Ruby and Nathan move in with them. And then the cycle of abuse would have begun all over again. With no money and a failing relationship, Ruby and Nathan allowed themselves to be steered by her mother, and so they had given their baby up in the hope she would be afforded a better life.

With a sinking feeling, Ruby wondered if she was destined to be like her mother, battling a past that would not let go.

CHAPTER FORTY-SIX

Anita rubbed her hands against the back of her jeans as she answered the door. She was smiling, which seemed to be the default expression on her face.

Lucy was happy to see that smile. Today she was wearing a blonde wig cut into a blunt bob, which brought her hair to her shoulders. The rose-patterned dress she was wearing was similar to Anita's clothes, and she was disappointed to see her in a sweatshirt and jeans. Lucy put on a brave smile and took a deep breath. 'Hello, I'm sorry to bother you.' She took a deep breath and exhaled again. 'Oh my gosh, this is so hard.' Gracefully, she extended her hand. It was a swan-like movement Lucy had practised countless times. 'My name is Lucy; I think... I mean, I am your daughter.'

The colour left Anita's face as she stared, open-mouthed, her eyes wide in shock.

'Muuuuummmyyyy,' the little girl called from the kitchen.

Lucy bristled within at the irritating squeal. But it brought another smile to Anita's face as she called back: 'I'll be there in a minute, sweetheart.'

'Well, please, do come in,' Anita said, closing the front door behind her. 'I'm sorry, this has come as a shock.'

Sunlight streamed through the glass door panels bathing the women in a soft glow. There was something ethereal about their meeting. Lucy felt it in the air. This was meant to be.

A strange hiccup-sounding sob caught in the back of Anita's throat as tears clouded her eyes. 'This is crazy,' she said, giving another little gasp. 'Are you saying you're really my daughter? The little girl I gave up all those years ago?'

Lucy nodded, mirroring Anita's emotions. 'Yes. It's me, Mum. It's really me.'

Anita opened her arms wide. 'Well, in that case, give me a hug.'

Lucy had not been expecting the instant display of affection after all the times she had been turned away. It warmed her from the inside out, and she breathed in her mother's flowery perfume, gratefully accepted her embrace. But their perfect moment was rudely interrupted by that irritating sound from the kitchen.

'Mummy, I'm done.'

Lucy's eyes snapped open, narrowing over Anita's shoulder as she stared at the kitchen door. Something would really have to be done about her.

Anita caught the tears with the tips of her fingers as she pulled away. 'That's Sophie… your sister. Oh my gosh, I'm shaking. I don't know what to say.' Pulling a ragged tissue from her pocket, she lightly dabbed her face. 'Would you mind waiting in the living room while I see to Sophie? I'll get you a drink. What would you like? Tea or coffee? Oh my gosh, I can't believe you're here,' she said, breathlessly, showing her into her humble abode.

'A cup of tea would be lovely, thanks,' Lucy said softly. 'Two sugars and milk. But I can come back at a better time, if you prefer? I didn't know how to approach you. I wasn't sure how you'd react.' Lucy began to squeeze a couple of her own tears out, in keeping with her mother's response.

Anita grabbed her hands and grasped them tightly. 'Oh, sweetheart, I'm not letting you go anywhere. I've been searching for you for years, but I kept hitting a dead end. I'm so happy to have you here. Please tell me you'll stay.'

Lucy could not believe her ears. Even while she watched Anita she never dared believe that she would react in this way. After all the rejections it was a dream come true. She had been right to choose a mother who was naturally maternal, unlike the others who rejected her from the start: Emily, a wet rag, who allowed people to walk all over her, and Monica, a career-driven materialistic cow. 'Of course, I'll take a seat and wait for you.'

'I just need to speak to Sophie, tell her that we have a very special visitor. And I have to tell my husband. Oh my goodness, I just can't believe this. I can't wait to hear all about you.' Anita wiped away another errant tear, blew her nose, and pushed the tissue back into her pocket. 'I'll be with you in five minutes,' she said.

Lucy took a few deep breaths to calm herself. Her eyes danced over the pictures on the walls and she imagined *her* face in the pictures instead of the little girl lined up in the shot. Of course, Anita would be unhappy if anything happened to her, and Lucy would have to take that into account when disposing of the rest of the family. A tall gangly looking man stared out happily from the family photo, his arm draped around what looked like a younger version of himself.

Anita's husband, from what Lucy's investigations had uncovered, who was conveniently away with his son.

Lucy sighed. More people to be taken care of. If only the rest of the world could just disappear and leave her and her mother alone. She stiffened as footsteps approached, catching the tail end of a telephone conversation as Anita paced the hall.

'Yes, it's really her. She said her name is Lucy now. No, I haven't asked her. It might be all a bit overwhelming. I think it's best that we take things slowly to begin with… I know… I can't believe that she's here, sitting in our living room.'

Lucy strained to listen as the conversation faded away, and rising from her chair, she pressed her ear to the door. A kettle boiled in the distance while a children's cartoon played a happy tune. She stepped back at the sound of the clink of cups being carried on a tray down the hall. Lucy perched on the sofa, plastering a smile on her face. Her heart swelled at the sight of the tray laden with tea, chocolate digestive biscuits and sandwiches cut in triangles. Nobody had ever offered her refreshments before. 'You shouldn't have gone to all this trouble.'

Anita's eyes were alive with excitement. 'It's the least I can do after you've come all this way to find me. I've so many questions, but I was just saying to my husband, you must be feeling overwhelmed.'

Lucy nodded, dropping two cubes of sugar into her flower-patterned cup. It was all so homely; she felt like hugging herself. 'My stomach's been churning at the thought of visiting. I've come to your front door so many times and walked away.' It was enough to cover up the fact she had been there before, in case some nosy neighbours pointed her out. 'But the same must go for you, having me turn up out of the blue. I don't even know how you feel about having me here.'

Anita's eyes began to well up for the second time that day. 'Darling, I'm over the moon. I want you to meet everybody; after all you've got a half-sister and brother that will be dying to meet you,' she said, 'but I'll respect your wishes and take things as slowly as you want.'

Lucy did not consider the little girl in the kitchen as her sister. Her mind could only bend reality so far. And, in Lucy's world, there was no room for sharing.

CHAPTER FORTY-SEVEN

The faces of the dead stared from the whiteboard: Harry Edmonds, his nose crushed from the unprotected fall; Emily Edmonds, her expression locked in terror – mouth torn from being force-fed the baubles now exhibited in a glass jar; and Charlotte Lockwood: her crime-scene picture made the grimmest viewing of all. Above the picture of the blood-splattered pavement was a blown-up passport photo. Pale and unsmiling, the bags under her eyes suggested sleep was a luxury she had seen little of. Ruby glanced at Monica last. She could not help but feel she had let the woman down. Despite the warnings on TV and appeals to the public this intelligent career-driven woman had opened her door to a complete stranger. Ruby had thought about what she would have done without the benefit of hindsight. It was always the same conclusion. If she had received such a visitor claiming to be her daughter, she would have invited her in too.

'Right,' DI Downes said, rubbing his hands together. 'Are we starting or what?'

They were back in hell; Ruby's least favourite place. At least today she had remembered to leave the briefing room door ajar before their meeting. And morning briefing was preferential to evening when the lingering heat drew out the sweaty odour and magnified it tenfold. In the absence of Worrow, Downes took the lead. Unbuttoning his shirt sleeves he rolled them up his forearms. Given the way his tie was swinging loosely around his neck it was only a matter of time before that came off too.

'Go ahead, boss,' Ruby said, carrying out a quick headcount. 'We're all here.'

It took only minutes for the team to be brought up to speed because, despite the overwhelming number of enquiries taking place, they were yet to turn up any solid leads. The television appeal had brought in hundreds of calls and valuable police hours were spent chasing up dead ends. The frustration was evident on Downes's face as he spoke. He moved his hand to the picture of Emily's address on the whiteboard and prodded at the image of her front door.

'Why here?' Downes said, casting his eyes around the room. He reached to the picture of Monica's home, pressing his finger to the door. 'And here. Out of all the homes in London, why did our suspect come knocking on these doors? These are the questions we need to be asking if we've any hope of solving this case. Were the baubles found in Emily's stomach Christmas decorations, or were they used for another reason? And why were Emily's and Monica's bodies staged, but not the others'? Luddy, how did you get on tracking down the origin of their clothes?'

'The nightgown was the most distinctive piece of clothing. It was from The White Company. They're online as well as being dotted all around the UK. We haven't been able to narrow it down any more than that. We've spoken to friends, family, colleagues; they all say the same thing: that both Emily and Monica seemed relatively happy with their partners. Both husbands had clean records. But that's where the similarities end. Friends say that Emily was timid and barely left the house, while Monica was career-driven and outgoing and hardly ever in.'

'And what about Charlotte? Anything new?'

'Crimestoppers have come through with calls to say a man was seen in the area prior to the attack. But there's no description other than someone walking down the street in a hoodie.'

'Which could just as easily be a woman in disguise. Yes, I saw that,' Downes interrupted.

Ruby interjected, shifting the attention from Luddy, who was sweating from more than the humidity in the room. It was clear that the pressure of holding back their visit to Goldie was getting to him, and Ruby felt guilty for bringing him along. 'We've had a vast number of calls reporting neighbours acting suspiciously, noises in the night, strange comings and goings. We're still going through them.' She fanned her face with her paperwork. 'We're also trawling through the nearest CCTV leading to and from the address. Vehicles are being checked against ANPR, and we're liaising with other forces for similar incident reports. Our prolific offenders are being monitored and spoken to. We've checked the history of Emily's home address, as well as her neighbours and anything else that could lead to it being a case of mistaken identity.'

'It's too much of a coincidence that Emily and Monica gave up children for adoption. No leads on their real daughters? Any relatives with some warped sense of revenge?'

'No, boss. Emily's daughter, as you know, has since passed on. She was an only child, a high achiever who was popular in school,' Luddy said. 'We've spoken to her friends; none of them stand out as being capable of murder.'

'And Monica's daughter?'

'We found out today that she's a travel rep in Greece. She's had no contact with her mother.'

'Crack on with your enquiries in local care homes. I want you to speak to anyone you can find who worked there ten, twenty years ago. Find out if any of the children had an obsession with death and Victorian traditions, or if anything significant took place around Christmas Day. We can't leave any stone unturned.'

'I've also had some possible evidence turn up on my desk in the form of two letters. They're currently with Bones… I mean, Crime

Scene Investigators,' Ruby corrected herself. 'It may be a hoax, but they were addressed directly to me.'

'Letters? Why wasn't this brought to my attention?' Downes said, looking harried. He despised being out of the loop when it came to briefing. His macho pride did not appreciate being shown up in front of his colleagues. Ruby felt a flush rise to her cheeks. Because of her visit to Oakwood she did not have time to inform him. 'They've only just been discovered,' she said, before describing the card. She hoped he wouldn't ask about the postmark and the fact the first envelope was delivered days ago. Friend or no friend, he would chew the arse off her for that. Best to inform him in a less public setting. 'The envelopes were black rimmed, and the letter inside was a kind of death announcement. It's in line with the Victorian mourning tradition.'

'So they're some kind of death notice?' Downes said, tugging at the knot on his tie. Ruby shoved on her glasses and peered at the list of traditions Eve had placed on the board. Information on death notices was listed near the top.

'Yes,' Ruby said. 'The envelope was marked so back in the day; people knew it was a death announcement before they opened it. It gave them time to prepare themselves.'

'And what's the significance to our case? Have you worked that one out too?'

Ruby glared down her glasses at Downes. It was a look telling him to back off. 'I've been informed that the second card is exactly the same, apart from the name. Monica Sherwood.'

Eve raised her hand. 'But what about the other victims? Emily's husband, Charlotte Lockwood? Why haven't you received notifications for them?'

'I think it's because they're bit players who interfered with Lucy's plans. Which makes this killer even more dangerous, because they'll kill anyone who gets in their way. Safety plans are in place for the victim's family members, but it's more likely the killer will move on to someone else, and this is why we need to warn such women *before* she strikes. Their whole family could be in danger.'

Ruby sighed. She couldn't sit on it any longer. 'I'm currently researching an email address provided by an anonymous source. They said the owner was acting suspiciously, saying they were searching for her mother and had a score to settle. Luddy has located the IP address to an internet café, and we've got a vague description of the suspect which I've added to the briefing notes. I've put an intel report in.'

'Good. Well, keep me updated. It may be more valuable than you think.'

It was close enough to the truth. As much as Ruby wanted to catch the killer a small part of her was scared. Her emotions were tied up in knots as she worked with her team to hunt Lucy down. But it felt like she was in a room where the walls of her life were closing in. With her job pressuring her on one side and the Crosbys on the other, she was left in no doubt – no matter what she did this was not going to end well.

CHAPTER FORTY-EIGHT

'Out of all the places you could have asked to meet, why on earth did you pick here?' Ruby said, glancing around the shelves of the local library.

'Because we won't bump into anyone from the nick,' Downes replied, leading her to a table at the far corner of the room.

It was a good choice. Ten minutes into lunch time and there were only a handful of people there. Ruby slid a book from a shelf as she soaked up the peaceful atmosphere: so unlike her office where she sweated over files, overtime sheets and fresh leads. They sat in a shaft of morning light which peeped through the blinds above. She could see herself coming somewhere like here, if only she had the time to read.

Downes peered at the novel. '*Wuthering Heights?*'

'Uh huh,' Ruby said, flicking through the pages. 'We're in a library, aren't we?'

Downes gently closed the book and rested his hand on the cover. 'I'm worried about you. I've just spoken to Bones. I know that letter's been sitting in your tray for a few days.'

'Any joy with forensics?' Ruby asked, hoping to change the subject.

Downes shook his head. 'Not yet. Look, I'm willing to overlook the delay in finding the letter, but I've been hearing other things… your night vigil in the hospital being one of them.'

Ruby's fingers drummed the table for the want of a cigarette. It was the second time in as many days she had been pulled up by a superior officer, and it left a bitter taste in her mouth.

'What *are* you talking about?' she said, thinking it safer to deny all knowledge.

Downes rolled his eyes. 'Don't give me that bollocks. I had a phone call from the matron. You stayed there overnight.'

Ruby forgot how well Downes knew the staff from attending the hospital when his wife was ill.

Downes sat back delivering a weighty gaze. His hair was tousled from running his fingers through it, his shirt creased. 'I'm worried about your association with the Crosby family. You're compromising your position in the police.'

Ruby pursed her lips. 'Don't piss on my leg and tell me it's raining. You want to know if I'm seeing him, don't you?'

Downes shot her a glare. 'You're in no position to be making jokes.'

'I'm sorry, that was out of order,' Ruby flushed. 'But don't you think we should be focusing our efforts on our serial killer instead of my personal life?'

'I just don't want you to be the next job I'm investigating,' he said. 'What's going on with you, Ruby? If you're in any kind of trouble then tell me now, and I'll do my best to dig you out.'

'I appreciate the offer, but there's nothing to sort out. Now can we get out of here? I really need a drag on my vaporiser. Or are you going to tell me they're bad for me too?'

Jack slid his hands across the table, cupping them over Ruby's. They were warm to the touch. Strong. His gravelly voice was laced with concern. 'Just be careful, that's all I'm saying. People are beginning to talk, and if you don't have a legitimate purpose to be speaking with the Crosby family, then you should give them a wide berth.'

Ruby snorted. 'You were asking for inside info the other day. You can't have it both ways.' She tried to pull her hands away, but Downes was not letting go.

'There's a difference between making discreet enquiries and putting your job on the line.'

The words stung, because Ruby knew he was speaking the truth. But she was far too guarded to allow him to tell her what to do. 'Look, Nathan and I go back a long way, and as much as it pains me to say it I *do* care about him. But I would never put my job in jeopardy. We live in two separate worlds.'

'C'mon Ruby,' Downes said, with a hint of reproach. 'You're not kids playing with your Lego any more. Lenny Crosby is a vicious bastard and his brother isn't far behind him. How do you think they've gained so much control? Do you know what happened to the last person who pissed off the Crosbys?'

Ruby drew back from his gaze. She knew about Goldie, and there had been several more victims since then. But she had enough on her plate dealing with the murderer now labelled by the media as 'the door-knocker killer'. She did not want to hear what Downes wanted to say, but he was not letting her go until he had said his piece.

'Turns out that one of their own was a snout. Lenny and his brother went around there and nailed him to the door. I mean they actually nailed him – hands and feet. Crucified this poor guy and left him to bleed out. Is this the sort of associate you want while you're in the police?'

Ruby stared at the cover of the dog-eared book, her heart sinking.

'You know what they did to the guy who testified against Lenny before he went to prison? Scooped his eyes out with a spoon.'

She glanced around as a photocopier whirred in the background. Satisfied they were not being overheard, she turned back to her boss. 'Is Nathan wanted for any of that stuff?' Ruby asked. 'Is he actually wanted by the police for *any* offences?'

'Of course not,' Downes said, shaking his head. 'He's as slippery as Teflon. But I'm telling you now, keep as far away as you can from that lot.'

'You don't need to worry about me. Besides, Nathan distanced himself from that sort of violence a long time ago.'

Downes snorted. 'Take off the rose-tinted glasses and step into the real world. If you keep trying to merge the two, you'll be up to your neck in it.'

'I get the message,' Ruby said, her heart heavy. 'You're right, Lenny *is* a psychopath, and I'm under no illusion as to what they do for a living. But there are rules. And they do instil order on the streets.' She raised her hand as Downes opened his mouth to speak. 'I'm not for a second condoning their behaviour.' She rose from the table, her cheeks flushed. 'I think it's time we got back to work, don't you?'

Downes clamped a hand on her shoulder as he stood. 'You're a good copper Ruby, but you need to catch yourself on. There's no happy ending with that lot.'

As Ruby left the library his words rang in her ears.

CHAPTER FORTY-NINE

Nathan stood firm, hands deep in pockets, his brow lined in a deep frown. 'I'm sorry, Leona, but I want us to finish.'

The smile slowly melted from Leona's face. 'Finish what?'

Nathan cupped his hand over his eyebrows, briefly closing his eyes. He wanted this over with. He wanted her out. 'This. Us. I'm sorry. But I don't want to see you anymore.' He realised how cruel the words sounded, but he could not find better ones. He had no point of reference, because in his world people were direct and to the point. But she was staring at him now; her eyes brimming with tears as she waited for an explanation. Nathan cleared his throat. 'I need some space. I want to be on my own.'

Leona stared, open-mouthed, her chin trembling as the words slowly rose from her throat. 'I don't understand. Is this some kind of joke?' Then she nodded, quickly wiping away the tears that were beginning to form. 'It is, isn't it? It's some weird joke. Is this how you do it in your family?' She laughed, but it was a hollow sound, and Nathan knew she was fooling herself.

'How we do what? he asked, wishing she'd just leave.

'Propose, of course; that's what you brought me here for, isn't it?'

Nathan pulled in a terse breath. Just what had Mum being saying to her? 'I don't know where you got that idea from, but it wasn't from me. I've no intention of proposing to anyone. Right now I just want to be single.'

Leona pulled a tissue from her clutch bag and began to dab the mascara-stained trails running down her cheeks. 'No, that's not true.

Frances said that we were going to get married, that we could have kids of our own.' Intermittent sobs bounced between her words.

Nathan stepped back, distancing himself from the source of his irritation. His anger rose like hot steam searching for release. 'You know what I'm sick of? Everyone telling me what to do. You, Lenny, Mum, all plotting what's best. I never made you any promises.'

Leona opened her mouth to speak, and he raised his hand for silence.

'I can see you're not listening so I'll make it really simple. We had a bit of fun together, but that's as far as it goes. I think it's about time you left.'

'You bastard,' Leona sniffed. 'You just used me, just like all the others.'

'Well, maybe if you didn't make yourself so available there wouldn't be such a long list. Now get out.' He regretted the words as soon as he uttered them, but they had the desired effect. Most men would get a slap on the face for such a derogatory comment, but his reputation ensured he would remain untouched.

Turning on her heel, Leona slammed the heavy oak door as she left. Nathan wished he could have handled it differently and had hoped they could have parted on better terms. But cruel words came easily, whereas heartfelt ones had to be dug around for in the darkness of his soul – in places only Ruby could reach. His family had been whispering promises that were not theirs to keep, all for their own selfish needs. He would deal with them later. He would send Leona some flowers, try to apologise for his unkind words. But now he needed to get his life back on track. Without his family's interference.

CHAPTER FIFTY

Getting her hands on tranquillisers had not been as difficult as Lucy had thought it would be. You could buy anything on the dark web if you had enough money. It was the same place where people traded their services for money. Obtaining access to restricted records was one of the many services available if you were a trustworthy source of payment. The challenge was making sure it could not be traced back to you. But it was worth taking the chance for Anita. Lucy sat in front of her, having brought down a chair from the kitchen so they could spend time together. Not that Anita was aware, as she was gagged and bound in the chair, her blonde hair trailing down her face. Lucy stared, her head full of dreams for the future. She was smitten, and she could not bear to hurt the object of her affection.

She had not felt this strongly about someone before. Not really. And it was why she had gone to the extra effort to make everything just right. The cinnamon and orange scented candles filled the room with the smell of Christmas, and the sound of the dripping pipe was drowned by the gentle lull of Nat King Cole. She could not bear for anything to wipe the smile from her mother's face.

Here was the one person who could fix her, make everything right. But Lucy was wary. She had to guard against the dark side of her nature: the side that relished power and control. Scarred by past experiences, she was unpredictable and angry, just as she had been all those years ago. The sexual high she derived in the aftermath of murder was proving to be an addictive drug.

Anita stirred in her chair, a low groan emitting from her parted lips. She was so close, Lucy thought, but she had been close before. And now their bodies were lying in a morgue. But she had taken care of that. There would be nothing to trace those disappointments back to her.

Everything hinged on Christmas. If she could get it right, perhaps she could be free, without the need for props. Maybe they could live abroad, she mused, somewhere snowy like Austria or Switzerland, where it could be Christmas all year around.

Lucy reached out to Anita, pushing her wispy blonde hair behind her ear. A frown crossed her face as she wondered if the gag was too tight.

Anita blinked, her head slowly rising in a drug-induced stupor. She carried the same confusion as the others, but her eyes were swimming with another emotion. Lucy leaned forward, peering into their depths. It was like looking into her own soul. Instead of terror, Lucy saw confusion, hurt and betrayal reflected back at her. Anita had come around twice now, each time gaining a little more recognition of her surroundings. But unlike the others, she did not cry out. Her chest rose and fell as she drew in panicked breaths, but her throat remained hollow, devoid of the screams that had led her predecessors to their deaths. And when Lucy told her of her plans she simply nodded and took it all in.

'I'm going to untie your gag,' Lucy said, her breath carrying a shudder of excitement. 'But first, I need a hug.'

Leaning forward, she took Anita in an embrace, inhaling the fading scent of her perfume. Anita did not stiffen, but relaxed into her embrace, resting her head on Lucy's shoulder. Lucy pulled back to see tears trickling down Anita's soft pink cheeks. Little pearly drops of emotion melting into the dirty blue cloth bound around her mouth. A pang of guilt enveloped Lucy. Anita was far too good a person to be wearing such a filthy gag. Slowly, Lucy untied the knot; whispering a warning to Anita not to spoil things, because she did not wish to cause her pain. Anita took a breath as a gag was removed, licking her dirt-encrusted lips.

Lucy stiffened, closing her fingers around the material as she tried to read Anita's expression. But Anita blinked, completely subservient as she waited for her to speak. Lucy's heart swelled with the power and respect her new mother was affording her. 'Please behave,' Lucy said. 'I don't want to hurt you, but sometimes I get angry and I can't control myself.'

'I'll behave.' Anita's voice sounded like marshmallows, and Lucy warmed inside.

'Do it right and you'll be freed. But everything has to be perfect. You're my only chance,' Lucy said; the words running out of her mouth before she had a chance to control them.

'I'll help you,' Anita said, blinking against the strength of the bulb overhead. 'I want us to be together too. But you have to help me in return. I need to know that Sophie's safe.'

Darkness crossed Lucy's face at the sound of the little girl's name.

'But remember, you're my daughter too, and I'm here for you. You can trust me.' Anita's voice was so soft and warm that Lucy forgave her indiscretion.

'She's asleep in bed,' Lucy said, pointing above their heads. 'I made it nice, just like in her bedroom. She's just fine.'

Anita nodded in understanding. 'Thank you. And I want us to be together too. But I need you to do something for me so everything can be perfect between us.'

'What do you want?' Lucy said, her voice hardening. Anita's gag had been removed for only a few seconds and already she was making demands. It twitched in Lucy's fingers as she took a step back, distancing herself from the allure of Anita's voice.

'I need you to take Sophie back to my house, or leave her somewhere people can find her. None of this is her fault.' She coughed as the words produced a scratchy sound. 'She doesn't need to get hurt. Do you understand?'

Lucy shook her head. 'Time for you to be quiet now.' She raised the gag, turning the slimy blue bandana so the dry side pressed against Anita's face.

Anita's shoulders slumped, her eyes glazing in resignation.

Lucy sighed, trying not to catch Anita's hair as she carefully tied the knot at the back of her head. 'I'll think about it. But the next step – and Sophie's life – depends on you.'

CHAPTER FIFTY-ONE

'Thank you for agreeing to meet with me, Mr Devine,' Ruby said introducing Eve as they entered his living room. Bodies lurked in the corridor: concerned family listening out for his best interests 'Can I close the door?' Ruby asked, rising to do it anyway.

'Please, call me Joseph,' he said solemnly. His face looked numb as if someone had injected an anaesthetic and he was waiting for it to wear off. A tall clean-shaven man, Ruby judged him to be in his fifties: at least a decade older than his missing wife. He walked slightly hunched, a habit which was probably picked up from being married to someone a good deal smaller than himself. Ruby met his gaze, and it seemed an effort for him to return it. 'I don't suppose you have any news?'

'I'm sorry, we don't; at least, not yet. I just wanted a quick word to see if you've thought of anything more since your statement.'

Her visit was purely on instinct, as, when they spoke on the phone, she had felt a hint of reluctance in his voice. She took a seat on the sofa, nudging up to make room for Eve. Mr Devine had already provided the police with a full account, but Ruby could not settle until she had met him in person. Joseph's missing person report had been taken extremely seriously, particularly when he spoke of a long-lost daughter who had allegedly turned up at his wife's door.

He glanced up at the family photo on the wall with puffy, red-rimmed eyes. A family of four, with two people missing; his anguish was evident on his face. 'I told Tim to stay on at university. He's studying journalism in Lincoln. His mum wouldn't want anything interfering with his studies.' He exhaled a long thin breath. 'The police keep asking if Anita and Sophie could have gone to stay with friends. But we're an insular couple, you know? We don't need anyone else when we have our little family.'

Ruby nodded, wishing Anita had not opened the door that day.

Mr Devine picked up a newspaper from the coffee table, pointing at the headlines emblazoned across the page. 'If it's true what they say about this door-knocker killer, surely they wouldn't have taken both Anita and Sophie?'

Ruby could not answer his question because she did not know. 'Mr Devine... Joseph, I do understand your concern, and as soon as we have any solid leads you'll be made aware. Can you tell me a little more about how Anita felt about the daughter she had adopted? You said there was no trace of worry in her voice when she called.'

'On the contrary, she was excited. The adoption was something she had come to regret. I thought that when we had Sophie it might help. For a while it did, until she told me that she felt guiltier than ever. I think it's why she did so much volunteer work with the Samaritans. Don't get me wrong, she adored Tim, her stepson. But the special bond she had with Sophie made her see what she had been missing out on all those years.'

Ruby nodded, trying not to be drawn into thoughts of her own past. It was something she had been struggling with since the case came to life. She filled the void with work and worrying about her mum.

'It's all my fault. I should have told her the truth.' A desolate sob escaped Joseph's lips. Bowing his head he failed to hold back the dam of tears welling in his eyes.

Ruby swallowed back the lump in her throat, feeling like an intruder in his home. She dug in her pocket for a tissue, gratefully accepting one fresh from the packet as Eve pulled it from her handbag. 'Here, take this,' she said, handing it over. 'What do you mean you should have told her?'

Joseph blew his nose before scrunching up the damp tissue in his hand. 'This is all my fault. I thought they'd be back by now and Anita wouldn't find out what I did.'

'Which is?... ' Ruby said, exchanging a glance with Eve. Pen poised, she was leaning on the pages of her leather-bound pocket notebook ready to take down whatever revelation Joseph blurted out.

'The truth is Anita's been trying to find her daughter for years, by making enquiries in the area. I told her it was a bad idea, but she wouldn't listen and they always reached a dead end. Then I got a letter from Samantha. That's her daughter's real name. She said that she didn't want to hear from Anita. That she had a new life with parents she loved. She said she was glad Anita gave her up for adoption because she couldn't have had better parents.' Joseph's Adam's apple bobbed as he tried to regain his composure. 'But the tone of the letter was bitter, and I wrestled with my conscience for a long time before burning it.' Joseph glanced up at Ruby before returning his gaze to the tissue knotted between his fingers. 'I know it sounds terrible but... I didn't want to upset her. Sophie had started school and Anita was feeling depressed. I didn't want any more setbacks.'

Ruby frowned. If there was one thing she hated it was having men make women's decisions for them. 'But wouldn't she have been happy knowing that her daughter was with a good family? Didn't you think she had the right to know?'

'I realise that now. I shouldn't have done it. It was pure selfishness on my part. I was angry with Samantha, and I didn't want Anita knowing how bitter she was towards her. Besides, you don't know what Anita was like. She would have pursued Samantha until she heard the words in person. She had just started accepting she would never find her. I was loath to start things up again.'

'And then you got a phone call from Anita saying her daughter had turned up at her door. Why didn't you say anything then?'

'She was so happy and excited, I thought maybe Samantha had changed her mind. I was taken aback; I didn't know what to say, and the letter wasn't something I was willing to discuss over the phone.'

'Anita hadn't received any letters prior to Lucy's visit?' Ruby said, thinking of the letters she found taped to the bath panel.

'No, not at all. She wouldn't have sounded so surprised if she did. Anyway, I offered to come home early, but she insisted I didn't need to because she wanted some quality time with Lucy.' Joseph shook his head as if delivering an internal admonishment. 'I should have told her about the letter from Samantha. If I had, she might not have asked this Lucy woman inside.'

'From what you told me, I think she would have opened her door anyway. It sounds like Anita was desperate to hear from her, and sometimes when you want something really badly you're willing to put aside any reservations you have in order to make it happen. Don't blame yourself. The only person to blame is the woman who turned up at her door.'

'And what about Sophie? She's just a little girl. You don't think they're involved in one of these… ' his face creased in anguish as he tried to deliver the words, 'paedophile rings, do you? You hear about these things on the news: children being bought and sold.'

'There's no evidence to suggest it. We've got almost a hundred officers working around the clock on this case in different capacities. But if you hear anything, I mean anything at all, let us know.' Ruby reached into her blazer and pulled out a dog-eared business card. 'Here's my mobile number; you can catch me anytime, day or night.'

Joseph grabbed Ruby's hands as she passed over the card. His fingers dug into her wrists, and it took all of her resolve not to pull back. 'Promise me you'll bring my wife and little girl home safely.'

But it was a promise that was not Ruby's to make. 'I promise that I'll do everything within my power to find them.' But she did not say she would find them alive. It was as near a reassurance as she could give. Exchanging a glance with Eve, she rose to leave. Safeguarding had already been completed with Joseph and his son, but leaving them gave her an uncomfortable, itchy feeling. 'It may be a good idea if you stay with family or friends for a few days, and you should urge your son not to go out alone.'

Joseph nodded as he bit into his trembling bottom lip. He emanated grief, and his features contorted with the need to keep a brave front.

Ruby wished she had answers to give, and her heart blazed with the need to find his wife and daughter alive. Her suspicions ignited a fear that Lucy was mentally deranged, fuelled by a hatred risen from a perceived betrayal. But how many more people would suffer at her hands?

'I feel like I owe you an apology,' Eve said, balancing her milkshake and carton of fries on her lap. The Drive Thru at McDonald's had been a welcome respite from a heavy day, but it was not over yet. Eve had looked pale and drawn, and a small pit stop was needed to get them back on their feet.

'Forget about it,' Ruby said, referring to their chat in the office. 'I shouldn't have been sticking my nose in. I just wanted to make sure you were OK.'

'It's not about that... well it is, but there's more to it.' Eve sighed. 'I'm babbling aren't I? I always babble when I'm nervous, people say that—'

'Eve,' Ruby interrupted, in between a mouthful of burger, 'don't be nervous. I promise not to bite your head off. What's wrong?'

'Luddy said you had a go at him the other night for complaining to Ma'am Worrow.'

'I don't see how that's anything to do with… ' Ruby's eyes widened. 'Was it you?'

Eve nodded, dropping her gaze to the car footwell.

Ruby stared until she lifted it again. 'Why? What did I do to deserve that?'

'I was angry. It was after you called me into your office. I bumped into Ma'am Worrow in the hall. She asked me what was wrong and… '

'Encouraged you to have a moan about me.' Ruby sighed. 'Why are you telling me this now?'

'Because I feel I should explain. It wasn't about you. Worrow just got me at a bad time, and I couldn't tell her what was really wrong.'

'Which is? C'mon, spill the beans; you owe me that,' Ruby said, despite apologising for prying before.

'I'm pregnant,' Eve said, tears springing to her eyes.

Ruby reached out and gave her shoulder a squeeze in an act of solidarity. It was a mannerism she had picked up from Jack. Eve had been married less than a year and had just taken out a joint mortgage on her home. 'I take it this isn't welcome news?'

'Scott's over the moon,' Eve replied, using her napkin to dab her tears. 'He hates my job, and now I'm pregnant he wants me to leave. He says it's too dangerous for the baby.'

'What are you going to do?' Ruby said, at a loss for what to say. She was in no position to give advice given the state of her own personal life.

'I don't know. All I've ever wanted is to be a detective. It's so unfair. If I was a man I wouldn't have to choose.'

'I'm not disagreeing with you there,' Ruby said, keenly aware of the sacrifices she had made to keep her job. 'But you should be on restricted duties at the very least. I can speak to your husband if you like, reassure him that you'll be taken care of.' At least now she knew why Eve had refused to fight at the raid, and sworn off alcohol during their night out.

'I'm not sure he'd listen,' Eve sniffed. 'I've been a right cow lately. My hormones are all over the place. One minute I'm fine, the next I'm angry for no reason at all.'

'Hormones, who needs them, eh?' Ruby said. But things had changed between them. It would be some time before she would trust Eve again.

'I'm so sorry, Ruby, you're a good sergeant. I shouldn't have said what I did.'

'What *did* you say? Worrow was very vague.'

'Luddy confided that you'd visited Goldie that day. He told me not to say anything, but I had to go and blurt it out, didn't I? I told Worrow you were visiting known criminals and not following procedure. It was a stupid thing to do, and I've felt terrible ever since. I can go back to her if you like, tell her it was all a mistake?'

'It couldn't do any harm,' Ruby said, exhaling a sigh of relief. 'Best not to mention we had this chat, or she'll think I coerced you.'

'Of course. Thanks for being so understanding. I'm happy to go on restricted while I sort things out.'

'Just do what's right for you. And if you ever need to chat, my door is always open… literally.' Ruby popped a chip into her mouth. She should have been happy, but she was feeling betrayed. The knowledge that Luddy had been gossiping behind her back felt like a punch to the gut. What else had he been saying? Was there anyone in her team that she could trust?

CHAPTER FIFTY-TWO

Ruby stripped out of her suit and threw it on the bed. There was no soft music or candlelight for the meeting she planned with Downes. She wondered if he had really wanted to come at all. He had looked so tired at work. A good night's sleep would be more beneficial than a night of rampant sex. She gave her leggings a quick shake before pulling them on. There was no need to dress up for what she had planned, and Ruby was pretty sure he would not want to stay when he discovered just how far she was entrenched with the Crosby family.

The deceit had wrapped itself around her like a cocoon, and the longer it went on, the stronger the lies became. Why was she doing a U-turn and telling him anyway? To ease her guilt? To allow him to take on the burden and decide what to do with her? Was she being selfish? She could peel off her clothes right now and forget about her full confession. Her encounter with Worrow was still playing on her mind and she needed someone in her corner in case the shit hit the fan. The doorbell emitted a weak whine. The batteries were going again. It was not as if she had many visitors. Pulling on her sweatshirt, her heart began to pound as she pulled back the latch on the door.

'Am I early?' Downes said, looking crestfallen. For as long as they'd had their arrangement, she had always answered the door in a state of undress. It separated work Ruby from sexy Ruby, but tonight the lines were blurred. The look on her face told him that sex was not on the agenda.

'I'm sorry to lure you here under false pretences, but I really need to talk and I didn't want an audience.'

Downes took a seat, his long legs stretched out in front of him. Tugging off his tie, he rolled it up and pushed it into his jacket pocket. 'I knew you were in trouble.'

Ruby handed him a glass of rum and coke. Something to take the edge from what she was about to say.

'You could say that. But first I need to ask you a question. Can I trust you? No bullshit; give it to me straight.'

Downes tilted his head as he offered a bemused smile. 'Of course. And while we're here I'm just your friend. Whatever you say won't go outside these four walls, unless you want it to.'

Seconds passed as she tried to assemble her words. 'You're very near retirement; I don't want to drag you down.'

Downes clasped her knee and gave it a squeeze. 'It can't be that bad, can it?'

Ruby knocked back her drink, taking comfort in its warmth as it slid down her throat.

Downes frowned. 'Now you're worrying me. Are you pregnant or something?'

'Good God no. It's about work.' She paused. Did she see a trace of disappointment flicker across Downes's face? It must have been relief in disguise.

He gave a soft chuckle. 'Then pour me another drink, girl; sounds like it's going to be a long night.'

The words felt like rocks in her throat: each confession worse than the last. Her on-off affair with Nathan, their adopted daughter, her visit to Goldie, and the unreported emails directed solely at her. Downes's face was expressionless throughout, but by the rate he was sinking her booze the words were having their effect.

'And you kept all of this to yourself? Why didn't you come to me earlier? It's not as if you didn't have the opportunity.'

'I didn't want to involve you; it wouldn't have been fair.'

'So what's changed?'

'I think I know who the door-knocker killer is.'

'Shit,' Downes said. 'Who is it?'

'I've got a suspicion it's my daughter. Lucy, or whatever she calls herself now. It's why I've come to you. I need your help bringing her in tomorrow. I think I know where she's going to be.'

'And how did you get that information?'

'Through my contacts,' Ruby replied, staring into her empty glass.

'The Crosbys.' It was a statement, not a question.

'Lenny. Nathan knows nothing about it. Please don't ask me any more.'

'Meaning,' Downes paused, 'you had to give something in return? Did he hurt you?'

'Oh no, nothing like that. But you're right; there was an… exchange. It's finished now. Nobody got hurt.'

'Hmm… but there was that drugs raid. The one they'd been planning for months. The one that fell apart because someone had tipped them off?'

'And there's this,' Ruby said, changing the subject swiftly as she pulled a sheet of folded paper from her pocket. 'These are the stills from the internet café that I mentioned in briefing. Judging by the times, we're pretty certain this is our suspect.' She handed over the grainy image of a person with short dark bobbed hair.

'Looks a bit like Worrow,' Downes joked, squinting at the image.

'It matches the description of the woman Goldie told me about. I'm going to disclose it to Worrow at first light. But I'm not telling her about my daughter, or how I got this information in the first place.'

Downes tutted. 'Ruby, Ruby, Ruby. What a tangled web we weave.'

She looked at him uncertainly. 'What are you going to do?'

'What do you want me to do?'

Ruby shrugged, feeling like an axe was about to drop at any minute. 'Do what you feel is right.'

'This does my head in, you know that? You're getting paid to lock up criminals, then sneaking off to see them on job time. You could lose your job.'

Guilt and shame washed over Ruby and she bit back the tears that threatened to flow. She drew in a deep breath. Crying had brought her merciless teasing from her brother as a child. It was a sign of weakness, and she hated herself for being at such a low point in her life. She wanted to tell Downes that she realised how stupid she'd been, that she was disgusted with herself for risking her career and felt every inch the loathed 'bent copper' for providing evidence which could have collapsed the raid. She opened her mouth to speak, but the lump in her throat grew and she could not trust herself to utter the words. Her chin wobbled and she shielded her face in her hands, catching the tears which were now trailing between her fingers without her permission.

'I'm sorry, I never meant for any of this to happen.'

Downes squeezed her shoulder. 'Hush now, you're not the first copper to get themselves in hot water and you won't be the last. I don't suppose you've eaten, have you? Let me order in some food. You'll feel better with some grub inside you.'

Ruby nodded, her sobs subsiding. Downes looked around the room for a takeaway menu. A rush of loneliness hit her. The dynamics in their relationship had changed, and they had broken all of the rules. No discussion of work, no sharing a meal, and definitely no crying on his shoulder. It begged the question: was their friendship over? And how would she cope on her own?

But Downes was not leaving her any time soon. The next few hours were spent discussing options over a takeaway Chinese.

Relief swept over Ruby as it became apparent he had no intention of reporting her to her superiors. She would have to ensure no evidence of any kind could be traced back to her, then deny any involvement if she was questioned. At least she hadn't taken any payment from Lenny. If she had, Downes might have turned her in, and she wouldn't have blamed him. But she was as much a victim in this sorry affair as anyone else, and all she wanted to do was to put it right.

Ruby rubbed a bleary eye as she looked at her watch. 'It's gone one a.m., you'd better be going.'

'I'm not leaving you here on your own. Do you want to come back to mine and stay the night?'

Downes's townhouse was five minutes' walk from the station, and the pretty tree-lined estate where he lived also housed other police officers on her shift. 'No, someone will see us and put two and two together. I'm OK, honestly.'

He stood up from the cramped chair and stretched his limbs. 'In that case, I'm staying with yous. Try not to abuse me in the night, I'm too tired.'

Ruby gave a short laugh and followed him to the bedroom. They spooned, listening to the gentle howl of the wind through the crack in her bedroom window. His strong arms gave her comfort, and she had the best night's sleep in weeks.

She awoke the next morning to the sound of the shower and pushed back her tousled hair as Downes emerged from a puff of steam.

'For the love of God, how do you use that shower? There're two settings: Baltic or lobster boil. I'm fecking freezing.'

Ruby cast an eye over his muscular shoulders, trailing down to the small towel draped over his torso. The slight paunch did not detract from him in the slightest. Ruby didn't want to return to reality yet. Tonight was a late shift, and it was an hour before her alarm clock was due to go off. Snuggling back under the duvet, she pulled back a corner, enticing him inside. 'If you want I can warm you up.'

Downes smiled in return, whipping off the towel to rough-dry his hair. 'I know your game, lassie: fiddling with the temperature to get me into bed. You only had to ask.'

CHAPTER FIFTY-THREE

The battered computer processor whirred as it fought to keep up with the programmes she had opened. Ruby clicked on the search engine, typing in scenes describing how the bodies had been found. Forensics on the memorial cards had been disappointing because whoever sent them had covered their tracks. But it gave Ruby the incentive to clear the paperwork from her desk. She had declined Downes's offer of a cooked breakfast, her mind too occupied with thoughts of Lucy to spend the morning relaxing in a café. Today was a late shift, which afforded her more time. But Ruby did not want to be anywhere else. A quick visit to her mum and she was back at work, four hours before she was due in.

Her search history consisted of some very strange phrases, but 'eating cucumber sandwiches in lounge scene' had to be in her top ten. But the return was so vast she did not know where to begin. She clicked on the images, pausing to change the search term. 'Victorian, book, movie, scene in lounge, cucumber sandwiches.' Like her other searches, it was random, but worth a shot. She found it on the third page of results. The image of a woman on a patterned chaise longue made Ruby's heart patter in her chest. A table was displayed in front of her, triangular cucumber sandwiches on a neatly laid tray.

This was it. This was the re-enacted scene.

A memory resurfaced of a movie Ruby had seen over ten years ago. *Lucy's Christmas*. It was too close to her own life for comfort, and she had vowed never to watch it again. A corny feel-good story set in Victorian times, it featured a little girl that had been given up for adoption. A blonde-haired, blue-eyed little girl named Lucy. The first time Ruby had watched it she'd sobbed the whole way through. Like an old-fashioned version of *Annie*, it was a story of past regrets and new reconnections, as the little girl found her real mother again. A tragic parting, a fairy-tale reunion, with both lives intertwined. The movie began as Lucy's biological mother sat sadly in her living room mourning the loss of her own mother. The death notice, the Victorian mourning traditions: they were all part of the scene. Having lost the one person who made her give up her daughter the woman vowed to reclaim her little girl. Several obstacles crossed her path, but all was resolved on Christmas Day. Ruby hated that movie because real life was not made of fairy tales and she couldn't bear the fact her child shared the same name. She grimaced as she looked up an online movie site to find more information. The details were vague. She would have to watch it again.

But Ruby did not cry when she saw the film again because this time she was in her office watching with the eye of an investigator. The mother figure named Melissa looked nothing like victims Emily and Monica. But the scenes were exactly the same. Ruby held her breath as the film began with Melissa staring mournfully at a death notification: a black-edged card just like the ones delivered to Ruby's desk.

The scenes could not have been any more exact. Melissa, in a floral dress, having tea and cucumber sandwiches, a temporary respite after being misdirected to her daughter's true whereabouts. Falling asleep in her Victorian nightgown, her hair spilling out on the pillow as she dreams of being reunited with her daughter. Ruby watched through to the final scene. A touching moment, when the woman was sitting in the car ready to drive away into the sunset with her little girl. It had all been focused around that special Christmas Day when Lucy asked Santa for her true mummy. At last they were reunited, and the wicked woman who ran the orphanage was taken away, replaced with someone kinder to care for the children who were left behind. It was an old-fashioned, heart-warming fairy tale. Ruby could imagine her suspect watching it over and over until she knew every word, every scene, every detail off by heart. But nowhere in the movie had glass baubles found their way into the mother's stomach. Was it an action born out of anger because Emily had not re-enacted the scene to perfection? And had Anita Devine ever watched this movie too? If so, it might give her a slim hope of survival. Ruby looked up a number and picked up the phone.

'Mr Devine, this is Detective Sergeant Ruby Preston from Shoreditch Serious Crime Unit. We've spoken before.'

'Yes?' Joseph breathed down the phone, his panic audible. Ruby could have kicked herself for her insensitivity. It was obvious he was expecting bad news.

'It's nothing really, just a quick question. Has Anita has ever seen the movie *Lucy's Christmas*? It's an old feel-good film, not very well known.'

Joseph started speaking before Ruby had even finished her sentence. 'Yes, she must have watched that movie a hundred times or more. She ordered it on DVD from some obscure website and tortured herself with it. In the end, I threw it away. Why? What's that got to do with anything?'

'It's just a line of enquiry I'm pursuing. And Joseph? If we have any real news, good or bad, we'll tell you in person. It won't be delivered over the phone.'

Ruby bid her goodbyes, grateful for the lead. It was also a small glimmer of hope. And right now, it was Anita's only chance of keeping her and Sophie alive.

CHAPTER FIFTY-FOUR

'La la la la.' Lucy danced down the steps, giggling as she reached the last one, and jumping with both feet together. Her voice carried in a forced high-pitched tone, and Anita prepared herself for her visit. She wanted to scream. She wanted to cry, to bunch her fists and launch herself at her captor until she broke free. But she knew from experience that her best chance of being released was to stay calm and give her persecutor whatever she wanted.

The last few hours had been hell, and she had no choice but to believe Lucy's reassurances that Sophie was still alive. Being good in emergencies was a trait which had got her out of a few sticky situations. The worse things got the calmer she became. It was uncanny. She used to worry about it until she found her niche in counselling. Her husband joked that she attracted all the crazies. It was all the more reason for her to have picked up on Lucy's mental state when she visited. But she so wanted it to be real she had put aside any niggling reservations. For now, Lucy was happy and it was up to Anita to make sure she stayed that way.

'Mummy,' Lucy said; the childish words strangely out of place for her adult frame. 'It's going to be Christmas soon.' She rushed forward, opening her arms for a hug. She was dressed as a little girl now and freakishly frightening. Her eyes flitted back and forth while narrow lips mumbled as she spoke under her breath.

Anita counted to ten in her mind, forcing her body to relax, leaning her head into Lucy's bony frame to accept her affection. It was going against every natural instinct, but she forced a deep, calming breath and was rewarded by the look of surprise on her captor's face. She had not been expecting her compliance. Not a second time. But Anita would do what it took to keep her baby alive.

Lucy stepped back and clapped her hands. 'Oh Mummy, this is so exciting. Do you like Christmas? Do you?'

Anita nodded, mumbling 'mmm' under the slimy gag which was making her stomach churn.

Lucy bit her bottom lip. 'Silly me, let's get this off,' she said, her fingers hastily undoing the knot. 'Now don't do anything silly, will you? Because the last lady did something silly and she's not around anymore.'

Anita's eyes fell on the bloodstained floor and she nodded. The smell of decay, the broken floorboards: everything about this room screamed danger. She focused on her lungs, drawing in breath and exhaling it again. In... out... in... Anything rather than allow her natural instincts to emerge. Because every sinew in her body was battling to punch, kick and fight. She took a slow breath as the gag was removed, licking the bitter taste from her lips. This was not the time to scream. This was the time to take things calm and slow. She smiled, looking at Lucy as if she was the most precious thing in the world. Because that was what Lucy wanted and keeping Lucy happy was her best chance of saving her and Sophie's lives.

Lucy stared as if observing a new species in the zoo. She clearly was not used to Anita's behaviour and seemed at a loss as to how to react. Anita wanted to ask about Sophie, demand for her to be set free. But instead she gave her a sad smile and waited for Lucy to speak.

'Aren't you cross?' Lucy said, folding her arms.

'No. I'm a little sad for you and feeling uncomfortable in this chair, but I'm not cross. Why would I be cross when I've found you?'

Lucy frowned. 'So you're happy to see me?'

'Of course I am, darling; I've waited all my life for you.'

Lucy jutted out her bottom lip in a pout. 'You're lying. You want to trick me – because you're scared.'

Anita smiled, pushing back the hysterical laugh bubbling up in her throat. She swallowed it back, emitting a gentle chuckle, her words calm and even. 'Don't you remember how happy I was when you turned up at my door? I said I'd waited all my life for you to come knocking. Seeing you was the happiest day of my life.'

Lucy nodded. 'I remember. But this is different. I took you here; you must hate me for that. The others did.'

'Sweetheart, I don't know about any other people, but I do know this: you're my daughter. From the second I saw you I knew that it was true. You must have been hurt by some very bad people to bring you to this dark place, and that breaks my heart. So it doesn't matter how I got here. You don't even have to tell me why; because now we start our lives afresh. Forget those other people who let you down. It's you and me now.'

Lucy eyed her suspiciously. It was the longest conversation she had ever had with her guests. And it was way too good to be true. Lucy's childish tone had dropped for now as she spoke with the voice of an adult. 'What about your other family? Your husband, your son and daughter?'

'They've had me all their lives. And I'm guessing that you've had no one. This is my chance to make things right. But there is something I need you to do for me so we can start on the right foot.'

'What do you want?' Lucy said, her voice flat.

'I need you to tell me where Sophie is.'

'She's asleep upstairs.'

'Good girl. Now we have an exciting adventure ahead, don't we?'

Lucy nodded; a slow bob of the head, her eyes uncertain.

'But it needs to be just you and me, nobody else, right?' Anita said.

Lucy nodded faster this time. 'You want me to get rid of Sophie?' She flashed a smile as if she had just been waiting for permission all along.

Anita cleared her throat, feeling as if she was drowning on the inside. 'No. I need you to see that she's returned home safely to her father. She's just a little girl, just like you, and we don't want anything bad to happen to her now, do we? If Sophie gets hurt, then the police will be looking for us and we'd be all over the television and in newspapers in all the countries. But if she is returned home I could write a letter saying I'm safe and I want to be left alone. Do you understand what I mean?'

'So you want me to take Sophie back home alive?'

'Yes. Then we'll be free to start again. And how exciting would that be? Because that's what you want, isn't it?'

'I guess I could do that. But there's something we have to do first. You have to pass the test. If you don't pass the test, then you're not my mother.'

Anita's stomach grumbled. All she'd had to sustain her was a glass of water, which brought with it the understanding that if she'd had nothing to eat then neither had Sophie. Was she still under the influence of the same drugs that made their capture possible? Anita realised that Lucy was staring at her. Fists clenched, they rested on the hips of that ridiculous outfit. She looked like a reject from *Oliver Twist*. 'Oh I do hope I pass,' Anita said, grateful she couldn't read her mind. 'I've got my hopes up now. I can't imagine us not being together.' She considered asking Lucy to untie her, allow her to speak to her daughter. But slowly slowly catchy monkey. Her senses told her to take things gradually. Lucy could change with the click of a finger, and she had made it quite clear that the other women had met a bad end. There was no doubt that this was a life-and-death situation. All she wanted was for Sophie to be returned home, safe and well.

'Do you like Christmas?' Lucy said, her face illuminated by the flashing lights on the tree.

'It's my favourite time of the year,' Anita replied, hoping it was the right answer.

'And do you like my clothes? Strike a chord, do they?'

'They're beautiful. I have seen them before but… ' Anita paused, wracking her brains for the answer. The Victorian clothes, the Christmas tree, and the music box she left on the shelf. She *had* recognised something about her. 'Silly me. Can you help?'

Lucy shook her head. 'I'm going to play my music box. Perhaps that will jog your memory.'

Anita nodded. 'Can I please use the toilet? It's just that… '

'Not yet. It's time. First the music. Then you'll know what to do. If you're my *true* mother, that is.'

As Lucy wound the music box, Anita felt as if she were part of a macabre bedtime story, being tested for her worthiness like 'The Princess and the Pea'. Only in this case, her life was hanging by a very fine thread.

CHAPTER FIFTY-FIVE

Ruby stared at the phone number, kicking herself for missing the call. It was not one she recognised, yet the recording of the young woman's voice left her in no doubt. It was Lucy – and she was trying to get in touch. Lenny had promised he would find her. Had he passed her phone number on? Ruby played the message back a second time. Silence fell as the answering machine picked up, followed by a resigned sigh: 'This was a bad idea,' the caller said, before ending the call.

Immediately she dialled the number. Her heart cranked up a notch in her chest as she waited for an answer. After six rings she was about to hang up when an unsteady voice came on the line. Ruby gripped the phone tightly to her ear, trying to distinguish its owner.

'Hello?' The voice was frail, but far from young and Ruby wondered if she had misdialled.

'This is Ruby Preston,' she said authoritatively. 'With whom am I speaking?'

'Hello?' the voice repeated.

Ruby tutted, wondering if it was one of those daft answer machines that played a trick on you by pretending to answer the phone. 'Is there anyone there?'

'Hello? Ruby? Is that you?' the woman responded.

Ruby's heart faltered as recognition kicked in. Surely not? How could it be? She took a deep breath. 'Mum? Is… that you?'

'Yes, dear. Why are you calling? Have you lost your phone?'

Ruby rubbed her forehead as she tried to clear the confusion. Where was her mother? Was she still at the home? And if so, why was she answering the mobile phone that had just called? 'Have you got a visitor?' Ruby said, her heart racing. It was the only plausible explanation she could think of. Either she was on someone else's phone, or her mother had been kidnapped. She prayed Joy's lucid phase would continue long enough to answer her questions. Pushing her hand in her pocket, she pulled out a set of car keys. She needed to get to Oakwood to find out what was going on.

By the time Ruby got to the car, all she could hear was the background noise of teacups rattling on a tray and the familiar sound of the inoffensive television programmes that played on a loop in the home, *Countryfile* being a particular favourite.

A muffled noise erupted as the phone seemed to switch hands, and the call was abruptly brought to an end. Swearing under her breath, Ruby redialled the number, but was rewarded with the deadening tone of a phone that was switched off. But she knew the number of Oakwood off by heart. Her nails tapped on the steering wheel as she willed staff to pick up the phone. It felt like a lifetime to Ruby, and at last, a woman's voice chanted on the other end. 'Hello Oakwood Care Home, how can I help you?'

Ruby was less gracious with her response, but her abruptness was fuelled only by concern. 'This is Ruby, Joy Preston's daughter. Can you tell me if she has a visitor with her? I'm on my way over, but I've had a strange call from a mobile phone. Mum was on the other end.'

It was a slight fib, but Ruby did not have time to go into details of how she came across the number.

'Oh, I don't recall Joy having any visitors, but I'll go and check,' the woman responded.

Ruby set her phone to hands-free and allowed it to echo through the speakers of the car as she drove. It had not occurred to her to tell her colleagues where she was going, because she was too wrapped up worrying about Joy. Was it really Lucy's phone number she had just dialled? And if so, what were her intentions towards her mum? Ruby felt jittery as the staff member's voice boomed through the speakers. She grasped for the button to turn down the volume.

'Hello again, dear, there's nobody with Joy now. I've checked the visitor's book and as I thought there's nobody signed in for a visit, but…'

'Yes?' Ruby responded, growing increasingly agitated. Visitors had to pass reception to enter and needed to know the pass code to open the second set of doors. So how did her mum have a visitor without anybody knowing?

'Well, I've spoken to some of the other residents. They seem to think that there *was* a visitor with her earlier: a young lady. But they're not there now. I'm sorry dear, but until we check the CCTV we've no way of knowing who it was.'

Ruby sighed with relief. At least Joy had not been kidnapped. After recent events with the door-knocker killer anything was possible. She replayed her late-night visit from Lenny in her mind. He had threatened to pay a visit to her mother if she did anything wrong. Had she said or done something out of turn since then? What about their recent rendezvous in the car? But he had looked more than happy when she provided him with the information of the proposed raid.

Ruby chewed the cherry red lipstick from her bottom lip. Oakwood was not a prison. Her mother was allowed as many visitors as she wanted. Sometimes old school friends would come, an occasional neighbour, or a distant relative. Ruby liked to keep tabs on people's comings and goings and always checked the visitor's book when she attended the home. Her continued acquaintance with Nathan ran the risk of Joy being a victim of a revenge attack. When the attacker could not get to the focus of their hatred their nearest and dearest became targets instead. It was why they gave each other such a wide berth in public. And God knows she had made enough enemies in her own job. She would be speaking to management about this. If they did not tighten up their security she would have to think about moving her mother elsewhere. But Joy was settled at Oakwood, and she did not want to put her through the distress of a new environment.

After questioning her mother the identity of a visitor was discovered; the same description as her suspect: slim, dark haired, with sunglasses shielding her face. A woman who went to the toilet and left her mobile phone behind. By some miracle, Joy had answered the call. This was usually beyond her capabilities; phone calls only served to confuse her. But today Ruby had been in luck. When her visitor discovered Joy on her phone she snatched it from her grasp and wasted no time in leaving.

CCTV revealed a figure entering the home behind a large family; a good disguise for someone who didn't want to sign in. Upon leaving, all Ruby could see was the same dark-haired figure cloaked by a delivery man as he made his exit. That was someone who was aware of CCTV and how it worked, and they had bypassed the door code by tailgating someone on the way in. Ruby did not hesitate in recommending that the home tightened their security.

But for what purpose was the visit? Was it to shake Ruby up? Or test the waters for what lay ahead? After a quick goodbye to her mum, she headed outside.

Rubbing the nape of her neck, Ruby was unable to shake off the sensation of being watched. She glanced around the tree-lined car park. The dining room was filling up, and as they sat at the window some of the old-age pensioners were looking her way – but their gaze was soft and yielding. Ruby exhaled in frustration as she rooted in her bag for her keys. Was she being paranoid, or was Lucy closing in? Involving her mother had brought things to a whole new level, and she had to report the incident if she was to keep her safe. As Ruby drove away, she wondered how much longer it would be before all her secrets came tumbling down around her.

CHAPTER FIFTY-SIX

The hair on the back of Anita's neck stood sentry as the music box tinkled in the stifling air. Each pin slowly plucked the steel drum, enhancing the terror of her surroundings. As the tune slowly wound down, Anita took in Lucy's hopeful features, her eyes roaming over her clothes. The blonde wig, the old-fashioned clothing, and a little girl in search of her mummy… a spark of recognition lit in her brain. Could it be? She replayed a movie soundtrack in the confines of her mind. *Lucy's Christmas*. Of course. She had watched it dozens of times. It was the music box that had put her off. The tune wasn't the same. But it was close enough for her to recognise the meaning. Her pulse quickened. So this is what her captor meant. Images flashed in her mind, aiding her recollection. As if she herself was in a scene of a movie. But there was no kidnap scene involved. She had to find her own way out of that. 'I remember,' Anita said, her voice raking through her dry throat.

A raspy breath cooled her cheek. 'Good. Then you'll know what to say.'

The others could not have known what Lucy meant. And perhaps Lucy had set them up to fail all along. But as the music box was tightly wound for the second time the answers instantly appeared to Anita. For it was a movie she had cried over many times, her lips forming soundless words as she relayed each scene. Lucy's eyes flitted up to the basement door which had been left tantalisingly open. Anita jerked against her bindings as Lucy looked away. But it was no use. She could barely move. Frustrated tears sprang to her eyes, and a sob escaped her throat before she could close her mouth to stop it. She hadn't eaten a thing. Nor had she been allowed to use the toilet and had suffered the shame of warm urine trickling down the thin material of her jeans. Each moment of discomfort made her heart ache for Sophie. Where was she? And how was she coping? She would not survive much longer, if indeed she was alive at all. She had to face the truth. Help was not coming. It was up to her to break free.

Lucy's eyes narrowed as she turned to face her. Her voice was churlish, spoken in a tone better suited to a sulking child. 'You're crying. Why are you crying?'

Anita sniffed, delivering a watery smile. 'It's because I'm so happy.' Her heart faltered in the hope that she would be believed. Her voice was smooth, her words delivered in the same calm tones she had learned in her training as a counsellor.

Lucy regarded her for a few minutes before nodding her head and laying down the music box. It gave a little tinkle, the last strands of 'Hush Little Baby' echoing in their darkened chamber. Her blonde curls looked freakishly out of place, and now that her face was scrubbed clean Anita could see her for what she really was.

'Are you ready to play?' Lucy said, tongue darting across her teeth like an animal about to devour its prey.

Anita nodded. She knew what would happen if she got it wrong. She wanted to scream Sophie's name, to know that her little girl was safe. She told herself that she was still alive. Their bond was strong, and in the depths of her being she felt her daughter's life force pulsating faintly, just as it did when she was pregnant.

Her flesh and blood. Unlike the creature before her.

She stared at the back of Lucy's head, sending invisible daggers of hate. There was something about their demeanour that told Anita this would not end well. The least she could do was to give herself a fighting chance as the final moments drew near. 'Could you untie me? The woman in the movie was standing beside the tree; I think it would be better if we got it right, don't you?'

Lucy frowned. Her childish voice dissipated as she spoke, and her tone was low and guttural. 'You better not play any tricks. If you play tricks I'll kill Sophie. I mean it.'

Anita's heart pounded in her chest surging a shot of adrenalin through her veins. Her body was preparing for the fight, and she fought hard to portray an expression of calm. She was weak and dizzy and needed time to gather her strength. She made a silent vow. Once unbound, she would never allow Lucy to bind her again. 'As I said, I've been waiting all my life to meet you. Why would I want to run away now?'

Lucy delivered a narrow-eyed glance. It was a look that said she was not so easily fooled, and she turned to delve her hand into the shoe box she had rested on the shelf.

Anita caught the glint of steel as Lucy drew near. It was a boning knife with a six-inch blade. Anita recognised it as she had a similar one at home. One she had lost. Or had she? Lately, things had been going missing, objects had been moved. She had thought she was going mad, but now… her eyes widened as Lucy approached. How many times had she been in her home before they met? Lucy's eyes held a manic stare, her tongue darting from between her teeth to lick her lips once more.

'Please don't,' Anita whimpered, as Lucy stood behind her; the cool blade kissing the skin on her wrists. Anita closed her eyes: blocking out the basement, the smells, and the lunatic tugging at her wrists… until all she could see was Sophie's face. If she was going to die, she would take love with her in her final moments, not terror or despair.

CHAPTER FIFTY-SEVEN

Flecks of rain sprinkled Ruby's face as she ran down the narrow path. Being fit added another layer to her armour. She had good legs and strong biceps and wanted to keep it that way. With her fitness test coming up, her superiors did not begrudge her a run during her break. But her mind was on the figure behind her who had been following for some time. The grate of their heavy breath came thick and fast as they struggled to keep up with her pace.

Coming to an abrupt halt, Ruby bent to tie her shoelaces. Her follower was close. Extending her foot, Ruby knocked them off their feet, sending them stumbling to the pavement below. Launching herself upon them, she wasted no time in pinning their wrists to the ground. The person did not put up a fight as Ruby pushed back their hood.

'What are you doing here?' she said, glaring at Helen with disbelief. It was not the first time Ruby had bumped into a journalist, but never while she was out on a run.

'It's not illegal to exercise, is it?' Helen said between breaths, sweat clinging to her mousy hair.

Patting her down for weapons, Ruby sprung to her feet. 'Don't give me that bullshit; I know you've been following me.' Grabbing the front of Helen's hoodie, she pulled her back onto her feet. Keeping hold of her sweater, Ruby gave her a quick shake. 'Come on then, I'm waiting.'

'Alright, alright, let go of me, will you?' Helen blurted, smoothing back her sweater as Ruby released her grip. 'I just wanted to see where you were going. There's a lot of buzz around this case, and I heard you might have some contacts.'

'And I was going for a run,' Ruby said, unimpressed. 'Next time I catch you following me I'll have you arrested for harassment.'

'Harassment?' Helen said, her eyes wide and disbelieving.

'Just keep out of my way in future. I was going to give you the heads up after our chat in the café. But now you can go through the official channels like everyone else.' It may have seemed harsh, but she'd had enough of people picking over the bones of her personal life. Lately, the lines between work and home seemed more blurred than ever.

Ruby replayed their conversation as she clicked through her emails trying, but not succeeding, to maintain a level of concentration. She hated admin. Loathed it, in fact. But if she didn't get the overtime and leave requests signed off she would be the least popular person in the station. Apart from Worrow, of course; although Ruby was back in her good books after coming up with the movie that seemed to fit the killer's MO. Luddy had been tasked with contacting the websites that sold it online. But there were so many, not to count the free online pirate sites where you could watch it for free. The killer could have obtained it anytime in the last twenty years, and Ruby could not help but feel she had loaded Luddy down with another fruitless task. Her thoughts floated back to Lucy. Was she really capable of taking a mother and child? And if so, where were they? Outer London was a hive of rat-runs, derelict council buildings and vermin-infested squats. Could she be holed up there? Or were her claims of homelessness a cover for what was really going on? Her efforts at tracing the number that called her had come up blank. Like Nathan, the caller had used a pay as you go: it was now permanently switched off. There was no doubt that

Lucy was playing games with her and communicated at a time only of her choosing.

The information she obtained from Goldie had not been worth the trade-off for her integrity, and Ruby buried her head in her hands feeling the magnitude of it all. This wasn't just about Anita. Sophie's life hung in the balance as well. She should be doing more. She drummed her fingers against the desk, resisting the urge to call Nathan. Lucy was his daughter too. If anyone could trace her Nathan could. But what if he found her? What then? She would go underground faster than a rabbit at a shoot, along with any chance of locating their missing people.

But there *was* someone else who could help. Someone who owed her. She plucked her mobile from her blazer pocket, straining her neck through the open door to ensure five minutes of privacy while she sent the text. She drew up 'L' for 'Lenny' on her contacts list, trying to keep the words as ambiguous as she could.

'Found her yet? Fed up chasing my tail.'

Ruby chewed her bottom lip. It was the politest way of getting across what was playing on her mind. 'Let's see what you make of this,' she mumbled under her breath; pressing send before she changed her mind. Two seconds later she deleted the sent text and prayed it would not come back to bite her. She diverted her attention to her computer and the work screaming out to be completed.

At the top of her bulging email inbox lay a response to an enquiry she had forgotten all about. The credit checks on Worrow's frantic caller. She knew she was taking a chance investigating one of their own, but it was with good reason – although, if she was picked up on it, she would have to come up with a valid excuse. Having a bad feeling about her superior did not qualify as a legitimate use of police systems, but she had made the enquiry on the grounds of the prevention and detection of crime. Downes had trusted her enough to authorise the request so it was more than her neck on the line. As Ruby clicked through the file it seemed she was right to be suspicious. She pored over the information, her mind working overtime.

CHAPTER FIFTY-EIGHT

Death did not come as Anita expected. The tugging sensation lasted seconds as her bindings snapped against the pressure of the knife. First her wrists, then her ankles. It took a few seconds for full feeling to return, and as Lucy stood over her, knife in hand, she knew it would not pay to aggravate her captor.

They regarded each other with suspicion as Anita forced out a 'thank you', rubbing the redness from her torn wrists. She wanted to cry, but she had to hold it together because there was still a faint hope of escape. Lucy's eyes never left hers as she took her place beside the tree, waiting for one false move.

'Well, come on then, time to begin,' Lucy said, still gripping the knife.

Anita rose, feeling like something from an old zombie movie as she hobbled, stiff and erratic, towards the tree. One foot in front of the other, she thought, resisting the temptation to glance up at the open door. Freedom was so close she could taste it, but she was not strong enough to run. Not yet. Her jeans had dried of their own accord, and the damp canvas swished as it rubbed against her thighs. Hunger consumed her. Her parched throat cried out for water, but, most importantly of all, she needed to find her daughter. Lucy grinned lewdly as Anita pretended to admire the decorations so carefully applied.

It was only then that Anita noticed the painstaking attention to detail. Shiny baubles, tiny wooden rocking horses, and glossy candy canes; they all graced the bent-up branches of the cheap synthetic tree. Anita imagined the previous victims cloaked in terror and confusion as they tried to understand their task. She suppressed a shudder. It was too late for them now. She had to focus on saving Sophie.

It was just her and Lucy now, whoever or whatever Lucy was. Anita was a naturally compassionate person, but she had carefully removed any remnants of pity for her captor. It was the only way if she was to kill without mercy in order to survive. She was confident there was nobody else involved. Lucy had made it very clear that she wanted it to be just them.

Lucy smiled that lewd grin as she fingered the decoration. There was a thirst behind her eyes and a storm cloud passed her face as light and dark battled for supremacy. Anita averted her gaze as panic rose in her chest, crawling like a long-legged spider up her throat and threatening to release the scream she had been suppressing since she awoke. She pressed her fingernails into her palms. If it were just her she might accept her fate, but the involvement of her daughter was something entirely different. She had allowed this woman into her home. And she would be the one to end this.

'It's almost Christmas,' Lucy said, staring at the tree.

Anita touched the wiry green branches and smiled. Lucy was still holding the knife, and she wondered if she was waiting for the excuse to plunge it in her chest. 'Yes, it is, and I'm so excited to be spending it with you.'

'But what if Santa doesn't bring me what I want, Mummy?' Lucy's knuckles whitened as her grip on the knife grew tighter.

The music box played eerily in the dim light. Like Lucy, it was off kilter, but Anita did not miss a beat as she recited her lines. Eyes shining, she stared at Lucy, praying that behind the ghoulish smile and freakish wig there lay a spark of compassion. 'Do you hear that? I played it the night you were born. I promised you the world. And it's time to keep my promises.' She paused, placing her left hand on Lucy's shoulder, just like they did in the movie scene.

Anita's face creased in a smile as she delivered the last line. 'My car's waiting outside, sweetheart. You're coming home with me.' The music box wore down and came to a halt. Anita had delivered the line word for word. Lucy's expression was one of wonder. Anita's heart hammered as she considered her options. What now?

'You did it,' Lucy whispered, her mouth open in amazement. With icy fingertips she reached out and touched Anita's face. It was as if she had never considered what to do when she got this far. 'You actually did it.'

'Of course I did, because every time I watched this movie I thought of you. Were you watching it too?' Anita said, but her words were mechanical as fear robbed her voice of its empathy.

'Yes, I was.' A shadow crossed Lucy's face and she narrowed her eyes. 'Why did you give me up? You said I meant the world to you and you wanted us to be together; so why did you give me away?'

Anita's glance flicked from Lucy to the knife which she was now clutching tightly to her chest. Was she imagining it or did Lucy seem disappointed because she had passed the test?

'I was fifteen when I got pregnant. Mum had died the year before and Dad wasn't coping. The first night I brought you home he threw you onto the bed because you were crying. He could have killed you. He had a terrible temper when he drank, and I could put up with him hurting me, but not my little girl. So I gave you up to keep you safe.'

Anita sighed as she recounted the fake story, hoping she was delivering a convincing performance. The reasons behind the adoption were personal and not to be shared with the monster she had come to hate. She blinked twice, conscious of the passing seconds as her daughter lay alone. 'You were so beautiful, a perfect child. It was the best chance you had of living in a normal, happy home.

But I never stopped hoping that you would come knocking on my door. And now here you are.'

'Here I am,' Lucy echoed, but her expression was vacant as she withdrew into herself.

Anita had dealt with many disturbed people and she recognised the signs. Lucy was totally unpredictable and could react without warning. Anita glanced from the knife to the door, her heart sinking. It took all of her strength just to stand. The time it would take for her to reach the stairs would not ensure her safety. But how long was Lucy going to continue with this charade? She could not afford to wait hours, days or weeks for this game to reach a conclusion. Perhaps it was revenge for years of abuse; a way of killing her mother for surrendering her to the wolves all those years ago. Anita knew deep down that it was not going to end well, because she could see that a part of Lucy relished the kill. She had no intention of returning her daughter to safety as promised, or of setting her free. Because, despite Lucy's twisted desperation to recreate an idyllic family scene, in the real world, dreams didn't always come true.

'Lucy,' Anita said, bringing her thoughts back, 'I need to use the toilet. Can you show me where it is?' She longed to escape the stench of the pit they were in and raked in a breath as anxiety pressed down hard on her chest.

'Do you like the decorations? They're pretty aren't they, especially these baubles,' Lucy said, touching them gently.

Fear tightened its hold, and Anita's chest heaved as the warm birth of panic made itself known. Slipping the glass bauble from the tree, she held it up under the light. 'I like this one the best. See how it sparkles, just like the one in the movie.'

Anita allowed it to slip through her fingers and fall on the floor. She knew it would provoke anger, but just a few seconds of distraction was all she needed to make her escape. It was now or never. Because she knew that Lucy would never let her go.

'What have you done?' Lucy said, bowing her head to stare at the bauble, which had broken into a hundred pieces against the wooden floor.

Drawing up all of her strength Anita brought forward her knee, smashing Lucy hard in the face. A strangled scream erupted as cartilage cracked upon impact. The clang of a knife reverberated in the room as she dropped the implement, clutching at her bleeding nose. Staggering back, her legs buckled, making her cry out as she hit her head against the floor. With shaking limbs Anita darted for the stairs, taking them two at a time.

Slamming the door behind her, she swivelled her head left and right, limbs shaking, eyes straining against the natural light. Just as she had imagined, she had been held captive in somebody's home. The scent of disinfectant overpowered her senses, but it was a blessed relief compared to what she had been forced to endure below. 'Sophie, where are you?' Anita cried, barely recognising the sound of her own voice as it rebounded around the cluttered rooms.

A cat mewed on the landing, curling its tail around her legs. Anita drew away, clouded in confusion. Here in the midst of all this horror was a family pet. A symbol of everyday life, out of place with the monstrosity of the situation.

She glanced at the back door: the promise of freedom so close to hand. But she was not leaving without her daughter. Lucy said Sophie was asleep. She had to be upstairs. Stumbling into the hall, she forced her legs up the narrow stairs. If she could just grab Sophie and run there was still time to get away. Turning left and right, she flung open doors, peering inside each room before moving on. Hot press, bedroom, bathroom. With each empty room her despair mounted, until she came to the last door on the right. Her eyes fell on the protruding metal padlock. For once, luck was on her side. It wasn't locked. A cry of relief rose from her throat as she threw it on the floor.

Slamming back the door, her jubilance was short-lived as she caught sight of the small figure on the single bed. 'Sophie,' she cried. 'Oh my baby, what has she done to you?' Relief and anger rose in equal measures. The cheap grey tracksuit Sophie was wearing was bulked at the crotch from the nappy underneath, and a thin layer of sweat glazed her brow. 'Mummy's here,' Anita cried, laying the tips of her shaking fingers onto her daughter's face. She was still alive; there was still time. Slowly she peeled back the plaster holding the drip in place. But as she did so the image of a face fell into her peripheral vision.

Heart hammering, Anita glanced to the side, a cold trickle of fear encasing her in an icy grip. It was not a person, but an array of wigs on styrofoam heads. Her lungs expelled the breath she was holding as she peered at the dresser to her right. Eyeshadows, foundation, perfume; every spare inch was covered with make-up and jewellery of varying colours and brands.

Above them, a dozen photos were sellotaped to the mirror. It was her: walking to school with Sophie, driving the car, and even in the supermarket on the weekly food shop. Time stood still as Anita glared in disbelief. The creak of a floorboard brought with it a renewed sense of urgency, and she babbled nonsensically, kissing her daughter's cheek as she scooped her up from the bed.

Sophie was alive, but for how long? She had to get out before her legs gave away. She turned for the door, fear slicing through her like an icy spear. But it was not a wig that made her recoil in horror. It was the person in the doorway, standing with their fists clenched.

'Help me,' Anita whispered, clinging to her child with the last of her strength. But as the stranger advanced upon her Anita knew that help was very far away.

CHAPTER FIFTY-NINE

'I knew you were going soft,' Lenny Crosby said, cracking his knuckles as he paced the polished oak floor. 'She's like a drug to you, isn't she? Why else would you turn your back on your own family for a stinking copper.'

'Fuck off, will you; I don't need this right now,' Nathan replied, knowing it would take more than a few expletives for Lenny to pack it in. Tweedy Steve stood, a giant of a man, closely monitoring the arguing brothers. But Nathan had no intention of getting him involved. He would allow Lenny to rant until he ran out of steam. No doubt their mum had sent Lenny over after Leona had gone around there crying that she had been dumped. Nathan rolled his eyes as Lenny continued with his tirade, delivering his words with spittle-laced venom.

'You want to end up penniless, is that it? Because that's what's gonna happen. I can't run the family business on my own. The clue is in the name... *family* business.' Lenny elongated the word, driving his message home.

'Jesus, Lenny, you talk as if it's the only way of making money. You got to move with the times. Look at the escort service. Half those girls are hooked on coke. You're only a few steps away from being like Frenchie. It's disgusting, that's what it is.' Nathan took a step towards Lenny. Judging by his dilated pupils, he was amped up himself. There was no reasoning with him when he was like this.

'So what about that nice bit you took on the other day?' Lenny said, a smile curling on his face.

Nathan folded his arms across his chest. 'It's because of her that I'm putting an end to it. We're taking advantage. It's not right.'

'Just listen to yourself, will you?' Lenny tapped his finger to his forehead. 'Have you lost the plot? Since when did you start taking the moral high ground?'

'Being in hospital gave me time to think. And it's not about Ruby, before you ask. I've had enough of being on the wrong side of the law. We've made our money; we don't need that shit anymore.'

'You haven't got a clue, have you? Ruby, the saint, who hates what we do. Well, your precious Ruby's a bent copper, and she's been plotting against you all along.'

'What? No. You're lying,' Nathan said, his face thunderous.

'She's as bent as they come. Where do you think we got that intel on the raid? She gave it to me. Here. Check my phone if you don't believe me.'

Lenny slid the mobile from his pocket, his fingers bringing up his latest text. The raid. It was because they had called it off that Nathan had got stabbed. It was a message from his suppliers who thought he was reneging on payment. In his line of business crossed wires could cost you your life.

Nathan looked at the text as Lenny shoved it under his nose.

'Found her yet? Fed up chasing my tail.'

He frowned as he checked the number. It was true. Ruby *had* texted Lenny from her phone. 'What's this all about?' Nathan said, thrusting the phone back into this brother's hand.

'She came to me a few days ago; said she had some intel that would be of use. Ask Mum if you don't believe me. She had the cheek to come to our house.' Lenny paused to light a cigarette, savouring his brother's reaction. 'I wasn't gonna look a gift horse in the mouth now, was I? But she gave it to me on the proviso that I deliver something in return.'

'What could she possibly want from you?'

'Something very precious indeed. And I delivered her, just as promised.' He took a drag of his cigarette and exhaled a plume of smoke from the corner of his mouth. 'Don't tell me you didn't notice the resemblance? Lucy? Your daughter? Remember her?'

He was talking about their little girl: a subject guaranteed to wind Nathan up. Nathan strode over, clenching Lenny's jacket as he lifted him from his feet. 'Don't push me, brother. I've told you before. You're not to mention her name.'

The cigarette dangling from between his lips, Lenny broke his brother's grip. 'Don't shoot the messenger, bruv; I'm the only one telling the truth.' He straightened out his jacket before taking a step back. 'I found Lucy and gave her Ruby's number, but she wasn't in any hurry to speak to her mum. Probably just as well given she's gunning for her. Ruby's got it in her head that Lucy's the door-knocker killer.'

Nathan paled. 'This is bullshit. I don't believe you.'

Lenny shrugged. 'So I thought I'd keep Ruby busy until I figured out what to do. I gave her a couple of leads, hoping she would come to her senses, but she's intent on sending her down. Your own flesh and blood. She didn't even have the decency to let you know.'

Nathan stared in disbelief as he tried to comprehend the words. It couldn't be true… not Ruby. She was the one good thing in his life. The only person that could pull him out of this murky world. Now she was up to her armpits in it, just like the rest of them. Questions rose in his mind amidst the confusion. Why hadn't she told him of her suspicions? But the answer was clear. Because she knew he would stop her. 'Where is Lucy?'

'You've already met her. She's been right under our noses all along. Just a street urchin, although she looks like she's been around the block a few times.'

'You're not saying… '

'Yeah, it's that bird you took on at the club. Cathy, her name is. I found her sleeping rough under a bridge, told her that her mum was looking for her. She was embarrassed, wanted to straighten herself out, so I sent her to the club to ask for work. I thought it would be better for you to break the news that you're her dad and all.'

'Jesus,' Nathan said, running both his hands through his hair. And there she was, offering to take off her clothes for him. His stomach churned at the thought.

'Shame,' Lenny said, taking a final drag on his cigarette before stubbing it on Nathan's oak flooring with the heel of his shoe. 'I was going to invite her round, but she's already gone out on a job.'

'What job? I told her to stay behind the bar.'

'Are you sure?' Lenny sneered. 'Because as far as I know she's gone to work on her back. She must have inherited that side of things from her mother.' He glanced at the expensive watch decorating his wrist. 'Speaking of filth, you'd better get around there before the old bill turn up. Ruby's been keeping tabs.'

'Where is she?' Nathan said, between gritted teeth.

'Fat Barry's place.'

Tweedy was already standing by the door, car keys in hand.

His muscles tensed, Nathan shouldered his brother aside. Hot fury had descended, leaving little room for rational thought. He had to get away. He could not be held responsible when anger like this took hold. His body shook with the need to expel it, but he had barely stepped forward when Lenny spoke in a low, gloating tone.

'Turns out Fat Barry's more than happy to break her in.'

Fist connected with bone as Nathan swivelled around, punching his brother hard in the mouth. He followed it up with a winding blow to the stomach, taking Lenny to his knees. He had raised his bloodied fist, ready to pummel Lenny's head, when a pair of strong arms wrestled him from the floor.

'Boss, c'mon, we've no time to waste.'

It was Tweedy. And he was right.

Gasping and choking, Lenny spit blood. 'My toof. You've broken mah fucking toof,' he lisped, clawing back the breath his brother had expelled.

But Nathan was already halfway out the door. If what Lenny said was true, he had to get to his daughter. He had let her down once. It would not happen a second time.

CHAPTER SIXTY

Ruby pushed down on the stiff doorbell, the noise producing a delicate chime out of place with the surroundings. Lenny had surprised her by texting the address, although he was the least trustworthy source of them all. Her heart skipped a beat as she contemplated meeting her daughter. Just how was she going to handle this? Flash her warrant card and blag her way inside? And what if her daughter *was* there? Could she arrest her own flesh and blood? It would end all ties with Nathan if he found out. Ruby took a deep breath as footsteps approached the door. The thought of losing her one constant in life made her scared. But a child's life was at risk, and she had no choice but to try.

Yet it was not 'Fat' Barry Sedgewick opening the door, but Nathan. And his face was like thunder. Grabbing her by the elbow he pulled her inside. The long narrow corridor offered little room for movement and she found herself with her back against the woodchip paper. Nathan stared with an intensity that frightened her, and her heart picked up a notch as she tried to break free.

His breath fell warm and heavy against her skin as his hands pressed against the wall either side of her face. Why is he here? Ruby thought, listening out for signs of Lucy, but the only sound was of the traffic outside. If her daughter was here, she was being very quiet about it. 'What's going on?' she said, keen to get moving. She was not here to play games.

'I could ask you the same question,' Nathan growled, every sinew in his body tensed. Ruby had seen him like this once before, and in times like these he was best left alone. But she had come here for a purpose, and she needed to know.

'I'm here to speak to Barry Sedgewick. What's your excuse?' She could tell by his demeanour it was not a social visit, and she was not in the mood for an argument. Lenny had sent her the address. Had he been setting her up all along? Ducking under Nathan's arm, she checked the downstairs rooms before making her way up the stairs.

'If you're looking for Lucy, she's not here. Neither is Fat Barry. He wasn't too keen to speak to you, funnily enough,' Nathan said, standing on the landing as she returned from checking the empty bedrooms.

Ruby's eyes fell to his grazed right fist and the blood splatters on his white shirt. 'What's your problem, Nathan?'

'I'll tell you what my problem is,' he said, jabbing her on the chest. '*You're* my fucking problem. How could you do it, Ruby? How could you set up our daughter? Did you really think I was going to allow you to arrest her?'

'Ow,' Ruby frowned, rubbing her breastbone. 'What are you talking about? You're not making any sense.'

'What's the view like from that high horse of yours? Lecturing me on what's right, then trading information so you could nick our daughter for murder. And here was me thinking you were beyond reproach.'

Ruby's face fell as she realised what it looked like. She had been played. And Lenny was pulling their strings. 'I can explain… '

'You *knew* how much I wanted to see her. Yet you chose to keep it quiet because you wanted to take her from me all over again.'

'What the hell? We both agreed, remember?' Except Ruby knew that was not strictly true. Her mother's recent ramblings had brought Nathan's reluctance to light. 'Anyway, it's a bit late to start laying blame, don't you think? If your family had any sort of normality, we wouldn't have had to give her up in the first place.'

Ruby knew from the expression on Nathan's face that her words were hitting home.

'I had no choice,' Nathan said, his voice choked by the anger backed up in his throat. 'Your mum railroaded me into it when I was at my lowest point. And what about you? You have the cheek to tell me my family is inferior to yours? At least my mum knows what day of the week it is.'

Ruby drew back her hand, slapping Nathan hard on the cheek. Nathan had grown up learning that pain does not come from the fist alone and was adept at pushing her buttons.

He carried on as if nothing more than a fly had landed on his skin. 'I should never have listened. If I did, then Cathy wouldn't be the state she's in now.'

'Cathy? Who's Cathy? And what do you mean "the state she's in"?' Ruby said, touching the stairwell to ground herself. Her phone buzzed in her pocket. No doubt it was work wondering where she was.

'Her adoptive parents changed her name. And it's a bit late to start acting the concerned parent. First you abandon her, then you try to nick her. And you have the cheek to lecture me about blood money. You disgust me. You're nothing but a joke.'

'How dare you talk to me like that,' Ruby said, her voice rising. 'You know nothing of this investigation. There's a child's life on the line here. If you just took the time to hear me out… '

'Well, I'm too busy looking out for our own flesh and blood. Go and find your killer elsewhere, because I can tell you now it had nothing to do with her. Now fuck off back to the job you love so much. We don't ever want to hear from you again.'

'Nathan, you've got this all wrong,' Ruby said, following him down the stairs. 'It's Lenny. He's set this all up. Just give me the chance to explain.'

'We're not interested. Cathy's safe now, somewhere you'll never find her.'

'Please. Just ask her one question. Has she ever watched the movie *Lucy's First Christmas?*'

Nathan looked at Ruby as if she was speaking a foreign language. 'What are you on about? What movie?'

'It's part of the investigation. The killer's recreating scenes from the film. I've got to know. Has Cathy watched it or not?'

'You're a piece of work, do you know that? Even now, you're taking the side of the police.' Nathan made towards the door, wrenching it open until it rebounded against the wall. 'I'll never forgive you for this, Ruby. You can go to hell.'

Ruby flinched as he slammed the door, leaving her alone in the hall. The energy of their disagreement still hung in the air, and she could not bear to leave it like this. But there was little point in chasing after him, and who could blame him for being mad? It was bad enough that she hid Lucy's contact from him, but to hear it from Lenny... Ruby had walked straight into his trap and had nobody but herself to blame. *She* went crawling to *him*, and she should have known better than to trust Lenny Crosby. A wave of grief rose from within as long buried feelings of shame and regret made themselves known. She should have been stronger. Had she not given her baby up, things would be very different now. They could be together as a family. This was all her fault. Warm tears moistened her cheeks, and she swiped them away with the back of her hand. She would not allow herself to go there; at least, not until she had sorted out the mess her life had become.

CHAPTER SIXTY-ONE

Lavender bath salts mingled with the scent of warm sticky blood. It rose with the steam clouding the glass, blotting out the outside world. Lucy inhaled deeply, drawing it deep into her lungs. This had been her best yet. And the most satisfying. She had fooled herself into thinking that it would end any other way. She didn't want to find her mother. She wanted to end her. And once was never enough. She had to pay her whore of a mother back ten times over for abandoning her as a child. Trying to recreate a happy ending was a façade. She understood that now. *But every cloud has a silver lining...* The nearer she came to perfection, the more exquisite the payback. Her body shuddered from the afterglow of her satisfaction. Who was she to deny that part of herself? Deep down she had known, even as Anita recited the lines, word perfect, that it would never work. How could Lucy live a normal life when everything about her was an aberration?

At first she turned the blame inwards. She was a freak who had committed crimes in the eyes of society. Her happy ever after was never going to come true. But who wanted normality if all it brought were rules and boundaries? It was easier to give into the longing rising within her. Inflicting pain on others made the horror go away. And the reward... oh what a bounty that had been: wave upon wave of ecstasy as she purged herself in a bath tinted with blood.

But now she had another problem to deal with. Sophie. The little girl was still sleeping on her bed. Now Anita was gone she was just a stranger: no longer a competitor for her mother's affections.

Like her she was motherless; cast adrift in a cruel world for wicked men to do what they would. And there were plenty of wicked men. She pulled the plug, allowing ribbons of blood to swirl into the void. What was she going to do with her indeed? She was not a child killer. But Sophie had to be disposed of. And there was no way she could return her home. She knew from the start that was never going to happen, despite her reassurances stating otherwise. If only she could just make her go to sleep: a deathless death, never to awaken. She was only a little thing, soft and pliable, free of the threat of rigor mortis. A slow, thin smile spread across Lucy's lips. She thought about the final death note which lay on her dresser. Sophie would fit nicely into the suitcase. And Lucy knew just where to take her.

CHAPTER SIXTY-TWO

Ruby slammed the office door behind her, digging her hand into her leather jacket to check her phone. 'Yes?' She answered it stiffly, heat still inflaming her cheeks from her encounter with Nathan.

'I take it things didn't go as planned?' Downes said. It was with great reluctance that he had offered to cover for her, but only on the proviso that she would call if she got into bother.

'No. And I'm beginning to wonder if Lenny wasn't just playing with me all along.'

'Where are you?' Downes said, an echo in his voice.

'Back at work. Where are you?'

'Oh.' He gave a soft chortle, 'so you are.'

Ruby turned her head to see him enter from the corridor. He sank back the last of his diet Coke before scrunching up the can in his fist and throwing it into the waste paper bin.

'How was evening briefing?' Ruby asked, trying to keep the scowl from her face. 'Did Worrow miss me?'

'I told her you were called out to Oakwood because of an emergency with Joy. Sorry, it's all I could think of.'

'How did she take it?'

'She had a face on her that'd cut tin, but that's her usual expression so I wouldn't worry.'

Ruby sighed. She hated to use her mum as an excuse, but it seemed a valid enough reason for her sudden disappearance. 'I don't suppose there's been any breakthroughs in my absence?'

Hands deep in pockets, Downes puffed out his cheeks as he exhaled. 'They're still going through all the CCTV, transport links, and phone calls. We believe the women were stalked prior to abduction. The victims kept to a routine and the killer's profile suggests she was aware of that.'

Ruby had seen the suspect profile, which was too broad for her liking. 'Let's hope they catch something on CCTV.'

Closed circuit television was everywhere and it was easy to build up a picture of someone's day, particularly if they had a set routine. Supermarkets, buses, trains, tubes stations and the streets of London – all sources of valuable information, with better image quality than in their rural counterparts. The team had already spent hours hunting down the victim's last movements. Armed with a vague description of the suspect, they were feeling their way in the dark with a dimly lit torch. She needed to see Cathy, the person purporting to be her daughter. Then at least she would have something to look for in the sea of faces. Without a clearer description, Anita's stalker could have been any of the women recorded out shopping that day.

'I take it they've not got any further on my movie re-enactment theory?'

'It's a long film; the next placement could be from any number of scenes.'

'Yes, but if Anita knows the movie as well as she should, the next scene should be the hotel reunion.'

Downes nodded. 'They've notified hotels and guest houses; they'll report anything suspicious.'

Ruby was in no doubt of that. Finding a corpse on their grounds was hardly good for business. The media had a strong grasp of the story, and she had read the headlines featuring the door-knocker killer all over the *Metro* newspaper that morning.

But there was something bothering Ruby: a feeling of being played. If Lenny had set her up by giving her the address, could he have been responsible for sending the emails too? She couldn't see how the lost young homeless girl now in Nathan's care could have the mental dexterity to carry out serial murders, particularly kidnapping a mother and child. But she would know for sure soon enough. Nathan did not trust anyone and would have Cathy under observation twenty-four hours a day.

Cathy. Ruby loved the name. It reminded her of her favourite book, *Wuthering Heights*. Could she really be her daughter? Or was it all part of some elaborate plan? Perhaps it had been a ruse to distract her all along. Ruby picked up the file containing the photographs of Monica's post-mortem. There were inconsistencies that had been bothering her and now was the time to delve further.

CHAPTER SIXTY-THREE

'You need to give up the smokes,' Downes said, as he took the stairs two at a time. The lift was out yet again, and Ruby was made to feel wholly inadequate as she clambered behind him in between heaving intakes of breath.

'I'm working on it,' Ruby said, the craving stronger than ever. 'Now if you just let me catch… my breath… '

Fumbling in her pocket, she produced a shiny new key. It wasn't good enough that she had replaced the locks. Downes had insisted on walking her back to her flat, reasoning that her daughter could be waiting to pounce. Given that Nathan had taken her in it was highly unlikely. In fact, the idea of Cathy being the killer was sounding more ludicrous by the minute. But there was a personal connection: how else would they have known her middle name?

As her eyes fell to the floor the world stopped turning. The black-edged envelopes were something she dreaded, and this one had been shoved under her door. A low groan escaped her lips. They were too late.

'Don't touch it,' Downes said, as if they were dealing with a poisonous snake. Pulling a glove from his pocket, he pointed towards her bedroom. 'Check the rest of the flat, just in case they got in.'

But her search proved fruitless. She returned just as Downes gently plucked the card from the envelope with the tips of his gloved fingers.

'In Memoriam:
ANITA DEVINE
Died in her sleep
Rest in Peace'

'Oh God,' Ruby groaned. 'What about Sophie? What about the little girl?'

Downes checked both sides of the card before sliding it into an evidence bag. 'There's no mention of her,' he said, his voice low. Pausing only seconds, he slid his phone from his pocket and updated control.

Ruby clasped both hands behind her neck, bowing her head as responsibility formed a physical weight on her shoulders. A thought lit like a beacon in her mind. 'I checked the flat after Nathan took Cathy in, which means she couldn't have sent the death notice.'

'Someone could have sent it for her,' Downes said.

'But it's not just the notice, is it? She's been with him all morning. Anita's out there waiting to be discovered. It would have taken time to stage the body, put it in place. They'd need transportation too. It couldn't be her.'

'As you said, she's been with her father. How far would Nathan go to keep her out of prison?'

'You're so bloody cynical. It wasn't Nathan, alright?' Ruby snapped, unwilling to allow the thought to cross her mind. As far as she was concerned, her ex would never hurt a woman. Growing up in a cycle of domestic abuse repelled him from any such act.

'Steady on, girl, I'm just saying keep an open mind.' Downes lumbered towards the door. 'I'm heading to the Park Royal Hotel. It's on the watch list as a possible dump site. You coming with me?'

It was the name of the fictional hotel featured in the movie. There were a few variations of the name in several London hotels: The Park Royal, The Royal Park; police were attending them all, and judging by the updates Downes had received they had all turned up blank.

'Has it been under surveillance?'

'Yes,' Downes said.

'And it's a no-show so far?'

Downes nodded in affirmation.

'Then there's got to be another location.'

For once, Ruby asked Downes to drive. He negotiated the traffic with as much haste as he could while Ruby tapped on her phone, seeking out possible dump sites.

'The hotel in the movie: it could be any number of places. How would someone dump a body, if they're all on high alert?'

'Don't ya think we've been asking ourselves that? How did they get into those houses and leave Emily and Monica for us to find?'

'Those houses were empty…' Ruby's voice trailed away, unwilling to admit that they were all on the Crosby Estate Agents' books. 'Of course! Turn left here.'

'Where are you taking me? This isn't the way to the Park Royal,' Downes said.

Ruby tapped on her phone, indicating he take the Marylebone flyover. 'Bear with me, boss; I have a theory. Emily and Monica, they didn't know the movie. That's why they suffered violent deaths. But Anita did. In fact, she probably knew it off by heart – her husband said she used to watch it over and over again. So the happy ever after wouldn't be the reunion in the hotel: it's where they drive off together into the sunset.'

Ruby was referring to the final scene. It wasn't set in a grand house or hotel but a car. Having found her daughter, the mother of the little girl sat behind the steering wheel waiting for Lucy to jump in beside her, before driving away.

'Except it's not a happy ending, is it?' Downes said in a gravelly voice. 'We've just been served a death notice.'

'I know. But maybe the killer's come to the conclusion there's no happy ending to be found.'

'Where does this leave Sophie? Is she a replica of the adopted child? Are we going to find her in the car too?' Downes said.

'Maybe, maybe not.' Ruby replayed the final scene in her mind: mother and child driving away; Lucy's suitcase on the back seat of the car. A chilling thought surfaced. Emily had been found in the foetal position, the forensic pathologist surmising she had been kept in a box-like space. What better way to transport a body in broad daylight than in a suitcase?

'All the local hotels have been on high alert,' Downes said. 'I can't see how our killer could just turn up and dump a body in a car with people walking by.'

'Neither do I,' Ruby said. 'That's why we're going to a derelict hotel. It's empty, just like the houses where the other bodies were found. It doesn't matter if it's no longer in use. They can park outside and still be in keeping with the theme.'

'I never thought of that.'

'I could be wrong. But it's worth checking out.' She could have asked a local unit to attend, but she had an unofficial ownership of the case and could not relinquish it now. The hotel in the movie was grand: the building looming into the view looked anything but.

'The Magnat?' Downes said. 'Why have you brought us here?' The Magnat Polish Pub had been derelict since 2012, closing down after numerous reports of violence. The drab two-storey building was a shadow of the once beautiful 1930s hotel.

'It hasn't always been a pub,' Ruby said. 'It used to be called the Park Royal Hotel.'

'The same name as the one in the movie,' Downes said. 'Good thinking.'

'I've found it on a site on my phone: *Derelict London*.'

Downes pulled up a small distance away. 'Let's walk,' he said. 'We don't want to spook them if they're already here.'

But as Ruby's heels echoed on the gritty pavement all she could see was a lone, rusted Fiat Panda. And in it was a blonde woman wearing sunglasses, her face tilted in the direction of the road ahead. Her hands gripped the steering wheel as if she was waiting to drive away. Ruby's heart plummeted as she drew near. Dressed in a black netted hat and skirt suit was the body of Anita Devine.

'Don't touch anything,' Downes said, signalling he was returning to his car. 'There's crime scene tape in the boot. We'll cordon the area off and call for backup.'

Soon the street would be buzzing with crime scene investigators and police. But for now it was deathly calm. Nobody had noticed that the woman sitting behind the steering wheel was a corpse.

Ruby peered through the dust-streaked car window. Her pallid face, her bloodless lips; it was a heart-breaking sight to see such a young woman trussed up in this way. Cable ties looped around the steering wheel under the black leather gloves tied Anita's hands into position. A thin rope looped under a neck scarf attached to the headrest kept her upright. Blood bloomed from the centre of her suit jacket, difficult to see against the dark fabric. 'I'm sorry,' Ruby whispered, her words sticking in her throat as she noticed a thin layer of fog on the inside windscreen. Could it be?... Wrenching back the door she pushed her two fingers against Anita's carotid artery. The faint soft pulse of a heartbeat. 'Shit,' Ruby whispered, ripping open her blouse. The wound was superficial, but the bruises on Anita's neck told a different story. Had an attempt at asphyxiation brought her to the brink of death? Ruby swivelled her head to call for Downes. 'She's alive. Call for an ambulance, she's alive!'

Downes raced towards her, his radio pressed to his ear. Wasting no time they performed emergency first aid. But one thought was drowning out all others in Ruby's mind. *Where was Sophie?*

Ruby felt a jolt in her chest as she caught sight of the oversized suitcase on the back seat. Please don't let that be what I think it is, she thought, as Downes's radio broke the silence behind her.

Death had almost touched Anita, but what about her child? She thought about what Anita must have gone through, and the panic she must have felt for her daughter. 'We've got to get that suitcase open,' Ruby said, turning to her superior for permission. 'Sophie could be in there.'

Downes nodded, handing her a set of PVC gloves. 'Do it.'

Pulling back the door, Ruby forced herself to take cool steady breaths. She didn't know if the killer had meant to finish Anita off, but after seeing what she did to Emily's husband, Harry, little sympathy would have been afforded to her child. Kneeling on the seat, she leaned over the brown canvas suitcase, her heart sinking as she felt its weight. Her internal voice shot a warning down the corridors of her mind. *Prepare yourself. It's a dead weight.* She glanced around the car, her heart beating against her ribcage. She was encompassed by the promise of death; the tar-stained ceiling felt like it was closing in. She tugged the zip across the jagged silver teeth. Discovering Anita was harrowing enough – the thoughts of finding her dead child was horrific.

Ruby pulled the zip harder, cursing under her breath as it jammed. These were the times she wished she worked as a school teacher, or in a supermarket checkout. To have the luxury of falling asleep in bed worrying about simple things, such as telephone bills and if the bins had been put out; not whether the suitcase she was opening was going to house the corpse of a murdered child.

Finally, the zip became free. She opened the suitcase preparing for the worst.

CHAPTER SIXTY-FOUR

'Fucking Bastard.' Ruby exhaled as a pile of bricks wrapped in a blanket tumbled out. Lucy had done it to taunt her: weighing-down the suitcase to mimic the weight of a child. A pinprick of light lit her troubled mind. Sophie may still be alive. Staggering from the car, Ruby took Downes's arm when it was offered. The paramedics were here now, talking in urgent voices as they worked on getting Anita from the car onto an awaiting stretcher. Evening was closing in, and people were gathering behind the police tape. This was not the time to fall apart. 'I'm OK,' Ruby said gratefully, taking a couple of deep breaths. iPhones were lifted; her distress filmed for other people's viewing pleasure. Ruby's glance fell back onto Anita. She wanted to tell her that everything would be alright and she would save her little girl. But there were no guarantees in a world where God did not listen.

By the time she got back to the station, Ruby knew where her focus lay. Taking a sip of tea that had gone cold, she worked her way through the recent updates on the case. The list of keyholders for the body dump sites had been spoken to, but there was one name that stood out from the rest. Her brow furrowed as she turned her attention once again to the post-mortem photos. And now, peering at the images, a piece of the puzzle fell into place. The truth was, she had had a suspect in mind. The idea had seemed preposterous; she had kept pushing it away. But how many times does someone need to pop up on the periphery before you start taking them seriously?

She could not ignore the facts. But what if she was wrong?

Ruby knew exactly where she had to go. An unknown number flashed up on her mobile phone as she climbed into her car. Her finger hovered over the answer button. She could not rule out the possibility that the killer was on her tracks. She answered, breathing a terse 'yes?' down the line. It was ten p.m. This was not the time for pleasantries.

'Where are you? We need to talk.'

Ruby did not see the point in taking Nathan's calls. He had made his feelings perfectly clear during their last meeting. 'I don't have time for this, I'm in a hurry.'

Nathan replied flatly as if she had never spoken at all. 'You're wrong about Cathy. I've spoken to her about the movie. She's no murderer. So don't come looking for her.'

'I know. And I'd like to point out that *you're* the one calling *me*. So why don't you let me get on with finding the real killer?' Ruby took a breath to accommodate the words erupting in her throat. 'And you can tell our daughter, if she *is* our daughter, that she can come and find me as soon as she's seeing sense. Now if you don't mind, I've got work to do.' Ruby terminated the call, pushing aside her anger.

It was pointless hoping for a reunion. Nathan, Frances and Lenny had made it quite clear that it was over. She had been silly to think things would work out any differently. As for her daughter? Trust had to be earned in the Crosby family. Nathan may have readily taken Cathy in, but when his mother Frances got over her shock she would not waste any time in having a DNA test completed.

Ruby turned the ignition of her car. She couldn't think about that now, not while a little girl's life was hanging by a thread.

The closer Ruby came to her suspect's home the more she doubted herself. She thought about ringing Downes to voice her suspicions. But that's all they were: suspicions. What if she was so desperate to find the killer that she was plucking suspects out of the air? But a work colleague? Would they really be capable of such horrific acts? The idea seemed ludicrous, and the last thing she wanted was to be made a laughing stock. She pressed down her indicator; her mouth dry as she approached their home. She was just going to talk to them, get some feelers out there. A quick call wouldn't look out of place given they were so heavily involved in the case. But as she parked outside the address she had almost persuaded herself that she was wrong. What would the others say if they could see her now? Surely this was not the home of a murderer. She must have been mistaken. But killers took many guises. Far removed from the bogeyman, or horror movie villains. Many were people you wouldn't look twice at on the street.

She pressed hard on the doorbell, the shrill ring drilling into her brain. Ruby was tired. She hadn't eaten in hours and sleep was just a memory. Every day she hated her flat a little bit more. Would there be another letter waiting for her when she got back? The thoughts of going home alone made her flesh creep.

The door opened, cutting into her thoughts. In front of her stood Christopher Douglas, the forensic pathologist.

'Ruby,' he said, his eyebrows raised. 'What are you doing here at this hour?'

'I was passing and… ' Ruby sighed, 'actually that's a lie. I came here because I need some advice. Can I come in?'

Chris paused at the door; his features clinging to a smile that did not reach his eyes. 'What am I like? Of course, come inside.'

Steady, Ruby told herself. He was surprised to see her that's all. Being shifty was not a prelude to guilt. It certainly was not enough to gain access via a warrant, which was what was needed to search his house. Such an old building was bound to have lots of hiding places. She sniffed the air as she entered the hall. Isopropanol. The smell of the morgue.

Chris turned to catch her eye as he led her inside. 'Excuse the smell. I've been looking after the neighbour's cat. She's been shitting everywhere except where she's supposed to. I brought home a couple of bottles of disinfectant from work. You won't tell on me, will you?'

'Not at all,' Ruby said. 'Gone back now, has she?'

'She's at the vets. Stomach problems. They're keeping her overnight. Can I make you a tea? Coffee?'

'A cup of tea would be lovely,' Ruby said, her senses on high alert. She had smelt enough decomposing bodies to believe he was lying through his teeth about the cat.

Two flowery teacups were placed on the table in the living room, where Chris insisted they sit.

'Thanks,' she said, wishing she had not set her phone to silent. Her unease was growing by the second. She shouldn't have come here. If he had the slightest suspicion the police were onto him, all evidence would be destroyed.

'Biscuit?' Chris said, pouring the milk.

'Oh go on then,' Ruby said, although her stomach was churning.

The second his back was turned she swapped the cups of tea. It seemed silly, suspecting her colleague of poisoning a harmless drink, but the minute she had entered the hall he had become someone else. Ruby took a sip, smiling at Chris as he took a seat across from her. But her stomach was doing butterflies, and she forced herself to nibble on the ginger snap as he watched.

'So what brings you to my humble abode?' Chris said, sitting bolt upright in the chair. He looked ready to jump up at any second, and his jitteriness was catching.

'Sorry, just let me check my phone,' Ruby said, turning on the sound. No calls. She frowned before returning her attention to Chris. Her mind was racing as she tried to formulate a reason for her visit. 'It's Worrow. I was hoping for some advice, but it's a sensitive issue,' she said. 'You're friends, right?'

Chris nodded slowly. 'Sounds ominous. Well, I can assure you, anything you have to say won't go beyond these four walls.'

'I know.' She took a mouthful of tea to ease the dryness in her throat. 'It's just that I overheard her having a heated phone conversation the other day. She mentioned her job being compromised. I'm worried something's wrong.'

'Why didn't you ask her?'

'It's not my place. Besides, I got the feeling she was trying to distance herself from whatever mess her friend was in.' Ruby swallowed back another mouthful of tea. 'I dunno, I've been thinking of asking her about it, but I don't want her to take me up the wrong way.'

'In my opinion, if you've something to say you're best off not pussyfooting around. You never struck me as a game player, Ruby. Why start now?'

Ruby fell silent. His words were leaden, delivered with a double meaning she could not ignore. He knew she was onto him. She raised her hands in mock surrender. 'You're right, I'm sorry. I came here with every intention of being upfront with you. I know it was you on the phone.'

Chris gave two slow nods of the head. 'So you've been snooping in on our private conversations. And the real reason for your visit is?'

'To offer my help, of course. It was just the once, but you both seemed really stressed. I promise it won't go any further if you need to talk,' Ruby added.

Chris crossed his legs, squirming in his seat. 'I've had some unexpected outlays, but it's under control now. So you can bury that little problem. It won't raise its head again.'

Ruby was well aware of his finances. Chris was in debt for a considerable amount of money, and it had come on suddenly, plunging his credit record from full health to being in the red.

'Thanks, Chris, I didn't mean to pry.' Ruby glanced at her watch. 'Gosh, look at the time, I'd best be off.' She wobbled as she stood, blinking at the pinpricks of white lights which dotted her vision. The adrenalin rush that flowed through her veins had come to a halt, making her feel out of kilter. She glanced around the messy room, taking a breath to regain her strength. 'This is a nice big house. Have you lived here long?'

'Oh yes, quite a few years. I was very fortunate to inherit it. I could sell it for a packet and live a bit further out, but I'm attached to the old place. It's got a bomb shelter you know; I even found bits of memorabilia down there.'

'Really?' Ruby said, knowing she should leave while she could. But she needed to have a nose around while she still had the chance. 'Mind if I use your bathroom?' she said, trying to shake off the feeling that Chris was onto her.

Chris smiled, a slow narrow-lipped grin. 'Would you like to see it? The bomb shelter that is,' he said, walking with her. 'I'll show you the bathroom on the way out.'

'I'd love to,' Ruby said, taking a wobbly step forward.

'Steady, are you OK? You've gone a funny colour.'

'I've not eaten much today. I'll be OK,' Ruby said, following him out to the hall. 'So you've got a bomb shelter, eh? That's pretty cool.'

'Yes, it is: good for storage, gardening tools. Handy for all sorts of things really.' Walking to the cupboard under the stairs, he opened the door, then pulled back a rug to reveal a trapdoor underneath. 'Here it is,' he said as the door to an underground chamber gaped open. Ruby peered into the darkness, wrinkling her nose as the pungent smell rose up to greet her. The liberal coating of disinfectant in the hall was no match for the overpowering stench from below.

'Go on then,' he said, gesturing for her to go first. 'You wanted to see it, didn't you?'

Ruby peered in. She should go down, and if enough evidence was gained she might be able to arrest him. But every fibre of her being was screaming at her not to do it. There was no way she was turning her back on Chris, who was now carrying a maddening look in his eyes. 'You go first,' Ruby said. 'It's a bit too dark for me, don't want to fall arse over tit.'

'No,' Chris said. 'I insist, you first. It's what you came here for, isn't it?'

'I'm sorry?' Ruby said, unease creeping up her spine like a long-legged spider.

'Come off it, Ruby, you really think I'm buying that lame story about Worrow? As if you'd come all this way just to talk about a stupid phone call. I know why you're here.'

'Chris, I don't… '

'You saw, didn't you? The dirt on Monica's feet. You noticed it at the scene when you looked under the duvet. I had a feeling you did.'

There was no going back from that admission. Ruby nodded. She didn't want her colleague to be under suspicion for murder. She didn't want any of this. But the sooner she could get an admission, the quicker she could trace Sophie's location. 'I couldn't understand why the post-mortems were drawing a blank. So I checked and rechecked the photos. I was going to suggest soil sample analysis, because the soles of Monica's feet were dirty at the scene. But then when I checked the crime scene photos her feet were clean. How did you do that? I know what I saw. Emma was there taking photos when we pulled back the duvet. How did she miss it?'

Chris folded his arms. 'Emma was thrilled when I told her your DI had a soft spot for her. So when she followed you all out to the door I cleaned Monica's feet with some wet wipes. When Emma came back in, she carried on taking photos. People don't question the forensic pathologist. It's one of the perks of the job.'

There was one last piece of the puzzle that was not fitting in. The door-knocker killer was reported to be a woman. She had to be, to be invited into people's homes. But Chris had displayed enough guilt to warrant an arrest. They would discuss the finer details back at the station. Straightening her posture, she recited the caution. 'Christopher Douglas. I'm arresting you on suspicion of murder. You do not have to say anything… ' A wave of nausea passed over her and she swept her hair from her face. 'You do not have to… ' she repeated, trying to focus on the figure before her. His image split in two and he blurred in and out of focus. Ruby swallowed, taking a step back to support herself against the wall.

'Did you really think I wouldn't notice you switch the teacups? You can't kid a kidder, Ruby; isn't that what you always say? Oh, and by the way, they were both laced with sedatives. It's why I didn't fancy mine.' Reaching into his back pocket, he pulled out two black-edged envelopes and waved them in her face. I'm playing postman today. Guess who these are for? One for you and one for Sophie. Perhaps I'll deliver them to Jack Downes instead?'

Jack. Ruby slipped her hand into her pocket and pressed the call button on her phone. For once, she was grateful for the push button pad, and could only pray that some kind of a call went through. She had to get out, but as the sedatives hit her system every step felt like lead.

'Where's Sophie?' she asked, her words slurred as what felt like the world's worst headache wrapped around her skull.

'She's safe. For now. But the question is, what are we going to do with you?'

CHAPTER SIXTY-FIVE

'What do *you* want?' Downes said, his eyes narrowing in distrust.

The last person Nathan wanted to turn to for help was a copper, much less the one Ruby had taken to her bed. But the phone call he had received left him no choice, and he used the swiftest way to get the man on side as he uttered three words: 'Ruby's in trouble.'

'How did you find my address? No, don't tell me, I don't want to know.' Downes led Nathan into the living room of his two-bedroom London townhouse. It still carried the feminine touch of the wife who had passed on a year earlier. Floral patterned wallpaper, soft furnishings and a collection of Swarovski crystals in a cabinet. Hardly the décor of a bachelor pad. Nathan knew all about Downes, because he made it his business to investigate Ruby's closest friends. The two men eyed each other warily as Nathan dipped his hand into the pocket of his black combat trousers. Not his usual weekend attire, but the concealed pockets were effective for carrying weapons and he had a feeling that he might need them.

'I got a voicemail from Ruby. Listen.' Ruby's muffled voice came into life as Nathan pressed the speaker button on his phone. He had listened to it three times now, and the slur in her voice set him on edge.

'Where's Sophie?' A rustling noise ensued. Phone against cloth. Or a pocket, Nathan thought.

A voice responded. 'She's here. Would you like to meet her?' Downes frowned as they leaned into the phone. Nathan caught his expression and mouthed, 'who?'

Downes pushed his finger against his lips as the conversation continued.

'Why, Chris, why did you kill those women?'

Nathan tensed as he caught a glint of recognition in Downes's eye. He wanted to get going, but he didn't know who Chris was. Was it a male or female name? It was impossible to tell. The conversation continued as Chris spoke in a taut voice.

'It doesn't matter anymore. It's over. Now down you go like a good girl; it's OK, you'll have company.'

'I'm not going down there,' Ruby replied before the phone went dead.

'Where's Ruby?' Nathan said. 'And who the hell is Chris?'

'Chris Douglas, by the sounds of it. He's our forensic pathologist. I wondered what Ruby was up to when she requested that credit check.' Downes rubbed the stubble on his chin. 'But how? All this time we thought it was a woman… ' Lacing his shoes, he craned his neck up at Nathan. 'I've got to go.'

'You've had a drink,' Nathan said, eyeing the half-empty decanter of whiskey on the coffee table before him. He would have gladly left without him, but he needed Chris's location. Nathan gave him a wry glance. 'We'll get there quicker in my car.' Downes did not argue. Nathan's Mercedes SL 400 was far superior to Downes's Ford and having a detective inspector in the front seat would negate any police stops along the way. It would not do his street cred any good, but Nathan was beyond the point of caring.

All he wanted right now was to find Ruby. And if he could trace the location of the missing child, then all the better. But as he tore up the streets he had a feeling it would not end well.

The car purred under pressure, attracting admiring glances from pedestrians as the grey metallic paintwork gleamed under the grimy street lights.

'When did you last see her?' Nathan said, flipping on the wipers to negate the shower of rain.

'A couple of hours ago,' Downes replied, 'at work,' he hastily added. 'But she's been getting death notes addressed specifically to her.'

'Shit,' Nathan said, his voice softening. 'Ruby... we have a daughter together. She thought she was to blame. But when I last spoke to Ruby she said she was on someone else's trail.'

'I know,' Downes said.

'You know?' Nathan repeated, his eyes fixed on the road. It added a new layer to their friendship. Ruby rarely confided in anyone, unless she was at a low ebb. So either Downes and Ruby were getting closer, or she was in a bad place.

'I was digging into local adoption records so she knew I'd find out anyway,' Downes said, easing Nathan's concerns. 'She was getting emails. She thought Lucy was stalking her.'

His daughter had admitted to Nathan that she had rung Ruby once and visited Joy in the care home, just to say hello. Oakwood's address had been provided by Lenny: an effort to stir the pot. But further probing revealed that that was as far as it went, and no emails had been exchanged.

'And now she's been drugged by some psycho posing as our daughter. Fuck it!' Nathan said, smacking the heel of his hand against the steering wheel. 'All these years I've been keeping an eye on her and the moment I step back this happens.' He jabbed a finger at Downes, taking him by surprise as fury raged in his eyes. 'You were meant to be looking after her. Where were you tonight? She's being stalked by a nutter and you let her find her own way home?'

'It wasn't like that. She said she was working late. She was meant to get a taxi.'

Nathan returned his gaze to the road. 'You should never have left her alone. You're all the same you lot, no loyalty. Well, let me tell you, if anything happens to her... '

'Ruby's not an ornament that you put aside to look at. She's her own woman.' Downes turned his attention back to his phone as units called to say they were en route.

'ETA in five minutes, that means... ' Downes said.

'I know what ETA means.' Silence fell between them as Nathan navigated the road.

Downes frowned, lowering his window to take in some air. 'Your family have caused Ruby nothing but grief. I know what you and your brother have been getting up to. The sooner he goes back to prison, the happier I'll be.'

'Don't give me that,' Nathan said. 'Ruby knows the score. If we weren't there to keep a lid on things there'd be anarchy. If my brother's been involved in anything, it's been restoring order upon his return.'

'Is that what you call it? Restoring order? And what about Ruby? Was he restoring order when he put a knife to her throat?'

'What are you talking about?'

'So you don't know? Is that how you do business then? I thought you two were tight.'

Nathan's jaw tightened. 'If you've got something to say then spill it now.'

'Lenny's got a screw loose. Ruby was going home when he pulled a knife on her in the lift. Threatened rape, by all accounts. So why don't you look closer to home before you start lecturing me about looking after her?'

Nathan shifted in his seat. He had no reason to disbelieve what Downes was saying. That must've been the night that Ruby went to the flat, and it explained why she took a knife to bed. Yet she had not told him. This was all his fault.

'I wanted to have him arrested, but she wouldn't allow it. Lenny threatened to pay her mother a visit and finish her off. Such a kind and compassionate man your brother: picking on women and the elderly. Yeah, I'd say he's a real asset to the community.'

'What do you want me to do?' Nathan said, pulling up to a set of traffic lights.

'Sort him out. If you won't, we will.'

Nathan inhaled a deep breath; his fists clenched over the steering wheel. He needed to regroup, focus on the task ahead. 'What's the killer's MO?'

Downes silently stared out the window, seemingly incapable of relinquishing the words. Finally, he cleared his throat to speak. 'The victims have died from stab wounds, with attempts at asphyxiation. They had ligature marks on wrists and ankles. Splinters of baubles were found in Emily Edmonds's stomach.'

'What kind of weird shit is that?'

'It's the kind of weird shit we're dealing with.'

Nathan negotiated the traffic until the streets of Inner London melted away, bringing them to a tree-lined avenue on the outskirts of Greenwood. Thoughts spun in his head like a fairground waltzer as he tried to concentrate on the road. Why had he gone for Ruby like that when she was only doing her job? He'd come so close to giving up everything to be with her. Was he self-sabotaging because he was scared of letting her in? It was obvious Lenny was pulling his strings and had set the whole thing up. If he hadn't got to his daughter in time... And she *was* his daughter. The DNA test had made that clear. She was holed up in a spa with his mum now, trying to comprehend the situation. As much as Frances proudly referred to her as a Crosby, she carried her mother's dark features. Eyes you could fall into, never to return. Ruby. He needed her more than ever. He couldn't do this on his own.

'Turn left here,' Downes said, his ear glued to his phone.

Nathan recognised the houses from his estate agent's listing. It was the same street Monica Sherwood had been discovered: one of the latest victims of the door-knocker killer. It had not taken Downes long to find out Chris Douglas's home address and they'd arrived on par with the police units he had alerted. The strength of Nathan's heartbeat swished in his ears as he abandoned his car to run up the driveway to Chris Douglas's front door. The steady thump of his 9mm Glock pistol thumped against his thigh as he ran.

CHAPTER SIXTY-SIX

A vice-like pain gripped Ruby's forehead as she raised her head from the unforgiving floor.

'Where am I?' she said, her voice echoing in the darkness. Waking up disorientated was not unusual, but the blackness of her surroundings grew fresh fears as she failed to seek out the chink of light that spoke of home. Groaning, she struggled to rise. A wave of dread washed over her as she realised her ankles and wrists were bound. Groping in the darkness, her fingers traced the outline of woollen fringes. It was a rug. Was she in the basement of Chris's home? She needed to think quickly in order to get her bearings.

Sliding into a sitting up position, Ruby scooted back until she felt a bare brick wall, leaning against it long enough to ease the dizziness penetrating her brain. A dry bitter aspirin taste permeated the roof of her mouth, but the full memory of her most recent event was slow in coming. She desperately needed to regain some focus. There had to be an opening, she thought, a doorway out. A sudden breath made her heart work double time. She was not alone. 'Who's there?' she said, her voice echoing against the oppressive brick walls.

Torchlight seared her pupils and she blinked as she focused her gaze. Ruby recoiled as the memories finally returned. Chris confessing to being the killer, then admitting to drugging her tea. How long had he been sitting in the darkness with her? The figure chuckled as it watched her flounder.

Ruby leaned against the wall, forcing herself to her feet. The room was a cavernous chamber, long and bare, with furniture cloaked in dust curtains further down. To the left was a staircase leading to a closed door. Slime laced the walls, and Ruby inhaled a fetid smell. Somewhere on the periphery the urgency of the case made itself known. Sophie. What had he done with the little girl? Ruby gained enough composure to challenge her captor. 'The police are on their way so you'd better untie me now.'

Another low laugh. But this time, Ruby made out a feminine lilt. She blinked in quick succession, her eyes darting around the room for a weapon. The echo of footsteps filled the hollow chamber as her captor flicked on the light overhead. It was not Chris before her, but a woman; the white smock covering her dress like a butcher's apron was decorated in a smattering of dried blood. She stepped under the dim light bulb revealing her identity, and in doing so she stole the air from Ruby's lungs.

'Goldie? Is that you?' Ruby whispered, peering around the darkened room for her accomplice.

At least she had been spared a gag. But then why would her captor gag her when she had gone to so much trouble to reel her in?

Goldie's smile lacked the gold-plated teeth and the beehive hairstyle. Now, with her shaven head, hastily applied make-up and peculiar dress, she didn't look like herself at all. 'Hello, Ruby. Would you like to play a little game?'

Ruby wanted to launch herself at her to pin her down and extract Sophie's whereabouts. But she was in no position to fight; the only thing holding up her shaking legs was the firmness of the brick wall behind her. 'Where's Chris?' Ruby said, seeking out Goldie's accomplice in the darkened room.

'Serving a higher purpose,' Goldie said, still wearing a fiendish smile. 'I thought it would be cosier with just us girls.'

'And Sophie?'

'Asleep.' She tilted her head to one side as she examined her nails. 'How is Cathy by the way?'

'Cathy? Just what's going on?' Ruby said. If she could get answers to the smaller questions, perhaps she would get clues to the bigger ones too, such as Sophie's location.

'You're dying to know, aren't you?' Goldie smiled.

'You were placed in care,' Ruby said, pre-empting her response. Just like with Anita, time was ticking, and she might not be as lucky this time. She bit the inside of her gum and was rewarded with a sting of pain that brought with it sharp focus.

'Cathy and I were fostered by the same parents after her adoptive mum died. I'd forgotten all about her until she found me on Facebook and asked to meet up.'

'Oh,' Ruby said, feeling a pang of sadness. Goldie was a born liar, but that piece of information made sense. 'That's how you saw her birth certificate, wasn't it? How you knew my name, and the time of birth.' She knew by the glint in Goldie's eyes that she had been responsible for the death notes, as well as the murders.

'I went through her stuff when she wasn't looking. How could I forget a name like that? "RIP". You looked so alike I thought it had to be you. Sure enough, when I tested the waters you emailed straight back.'

'So you tried to pin the murders on Cathy. That's what it was really all about.'

'What it was about was finding my happy ending. But I had to get rid of the bodies, and Cathy was there.'

'Until you found out that Nathan was her father. I saw the look on your face when I told you he had a vested interest.' As they were unmarried, Nathan had not been listed on the birth certificate. It suited Ruby at the time. The fact her daughter had originated from a family of criminals was something she had not wanted her to know.

'So you switched the blame to someone else. Chris. You were blackmailing him because he was a client. That's why chunks of money kept disappearing from his bank account.'

'I'm impressed,' Goldie said, pushing her hand into her apron pocket and pulling out a lighter and packet of cigarettes. Her face lit in an orange fuse as the lighter clicked into life. Closing her eyes, she dragged on the cigarette, blowing the smoke towards the cobwebbed ceiling. 'You want one?' she said, holding out the cigarettes.

Ruby nodded. Anything to escape her bindings. She had grazed her knuckles from rubbing the rope against the wall, but it was showing no signs of loosening.

'Well tough,' Goldie said, pushing the packet back into her apron. 'Chris had mummy issues. Liked to do it in all sorts of places, including his workplace. He would have paid anything to keep me sweet. So when the money dried up he let me use his place instead.' She took another drag of her cigarette. 'Want to know a funny thing? He got a kick out of that too. Started advising me on how to cover up my tracks, told me where to dump the bodies. Even came to the house after I killed Harry Edmonds. Then he'd turn up later on, with you, ready to make sure nothing was traced back to me.'

'If you were such good friends why was he ringing my DCI asking for help?' Ruby said.

Goldie gave a half-shoulder shrug. 'Doesn't matter now, it's all over. There's no happy ending. Not for any of us.'

Ruby felt chilled by the words. Goldie was referring to Chris in the past tense. He had outlived his usefulness, just like the others.

'I don't believe you,' Ruby said, trying to buy some time. If backup was on its way, they needed Goldie to tell them what she had done with Sophie. 'Those murders took time. You said yourself that Frenchie never gave you five minutes' peace.'

Goldie gave a low, mean chuckle. 'Frenchie's dead. I've been running the girls, not him. Chris helped me get rid of him too. We hid his body under the floorboards, but it isn't half kicking up a stink.'

'It's not too late to recover this. What have you done with Sophie?'

But Goldie was gazing beyond Ruby, somewhere she could not reach. 'None of those people deserved to live. I gave them every chance and they all failed miserably, just like you.'

Ruby's heartbeat thundered in her ears. The room was quiet. Too quiet. She needed the sounds of the streets, the scent of pollution, voices from the room next door. An insect scurried over her hand, and she pushed herself away from the wall, kicking off her heels in order to stay upright. Ruby forced her focus back on Goldie.

'You took refuge in the movie *Lucy's First Christmas*, didn't you? Waiting for a mother that never came.'

'And I waited so long… ' Goldie said, her voice etched with pain. 'I'd sleep to the tune of my music box, praying I'd wake up to see her waiting to take me home. I really thought I'd found her this time. But Anita was just liked all the others.' Goldie pulled at her thumb, ripping off the prosthetic piece and throwing it on the ground. 'I made myself look nice so she'd take me in. But she only cared about her perfect little girl. There was no room for me.'

'Where is she? Where's Sophie?' Ruby said, her words falling on deaf ears. She wrestled with her bindings, loosening them a fraction, then realised that Goldie was staring at her. Silence passed between them, two souls forced into solitude.

'My birth mother's dead,' Goldie finally spoke. 'Suicide. Couldn't live with the disappointment, I suppose.' A bitter laugh escaped from her mouth. 'But then, I've done some terrible things.' Goldie sighed, a smile touching her lips as she briefly closed her eyes. 'Have you ever killed anyone?'

'No.'

'Let me tell you, the rush of a kill is better than any drug. It surprised me in the end. The reward became more important than fulfilling the dream.'

'So the childhood fantasy was not so innocent after all,' Ruby said, the disgust evident on her face. 'It's over. Untie me and take me to Sophie.'

Goldie extinguished her cigarette with the sole of her lace-up boot. 'You forced my hand when you knocked on Chris's door. If you'd brought backup she'd be safe in your arms now. Her death is on your head.'

'Where is she?' Ruby asked, her chest rising as she battled the rising tide of frustration. If she didn't get out of this place soon… she couldn't be held responsible for her actions.

Goldie smiled. 'I told you, she's asleep, frozen in time like Sleeping Beauty. But the minutes are ticking away.' She waved a finger from left to right. 'Tick-tock, tick-tock. If she's not dead already, she soon will be. And you've nobody but yourself to blame.'

'You monster! She's just a little girl!' Ruby raged, unable to hold it in.

Within three strides Goldie was upon her. And it was only then that she caught sight of the scalpel: an instrument Chris must have used countless times before.

'Get back!' Ruby pushed herself back against the wall.

With one sweeping kick, Goldie took her legs, and the floor rose up to meet her as Ruby's face connected with a thud.

Dropping to her knees Goldie dragged Ruby's head onto her lap. 'Shhh, hush now, Mummy,' Goldie said, stroking her hair. 'It's time. I have to make the bad stuff go away.'

'Get off me,' Ruby said, wriggling her entire body. But her movements were halted as the metal blade was thrust under her jaw. Ruby gasped and became very, very still. But unknown to Goldie her hands were still moving. Inch by inch she twisted her wrists against the bindings, loosening the badly tied knot.

'It's good that we're together. You wouldn't want to die alone, would you?' Goldie said sadly. 'I don't like the thought of that at all.'

'Think about what you're doing… Please, I can help,' Ruby said, staring up at her face. She worked her wrists against the prickly rope, her flesh stinging against the insistent pressure. Beads of sweat broke out on Ruby's forehead as the knot loosened. She needed time. There was still hope.

Briefly closing her eyes, Goldie re-emerged with a smile. It was a clown-like grin which spread across her features in fetid glee. 'My name's Lucy. Are you my mummy?' The child-like voice echoed around them.

'I can be, if you want,' Ruby said, wearing a tight smile.

'Then say it, Mummy, please. Say you love me. Tell me you'll bring me home.'

Ruby did not think twice. She would say anything to extend precious seconds of their time. She took a deep breath. 'I lo—' But her words were cut short as an arterial spray of warm blood slapped against her skin.

CHAPTER SIXTY-SEVEN

Cathy was a good kid, and despite everything she said she needed her mother. Nathan knew so little about her, but it was not too late to repair things – as long as he could get Ruby back safely. The thought of her being buried in a casket in the ground struck cold fear in his heart. It was an alien emotion, and he tried to shake it off as he followed Downes down the driveway of Chris Douglas's house. He curled his fists. Replacing the emotion with the familiar lust for revenge had sharpened his focus. If Chris Douglas hurt a hair on Ruby's head, he would blow his fucking brains out.

Thundering behind the police unit, he and Downes pushed their way through the front door. Broken-hinged, it had been battered to submission. The last thing he expected to see was a man lying in a pool of blood on the kitchen floor.

'Fuck,' Downes said. 'It's Chris.'

But Nathan had no sentiment for Chris; his focus was solely on Ruby. A lump of dread rose in his throat and wedged like a hard ball. 'There must be a basement,' Nathan barked at the officers. 'She said something about going down. Try the garden too.'

Downes gave him a look which told him who was in charge, but Nathan didn't care. The detective inspector might have to play it by the book, but he didn't. Nervous energy erupted in his bloodstream as he pulled back the door of a cupboard under the stairs. 'Here,' he shouted, lifting a panel on the floor which led him to an underground stairwell. Feeling for a light, he adjusted his eyes to the darkness. The stench of bodily fluids and human remains were overpowering. These were smells he had encountered from a young age when he was forced to watch his father's 'work'. He entered the bowels of the room, resisting the urge to draw his pistol. Carrying a firearm would land him a prison sentence, and judging by their sideways glances there were lots of officers here who would be too glad to collar a Crosby. Flicking on the light switch, he descended the steps to the basement. 'Ruby?' he called out, his voice echoing in the dank space.

Nathan's heart plummeted as he gazed around the empty room. Nothing but a swivel chair, a bent-up Christmas tree, and some old stains on a splintered wooden floor. Sure, the basement harboured life. The rat droppings and cobwebs were testament to that – and the smell of death reeked from the floorboards. But if Ruby *was* here she had since been moved. They had found their killer alright. But where was Ruby now? Police boots echoed on the stairs as officers warily followed him down. They did not question their superior about Nathan's presence, and Downes did not offer any explanation.

Who knew what they would uncover from beneath the floorboards? But Nathan was not here to solve past crimes.

Downes rubbed his chin, disappointment evident on his face.

'Where's he taken her?' Nathan said. 'You said he was a pathologist. Where does he work?'

'We need to get to his office. I'll take it from here,' Downes said.

'You're having a laugh if you think I'm stepping back now,' Nathan replied, pushing past officers to hike up the stairs. But Downes was not far behind, matching him step for step. He must have known what Nathan was planning because he was not allowing him out of his sight.

Downes grabbed the door handle of his Mercedes and launched himself inside. Revving the engine, Nathan tore up the road.

'Listen, we both have one thing in common and that's Ruby's welfare,' Downes said, pushing his seat belt into its holder. 'Just leave this to the police. If Ruby comes out of this in one piece, then you've got your futures to consider. I won't come between you.'

'That's very magnanimous of you,' Nathan said, bemused. As if Downes ever stood in their way.

'I'm thinking of Ruby and what she'd want for her daughter. Having you in prison isn't one of them. Drop me off and then go home. I'll call and update when I get inside.'

'Don't worry, Downes, I won't throw any punches. It's not how I do business,' Nathan said.

Downes raised an eyebrow, as if to say that was not what he had heard, but he stayed silent.

Nathan pulled up outside the building and killed the engine of the car. Police sirens echoed in the distance, indicating they would not be alone for long. 'I'll give you five minutes, then I'm going in.'

Downes nodded in acknowledgement. A thin layer of perspiration shone on his forehead. Scrambling out of the car, he took long strides in the darkness towards the building. Neither of them noticed the thin sliver of crepe which had come loose from the front door. Edged with white ribbon, the breeze carried it away, along with any clues to Sophie's whereabouts.

CHAPTER SIXTY-EIGHT

Ruby heaved a gasp, involuntarily swallowing the fluids which had sprayed on her tongue.

Goldie's head connected with the floor, the clang of the scalpel jerking from her hand. Goldie knew exactly where to slice for maximum impact. And now she was as good as dead.

Pulling and tugging on the rope, Ruby cried out in frustration. The more her head cleared, the louder the voices became. *You're trapped down here. They'll never find you. Trapped in the ground with a corpse, and a million insects for company.* 'No,' Ruby whispered, her skin clammy with blood and newly formed sweat. Shuffling over to the scalpel, she grappled for purchase, being careful not to touch the blood-tinged blade. Razor sharp, it could have her fingers off in seconds. Goldie twitched behind her; her strangled breaths growing weaker. Blood pooled around them; the last few beats of a dying heart pumping it through the open wound. Ruby could feel it providing warmth as it soaked into her trousers. Wrapping her fingers tightly around the handle she inched the blade towards her bindings and sawed. The rope parted with a satisfying crack, leaving her free to undo her ankles.

Ruby was flooded with relief. It could so easily have been her lifeless on the floor.

Pulling off her blazer, she wrapped the sleeve around Goldie's throat in an effort to plug the wound. It was like trying to stop the tide. But in this case the tide was blood red. She had to leave, search the house for Sophie and call for help. Goldie stared at the ceiling. Her lips parted, but, devoid of breath, she had taken Sophie's whereabouts to the grave. Ruby rifled for her phone before rising to her feet. No signal. She needed to get out of here and call for help. Goldie's words replayed in her mind as she took the stairs, praying for an unlocked door. 'Just like Sleeping Beauty'. The truth finally dawned. She knew exactly where Sophie was. And if she was right she had just minutes to save her.

CHAPTER SIXTY-NINE

Ruby launched herself up the stairs, clinging onto the narrow railing for support. After checking Goldie's pockets, there were no keys to be found, and she prayed that the door had been left unlocked. Pulling back on the door, she was met with resistance. Without a phone signal, she had no way of alerting anyone of her whereabouts. She had pinned all her hopes on the fumbled call she made. But it must not have gone through. Banging on the door with clenched fists, she pounded the wooden barrier between her and the outside world. And then in the silence, a crash of glass.

Somewhere in the distance, someone was coming.

Heavy footsteps drew nearer, approaching the other side of the door.

'Help,' Ruby shouted, 'I'm locked in, can you get me out?'

'Ruby, it's me, Nathan. Stand back from the door.'

Ruby had never been so happy to hear his voice. She took a couple of steps down the stairs. Shielding her eyes, she waited as the crack of timber shattered the desolate air. Ruby caught Nathan on the top step as he kicked open the door.

Drawing back a sudden breath, he took in her appearance. 'You're hurt,' he said, the words tumbling from his mouth as he checked her for injuries.

Of course. The blood. She must have looked like something out of a horror movie. 'It's okay,' she said, batting him away as she stepped through the splintered door. 'It's not mine. But we need to get to Sophie. I think I know where she is.'

Ruby wanted to ask how Nathan had found her, but such questions could come later. For now, there was a young life hanging in the balance. 'Where's Chris?' Ruby said, throwing a glance over his shoulder.

'He's dead,' Nathan replied, leading her into the long dark corridor.

So that was what Goldie meant when she said he was serving a higher purpose. Chris was her accomplice, and she had killed him to shift the focus from her. Ruby looked around the hall. It carried the same smell of disinfectant, but this was not Chris's house. 'What?... Where am I?' she asked, her words laced with confusion.

Nathan frowned. 'You're at the mortuary. Don't you remember?'

'I passed out. I... I thought I was in his basement.' But as she got her bearings she remembered why she was there. 'But this is better. Come with me.'

Running with her bare feet slapping against the cold tiles, everything felt surreal. As if trapped in a nightmare, she galloped down the corridor, searching for the door which would provide her escape. She turned left. Pushing through the double doors, Nathan was right by her side.

Laced with Goldie's blood she must have looked a strange sight. Wild-eyed, she pushed her way through Downes and attending officers; their faces clouded in confusion as they stared at her bloodied face.

'Call an ambulance,' Ruby shouted. 'Goldie's in the basement. She's cut her throat. I think she's dead.'

'Goldie?' Downes said, holding his hands out in front as if he was calming a wild animal. 'Ruby... stop for a minute, tell me, what's going on?'

Ruby darted past him, making her way to the mortuary freezers, where the bodies of the dead were kept. 'I know where Sophie is.'

There was no time for questions. Downes and Nathan exchanged a glance before following Ruby in haste.

'You start down there,' she said, pointing to the end. 'And I'll start here.'

Ruby grasped the handle, pulling back the long heavy drawer. It rolled on its wheels to reveal an elderly woman. Ghostly white with sunken eyes, she was queued for the autopsy that was yet to come. But Ruby had no time to afford her the respect she deserved. Slamming back the door, she paused only to turn and pull out the next drawer. Nathan began in the middle, and Downes was at the end. Under the glow of strip lighting and the faint tang of disinfectant in the air, the only sounds were police boots pounding down the corridor to the basement and the ominous rolling backwards and forwards of freezer drawers.

'Ruby,' Nathan said, his voice flat. Pulling open the rest of the drawer, he revealed a waif-like little girl who was lying fully dressed, with hands bound in prayer. Frozen in time, just like Sleeping Beauty.

'Help me get her out,' Ruby breathed, clasping her hands under Sophie's armpits. She was cold, so very cold, and Ruby pressed her hand against Sophie's coat, praying for the comforting thump of a heartbeat. But there was nothing. 'Over here, to the radiator,' Ruby said, as Nathan gently lifted her up. For once, she was grateful for the stifling heat pumping through the building. Placing her on the ground, Ruby pressed her cheek against the little girl's face. Touching the artery in her neck, she held her own breath, willing Sophie's to return. She gasped a sigh of relief. 'We've got a pulse.' But the child was barely breathing.

Nathan pulled off his jacket, wrapping it tightly around her as Ruby drew the little girl into her arms. Like a life-sized doll, she lay with blue lips and hands forced together. Reaching into his back pocket, Nathan drew out a Stanley knife, cutting the bindings and releasing her wrists. Downes stood, rooted to the spot, as he watched the couple try to breathe life into the little frozen girl.

'Your coat,' Nathan barked at him. 'Give me your coat.'

Pulling off his heavy woollen coat he threw it to Nathan; for once in his life devoid of words. Working together, Nathan and Ruby wrapped it tighter around Sophie. Pulling off her shoes, Nathan massaged her feet, then her fingers, cupping his hands and breathing hot air, pressing her to the radiator for warmth.

Ruby drew her tighter, hugging her to her chest. Gently rocking, she begged in ragged whispers for the little girl to come back to them. 'You're alright, you're going to be alright, please, wake up now, there's a good girl.' And then she heard it: a little sigh of breath. Followed by a tiny flush of colour to her cheeks.

Nathan wrapped the coat tighter, encouraging murmurs passing his lips. In those few seconds it was just Ruby, Nathan, and the skinny little dark-haired girl.

'I'm sorry,' Ruby whispered as she rocked, kissing the top of her head. But she did not know what she was sorry for. Was it for her own daughter, for Sophie, or for her mother, Anita, who was lying in hospital recovering from her ordeal?

Downes turned to the window as he raised his radio to his lips; his face illuminated in the blue flashing lights.

Ruby gently rocked the sedated child, unwilling to release her to the uniformed bodies bustling into the room. Police, ambulance and crime scene investigators flooded in. Head bowed, Downes updated his superiors by phone, pressing a finger against his ear as he engaged in conversation.

'It's OK, you can let go now,' a soothing voice spoke in Ruby's ear. She swivelled her head to see the green paramedic uniform and a pair of outstretched hands waiting for the precious bundle. She glanced at Nathan, tears pricking her eyes. And in that moment they both saw the pain that giving up their daughter had caused each other. Getting to her feet, she allowed them to work. Her arms were empty, her body hollow. Nathan put a comforting arm around her and squeezed. Unconcerned by her witnesses, she allowed her hand to slip around his waist, taking comfort in his strength.

'You need to go with them,' Downes said, nodding at the paramedics.

'I'm fine,' Ruby said.

'She's coming back to mine,' Nathan spoke at the same time.

'We need statements,' Downes replied, his voice laced with disapproval.

Nathan stared, hard faced. 'In the morning. You'll have your statements then.'

Ruby allowed him to steer her away. Downes would send someone to the house, have them bag up her clothes and swab her face for forensics. A nod passed between them, and Downes let her go.

CHAPTER SEVENTY

Switching off the hairdryer, Ruby gasped as she caught sight of a figure in the bedroom mirror. Nathan. A jittery laugh escaped her lips as she caught her breath in relief. Here, in the home he bought for her, she could not be any safer. It had taken guts for Luddy to attend Nathan's house last night, but it was worth providing a full statement to be allowed a late start today. Ruby had been prepared to go home, but, in his wisdom, Nathan had brought her here. He was right: it *was* their safe house. And she had never been more grateful for it than today. Exhausted from the emotional turbulence she had fallen into a nightmarish sleep; her dreams filled with running barefoot down empty corridors, searching for her daughter.

'I made you some coffee,' Nathan said, his eyes falling on her hair. It had taken three boiling hot showers to satisfy her that all traces of blood were washed away.

'Thanks,' Ruby said, pulling the towelling robe around her before following him to the sofa.

'How did you find me? In the basement, I mean. How did you know where I was?' Ruby asked. She couldn't figure out why Nathan had smashed a window to gain entry to the back while Downes and his colleagues were at the front.

Nathan took a sip from his mug, staring straight ahead. 'I was waiting in the car when I searched up plans of the building on my phone. As soon as I saw there was an underground basement I went in.'

Ruby smiled. That was Nathan all over. Action first, ask questions later.

'My turn now,' Nathan said, giving her thigh an impromptu squeeze. 'How did you know that Chris was mixed up in it?'

'It was little things at first. He insisted the corpses had been washed. But I could tell by Emily's hair that it wasn't clean. Then I saw stamen powder on his coat when I hung mine up next to his at the post-mortem.' Ruby lifted her feet and curled up on the sofa, hugging her cup for warmth. 'There were lilies at Emily's address, but we wore forensic suits at the scene. Anyone can buy lilies, so I dismissed it from my mind.'

'What about the others?' Nathan asked. 'Monica and Emily?'

'He disposed of any forensics during the PM. It worked out fine, until I saw Monica's dirty feet.'

'It didn't help that the bodies kept turning up in properties on our books,' Nathan said.

'That was just a coincidence. Chris lived a couple of doors down from where Monica's body was dumped. Then I read the witness statement saying he used to be a keyholder for the last lot of homeowners when they went on holiday. That's when it all started coming together.'

Nathan shook his head. 'I've come across some messed up shit in my life, but that… why do it? And why did Goldie kill herself afterwards?'

'Because she never found her happy ever after. I think all she really wanted was for her mum to love her for who she was, just like in the movies.'

'Lots of us have crappy childhoods,' Nathan said, giving Ruby a knowing glance. 'We don't all turn out to be serial killers.'

'Think about it. Why do you carry a gun?' Ruby asked, staring intensely into his blue grey eyes. Silence fell between them, and Ruby took another breath before delivering her next question. 'Have you ever used it?'

Nathan averted his glance. His reluctance to respond was answer enough.

'I'm not excusing what Goldie did,' Ruby said. 'Ending those women's lives, and almost costing Sophie hers… it was brutal and a needless waste of life. But if you're brought up to believe that someone's warped viewpoint is the absolute truth, it's hard to shake it off. Goldie carried the scars of her childhood like a cancer; they infected every aspect of her life.' It was the best example she could give to make Nathan understand. Nathan carried a gun; Goldie unleashed her demons.

'I heard they found Frenchie's body buried in Chris's basement.'

Ruby nodded; the excavation of Chris's home was ongoing. 'It's why she sent me the death notices. When she saw I had given up my daughter, I think it triggered something inside. Deep down she wanted to be caught.'

'Or she hated you for what you did and was messing with your mind. Why do you always see the good in people? Even after all these years in the police. Why can't you see these nutters for what they really are?'

Ruby delivered a teasing smile, stretching like a cat as she kissed him on the cheek. 'I see the good in you, don't I? Thanks for coming to my rescue, Action Man.'

Nathan tried but failed to hide his smile. He looked at his watch and rose. 'I'd better get going. There's clean clothes in the wardrobe if you want to go to work from here.'

Ruby rose with him. 'I'm still going back to my flat you know; this isn't permanent.'

'I know,' Nathan raised a hand as he made for the door. 'Call me if you need anything.'

She stood wanting to call him back. The sight of Nathan leaving sent a bolt of regret. Why was she joking when her daughter had come home?

'What does she look like?' Ruby said, the words feeling too big for her throat.

Nathan paused at the door. 'She's thin, dark hair. Has your eyes, my attitude. She's a bit wild, keen to get involved in the family business.'

Ruby arched an eyebrow as he returned and took her hand. Drawn like magnets, one always returned for one last touch, one more word. She hoped that it would be the same for her daughter, that some way Cathy would find her way back to her. At least now she knew who had been visiting her mother at Oakwood. It gave Ruby hope that Cathy wanted to engage with her grandmother.

'I'll make sure she keeps her nose clean; help her get an education, a proper career.'

'It wasn't that long ago that you were telling me that being a criminal was a career,' Ruby said, half-joking.

'It's not the one I have in mind for my daughter.'

My daughter. Not *ours*. Ruby knew she had no right to be upset by his turn of phrase, but it hurt like hell anyway. She thrust her hands into the dressing gown pockets, swallowing back the tightness in her throat. 'Will you tell her that I've always thought of her? That I'd like to meet?'

'When she's ready to hear it I will.' He sighed. 'She's a very troubled girl. And I'm going to need your help... when she comes around.'

'I'll be right here when she does,' Ruby said. 'So what about you and Leona? I've heard you're getting married. I don't suppose you'll have much room in your life for me then.' She knew what she sounded like and hated herself for it, but she had to know.

'Me and Leona are through,' Nathan said, ruefully. 'And what about you? I guess that Jack Downes doesn't seem that bad now I've met him.'

Ruby smiled at Nathan's efforts of being diplomatic. 'Work relationships are messy. We're back on a professional basis only.' It was a decision she had not been aware of until the words fell from her tongue.

Nathan reached out and touched her hair, pushing an errant lock behind her ear. His knuckles brushed her cheekbone, sending a tingle down her spine.

'I guess I'll see you around,' he said, before turning and walking away.

'Not if I see you first,' Ruby called after him, her smile filtering through her words.

She padded to the window, opening it wide, absorbing the noise of the streets below. London. The sounds of the traffic were her lullaby; the scent of the streets her perfume. She did not know what the future held, but as long as she was here she was home. She leaned on the windowsill, basking in the morning sun. Her phone beeped in her dressing gown pocket, alerting her of a text. It was Downes.

'Are you getting your arse back in here or what?'

Ruby smiled. Time to get back to work.

LETTER FROM CAROLINE

Writing a new series can be a daunting experience, as you wait to see how your new character will be received. DS Ruby Preston sometimes bends the rules, but she has a good heart, and I hope you have enjoyed meeting her for the first time.

I'm really enjoying setting this series in London. I'm currently plotting books two and three and am very excited about what the future holds for Ruby and the people around her. Having worked in the police for many years, I do hope I've been able to portray a good account of the type of interesting and varied characters I used to meet. I have had to stretch reality slightly when it comes to the role of a Detective Sergeant, as we all know there are just some days that paperwork prevails – I do hope my ex-colleagues forgive me for the freedom Ruby is sometimes allowed.

Thank you so much to everyone who has supported my books. I truly value my readers and the wonderful book bloggers and clubs who discuss my work. There's lots more to come, to don't forget to subscribe to my newsletter to ensure you are kept updated of each new release.

www.bookouture.com/caroline-mitchell

You may also be interested in my previous crime thriller series, featuring DC Jennifer Knight, which is available now. Like Ruby, Jennifer investigates crime, but her stories come with a spooky twist.

If you have enjoyed this book, I'd love to hear from you. My Twitter and Facebook links are below if you would like to get in touch.

Until next time,

Caroline

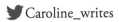 Caroline_writes

paranormalintruder

www.carolinemitchellauthor.com

ACKNOWLEDGEMENTS

I am hugely grateful to the people who have helped bring this book, the first in the DS Ruby Preston series to fruition.

To Oliver Rhodes and the team at Bookouture – thank you, your support has been phenomenal. A special mention must be given to my publicity manager Kim Nash, who never seems to sleep, and top editor Keshini Naidoo, whose mind is darker than mine – and that's saying something!

Speaking of dark minds, this acknowledgement would not be complete without mentioning two of the darkest in the business – authors Mel Sherratt and Angela Marsons – you know I love you really! Also to the fab Helen Phifer, whose name was used in this book, thanks to her support for the CLIC Sargent charity auction.

I'd also like to thank my agent, Madeleine Milburn, who I feel extremely fortunate to know. I'm so pleased to have her at the helm of my career, guiding me every step of the way.

To my fellow authors, and a certain Facebook group (or should I say scene). Thanks for your support – I'm so pleased to know such a fantastic group of people.

To my police colleagues and those who have walked the thin blue line, in particular Tracey Allen, Ian Rutherford, Sally Keeble and Scott Jamieson. Sorry I couldn't include everyone, but I've enjoyed working with you all. It's been eventful! Also to Garry Rodgers for his assistance with my questions about mortuaries and ongoing support.

Thanks to the band of dedicated book reviewers, book club members and readers who have championed me from the beginning – I truly appreciate your support.

To my husband Neil and my children who are growing up far too fast - thanks for putting up with me. I love the bones of you all.

Printed in Poland
by Amazon Fulfillment
Poland Sp. z o.o., Wrocław